YOU CAN'T IRON A WRINKLED BIRTHDAY SUIT

BY SHARON PHENNAH

You Can't Iron A Wrinkled Birthday Suit

This is a work of fiction. All of the characters, names, incidents, organizations, and dialogue in this novel are either the products of the author's imagination or are used fictitiously.

First published in 2010 by Outskirts Press

Published in the US in 2011 by BQB Publishing
(an imprint of Boutique of Quality Books Publishing)
www.bqbpublishing.com

ISBN 978-1-937084-14-1 (p)
ISBN 978-1-937084-15-8 (e)

Library of Congress Control Number: 2011938626

Cover illustration artwork is "Happiness - A Study" by Des Brophy who agreed to its use for the update of this book.
Book interior by Robin Krauss, www.bookformatters.com

I dedicate this book
To the Source of All from whence it came,
To the professionals who helped me make it right,
To my friends and supporters.
You know who you are, and my gratitude is boundless.

—Sharon—

Acknowledgements

A huge thank you to artist Des Brophy who agreed to the use of his painting "Happiness - A Study" for the new cover of this book.

Mr. Brophy's painting so concisely protrays the delight that can be found in the "Golden Years" if we're open to pursuing it.

Table of Contents

1

Operation Wonder Woman

Silhouetted against the denim sky, two women ascended a ladder behind the yellow brick McClellan building, Pine Crossing's defunct five-and-dime store. The third woman, meant to be steadying the ladder, threw up in a forsythia bush. She assigned her queasiness to the hour—four in the morning—and the garish green view through her night-vision goggles.

With ease, the three-part extension ladder reached the parapet of the second-story roof. Seventy-something Grace, clad in a black spandex outfit, her Tide-white hair stuffed under an ancient black bathing cap, went first. The most athletic of the three women, she scampered up the ladder like a spider in a hurry, her grandson's paintball gun bungee-corded to her backpack, her waist pack bulging with paintballs.

As she climbed, Grace reflected on the moment. How exactly had she gotten here? Wacky ideas were the trio's forte, Grace realized, but this caper was off the charts. Hazel, now wiping her mouth at the bottom of the ladder, had been one of her more creative physical education students in high school. Hazel had married the day after graduation, then vanished for many years into Grace's mental file labeled "former students."

Recently retired from New Jersey to Pine Crossing, North Carolina, Grace had been passing a Humane Society Adopt-A-Thon at the local pet supply store one day when she stopped in her tracks. There was something familiar about the woman returning a kitten to its crate. *What was her name? Hazel? Yes, Hazel.*

In the conversation that had followed, Grace discovered that Hazel, now a widow, was also a recent émigré from New Jersey. The friend with Hazel that day, Gus, was her newly rediscovered college friend, a transplant from New England.

Now living in the downtown home she'd inherited from her parents, Hazel insisted Grace and Gus come to dinner that evening, and the rest, as they say, became wonder woman history.

In Grace's mind, Hazel was an ordinary woman with a middle-class upbringing and outlook, but now and then, she became a radical activist—this morning being a case in point. Hazel's support for Bruce, her significant other, was unqualified. As board member and pro-bono counsel for the Historical Prevention Society, he wanted with all his heart and soul to save the McClellan building. Therefore, so did Hazel; and therefore, here they were on this ladder.

Looking down at Gus, Grace smiled to herself—Gus was a good friend. Not quite sixty, Gus still worked part-time as a vet tech, so she didn't have as much free time, but she showed up for every plot and plan, kvetching, just like now.

"Let's move it," Gus said, groaning as she tested the second rung. She, too, wondered how she got here. Time and sleep were precious commodities and this wasn't on her to-do list. Nevertheless, friends were friends. Hazel had helped her rescue countless animals from euthanasia and listened to her conundrums over the years. And even though there'd been that hiatus while Hazel was married and raising her kids, college friendships have a special glue. Gus smiled as she recalled the day her cart collided with Hazel's in the Pine Crossing supermarket a dozen years ago. Her interest in "straightening out" the offending party stifled, becoming tears of joy when she realized Hazel was the errant shopping cart driver.

Sighing, Gus struggled up the ladder. Her over-fifty-and-a-few-extra-pounds body with her mismatched black ensemble suggested an adventuresome tortoise. She mumbled into the cool spring air, "This is what friends do, it's only two stories, it's what friends do." She wondered about Hazel, but knew better than to look down until she reached the rooftop.

On the ground, brusquely wiping her mouth, Hazel collected her dignity and stepped on the bottom rung as if it were the first step to the gallows. Dubbed their "fearless leader" because this was her idea, she shifted her backpack to support the sling chair on her shoulder. Closing her eyes, she hoisted her XXL body upward, tilting the ladder.

"EEEK!" Gus screamed as softly as she could, "I almost slipped!"

"Sorry," Hazel mouthed. Then in frustration, she yelled, "You're supposed to hang on!"

"Sheesh! Hush you two! Pay attention!" The admonition floated down from Grace, now standing on the roof. Hands on her knees, she caught her breath and pushed her packs and paintball gun aside so Gus could plop over the wall. Shaking, Gus did just that, using the wall as leverage to lurch to her feet.

Hazel muttered, "I think I can, I think I can," into her bosom with each step on the ladder. Without warning, her mind overloaded with images of her derriere as viewed from the ground. *What if there are pictures, TV news?* Sweating in her night-vision goggles, Hazel focused her eyes on one rung at a time. She reached the top and froze.

"Hazel! *Look* at *me!*" Gus commanded as she and Grace hauled her over the wall, losing the sling chair, which landed in a small tree at the base of the building.

"Why did you two let me talk you into this?" Hazel wailed, righting herself and shedding her packs to bury her face in her hands. "You know I hate heights. What if this mission fails? And what about the media? All I could imagine on that ladder was my huge butt attached to wobbly, stretch-marked thighs." Hazel howled through her fingers.

Grace rolled her eyes and walked away to inspect their rooftop domain.

Trying to reassure Hazel, Gus exclaimed, "So, what . . . *I'm* a bathing beauty? *This* is a fabulous ensemble? So chic, yet so comfortable," she continued, yanking the crotch of her cut-off leotards below her knees. Next, she grabbed the spare tire around her belly, flapping it toward Hazel. "And *this* is my six-pack abs!" Into it now, Gus danced around, wagging her butt cheeks and flapping her underarm wings. "I'm a *real* sex queen if you're into flab, cellulite, and blue veins."

Gus waggled on until Hazel finally sniffed "okay okay" and pulled a tissue from the folds in her clothing. "How about some gum?"

"Sure," Gus replied as Hazel fished in her pack.

Grace appeared a beat later, her hands full of five-gallon plastic buckets she'd scavenged near the front of the building.

"Look what I found," she sang out. "Seats and a latrine! There's lots of stuff over there, and the roof seems solid to me. Who said there were holes in it?" Grace distributed the pails upside down with one in the middle for a table. She placed the last bucket, right side up, between the chimney and the air vent and stood back to admire her handiwork, spanking her hands together. *That's done.*

Hazel handed Gus a piece of gum and inhaled through her teeth, squinting doubtfully at the pail by the chimney. Gus grimaced as if she had just sucked a lemon or worse. *Latrine indeed*, Gus thought. *I'd explode first.*

"Where's my chair?" Hazel asked, looking around as she handed Grace the gum.

"It fell when we dragged you off the ladder," Grace explained, deadpan. "It's in a treetop. We couldn't save both the chair *and* your pack of coffee and scones."

"I took a swipe at the chair," Gus consoled, "but I missed."

"Well," was all Hazel said, so the women tested the pails and chewed their gum.

"Look yonder," Gus said, pulling off her goggles. "First light. It must be around six. Let's reconnoiter. What's the plan, Hazel?"

"In a minute," Hazel replied, pushing up from her pail. She walked to the wall and looked down at her chair in the tree, locking into a morbid fascination with the height, wondering if she'd survive a fall, what her injuries might be, what it would feel like.

"Looks way higher from up here than from down there," Hazel said as Grace and Gus flanked her. Hazel stepped away from the wall. "I can't believe I climbed that ladder."

"It's just two stories," Gus answered, raising her gaze to neighboring rooftops, most of which were similar to this one. "If there was a fire, you'd be the first to jump."

"Shut your mouth, Augusta Roberts," Hazel admonished, shuddering as she took a last look at the ground. "Besides, this is the floor of the *third* story!"

Regaining their seats, the women assessed their situation. They had plenty of supplies: coffee, water, granola bars, sandwiches, fold-n-stow straw hats, sunscreen, and charged cell phones.

"Okay. *Now*, Hazel, what's the plan?" Gus asked.

"You know the plan," was Hazel's retort.

"Let's go over it again; make sure we're all on the same page," Grace soothed, her goggles draped over her shoulder.

"Okay," Hazel sighed, placing her goggles on top of her head. She straightened her back and replied in exaggerated official-ese, "You have already been informed that my beloved significant other, Mr. Bruce D. Winston, pro-bono counsel for the Historical Preservation Society, acquired back-channel information that the Lewis and Son Devoted Demolition crew, employed by the United Fundamental Church, will arrive at this site between oh eight hundred and oh nine thirty with intent to demolish said building. Place of interment, the landfill.

"Now, we also know that The Historical Preservation Society versus The United Fundamental Church is the first case on the docket today in court. Court convenes at ten hundred and adjourns at twelve thirty sharp." Hazel pointed to the north toward the courthouse. "A verdict is expected at that time. If the verdict favors Bruce—I mean, the Society—it would be good for the building to be standing, yes? And that is why we are here. To prevent the demolition until the hearing adjourns."

"Okay, so we hold the fort no matter what, until reinforcements from Bruce materialize," Gus confirmed like a true soldier.

"A-plus!" Hazel clapped, sitting down hard enough to push her pail into the asphalt, stopping its wobble. "To answer your question about the roof, Grace, someone from the church said the roof's disrepair is so extensive that replacement costs would be more than the building's assessed value."

"Why am I thinking *Alamo defended by three blue hairs?*" Gus got up and rummaged in Hazel's pack. "Coffee anyone?"

Over coffee served by Gus and crumbled scones, the women watched the light brighten this misty spring morning. The shadows of nearby branches, stirred by a gentle breeze, seemed to finger and play with the litter on the rooftop. For a few minutes, this odd beauty in motion soothed their spirits until Hazel broke the spell by shrieking, "The *ladder!* We forgot to pull up the ladder!"

Making enough noise for a small machine shop, the women levered, yanked, and slid the ladder up and over, laying it along the wall. Puffing and red-faced, they returned to their pails.

"As to *how* we hold the fort," Gus began, "I'm guessing we'll stick to being undiscovered until the last minute, letting the wrecking ball or backhoe make the first move?"

"Yes," Hazel replied. "It's vital that they don't know we're here until the last safe instant. Once they know we're here, they will focus on getting us off the roof. The less time they have for that, the better. But if we wait too long, we may tumble down with the building. The hard part will be keeping them occupied until court is over."

"We can handle that," Grace said, leaning forward, elbows on her knees, face cupped in her hands.

"Yeah, but . . ." Gus answered, swallowing some coffee, "while they try to get us down, what if they hose or foam us, or whatever they do now, maybe net us?"

"Stop it, Gus," Grace commanded. "No matter what they do, someone has to get up here and physically remove us, even if they shoot us with tranquilizer darts from a helicopter."

"Okay, okay," Gus conceded, "so we hold them off, we get home, and we've accomplished what? I mean, yes, the building will stand, but what then?"

Grace stood, pushing Hazel, who was half risen and wholly irritated, back on her pail. "Gus, I know you think this building is just a bunch of yellow bricks laid in a two-story rectangle," she chided.

"You bet I do, Grace. There're thousands of old five-and-dimes all over the country." Gus got up and began pacing. "Don't be hollering at me, either of you, for what I think. If I weren't your crazy friend, I'd be asleep in my bed with my cat for a hat. A cold Corgi nose would wake me, and I'd begin my day like a sensible person with coffee and the paper." Gus stopped and looked at Hazel. "And today I'd be taking the dogs to the groomer instead of my neighbor Irene having to do it. I don't think she can handle all five dogs at once, and I *don't* want to end up with a pissed-off, used-to-be-my-friend neighbor."

"Aha!" Hazel said triumphantly. "*That's* what's eating you. The dogs!" She crossed her fingers in her pocket and said, "Irene will be okay. I told her to leave my Lady Labrador and just take the Poms, so she's just got four dogs."

"Thanks, Haze. I feel way better knowing she's only taking four. You *know* Shear Charisma's too close to the highway if, God forbid, one of them slips a leash." Gus sat with a resigned thump on her pail, adding, "Geez, it's already getting hot. What time is it?"

"Gus, your animals have you too well-trained," Hazel said.

"Gang, it's seven oh two on a fine, spring morning," Grace said at last, throwing her hands up. She was in no mood for their bickering right now. Sitting again on her pail, she picked up her coffee and lapsed into thought.

A few moments slipped past as the women sipped coffee. The sun was well above the horizon, over-warming their backs.

"Look," Gus spoke up, conciliating, "I know my history. This building is Pine Crossing's civil rights symbol. Our sit-in occurred the week after the first one in Greensboro. I even looked up our date, which I couldn't find, but Greensboro's was February 1, 1960, so our sit-in was around the eighth. Their lunch counter's in a museum, while ours is moldering downstairs. That's not right."

Gus went on, "I've been in protest marches and sit-ins since the sixties. I'm sorry if I act like a turkey, but I need a really good reason for being hot and upsetting all my fifty-something joints. I swore off doing this after Seabrook in the eighties, when I was scorched on all sides from the sun above and its reflection off the parking lot. We have a similar sun situation here, gang, and I'm not convinced that if we succeed, it'll make a difference. Can the Historical Society afford to buy the building? What is its planned use? This seems like an exercise in futility to me."

Hazel leaned over and patted Gus's hand. "This is hard for me too, Gus. The main thing is, *if and only if,* the court rules in favor of the Historical Preservation Society, we are gaining time to get money together and wrest, excuse me, buy this building from the church. The church has made it clear they intend to demolish the McClellan and create yet *another* park, period." Hazel's face was a study in disdain. "The building could be a museum, artists' studios, or a collection of small shops. I hate the thought, but a well-designed parking garage would be more practical than a park!"

Grace emerged from her rumination. "Think. How cool would it be if this old store were restored to its original state? Our collective childhood memories would be resurrected, and our kids and grandkids could experience what we talk about. Remember the sheer sensual pleasure of the fans chuff-chuffing over head, the popcorn smell, the feel and sound of hardwood under foot, especially bare feet? Do you think that angle would attract support?"

"Yeah, it might," Hazel said, smoothing her hair. "How about being able to play with the toys? And touching the grownup things too, garter belts and girdles? No plastic wrap! I bought my first bra in a five-and-dime after I examined all the others too. I was fascinated by the different sizes and shapes."

"Yeah, I couldn't imagine how someone would wear those *huge* D cups," Gus said, her eyes sparkling in recollection. "Even better, it was okay to play a 45 rpm record before we bought it. And they had the best grilled cheese sandwiches and rootbeer floats."

"Good lord, Gus," Hazel exclaimed, looking at her chest. "Doubt I'll ever wear a D cup again! We had it good in those days."

Grace looked at her watch. It was now eight thirty. "Yeah, I love the old days and I'd support a restoration of the five-and-dime, but we've got to do today right first. Let's move everything over by the chimney where it won't be seen. That's where any scrap of shade will be too."

"Incoming!" Hazel screamed, a decibel or two above the staccato of diesel engines, squealing brakes, and grinding gears. "What time is it?"

"Showtime," Gus shot back, putting on her sweatband. Grace duck-walked to the wall, while Gus and Hazel half knelt, half crawled in the soft, grainy asphalt.

The trucks and yellow crane stopped and took their places on the side where the ladder had been. The women held their breath. Could the men see the sling chair? They scuttled closer to the wall and, like three large Meerkats, popped up for a look, disappearing even faster.

Gus and Hazel, their attitude changing from excitement to impatience after fifteen minutes, leaned against the wall and communicated by mime and exaggerated facial expressions. Grace checked on the men every three minutes, frustrated with the seemingly endless posturing, pointing, crotch-scratching, and coffee-drinking taking place on the ground. "What's happening now?" Hazel whined, shifting her position yet again.

"Some of the men are leaving. Maybe they need more coffee or forgot something," Grace replied, irritation in her tone.

"You made a fine butt-print," Gus whispered to Hazel, who had turned and got on her hands and knees.

"Ouch! This feels like kneeling on grits!" Hazel sat back down.

"Daddy, when're we gonna *beee* there?" Grace chortled, glancing at her friends.

Gus flipped Grace the bird. Her butt was stuck on the roof, her feet straight out in front of her. Hazel was now similarly positioned. Two beached whales came to Gus's mind, but she kept quiet and the women waited.

At nine thirty, there was a new noise. While Gus and Hazel struggled to stand, Grace looked over the parapet and saw the reason for the noise. The crane was running, and its boom with a ball at the cable's end swung toward the building. Stark reality swept over them.

"Stop!" Hazel yelled, standing toes to the wall.

Gus shoved two fingers in her mouth and whistled the loudest whistle in her repertoire.

Grace had the paintball gun loaded. She took aim and shot toward the crane's windshield. "Damn! I missed the entire cab! Damn! Damn!"

"You hit the tracks, though," Hazel said, pointing at the red blotch.

"I hope he sees us!" Gus yelled, waving at the men, her triceps flapping like semaphore flags.

2

Let the Games Begin

Holy Sweet Mother of God!" the crane operator bellowed as he wrenched the boom and ball levers and throttled back the engine. The foreman jumped on the crane's tracks and yanked the cab door open.

"Am I effin' seein' things?" he shouted, a foot from the operator's ear.

The ball swung low, like a pendulum, parallel to the wall.

The operator turned off the engine and removed his ear protectors. "Quit yellin', I'm right here. There's friggin' people on the roof."

"Dammit, I *know* that," the foreman exclaimed, pointing at the red blotch on the crane track. "They shot something. Look at that red paint. Did you see that?"

"Effin' A, I did. I looked up and I'd swear I saw white hair. The sun gave 'em halos. Scared the crap outta me."

"This sucks. I'm callin' The Boss."

"You do that. I'll be in my truck with my coffee. You want some?"

"After I call The Boss, you bet. He'll be after our asses, big time. He wants the hammer down on this job."

Herman Lewis didn't like interruption or inconvenience, and his foreman had given him both. Still in his golf clothes, though he'd had to cancel his tee time, a red-faced Herman erupted from his truck and slammed the door. A swaggering, corpulent man, he behaved like a barnyard rooster. He got a bead on you with his shifty eyes, and when he had your attention, he jabbed you with his spurs. In every negative way, he was The Boss.

"What's the trouble here?" Herman demanded of the foreman and the crane operator. The other men, back with coffee and a part for the dump truck, lurked on the periphery, scoping out The Boss's mood. It wasn't good.

"There're three old ladies up on that roof, sir," the foreman replied.

"They shot the crane with a paint ball," the operator added, "That sure got my attention."

Herman shaded his balding brow, chewed on the tip of his cigarillo, and squinted into the sun, now bright behind the roof of the McClellan building. The church promised to pay him double for this job, but only if it was finished *today*. That meant everything to him. If removing just one remaining brick was left for tomorrow, pay would be regular rate.

Herman squinted upward to the roof. His men were right. He made out three old ladies, white hair shimmering like halos in the backlighting of the sun. "Damn!" Wiping his eyes with a monogrammed handkerchief, Herman turned back to the foreman. "Call the cops, call the fire department, call the Marines if you have to, but get them off that roof and tear that building *down*! No work, no pay," Herman sniggered. "Don't call me again until that building is *gone!*"

The Boss strode to his truck and sped away, spewing chunks of grass and gravel over his men and equipment.

Safe for the moment, the women retreated to a shady spot near the chimney and passed around sunscreen, an assortment of sandwiches, and bottled water.

"I know that guy from somewhere," Hazel mumbled as she chewed.

"Which guy? The Boss?" Gus poured some of her water on her head.

"Yeah, The Boss. I know him *and* that red, double-cab, dually diesel with hemi and indestructible bed-liner. I just can't place him at the moment." Hazel sighed and wiped her face. "It'll come to me. What time is it?" "Eleven thirty," Grace answered, peeling down to her tank top. Sweat flowed in twin rivulets along her backbone. She stuffed her shirt into her backpack.

Gus and Hazel were cutting their eyes at Grace and to one another, envying her wiry build, when sirens erupted from every direction.

Half a dozen police cars arrived, screeching to sidewise stops on Glover and Main streets. In moments, officers barricaded the sidewalk on Main

Street in front of the McClellan and cordoned off the whole block of Glover Street.

Hanging over the wall, Grace nudged Gus, "They've got a good protocol. The area's secure and it looks like that young guy on the phone is in charge. All in six minutes."

"OIC, Grace. He's the Officer in Charge. Could be my grandson," Gus reflected.

"Only if your kid had a kid at fifteen. He's way over thirty."

"You think?" Gus leaned further out to more thoroughly examine the officer. He was tall and well built, not all muscle, but not skinny either. Maybe he's a runner, Gus thought. The man lifted his hat and wiped his brow, revealing male pattern balding in the center of his head.

"You're right, Grace, more likely my son," Gus acknowledged. "He's forty-something, but he looks wicked fine to me."

"Uh-oh," Hazel said as she joined them. "I remember now who The Boss is. His name is Herman and he used to date Bruce's ex-wife." They watched as the OIC closed his phone and a few words floated up to the women.

" . . . around front . . . alley over there . . . fire department."

As his men dashed off to follow his orders, the OIC tilted his head back and stared at the women. *The wellbeing of the women comes first,* he thought, *but the Lewis crew has rights too, no matter how I feel.* For sure, he had the women for trespassing.

"You ladies up there okay? You know you're trespassing?"

"We're fine," Grace shouted back. "Hot, but we're fine."

Hazel drew on all her dignity, hoping it showed in her words. "We want to thank the crane operator for stopping. He prevented a disaster. He's a hero and everyone should know that."

"You don't belong there in the first place. You could have been hurt, even killed." The OIC appeared hot in his dark uniform, and his hat was sliding around on sweat as he peered up.

"You look uncomfortable," Grace yelled. She held up her phone, pointed at it. "Call me at five, three, seven, seven, oh, seven, oh."

"Get back from the wall," the OIC replied, now red-faced. He caught his cap slipping off his head and dropped it on the hood of his cruiser. He motioned to a returning officer. "Over here. What did you find?"

"The building's locked, sir. We have no idea how they got up there."

"They've got to come down. It was The Boss's foreman that called me. You know who I mean, Herman Lewis. He said this job must be done today." The OIC adjusted his belt and shifted his weight to his left foot.

"Sir?"

"Yes?" the OIC responded.

The other officer shuffled his feet. "Yes sir, I know Herman. Pardon me, sir, but I have to ask. Have you seen any paperwork for this demolition?"

"No, I haven't. Herman should know better than that after our last go-around. Well, Job One is to get those women down. Call the fire chief and see if he can spare a ladder truck while I talk to the women."

The OIC backed into the shade behind the forsythia where Hazel had thrown up and called the fire chief only to have his request denied. There might be a fire. A traffic officer suggested contacting the cable TV company for use of their bucket truck.

"Do it," said the OIC to the traffic officer as he punched in Grace's number.

A crowd had gathered behind the yellow caution tape: tourists, workers on lunch break, curious business owners, all asking each other and the officers what was going on. Half of them were on cell phones to friends and a small boy let go of his helium birthday balloon. For a few minutes, his howls drowned all conversation.

"Hi, officer," Grace answered efficiently. "How can I help you?"

Two TV sound trucks arrived, the reporters and cameramen hustling through the crowd, zeroing in on the OIC. He waved them to an officer beside a barricade, threatening them with charges for ignoring the yellow tape.

Frustrated and hot, the OIC chose a stern but fatherly approach, hoping it would have the desired effect on these women and convince them to come down without further ado. "You need to come down here. Then you can tell me what you think you're doing. If you cooperate, maybe we can help. You've already broken several laws—don't make it worse for yourselves."

"Just a minute, sir," Grace said, holding the phone tight to her chest while pulling Hazel closer with her other hand. "He sounds like a *Law 'n' Order* rerun. You better talk to him. He wants to know what we're doing."

Hazel took the phone, trilling in her best Hyacinth Bucket voice, "Officer, this is Hazel Hollister, resident of Pine Crossing. Did you ask why we're up here?"

"Yes, ma'am, I did. I must also inform you that unless you come down immediately, you will be considered under arrest and anything you say can and will be used against you in a court of law."

Leaving the phone on speaker Hazel said to the others, "If we don't come down immediately, we will be considered under arrest, and anything we say can and will be used against us."

"Guess half a Miranda's better than none," was Gus's reply. Grace just shrugged and said, "Ask what the charges are."

"What are the charges?" Hazel put the phone on speaker.

"Trespass, destruction of property, obstruction of lawful enterprise, and resisting arrest, for starters," the OIC responded.

"Excuse me, officer, we haven't destroyed a thing," Hazel said. "*Au contraire,* demolishing this building today is the un-lawful enterprise. This property is tied up in litigation as we speak, the United Fundamental Church versus the Historical Preservation Society. Check with your chief, the court, the district attorney. There should be a ruling from the court momentarily."

Grace looked at her watch. "Momentarily is right. It's just past noontime."

"And we're resisting arrest, how?" Gus muttered.

The OIC's voice boomed. "I am *not* joking, Missus Hollister. I *will* put you all in jail." The OIC mopped his brow. *This woman was making no sense–court, indeed.* Call-waiting cut in. "Ma'am, I have another call. I'll call you right back."

"*Mizzzz* Hollister," Hazel bellowed back.

The women retreated to the south side of the roof where the shade from the adjacent three-story building was expanding as the sun moved across the sky.

No sooner had Hazel ensconced herself on her pail than Grace's phone rang. It was the OIC again.

"Where are you? Come here where I can see you," he ordered.

"No sir. It's too hot there. We have seats in the shade. Come into the alley if you want to see us." Hazel laid her shoulders on the wall and exhaled. Gus leaned back too, shaking her gray curls like a mop. Grace was imitating Rodin's "The Thinker" on her pail, wondering *could this be sillier*?

"Okay. Have it your way. You will be coming down from there," the OIC's voice blared discord into the shady scene.

"Sir, with all due respect," Hazel continued, "if the court finds in favor of the Historical Society and this building is gone, it would mean your job. Call your chief."

"Ma'am, the cable TV truck will arrive to remove you ladies at one o'clock. Count on it!"

"Okay, it's your neck." Hazel clapped the phone shut and handed it to Grace.

At one o'clock sharp, the bucket truck appeared as promised. Court had to be adjourned now, the women realized. They had succeeded in keeping the building intact. Mission accomplished, the trio grinned, high-fived each other, and gathered their things, discovering exactly how hot and tired they were.

Grace's phone rang. "Un-huh, okay," she said into it. To the women Grace said, "The cable TV bucket is being raised. We're to come down now."

"Tell them we'll come down on our own if they'll get us some food," Hazel said to Grace. "Pizza, for instance, would be good. We're getting hypothermia here." She wiped her face with her bandana. "I think we miscalculated age and heat factors for this enterprise."

"Dehydrated," Grace said, not bothering to cover the phone. "We're not having hypothermia, we're dehydrated. I can't think anymore . . . Yes, you heard pizza," Grace replied to the OIC.

Hazel walked over to look down on the growing and curious crowd. Gus joined her. "I hope Irene's having a better day with the canines," Gus said. "Are there any granola bars?"

Hazel looked back at Grace still on the phone. Their packs were piled at one end of the ladder. She put her arm around Gus, took another look in the direction of the courthouse, did a double-take and leaped in the air, clapping her hands.

"Bruce! There's Bruce!" Hazel shrieked, standing on tiptoe, waving and pointing down Main Street past the TV news trucks.

Off the phone now, Grace stepped between Gus and Hazel, putting her arms around their shoulders. "Thank heavens, Bruce is coming. The bucket truck is stuck. Its basket is at half mast and won't move." The threesome, grinning like Cheshire cats, jumped and waved at Bruce. The crowd began to clap and cheer.

Bruce sprinted alongside two of his attorney buddies, their ties flapping about their ears. They carried their suit jackets, and their shirts had dark half circles under their arms. Bruce was giving the thumbs-up signal, while the others pummeled the air with their fists.

"Let's lower the ladder," Gus said. She looked down at the men now closing in on the OIC. "Bruce and his buddies can handle the police and the media. I've gotta eat. I'm woozy."

"Let's do it then," Grace replied, her arm around Gus.

"Crap," Hazel said, suddenly in a frenzy of straightening her clothes and hair. "Now I've gotta face the TV people! My Mahjong group will grill me for days!"

The women perched the ladder on the wall, its feet pointing in the air over the crowd like a giant teeter totter. As counterbalance, Gus and Hazel held the top while Grace guided the ladder ever more outward. As the ladder progressed to the tipping point, the raspy noise alerted all below. Halfway out in the air, the ladder plunged, feet first and downward, dragging Gus and Hazel across the roof, hands stretched over their head, their heels digging grooves in the soft asphalt.

Onlookers, cable TV men, and reporters stumbled and pushed each other away from the charging ladder, while two of the police officers grabbed the bottom rungs, saving the hood of the cable TV truck.

The crowd cheered Grace, who clambered down first. A female officer had arrived to take the women to the police station. She reached out to help Grace get both feet on the ground. Then she opened a pair of handcuffs.

"Not yet," Grace whispered. "I want to block the cameras. Help me."

The female officer, Tandy Sweet, according to her name plate, looked at Hazel coming down. Way too much flesh, she thought. She nodded a curt "yes" to Grace.

"Guys, give us some room here. We've got it covered," Tandy said to the male officers and motioned to the cameraman. "You, outta the way!"

Hazel was halfway down when she froze. Gus was still on the roof. "Come on, Haze," Grace wheedled from the ground. "You can do it. Put your right foot back and feel down for the next rung. Hang on to the side rails and close your eyes. You're almost there."

Quivering with exhaustion and covered with black, greasy spots, Hazel's thighs resembled two piglets after a greased pig contest. Above them, her butt cheeks wobbled and shook with each step like cats in a bag.

Hazel heard Grace's encouragement, but her mind clogged with images of what she thought Grace, the officers, and worst of all, the TV crews were seeing. Moving, she thought, would be even more horrible.

Still on the roof and out of patience, Gus needed something to eat, pronto. She fought to just remain upright, never mind climb down a ladder. Her mind faltered. Then the answer came to her.

Gus bent over the top of the ladder, cupped her hands, and screamed as loudly as she could, "Fiiiiirrrrrre!"

Thoughts of fire thawed Hazel's fear of photos, and she clambered down the ladder with feline speed, if not the same agility. With questions flying like darts and a zealous videographer behind her, Sergeant Tandy Sweet did her best to block the media while making sure Hazel and Gus disembarked the ladder in safety. She cuffed the women and put their packs in the trunk of her police cruiser, leaving Bruce and his buddies to deal with the OIC and the media.

Hours later at home, now clean and fed, the women discovered the local TV news cut the important things as always. The news didn't show Sergeant Tandy helping them off the ladder, or her smiling at them as they went to the station for booking. The news didn't show the scene where the women, with clean faces and combed hair, released on their own recognizance, shared a huge pizza with off-duty cops. Neither did the news make mention of the fate of the McClellan building.

However, on every half-hour segment, the TV video did show, and replayed several times, the women's ugly mug shots and the descent of Hazel's big butt.

3

Shear Charisma or Sheer Madness?

Gus's fears for the canines at the spa, while out of proportion, were not unfounded. Bedlam reigned at Shear Charisma Grooming Shoppe that morning, as the four canines arrived with their human escort, Irene. Taking longer than usual, check-in added to Irene's exasperation and made the ca-nines most unruly. Suspicious of Gus's request for canine transport, but unaware of "Operation Wonder Woman," Irene was irked by her uncharitable thoughts. An experienced woman and manager of Such Happenis Adult Toys, Irene could spot a con job, however clever. Her friends' reasons for needing her help were flimsier than a Victoria's Secret teddy. *What was going on?*

Butterbean, the Corgi (who belonged to Gus) was herding her two Pomeranian friends, Art and Gwen (who belonged to Hazel and Bruce), between the elegant and ticklish legs of HRH Queen Daphne, Greyhound Retired (who belonged to the women's younger friend Marigold). When Irene bent to untangle the dogs, they reversed direction, and the Pomeranians' leashes wrapped around Irene's ankles. Butterbean sat on Irene's left foot and thrust her head up, eyes sparkling, tongue lolling.

Queen Daphne batted Butterbean with her front paw and rebuked the Pomeranians with an elegant sneer, her raised lips and clenched teeth subduing the smaller dogs as if she *were* royalty.

"Oh, she's smiling! Isn't that cute?" chirped a perky client to the man with a Springer Spaniel, both behind Irene.

Ms. Perky Client gushed at Irene and then turned to the overwhelmed receptionist, who jotted down information as she talked on the phone and waited for a receipt to print.

Special attention denied, Ms. Perky stalked out the door in a huff.

Irene saw the relief in the receptionist's eyes when she began checking in her now well-behaved canines. Queen Daphne's information update and most of Butterbean's shot record was complete when the phone rang yet again. The receptionist made an "I'm sorry, I can't help it" face and picked up the phone. The folks in line began to shift from foot to foot, look at their watches, and get cross with restless canines.

"Oh no!" the receptionist exclaimed, bursting into tears. "How *awful!* Of course she won't be in. I understand, but I gotta go." She sniffed, snatched a tissue, and finished Butterbean's card.

The groom room was more frenetic than usual.

Joanie, one of three groomers, would not be in today. Something had happened to her dog Sassy this morning. The two remaining groomers would have to handle her workload.

Over the noise of the cage dryers, each canine voiced a new fact or opinion. One of the later arrivals, a Poodle named Henrietta, happened to live two blocks away from Joanie and Sassy. Often they met by accident on their walks.

"Well, you know how my human is," explained Henrietta. "We were late for our walk because her oatmeal boiled over and then a telemarketer called. I saved her from buying another sweater by circling my spot near the kitchen door. She noticed me, put down the phone, and out we went. There were sirens and people rushing about. When the hospital ambulance whizzed by, I dragged my human after it." Henrietta stopped and placed her shoulder in front of the dryer to protect her throat from the hot air.

"When we reached the scene, the nasty dog had been removed, half asphyxiated I might add, and a weeping Joanie was being herded into the ambulance. She had a wicked bloody arm. I didn't see Sassy, but talk among the humans was that she'd been wrapped in a blanket and taken to the vet. Someone said she was decapitated, another person insinuated she was shredded, and a few were screeching as only humans do when upset. I managed to see the blood, lots of it, but couldn't get close enough to smell whose it was. The street looked like a slaughterhouse, if you ask me."

Henrietta took a deep breath and continued, "A German Shepherd who saw the big, nasty dog being hauled away told me that the mean thing snapped and snarled all the way into the truck, threatening everyone on two or four feet. The Shepherd suspected either rabies or a deep psychosis, possibly from abuse. No matter, I won't go near there again! If his rabies shot is current, the psychopath will be home before we are. His human must be a piece of work!" With that smug pronouncement, Henrietta flexed her neck and lay down.

"Hmmph!" snorted Gwen, one of Hazel's Pomeranians. *Henrietta's human isn't very responsible either, she thought. What was she doing taking Henri near such a scene, leash or no?* "Damn!" Gwen whimpered. "Poor Sassy, she must have been scared witless. This is so . . . *so gross!*" Heartbroken, Gwen lay down, flat and still under her dryer, her nose running like a drippy faucet. She tried not to think about Sassy or a new groomer.

Gwen's brother, Art, was the last one bathed. In the cage adjoining Gwen's, he whirled clockwise with his left ear on the floor, then counterclockwise with his right ear down, allowing the dryer to blow on whatever part passed by.

"Things happen, you know. Was it a Pit Bull? I'd have Pit Bulls chained from birth, but who listens to me?" Art bellowed over the drying room hubbub. "I don't want to get involved, thank you very much. I need to get on with my drying."

Butterbean, not thrilled about grooming in the first place, was unhinged over the scene at check-in and now distraught over Sassy. She shivered in silence under her dryer. *What's wrong with canines?* she thought. *We used to treat each other with respect, or at least polite disdain. Now canines are behaving like human predators! Gwen must be a mess; she and Sassy are best buddies.* Butterbean howled her condolences and her frustration.

Consigned to a large crate in the drying room, Queen Daphne tried to set aside her aggravation over the front desk fiasco and to absorb the conversations around her. Like all the grooming clients, she always talked with Sassy in her bed under Joanie's grooming table.

How had Sassy's presence disturbed or threatened that huge dog? Daphne wondered, fuming at the pointless cruelty. Sassy was so small. Like certain human psychopaths, she felt these wing-nut canines should be removed from ordinary populations. Daphne sighed and continued listening to the din around her.

The morning's uproar at Shear Charisma declined after noontime. Even without Joanie, routine was re-established. Meals eaten, the two groomers made ready to finish the client canines. Rough-cut and bathed in the morning and then under the dryers as long as possible, the dogs would next have their final cut and primp.

Art, because he'd paid attention to his drying, got combed out and finished first. The pony-tailed groomer scissored his caramel coat into a neat roundness. His ivory tail fanned across his back like a white peacock displaying his tail feathers. Accustomed to Joanie and terrified that this new groomer would use nail polish, Art growled and grumbled the whole time she cut and filed his nails. When the polish bottle wasn't forthcoming, he relaxed and enjoyed his final fluff with the brush. A pat and a treat later, he was back in his cage.

Gwen was chosen next by Ms. Ponytail, and Butterbean found herself on the first groomer's table. Feeling Butterbean's dampness, the first groomer hauled over the super dryer and put on her ear protectors. Bracing herself against the force of the air, Butterbean leaned into the warmth and watched her undercoat float all over the room, way up to the ceiling fan. Her groomer followed Butterbean's gaze and said, "A black spider in the web of dust and hair on the blades would make a superb Halloween decoration." The blades poked more than stirred the humid air.

Butterbean enjoyed her final fluff as the air ran against the grain of her hair from tail to neck. She gave a shake and sat to scratch where a hunk of undercoat had blown away. It felt super good.

After blowing out every loose hair, the groomer cut and filed Butterbean's nails. On the second back foot, she understood that Butterbean's moans were motivated by self-pity, not by fear. She stopped, scratched behind Butterbean's ears, and kissed her on the head. "You wuss," the groomer whispered, laughing as she finished Butterbean's front nails.

Interrupted by a flurry of footsteps and voices, the dogs and humans in the groom room turned toward the doorway. Kurt, a Jack Russell Terrier, appeared for his monthly pedicure. A kennel girl plopped him on Joanie's table, muzzled him, and began the ritual.

Because Gwen, Butterbean, and especially Art found Kurt more annoying than desirable, they tried to avoid him as much as possible. The snub only encouraged Kurt, who passed endless sly and hurtful remarks. Not only had he no sympathy for Sassy, but through his muzzle, he launched a garbled tirade about some foolish old women in a breaking news bulletin on local TV. He mentioned they had been on the rooftop of a downtown building.

The kennel girl put Kurt down, released the muzzle, and stepped back to avoid his snap at her hand. Vexed that he'd missed, Kurt lifted his leg on the doorjamb. Looking back at Butterbean and Gwen on the grooming tables, he commented with a sneer, "By the way, *ladies*, on the TV video of those women coming down the ladder? They're *your* humans! I'd recognize those fat legs and butts anywhere!"

4

Wonder Woman Wannabe

Marigold Moon, the younger friend of the rooftop trio, fared no better than the women or the canines that day. Caught in a web of overbooked or mechanically disabled flights from Chicago to Pine Crossing, her delight in returning home after teaching another successful drama workshop annihilated by frustration. Marigold was tired, hungry, and desperate to keep her secret appointment with her new therapist. She took a deep breath for fortitude and dashed through the gates toward baggage claim.

"Marigold! Mari!"

Marigold stopped and whirled around, becoming an obstacle in the human torrent pouring toward the escalator. She stepped toward the wall, almost tripping a running businessman with her rolling carryon while she surveyed the crowd for the name-caller. At almost six feet tall and with a halo of red hair, Marigold wasn't easy to miss, even in a busy airport.

She saw a male hand waving in front of a grinning, cherubic face. It was Sam, the guy who lived across the hall. Cute, sweet, and sometimes helpful, he had a crush on Marigold the size of Mount Rushmore. He left home and moved into her apartment building five minutes after his high school graduation last summer, making him all of nineteen—half Marigold's age. He had become a part of her life like taxes, and like a St. Bernard puppy, he was marginally manageable. He *did* have a thick, wavy head of sandy-colored hair, and he knew how to fix anything.

Marigold's thoughts about Sam were interrupted by the local news on the television situated on the wall above the human flood. She saw a shot of a reporter standing next to an Animal Control Unit as two officers lifted a huge, unconscious dog into the back holding area.

"Early this morning, after mangling a small Poodle on Jefferson Street," the TV reporter pointed at a dark stain on the macadam, "a large, mixed-breed dog was removed by Animal Control. The Poodle's owner, badly bitten as she tried to rescue her dog, is at Pine Crossing Regional Hospital. We'll have more on this at five o'clock." He touched his earpiece and continued. "Breaking news downtown. Minutes ago, three elderly women were arrested on the McClellan building roof. We don't know yet what they were doing there or why, but we'll have updates as details come in. Back to you, Stephanie, for the weather."

Marigold turned to track Sam's approach, and there he was.

"Let me help you," he said. "I'm headed your way."

"To the Ladies Room?" she snapped, regretting her words as she watched the cheer leak out of his face, pinching his features into the theatre mask "Tragedy."

"I'm sorry," Marigold apologized. "My flight was awful. I had three connections, got bumped, spent hours stuffed between two obese men, and the complimentary beverages cost two dollars." Marigold waved at the TV. "Now I hear about a half-dead dog and old ladies on a roof. I have an appointment, Sam, and I want to get home."

A handful of hang-ups, one political robo-call, and four rants from coworkers disgruntled over next year's budget cuts filled Marigold's home answering machine—not as many as she expected for a ten-day absence. She exercised the delete button and pondered the messages she didn't get. There was no word from Gus, Grace, or Hazel. Apparently, her beloved greyhound, HRH Queen Daphne, was still at Shear Charisma. Disappointed and famished, Marigold decided to eat and unpack before dealing with absentee friends and a canine with delusions of royalty.

The phone rang. Marigold fumbled it, yelling "hello" as it slid to the floor.

"Who's this?" Irene bellowed.

"Marigold. Sorry."

"Aha! You *are* home." Irene's tone was touchy. "I hope you can pick up those crazy canines. It's been pandemonium everywhere today. Shear Charisma was sheer madness. Busy as a portside bordello, the place was insane! You won't believe this, but some enormous mutt almost killed Sassy, Joanie's Poodle, this morning. He bit Joanie's arm something awful, so there were just two groomers at the shop today."

"Oh crap," Marigold blurted out. "I heard that at the airport, but no details. What happened? How's Joanie?"

"I don't know," Irene replied. "I'm a New-York minute from a meltdown. Gus asked me to take the dogs for grooming because she and Hazel were going to the podiatrist. The dogs lost their manners during check-in, including your Queen Daphne. The Poms and Butterbean acted like it was a herding trial. Then at lunch I heard something on the radio about three old ladies and the McClellan building! I think I was hornswoggled!"

"Crap again! I apologize for Daphne. *What* old ladies? If you're right, and I bet you are, they'd plotz if they knew you called them 'old ladies.' Do you know for sure it's them?"

"I didn't call them old ladies, the TV did. I don't know if it's them, and I don't care. I can't get Sassy out of my mind." Irene's voice quavered. She lapsed into silence and Marigold waited.

Steadier now, Irene continued, "Can you get the dogs at five o'clock? I'm not worth fudge today, and I've gotta finish here. You know my boss, His Majesty Germy George. He gets pickle-faced if the shipping isn't done 'toot sweet.' My pile of outgoing boxes looks like the Washington Monument, and heaven forbid his customers don't get their toys the next day."

"I'd be glad to get the dogs. I miss Daphne. I'm sorry about Sassy and Joanie. Please call me if you find out more."

"Thanks, kid. And you call me if our AWOL pals turn up. They'll be gettin' a huge piece of my mind! Gotta go, bye."

Marigold sat at her kitchen table with her tea and tuna salad. In thirty minutes, she had to be at Dr. Olivia De Soto's office across town.

Dr. De Soto's waiting room and office was standard shrink in Marigold's estimation: soothing mauves, tans, and greens with gender neutral furnishings. Her shelves contained many books and several degrees hung on the wall. The only clock squatted on her desk, facing away from the client. One unusual item, a ponytail palm, sat in the left section of the bow window behind Dr. De Soto's dark cherry desk.

Of course, Marigold thought, as she flung herself into the waiting room two minutes before 3:30, this is my first real visit. Last week was eyeball-high paperwork. She had sat across from Dr. De Soto at the desk, filling out insurance, medical, and legal forms. Adding in the lists of legal, financial, and medical regulations as well as rules of conduct and privacy disclosures, they created a pile the size of the Raleigh white pages, leaving ten minutes to discuss Marigold's reasons for coming. Now, Marigold chose a chair by the forlorn-looking coat rack in the waiting room and rummaged in her purse to find and turn off her cell phone.

The office door opened on the dot of 3:30, revealing Dr. De Soto dressed in a tailored, pastel plaid shirt with tan cotton slacks. A turquoise scarf threaded through her belt loops, a pleasing visual condiment. Dr. De Soto smiled and stepped inside.

Seating herself in a comfortable chair beside her desk, Dr. De Soto motioned for Marigold to sit on the cushy loveseat facing the desk. The blinds were drawn against the western sun. Marigold decided this was the standard therapy arrangement.

"So," Dr. De Soto asked, "shall we begin?"

"Sure," Marigold replied, "any place in particular?"

"Sometimes I like to start with childhood, family of origin, and so on, but from our last session I gather you want to deal with current issues. Is that correct?"

"Yes," Marigold replied.

"Good. Perhaps we'll be led by those issues to an exploration of earlier times, but for now, let's start with the last few years."

"Okay. This has been a difficult day because I flew in this morning from Chicago. I teach drama at the community college, and I give week-long drama workshops for anyone who can pay for them. This one was at a small college in Chicago, and my flight was a nightmare and three hours late. I'm still rushing in my mind. Plus, I think a couple of my friends have been arrested and my dog groomer is in the hospital and I have to pick four dogs up from Shear Charisma as soon as we finish here. I'm telling you this because I'm not always this scattered, and I know it shows." Marigold reflected on her statement. It didn't sound very different from how she often answered the question, "How are you?"

"At least, I don't think I'm usually this scattered," she added, fussing with her bracelets.

"What made you hesitate, reconsider?"

"The answer I just gave sounded too familiar. I don't think I'm always scattered, but I *do* think I'm too busy."

"Why do you think that is?"

Marigold twisted a piece of her curly, red hair in her left hand. "I don't know. Can we save that for later? I want to outline my current situation."

"Sure, Marigold, we can do that." Dr. De Soto slipped a small pad and a pen from a drawer in the table beside her chair and wrote, "Busy-ness and control issues."

"I met a man, Fleming, at the Deco Gecko Gallery downtown a little over two weeks ago," Marigold went on. "He was attractive, interesting to talk to, said he was an artist. We seemed to hit it off, so he asked for my number and promised to call, but so far, no word. Somewhere in our conversation, he mentioned a trip abroad, but I didn't think it was imminent. Anyway, the workshop was a good one. The kids did a great job with a mediocre play written by their professor, and the stage manager, a really talented fellow, had me wishing I could be a cougar," Marigold stopped a moment, "but . . ."

"What's a 'cougar'?" Dr. De Soto asked.

"A woman in her forties who dates men half her age. Where was I?" Marigold watched Dr. De Soto smile as she wrote.

"Cougars, and before that, Fleming," replied Dr. De Soto.

"Fleming. I don't know him from Adam, but I'm interested. I check my cell phone like one of Skinner's rats, and he's all I think about, an obsessive hope against hope.

"I've got a terrible track record with men. I didn't want it to be that way and I don't think it's my fault, I mean, in the way of me being a bad person, you know, manipulating, gold-digging, castrating, those adjectives that come before the word 'bitch.' May I?" Marigold inquired, pulling her feet under her ankle-length skirt to slip off her sandals and curl up on the loveseat. Not missing the irony, loveseat, Marigold smiled to herself, stashing the observation for a later session.

"Sure, get comfortable. Can you tell me about your past relationships?"

Marigold adjusted her position. "I had the usual teenage crushes and supervised dating, but growing up in a commune, I was more open and trusting in some ways than my peers from nuclear families. At any rate, I became socially integrated in my high school years and comfortable with my status, whatever that was. College was fairly normal for me too. I lost my virginity in my junior year, more as a declaration of independence than as an act of love. I got engaged to the wrong guy, we mutually broke it, and I graduated with a decent grade point average. Two days later, I found a job as an assistant drama coach.

"It was in my first year of teaching that things changed. I met and fell in love with an English professor. We lived together after a few months and I was committed and deliriously happy. Then I caught him in the hallway with a student one day when I was supposed to be in rehearsal. It was unexpected, terrifying, and as life-changing for me as a gunshot. He begged forgiveness, promised it'd never happen again, and you know the rest of the story."

"I do? Will you tell me?" Dr. De Soto gently inquired.

"The Teflon Zipper story," Marigold quipped. "He was unfaithful again and again and I put up with it until I had no dignity or self-respect. One day, I slunk away to my girlfriend's apartment. In a few weeks, I got the courage to rent my own place, get my things, and move on. For the next two or three years, I went through men with a vengeance, seducing them and tossing them aside like wilted vegetables."

Marigold changed position and continued. "Once I understood the futility of that behavior, I went to a workshop in Raleigh, something about finding and keeping real love, and met Stuart. We dated semi-long distance for over a year and I thought he was The One. We shared humor, good manners, off-the-Richter-Scale passion, and economic parity. I considered moving to Raleigh and launched a job search there. Then came Act Three: the denouement."

"Specifically, how did that go?"

"We were in his posh apartment, a huge great room with kitchen on the side, one bedroom, one bath, high ceilings. His furnishings were swanky yet comfortable, and he'd chosen and arranged it, no decorators for my Stuart. The sofa faced a bank of fifth-story windows, his desk to one side and chairs to the other. Glass end tables held alabaster lamps and the accessories, paintings, and pillows were in primary colors.

"I was in my robe, returning from the kitchen with some iced tea. We'd had slippery sex and a shower together and were discussing where to have an elegant meal. Stuart was sitting in a chair, freshly dressed, backlit by the windows.

"'Sweetheart,' he said in a tone I'd not heard before. I tensed, sat on the arm of the couch nearest him, and talked myself back into the contentment I'd felt the second before he spoke.

"'Yes, darling,' I answered with a satisfied lilt." Marigold interrupted herself. "Dr. De Soto, whenever I think of this, I still wonder how I could have stopped his next words, but there's no answer. Such moments sweep over us like a flash flood, without our consent, irrevocable."

"Go on," Dr. De Soto advised.

"Okay, then Stuart said, 'I have something to tell you.' Naturally, my eyebrows flew to my hairline. I'd heard, read, seen these words before. They happened to characters in plays, novels, movies, to some of my friends. Nothing good was coming, I knew, but I grasped a thin hope. Perhaps it was a family illness, a financial loss, someone's house fire.

"He told me his ex-girlfriend moved back to town, they had lunch the day before, and he wanted to see her again . . . 'but I don't want to lose you either,' he had said. Impulse overrode upbringing as I drowned the rest of his sentence with my tea. Absorbing the shock of my behavior and reflexive distress over the stain on his expensive shirt, I sped into the bedroom, slammed the door, and dressed.

"I was packing when, without knocking, Stuart barged in wearing a honey-you-must-understand expression, and uttered those exact words. I felt so creepy, I wanted to unzip my skin and flee."

"The English professor all over again," Dr. De Soto remarked.

"Only I dumped Stuart right away," Marigold added. "I didn't subject myself to the degradation of trying to make a relationship where one didn't exist. But yes, the situational similarity was heart-stopping."

"How did you handle it?" asked Dr. De Soto, steepling her hands, fingers pressing her lips.

"Poorly. I couldn't believe it'd happened again. I wept for days, couldn't eat, scraped by at work, came within a hair's breadth of being fired.

"One day I heard about an injured Greyhound that was going to be euthanized. After some finagling, she was released to me with a broken hind leg, posttraumatic stress disorder, and a ratty collar. I named her, Her Royal Highness Queen Daphne, after Daphne Moon on 'Frasier.' The 'Royal Highness' part came from her elegant and aristocratic carriage even in those miserable circumstances. We healed each other." Marigold reached for a tissue conveniently placed on the end table and wiped her nose. "How long ago was that?"

"About seven years. It took almost a year of that time to get normal again and Daphne did much better than I did. Shortly after that first year, I met Frank at a party. He manipulated my heart in ways that blinded my eyes and drained my brain. Fear that I'd been too hard on Stuart made me too tolerant of Frank." Marigold plucked at her hair.

"When my girlfriends tell me about men like Frank, I suggest new identity papers and a plane to Brazil. I knew Frank's kind of guy, but I couldn't make myself use that knowledge for my own benefit. Emotionally paralyzed, I lived in terror of another romantic loss."

"What happened?" Dr. De Soto's voice was soft, inviting trust.

"What you'd expect. I won't tell it all right now. We've got plenty of time later. Suffice it to say, he became abusive, verbally at first, physically at the end. I was literally rescued by two of my older women friends and mentors." Marigold began to cry.

Dr. De Soto waited.

Marigold sniffed, blew, and composed herself. "Though he forged my signature, stole my savings and home equity, and I had to be rescued by Gus and Grace, I was nuts enough to miss him. A year of therapy improved things just slightly. That's how much I hate and fear being alone. How do Gus and Grace do it year after year?"

"These are your mentors? How old are they?"

"Sometimes mentors, friends mostly. It switches back and forth, depending. Grace is seventy and Gus is sitting on sixty. They've both lived alone since I was in high school.

"Maybe I'm a love addict. I know I want kids and a family. I'm thirty-nine and my biological clock sounds like dueling metronomes," Marigold blubbered. "I'm good at my job, responsible, caring . . . I've become the man I wanted to marry. I don't want to be a single mother. I want a committed partner who is into the adventure of raising a family."

Marigold wadded her old tissue and took three more. "I fret over this all the time, as much as men think about sex."

"What happened between Frank and now? How long has that been?"

"Hmmm. It's been about three years, maybe four. I've dated a little, but I get cold feet after five or six dates, when it looks like time to sleep with him. Yet I'm horny as hell too."

Dr. De Soto crossed her legs and rolled her shoulders, the unasked question hanging between them.

Marigold yielded first. "Yes, I can satisfy myself and I do. But we both know, good as it is, it isn't the same thing."

"No," Dr. De Soto admitted, "it's not the same, but it is self-caring and it takes the edge off."

Marigold smiled, "For sure." She looked at her watch. "I'm sorry to be looking at my watch, but I've got to be at Shear Charisma to pick up the dogs. They're closing early today."

"It's about time anyway," Dr. De Soto replied, getting up and walking behind her desk to check the clock. "Just one question, well, two, actually. Do you want to continue seeing me? Weekly?"

"Yes, I want to continue, and weekly is fine. Conversation makes me focus."

"What happened with your therapy after Frank?"

Marigold extricated herself from the loveseat cushions and stood. "It was fine, but my therapist's husband got promoted so they moved to Arizona. I searched for another therapist, but then this thing happened and that thing, and, well, at last, here I am."

"What do you remember most about your therapy?" Dr. De Soto wrote an appointment card.

"One sentence in particular stuck with me. When I was whining about one of the men, the therapist shot back, 'You know all your relationships had one thing in common,' and I asked, 'What?'" Marigold watched Dr. De Soto suppress an upward twitch at the corners of her mouth as she continued. "You know what she said next, don't you?" Marigold smiled at Dr. De Soto.

"Tell me," Dr. De Soto requested.

"You, Marigold, *you're* the common denominator."

5

The Morning After

The crescendo and finale of yesterday's events, like the crash and ebb of a giant wave, remained with the women the next morning, their physical beach of pain and exhaustion sprinkled with emotional landmines.

Hazel's reaction to the evening news, sobs followed by hysterical laughter, caused Bruce to Monday-morning-quarterback himself for not squelching "Operation Wonder Woman." Furthermore, Bruce was disappointed in himself for failing to mitigate or divert the media in their lust for scandal and embarrassment of the women. Never did it occur to him that both the media and the women were out of his control.

Bruised and sunburned, Hazel had asphalt in knee creases that wouldn't budge. Neither of them had a decent night's sleep, but intent on apprehending the paperboy first, Hazel rose before the sun. Not to waken Bruce, she left Lady Labrador asleep in her bed and took Art and Gwen downstairs to help her make breakfast.

Between trips to the front window, just in case the paperboy came early, Hazel set out breakfast Danish, but put off baking scones until she had the paper firmly in hand. Inevitably the aroma of coffee would spiral upstairs, waking Bruce.

Aware that Hazel's early rising related to the newspaper, and not concern about his sleep, Bruce showered, shaved, and helped arthritic Lady down the stairs. While lathering his hair, still impressed with "Operation Wonder Woman," he decided to procure and deliver appreciation gifts for the three women. Without their efforts, the McClellan would have been rubble this morning.

"Hi, Sweetheart," Bruce said, keeping his voice ordinary and neutral. "Coffee smells great!" Dressed in a red Rutgers tee tucked into pressed tan cargo shorts, he pulled on a short-sleeved chambray shirt against the early morning damp.

"It's raining off and on," Hazel said. "Want some Danish?"

"Sure. I had a brilliant idea," Bruce said, as he watched Hazel roll her shoulders. Her old pajama top was sheer and sexy from years of wear. She'd tossed a seersucker robe over it, and shuffled around in her pink bunny slippers. Her face, sunburned red yesterday, now had brown tones. Her freshly showered hair frizzed like a poodle's. He could tell she ached. She shifted and started as though she walked barefoot on gravel. *Or she heard the paperboy,* Bruce thought.

"What brilliant idea?" She trilled the l's and gave him a dazzling smile he didn't recall as one of hers.

"I'm off to get some lumber and plants for the privacy fence Grace talked about," Bruce said, taking some coffee, "and azaleas for Gus's backyard, not to mention a special gift for you, my sweet. Just a token of how much I appreciate yesterday. Do you think that's a good idea?"

"I think it's a fabulous idea! They'll both enjoy those things. What's my special gift?" She set the pot of coffee on the table, pulled some scones out of the cupboard, and sat down.

"Oh no, no, no, you're getting surprised too!" Bruce flashed the grin that convinced judges and juries his argument was the just one. "This smells great," he exclaimed, rubbing his hands together as he took his chair. His silvery hair was half dry—some of it curled, and some of it remained plastered in wet strands to his forehead and neck. He dove into the Danish as if he'd not eaten in three days and added all the milk that would fit in his mug.

Hazel studied this performance. *Bruce doesn't wolf his food.* Her expression inscrutable, she reached across the table and took his hand. "Slow down, Sweetie. I appreciate the thought, but you are not beating me to that paper."

Grace trundled downstairs two hours later than usual, her snooze button way overworked. Mindful that she wasn't fully functioning, she used the handrail and watched her feet. The stairs hadn't changed in the last twenty-four hours, but she had. Muscles on no known anatomy chart were screaming. Every inch of her skin hurt. The parts of her epidermis that were unscratched were otherwise blackened with asphalt or sunburned. Her stiff hands wanted to open her head and release the fogginess of exhaustion.

Grace reached the kitchen, sloppily gobbled two glasses of water, and turned on the coffeemaker. Wiping spilled water from her raggedy tee and cut-off paisley pajama pants, she groaned and hobbled to the front door, praying the paper would be on the porch this drizzly morning.

A movement in the living room window caught her attention. Then she heard a thump, bang, thud. *What in the hell . . . is that a tree on my front porch?* She grabbed her baseball bat from the umbrella stand and yanked the front door open. There was Bruce, straightening himself over a pile of lumber. He gave her that grin of his that reminded her of Rhett Butler, and put his hands on his hips, stretching backwards. "Hi, Grace! How are you this fine specimen of a morning?"

"How do you think I am?" Grace shot back. "On my way to get the dreaded newspaper, I see a tree float by my window. Then I hear what sounds like bodies being dumped on my stoop, and I find you in that bilious yellow raingear, turning my front porch into a lumber yard. Stop gawping like a guilty sixth-grader. What *are* you doing?" She put down her baseball bat.

Smiling a genuine sheepish smile, Bruce walked toward Grace, arms open, palms up. "Sorry if I startled you. I appreciate what you did yesterday, and thought I'd surprise you."

"You did that one hundred percent, you big oaf," Grace replied as they hugged. She stepped out of the hug and held his elbows like a grandmother might. "Want some coffee? It'll be ready in a minute. Then you can tell me about all this," she said, waving at the lumber.

"Great! Thanks, Grace. I've got a few more things to unload and I'll be right in."

Grace remembered the paper. Looser now, she traversed the porch steps and part of the lawn in her normal gait to retrieve it. *At least it wasn't buried in the hedge,* she thought, shaking out the wet plastic, grateful the paperboy wrapped it tightly.

Above the fold on the front page was part of a photograph, shades of gray and abstract patterns revealing a wall, sky, and the top of a ladder. She turned the paper over to reveal the remainder of the photo, and gasped. Gus's derriere was partially blocked by Hazel's head and shoulders, the remainder of the space filled with Hazel's butt and thighs.

Laden with bags of nails, hardware, and a toolbox, Bruce stopped beside Grace. "Have you seen the caption?"

"God no. Did Hazel see this?"

"Of course, she's seen it," Bruce replied. "You know Hazel. She was up before five thirty. Can I put these inside?"

"Sure. Let's have that coffee. I want to hear about Hazel."

A few minutes and half a cup of coffee later, Bruce began. "If I'd known how tough it was for you all on that roof, I'd have had the cops intercept you and you'd have been home for breakfast. I worked on the asphalt in Haze's knees with my super grease remover and it's still there. At the McClellan after court, it seemed that no matter what I or my buddies said, we couldn't penetrate the numb skulls of those TV folks. The paper's reporter was worse, if that's possible. They didn't care about court or the issue between the Historical Society and the Church. All they wanted was to talk about you three."

Grace's eyebrows were up like two question marks as she slathered butter and jelly on an English muffin. "Sweet, dear Bruce, women have been used to sell stuff from hand cream to Harleys. We're big commodities. What did you expect?"

"Who knows?" Bruce confessed, looking Grace in the eye. "Still, you three really impressed me and I appreciate it." He finished his muffin and reached for another. The front page of the paper, spread between them on the table, screamed in seventy-two-point type, "PLENTY OF BUTTS ABOUT THE MCCLELLAN BUILDING." Bruce poked it. "Only an avalanche or a tsunami would've stopped that reporter."

Grace looked at the article, turned to the continuation, and said, "Lots of words, no content. How much money does the Church want?"

"You don't want to know," Bruce answered. "We have a month to raise the money, which is next to impossible, but we'll try. Hazel is what matters right now." He buttered his second muffin and slathered it with jam, small globs falling back onto his plate.

"Did you watch Hazel look at the paper?"

"Sort of." He took a swig of coffee.

"No 'sort of.' You either did or you didn't." Grace shot him the no-nonsense look of a school teacher.

"After Haze announced she would be getting the paper first, I went to my desk in the den to figure out how much lumber I wanted. When I saw the paperboy outside, I got up to join Hazel. I thought she was hurt and achy, but the woman who zoomed down the hall and out to get the paper could have been nineteen. Anyway, I watched from the doorway."

"And?" Grace poured them each more coffee and took another muffin.

Bruce stirred some cream into the fresh cup before replying. "She turned the paper over a couple of times. Then she ripped off the plastic, unfolded the paper, and read it standing on the lawn in her robe and pink bunny slippers, clothing only her very closest friends have seen. Next, she strolled up to me, exuding nonchalance, and said, 'What do you think of this, dear?' Before I could answer, she shook the paper and screeched, 'No good deed goes unpunished!' She dashed in the house and slammed the door. I guessed she thought it was somehow my fault, so I followed her."

"How did she take that?" Grace asked, adding a dollop of jam to her over-buttered muffin.

"She was in the kitchen reading the article, and I put my arms around her. I had no idea what to say. Nothing seemed helpful, so I was quiet, just holding her. She turned to me and said, 'Bruce, I know this isn't your fault, but I've never been so upset, not even when Great Aunt Sally got arrested for smuggling pain pills in her walker.' Then she poked her butt in the photo, and asked, 'How can you love this?'"

"Oh. My. God," Grace said, bits of jam sliding down the river of butter running over her thumb. "The unanswerable question. What did you say?"

"'Very well,' came out of my mouth. It was the right thing, I think. I hope. She kissed me and said, '*You* are the only one allowed in this house and I'm not going out, not ever!' Then she went upstairs. I could hear doors slamming and water running. You know how you're supposed to leave a session of dog training on a positive note? Well, I couldn't improve on this, so I yelled, 'Bye, Honey,' and left."

"To get the tree and lumber and come here?"

"Yeah," Bruce said. His look reminded Grace of a Bassett Hound.

"And what is that all about? Why lumber and a tree?"

"Hazel and I were yakking one day and she mentioned you'd like to have a privacy fence up before the house next door sold. It seemed like a smart idea, so I got the materials for you. I thought we could work together, or I could do it, or maybe turn it into a fence party, whatever you wanted."

"Thank you, Bruce," Grace replied, getting up. "But you shouldn't have."

Semi-embarrassed, Bruce rose also. "Why does everyone say 'You shouldn't have'? Of course, I should have. I wanted to do this. I thought you might decide to put the tree near your living room window or maybe by the fence. It grows fast, but not too tall."

"Good thinking. What kind of tree is it? We'll have to see where the sun and soil is right for it."

"It's a fig tree and placement is your job. I was just thinking out loud." Bruce looked at his watch. "I need to shove off. I've got azaleas for Gus and I need to get something for Hazel yet.

They walked to the door. "Bruce," Grace said, "I'd do Operation Wonder Woman over again and so would Hazel, I'm sure. She thinks you're top drawer. You *are* a 'cool dude,' as they say."

Thinking of Grace as the older sister he never had, Bruce arrived at Gus's house, six blocks away. Neat and Spartan, Grace's two-story, foursquare house couldn't have been more opposite Gus's single-story, gingerbread home, featuring ornate carvings and "stuff" everywhere. Hard to believe both were Victorian. Instead of more "stuff," Bruce purchased half a dozen red azaleas to plant along her back fence.

Good, the rain has stopped, he thought as he backed into Gus's driveway. He cut the engine and tossed his raingear behind the seat. Coming down from his sugar high, Bruce surveyed Irene's place next door, now understanding why Gus called it "Plantsylvania."

Irene's porch, curtained with plants, green stalactites and stalagmites, could render two people and a donkey invisible from the street. Bruce couldn't remember which, "mite" or "tite," went up and which grew down. He made a mental note to look it up.

Except for the white picket fence, her front yard reminded Bruce of Vietnam. It was crammed full of tropical shrubs and trees, the ground heavily mulched and veined with soaker hoses. An arbor of wisteria canopied the short passage from the sidewalk to the porch steps. Irene's calico cat, Mandy, lounged in the shade of the arbor.

Good way to avoid lawn mowing, Bruce thought, as he exited his truck. Spacing the azaleas along Gus's back fence seemed to be the most direct way to test their looks before planting. If she wasn't awake, it would be a super surprise. Being sure to keep the gate closed with each trip in case her Corgi, Butterbean, came out, Bruce carried two plants at a time to the fence.

After satisfactorily aligning the azaleas, he stretched the kinks out of his knees. Trekking back to the truck, hoping to make a clean getaway, Bruce stopped in the middle of the yard to glance over his shoulder at his handiwork. His self-congratulations were interrupted by a shriek from inside the house. Bruce broke into a run toward Gus's back porch.

The instant his foot hit the first tread, the door opened, and the screen door shot out with G-force, banging the wall. Bruce caught a nanosecond glimpse of Gus tossing something toward him. He would swear later that she threw tongs at him and was topless, but now he quickly batted something cool, slippery, and wet off his forehead. The tail end of a snake fell at his feet and he instinctively jumped back, looking at the now-closed screen door.

Bruce squatted and examined the half snake. He heard the squeak of the screen door and glanced up to see Grizzie the cat in midair stretch. She gave a feline growl as she landed on his arm, climbed his head, and raced down his back, leaving claw marks with each step. Before he grasped what had happened, Bruce saw an oncoming Corgi at full throttle. He closed his knees to block her. She hit his shins and knocked him over.

Stunned by the impact, they looked at each other. Butterbean shook her head and Bruce clutched his shins. Finally recognizing Bruce, Butterbean dismissed all cat transgressions to fiercely lick the bloody gouges on his arm and to gleefully wash his face.

Inside, Gus was in a swivet over the front half of a stuck snake. It twisted in the leaves of the heat grate on her dining room floor, very much alive, hissing and striking the air. *Probably brought in as cat treasure, the snake had enough torment,* Gus figured. It belonged outdoors, but her tongs couldn't remove it from the grate. Gritting her teeth and using a week's worth of courage, Gus wiggled the grate out of the floor, holding onto it opposite the snake's head. She glided to the screen door, pajamas perilously askew, the grate and snake at arm's length. Apparently incensed at this turn of events, the snake slid across the grate toward Gus's fingers.

In one motion, Gus threw open the screen door and tossed the grate and snake over the porch railing, her eyes following the grate's descent. Then, she heard a canine screech. The snake had slipped out of the grate, hitting Butterbean, who jumped straight up, turned, and fled under the porch. Bruce sat up, dazed. Gus clutched her pajama top around her ample breasts.

Where is Ann Landers when you need her?

On the way home, Bruce couldn't help reflecting on the path of life that led him to this goofy place in time. He had been among several of Hazel's discarded college lovers. Theirs was a simple, and now more common, story of high school or college romances rekindling later in life. As a college student, Hazel had all she could do managing a full-time course load and two small children. Bruce, determined to become the next F. Lee Bailey, discovered he had even less time than Hazel did. Passionate hours snatched in odd locations became passionate fights over whose responsibilities were more important. In spite of magnetic attraction and a good dose of genuine love, it became clear they had incompatible needs and goals.

True to form, they both regretted the breakup, but went on to live full and satisfying lives. After graduation from college, Hazel married a coworker and quickly divorced, certain no one could match her dead husband. She had a successful career in marketing and raised her two children, now *émigrés*, one in Australia and one in Portugal. "Empty nest syndrome" wasn't in Hazel's vocabulary. She loved living alone, and though she inherited her parents homestead and moved from New Jersey to Pine Crossing, she intended to continue her same lifestyle.

Bruce meanwhile, not long after the breakup with Hazel, married a woman named Sheila and promptly had two sons. Once the boys were in college, the couple, at Sheila's behest, settled in Pine Crossing, her hometown. After just a month there, Bruce came home early and caught Sheila in bed—their bed—with her diving instructor. Immediately, he moved out and began divorce proceedings.

One morning after getting his final divorce decree, Bruce was answering the phones for National Public Radio, taking pledge information. Seated next to him was an attractive woman that seemed familiar, but then again, not. In between pledge calls, they engaged in casual conversation, both of them admitting to feelings of déjà vu. Over lunch, they resolved those feelings with much blushing and gales of laughter.

In the years since, they kept separate residences—at Hazel's insistence, but by mutual agreement. Because of the fenced yard for their dogs and greater human comfort, their time together was spent at Hazel's place.

"Honey, I'm hooomme," Bruce yodeled, keying open Hazel's back door. Greeted with silence, Bruce yelled again as he went into the half bath to clean himself up. He preferred to look his very best in public at all times, and he still had to get Hazel's present.

Painted with streaks of dirt, dog slobber, and probably snake goo, the women at the soup kitchen would have shooed him into line instead of letting him cook. However, his scratched arm was clean and covered with band-aids, as were two of the worst gouges in his back, thanks to Gus.

A quick inventory of his shirt and shorts led him to strip to his jockeys and slip into the laundry room to start a small wash. Lady, in her bed in the kitchen, raised her head with a woof and low growl until she caught Bruce's scent and lay down again.

Leaving his shoes by the washer, he padded down the hall and hurried up the front stairs, so focused on a shower and clean clothes that he opened Hazel's bedroom door without his usual knock.

On the phone with Irene and wholly unprepared for a disheveled, bandaged man in his jockeys, Hazel shrieked, dropped the phone, and flapped her hand around on the nightstand, seeking her pepper spray.

"Whoa baby," Bruce said, backing up with raised hands. "It's me, Bruce!"

"I *know* it's you, turkey," Hazel said, trying to finesse her reaction. "You scared the crap out of me. Look at yourself!" Hazel retrieved the phone, Irene's sputtering now audible to all.

"Who's there? Hazel, do you need help? Say something, Hazel, or I'm calling 911."

"I'm okay, Irene. It's Bruce. He's a mess. I'll call you back in an hour." She plunked the handset in its slot and went over to Bruce, turning him around and inspecting his bandages. "*What* happened to you?"

"Grizzie and Butterbean happened to me. I delivered Gus's azaleas, had them lined up along her back fence, and was taking a last look when . . ." Bruce made his Rhett Butler grin and Hazel cut him off with a quick kiss.

"Before you go on, can I make us a sandwich while you shower and change? We can tell our tales then. I've had quite a morning too."

They reconvened in the kitchen, "I'd like to get caller ID and new drapes," Hazel said. She was dressed in slacks and a cheerful print blouse. Bruce wore clean khaki cargo shorts, a neon green tee, and fresh bandages.

Hazel poured coffee and rummaged through the various pastries she'd set out. Bruce described his visit with Grace, excluding the newspaper discussion, mentioning his pleasure that Grace liked the lumber and the fig tree. On his second cup of coffee, he recreated his adventures at Gus's, giving Hazel her laugh for the day.

"*That's* why Gus hasn't called. Whatever could she say?" Hazel broke up a lemon Danish, still chuckling. "While you were getting mauled, Grace called to tell me she'd taken her phone off the hook. Lawyers, radio folks, and church members spewed solicitations and nastiness all over her answering machine. Then Irene called to say we landed on *Good Morning Pine Crossing* every hour from five to nine. They interviewed the OIC, who exuded commitment to law 'n' order."

"That's why you locked the back door?" Bruce mumbled, scone crumbs slipping into his coffee.

"Yep, and listen to this. Irene's life is headed for the crapper too. Her boss thinks the prescription erectile dysfunction drugs are dooming his business, so he's searching for any competitive pill or potion, never mind the risk. Irene hates them all—the side effects of prescription drugs and the complete risk of unexamined concoctions. She's looking for more, well, tangible devices.

"Then Marigold called. She dressed me down for not including her in our operation and I reminded her she wasn't home yesterday. Sheesh! Next she ranted about our health and age. She must think we've got one foot in the grave. Anyway, her neighbor Sam banged on her door as we were on the phone. He wants to do an article on us for the college paper. I hollered 'no' as loud as I could and hung up."

Bruce sighed and rubbed his stomach. "Let's go look at drapes then. I can call the phone company while you get ready."

"No! Not me!" Hazel cried, spilling her coffee. "You go. Get any color green but pea. *Please* go. I'm not going out ever again. I can't show my face, not with *that picture* on the front page. I'm not even sure I want to live here anymore. This is just the beginning, I think." Sobbing now, Hazel grabbed a paper towel, and blowing her nose, ran from the room.

Bruce put his elbows on the kitchen table, his head in his hands.

6

A Friendly Home Invasion

Five days passed. Gus survived the snake episode and Bruce planted her azaleas. Suffering heat exhaustion and endocrine imbalance from the McClellan debacle, she made copious mental notes about diminishing resilience. She taped a reminder on her bathroom mirror: "One learns good judgment through experience; one gains experience through bad judgment."

Tired of Hazel's truancy and resulting silence, Marigold took action. She and Her Royal Highness Queen Daphne marched to Grace's house, and Grace drove them the few blocks to Gus's, where they captured Gus and Butterbean in the garden.

Pouring out of Grace's car, the troupe launched an assault on Hazel's front porch, but the place seemed forsaken in the way houses do when the owner is out of town. They repeatedly buzzed the doorbell with no response. Gus stepped off the porch to glance at the second story windows, noticing no leaves hung over the gutter's edges. In the second or two she marveled at such cleanliness, Gus caught the flick of an upstairs curtain. Hazel *was* hiding out.

Now certain their quarry was present, Gus opened the side gate, letting Butterbean and Queen Daphne into Hazel's yard. The Poms raced from the back and greeted them while Gus closed the gate, returned to the front porch, and called Hazel's cell phone. Marigold rang the landline, and Grace leaned on the door buzzer.

"Okay, *okay!*" Hazel yelled over the sound of three clunks, one for each lock. She stood in a river of ecstatic canines that had burst in through the doggie door. Art and Gwen bounced and barked. Butterbean butted Hazel's ankles. Daphne nudged at her elbow. Lady stood behind the group, wagging her tail, her gray muzzle turned up in a smile.

"Get in here before someone sees you!" Hazel hissed at her friends. "Can't you tell when a person isn't home? I may *never* be home, maybe won't *have* a home in this town. What were we *thinking*?" Hazel grabbed each of them in turn by the forearm and pulled them inside, slamming the door behind Marigold, the last.

Everyone shuffled down the hall in a conga line to avoid stepping on furry feet. When they reached the kitchen, Gus, who was first in line, stopped in her tracks.

Hazel's kitchen, usually exuding rumpled warmth, offered all the charm of a furniture outlet. The table was polished to a military shine and held only two silver candelabra, the candles still wrapped in cellophane. Gone was the pansy print tablecloth, its stains testament to past holidays, birthdays, and personal celebrations. Gone were the scattered newspapers, stacks of mail, and Bruce's laptop.

"Wow," Gus said, keeping her voice emotionless. "Look at the new chandelier! And the Black Watch dog beds, a gi-normous one for Lady, and little ones for Art and Gwen. I can smell the cedar." She wanted to add, "Instead of coffee and baking scones," but she held her tongue.

The women took their accustomed seats, and the dogs found strategic spots under the table. Hazel put on coffee and brought out cream, sugar, and substitutes for same. She offered Danish, donuts, and with reluctance, scones.

"Stop gawking! You shouldn't be here anyway." Hazel's lips flat-lined like an ATM slot, a signal that more than coffee was brewing.

Marigold sat at the nominal head of the table. With her curly red hair in a single plait, she pulled her feet on the chair seat and tented her skirt over her knees, looking seven years old. Her tone soft, wary, she asked, "You mean, we can't visit?"

Hazel put out mugs, each making a solid thump as it hit the table. "I thought I was clear on the phone to *all* of you. We're to appear in court on Wednesday for misdemeanor charges, loitering on private property, and trespassing in a restricted area. The Preservation Society has one month to raise enough money to purchase the McClellan, period. If the money isn't raised, then bye-bye building. What else is there to know?" Her lower lip stuck out, and she squinted at her friends as if they were an alien species.

"Settle down, Haze," Grace admonished. "It's okay. We can't get more than a fine and a few hours of community service. We did all we could to save the building. It's over for us, out of our hands."

"How can you be so sure that's the end of it, Grace? People initiate civil suits all the time." Hazel plunked the butter next to the scones.

"Look at all the judge programs on TV," Gus grinned. "There must be five now. Folks love lawsuits, the crazier the better. We could be sued for slandering the church, assault on a building, or red blotch damage to the crane."

"Gus is right. A civil suit would have to be that ridiculous: red blotch damage!" Grace chuckled, pieces of scone slipping from her mouth. The dogs scrambled for the spoils.

Hazel plopped the coffee carafe on a new pot holder. Her mouth softening, she poured coffee.

Marigold unfolded herself, took a Danish pastry, and put cream in her coffee. She looked around the room and in a tentative tone asked, "Hazel . . . Hazel, how did this . . . I mean, did you . . . The room looks great, how did you do it?"

Hazel's eyes narrowed as Gus intervened. "I'm impressed, too, Hazel, and inspired. I have too much to do at my place. How did you manage this in just a few days?"

"You did all this yourself?" Grace chimed in.

Hazel's expression said her bullshit detector was in the red zone. "It's not great and you know it, at least not yet. The light yellow paint's good, but the neatness is because I threw everything out." Her voice cracked a bit as she went on. "I've been too embarrassed to go out and even more upset with myself for feeling that way, so I took it out on my kitchen.

"It was fun tossing that old wagon wheel chandelier with the milk glass globes, but Bruce claims he can't eat by candlelight, so he came home with *this* shiny thing." Hazel pointed vehemently at the new chandelier. "Sometimes he forgets we aren't married and that we have final say in our own houses." Hazel sighed, forestalling other comments by saying, "I know it's meant as a love message, and maybe the brass will tone down with some tarnish and dust, but right now, looking up blinds me like a camera flash."

"The new dog beds are cool," Marigold said. "I like Black Watch plaid."

"I do miss the old tablecloth and the clutter, though," Gus said, getting up. "Where're the napkins and dog treats?"

"In the pantry until I get new canisters." Hazel took a scone and dunked it in her coffee.

"Hey, Haze," Gus shouted from the pantry. "Change of subject. I wasn't kidding about the mess at my house. Who cleans your gutters?"

Hazel's eyes popped. "*What?*" she yelped, "*You're* asking for help?"

Returning with napkins and treats, surrounded by a troop of salivating canines, Gus sighed. "I can't do it myself any more. I'm choosing my battles, so to speak. My magnolia sheds worse than a Husky in August, covering everything with leaves, especially the gutters."

"No more balancing on your rickety ladder, hosing everything in sight, including yourself?" Hazel's voice dripped disbelief.

"Yep," Gus answered, handing Hazel some of the treats. "My spiritual advisor suggests I delegate authority, which means spend money. The gutters are first."

Grace poured more coffee and asked, "Why the sudden change?"

"Who's your spiritual advisor?" Marigold interrupted. "I need one."

Hazel flapped her hand and made a shushing noise in Marigold's direction. "What's up, Gus?"

Gus passed out her handful of dog treats and sat down. "I'll share my spiritual advisor later, Marigold. What's up is: I'm going to write. I've wanted to write since high school, but life got in the way."

Hazel and Grace nodded, and Marigold looked quizzical.

"*You* know," Gus looked at Marigold. "You think moving away from your parents will bring freedom and creativity. But you have to get a job, go to school, or both. Next, you find yourself with a family, a career, or both. Except for furtive moments or annual vacations, your creativity and fun revolve around shopping, meals, laundry, and money. If you love your life, freedom never crosses your mind, and if you don't love your life, it never leaves your mind."

The three women nodded agreeably, but Gus couldn't tell if Marigold was *really hearing* what she meant. She pressed on. "One day it's over. The career peaks or ends, the kids are grown, and you see yourself gray in the mirror. It hits you: you can't iron a wrinkled birthday suit no matter what you eat or how often you visit the gym. You come to a mental and emotional halt instead of the familiar full speed ahead. Past choices seem blasé, and you have no clue how to return to the road not taken, or even if you want to."

"Amen!" Grace interjected. "I saw a button that said 'Inside every old person is a young person wondering what happened.' I laughed and cried at once. Then I started Tai Chi classes and learned to garden. I'm used to seeing my mother in the mirror now, but I still hope I'll wake one morning and find I'm thirty-five again."

"Ei yi yi!" Marigold wailed. "I'll be gray before I find a decent man, never mind children or retirement. Please, let's change the subject."

Hazel intervened. "I'll make more coffee if you want."

"How about half a pot," Grace suggested. "You know, Mari, Gus's gloom-and-doom aside, you'll be okay. I married at forty and had two kids in three years. They grew up just fine, and I didn't get mirror trouble until after I retired from teaching Phys Ed." Grace swiveled in her chair. "And you, Gus, what will you write about? Dogs? You've been a vet tech a long time."

"I know what *I'd* like to read about," Marigold said with fervor, "a *functional* marriage. Not self-help-y, but a story with characters and dialogue that shows a working marriage. I know about having a childhood in a commune, how to do well at a women's college, and I think I'm a successful drama teacher, but, and this is a big 'but,' I haven't a clue how to conduct a nourishing, good-natured romance. Nor do I know what brand of man does. If there're twelve good guys and one jerk in a room, I'll choose the jerk."

"I'm sorry, Mari, what I know about love and romance wouldn't fill two pages," Gus replied. "I'm into family history, dogs, or living-single-and-loving-it, but maybe a novel, who knows?"

Marigold hiked up her long skirt and returned her feet to her chair seat, making a pouty face. "I'll pass on living alone for now. I'm so over it."

Hazel laughed, "I can see it now. Gus Roberts, Living Single Guru, touring the country with her inspirational message. Can I be your assistant?"

"How about we assist Gus back to her house and see what needs to be done," Grace offered. "I'll even drive."

"Okay," Gus agreed. "It's lunchtime. How 'bout sandwich at the deli first?"

As Gus opened the door to the deli, she caught Hazel's expression in the glass. It was the exact moment Hazel realized she was in public. Priceless!

7

Life Goes On

Whew! I'm glad that's over," Hazel exclaimed to Gus and Grace as they exited the courthouse. "Too weird, watching the orange-suited prisoners plead their cases. What a way to spend a Wednesday morning. A group of folks in the back appeared to be there for the fun of it."

"Some people do that, I guess, spend the day in court for entertainment," Gus grumbled. "My interest vanished when I realized how close we were to our own orange suits. One of those guys had charges similar to ours." Her left knee aching, Gus watched her feet on the steps.

"For heaven's sake, you two, we only trespassed and loitered. That fellow broke a plate glass window." Grace took Hazel's arm as they descended the last step. "I think our fines and a hundred hours of community service is fair."

"I don't mind the fifty bucks, and we'll all put in a hundred hours at the soup kitchen anyway, but the judge had no right to make his last remark." Hazel extricated her arm to blow her nose.

"Which remark? When he said, 'Ladies of your age and station should be home knitting and writing letters to the editor'?" Grace laughed. "We don't want to destroy that illusion. Old lady suits render us invisible in this society. Get over it, girl. Think about what we get away with!"

"That wasn't the remark I meant. When you two went to your seats, the judge whispered to me, 'Do you know why I went easy on you girls?' and before I could say 'giirrlls?' he said, 'That photo of you in the paper is punishment enough.' Some judge! I never want to see that courtroom again!"

"Ain't that the truth," Gus exclaimed as they reached the car. "I'm gonna do my community service as fast as I can. Once I get in the writing groove, I don't want interruptions." Gus pulled her blank signature card, a receipt for fifty dollars, and her car keys out of her pocket. "Now I know how the blokes sentenced to ninety days in AA feel when I sign their cards!" She smirked and unlocked the car.

"If we hurry, we can make the soup kitchen in time to work lunch. That'll dispose of a couple hours right away," Grace observed.

"Let's do it," the women agreed.

Two weeks passed. Gus's azaleas blossomed. Bruce and Grace built her privacy fence in sections. Marigold, with Sam's help, dug the post holes. One evening, the whole crew came over, planted the posts in the holes, added the quick-set concrete, and straightened and leveled the posts for the required five minutes. The next night, they attached the panels. Then, Bruce put in the lag bolts, and *voila*! There was a fence!

Grace, unsure of the best location for the fig tree, listened to Marigold and Gus who adamantly favored a spot by Grace's living room window, while Hazel and Grace lobbied for the center of her backyard. Bruce did the neutral dance, complimenting each location, smiling when Grace postponed the decision.

Readjusted to life in public, Hazel resumed her normal activities. Her Mahjong group, at last grasped the point of the "operation," and donated heavily to the Preservation Society. The soup kitchen managers, delighted to see the women more frequently, cooked up schemes to keep Gus and Hazel in minor trouble with the law, as did Grace's coworkers at the Habitat ReStore.

Marigold's desperation for male companionship seemed to be on hiatus. She hadn't heard from Fleming, but she didn't talk about it. She appeared calm and poised.

Meanwhile, the owner of Such Happenis Adult Toys, George Watson, known to the ladies as Germy George, continued to drive Irene nuts over erectile dysfunction drugs. He'd decided to fight prescription ED drugs with over-the-counter penile enhancement concoctions, and contacted every manufacturer on the Internet, offering to display and sell their items at his store. Never mind, Irene had screeched to Gus one day, never mind these weren't toys, but unproven drugs that might cause havoc similar to Phen-Fen or Yaz—a far cry from a blowup doll, stiletto heels, or even a dildo.

As they often did, Hazel and Bruce hosted Sunday dinner at Hazel's, accessorized by Gus's famous garbage salad. Everyone arrived at six, canines included, for a scrumptious meal, including hors d'oeuvres and drinks followed by pot roast, veggies, potatoes, and of course, the salad.

When they were finished, Grace ambled into the dining room to gather the hors d'oeuvre plates and scarf another deviled egg only to find that plate empty. Mystified, she queried the others, discovering that combined, they'd eaten only six of the dozen eggs.

The dogs, banished to the yard, slipped in and out the doggie door unnoticed. Lady lay under the table and Butterbean hid in the living room.

While Grace, Gus, and Irene put food away and loaded the dishwasher, Hazel rummaged in the pantry for Triple Sec, and Bruce retrieved cheesecake and ice cream from the freezer. Butterbean snuck under the table and lay flat on her side, breathing heavily.

After two rounds of liqueur and key lime cheesecake, Bruce and the five women at Hazel's dining table reached the silly, blissed-out state that occurs following too much food, spirits, and good company.

"Do we have wine, something not too sweet?" Bruce asked, turning to Hazel.

Hazel reached behind her and took a couple of bottles off the sideboard. Grace rose and gathered appropriate glasses from the china closet, while Marigold collected the dessert plates and liqueur glasses.

"So," Gus inquired, "what shall we talk about?"

Hazel began pouring and handed Gus a bottle of sparkling white grape juice.

Grace sat down and said, "How about you, Gus? How's the book coming?"

"Fffft," Gus stuck her jaw out and exhaled, blowing her bangs straight up. "Not well, I'm afraid. When I have the time, I can't concentrate. I have, however," she made a motion of drawing something out of her back pocket, "a few pages if you'd like to see." She smiled, pantomiming ruffling a huge sheaf of papers. "In all seriousness, I *have* a subject and a title, which wasn't easy."

"Which is?" Marigold asked.

"The working title is, 'Dog-Speak for Humans,' and the more I think about it, Marigold, the more it *does* relate to love and romance in one aspect."

"What aspect is that?" Marigold asked, leaning toward Gus, fully engaged.

Gus sipped the last of her sparkling grape juice. "One problem lovers or people have with each other is the misunderstanding of what I call 'love messages.'"

"Huh?" Hazel grunted and burped, covering her mouth with her napkin in a ladylike fashion. "We aren't getting a lecture, are we?"

"Shush, Hazel," Marigold put her finger to her lips. "I want to hear this."

"I'll be short. Growing up, we learn what love means in our families. Mom says 'I love you' with her food. Dad says it, or doesn't say it, by spending time with the kids and teaching them. In some families, money or gifts are signs of love; in others, love is confused with approval or even sexuality, through ignorance or manipulation.

"When we meet another person and, say, money equals love to that person and time equals love to us, the stage is set for misperceptions, misinterpretations, and conflict simply because the 'love messages' come in different languages. We've all had that happen and it's worse between humans and dogs.

"The biggest training mishap is with the command 'come.' So often the dog, not grasping that 'come' means not only coming, but coming instantly, wanders around as the owner gets louder and louder. By the time Fido reaches her human, the human's yelling, 'Get over here, you mangy mutt,' and Fido thinks, 'Un-huh, I'm not going anywhere *near* that angry person.' Then Fido dashes away and the human goes nuts.

"I want to write about a concise way of preventing that miscommunication. I also want to show that dog training is easiest when your dog thinks she's training you. Humor might help bring points home too." Gus finished her glass of grape juice.

Under the table, Butterbean rolled onto her stomach, preparing to slip into the yard. Instead, she let out a belch and fell back on her side.

"Hmm," Irene said, smiling. "Butterbean is a prime example of a dog who thinks she is training you. Is she going to be listed as coauthor?"

"I hadn't thought of that, but I will use her point of view. Enough about me, Irene," Gus said. "What's up with you? You said you wanted to devise something to compete with the erectile dysfunction drugs. Have you?"

Bruce rolled his eyes at this conversational turn. He slid his chair back as if he might leave.

"No, Bruce," Irene said, "don't leave. This is nothing personal, nothing you haven't run into somewhere, and your opinion is valuable." She thought a minute. Bruce didn't move his chair forward, but he didn't get up either. "Naturally Bruce, for you, this is all theoretical," Irene continued diplomatically, though curious how theoretical her assumption might be. "Women have a different view, so we need yours. I want to develop a penis prop, if you will, that will be as pleasing and fun for both parties as the bona fide thing, or at least wicked close."

Bruce made a face. "Never happen, but okay, I'll go for theoretical," he said, pushing up to the table.

"Okay," Irene said, "theoretically. Maybe one or both partners don't want to risk the side effects of ED drugs. Heart issues and blindness are the two biggies." She sipped some wine. "We all know the most emotionally explosive marital subject, besides power and money, is sex. If there are fun and interesting alternatives to the drugs, maybe, just maybe, good sense will prevail for some couples. There's also the advantage of no waiting. The guy doesn't *always* know he's going to score hours ahead of time, often not even the day. *And*," Irene gestured for emphasis, "by the time a guy has ED, he's probably not the athlete he once was in other areas. With the exception of sweet Marigold, we've all experienced something—arthritis, blood pressure issues, or cholesterol meds—that reduces our speed and endurance. As for agility, how many of us can put our ankles around our ears or hold weight on achy hips and knees?"

Bruce blushed to the roots of his white hair.

Butterbean had an attack of flatulence, rolled onto Bruce's feet by accident, and when he looked under the table, she lumbered up and out the doggie door.

Sniffing and coughing from aroma d'Butterbean, Grace hacked, "There's our deviled eggs, encased in Corgi."

The laughter subsiding, Bruce poured a round for all from the last bottle of wine, continuing on topic. "Getting back to our conversation, the penis needs accommodation and secure attachment." Bruce pushed back his chair and wobbled up.

Marigold stood up, "Sorry, but I gotta go. Early class tomorrow and no ideas about a supporting cast for penises."

After the goodbyes, Bruce opened one of the bottles, poured a round, and brought out iced tea for Gus. "Let me give you the male point of view about this penis prop, and then, I too must hit the hay. I'm not sure I'm making sense as it is."

"Thanks, Bruce," Irene said. Everyone gave him full attention.

"The substitute penis has to be flexible and comfortable for its owner/operator." Bruce smiled in spite of himself. "You'd probably need several sizes in both length and width, and its attachments can't cut or bind. It might turn out that a kind of undershorts would be the best attachment.

"But enough. The wine is talking now. I'm going upstairs." Bruce drained his glass and got up. He kissed Hazel on the forehead. "I see a lot of R&D in your future, Irene, and you'll need better men than I."

Irene got up and hugged Bruce, followed by Gus and Grace who said, "I love the privacy fence. It's just the ticket."

"My pleasure," Bruce replied, heading upstairs.

Grace and Gus helped Hazel clear the table.

"Do you have any cookies?" Gus asked as they finished. "I need something to soak up all that tea and grape juice." She put the last plate away. "If you devise this item, Irene, how will you advertise it?"

Irene folded her towel and hooked it on the towel rack. "The first thing is to desensitize impotence, make it a non-issue. Make it something your average Baby Boomer would, if not discuss with his boss, be able to share off-handedly with close friends, doctors, kissing cousins."

Hazel produced a plate of oatmeal cookies.

"The ads for ED drugs have helped a lot with that," Gus said, gobbling a cookie. "Soon we'll be hearing, 'Can't get it up? Neither can I, but here's how I do it. *And* my love life's better than ever!' After a dozen baseball players, NASCAR drivers, and down-home workers promote it, the emotional weight will be the same as for men's hair coloring."

Hazel giggled and snatched some cookies. The last bottle of wine was half full, and she and Irene passed it back and forth. Grace joined Gus in drinking tea because she was getting woozy.

"It's been fun," Grace said as she and Gus put the glasses in the sink. Irene drained the wine bottle and wrapped up the remaining cookies.

"You okay to drive home, Grace?" Gus asked, collecting Butterbean's leash.

"I'm fine. Are you walking?" Grace jingled her keys. "I can take you."

"Un-huh, a walk will be good for me and Butterbean. C'mon, Irene, walk with us."

"Okay. Hazel, wake up!" Irene shook Hazel, who revived enough to see them to the door.

"Thanks for the think tank," Irene said.

"My pleasure," Hazel slurred after her friends, who wavered down the driveway, singing off key. "Good night, Irene, Good night, Irene, Ireeeene, good night."

8

Canine Conference and Calorie Exorcism

Like their parents and others who had "gone before them" into retirement, Hazel and Grace wondered how they used to find the time to work. They had volunteer and social commitments to Habitat for Humanity, the soup kitchen, and the library. Hazel played Mahjong twice a week. Grace zealously attended Tai Chi Chuan class on Thursday mornings. Gus, a semi-retired vet tech, worked a variable three days a week. Prodded by Grace, she attended Tai Chi class on her free Thursday mornings.

Because teaching drama at the college included evening rehearsals and performance nights, Marigold's daytime teaching schedule was flexible in the extreme, yielding compensatory free days.

With artful manipulation, every so often their schedules coincided and the women met for lunch, afterward spending time exercising the dogs.

Today, their pants buttons popping, the women left an Italian restaurant to collect and cram five eager dogs into Gus's SUV. While Gus drove, the dogs placed themselves over, around, and in between the passenger humans—Daphne imitating "Driving Miss Daisy" in the back seat; Lady blanketing Hazel; Butterbean and the Poms acting like Mexican jumping beans.

Gus parked, at the Pine Grove cemetery, and everyone waddled and wagged out of the car.

A dozen yards from the street, Gus and Hazel relaxed on a raised tomb in the shade, avoiding the ivy that hid the name of its occupant. Opposite them, Marigold and Grace lounged on a weather-worn, cedar bench in the sunshine. Instead of walking off their gastronomic exuberance, the women engaged in their customary caloric exorcism–talking.

"Ouch," Grace moaned, clutching at her side. "Damn sciatica!" She switched from a teenaged slouch to proper sixth-grade posture. "That's better."

Unfazed, Marigold maintained her sprawl across most of the bench, pulling the back of her long skirt between her legs and hooking it under the waistband, looking like a swami with gender identity issues.

"So, Mari, what's kept you so busy?" Hazel inquired.

"Yeah," Gus chimed in, "You didn't say much at lunch."

"I was too busy eating," Marigold said, pushing herself into a more erect position. "How do kids talk and slouch? I can't move my throat. Except for Sam being a pest, I've been wrapped up in work." Marigold caught Grace's expression and made a cross in front of her face with her index fingers. "Unh-uh Grace, I haven't encouraged him. His fantasy of me is all his own. If I treat him badly, he gives me the smile you see in paintings of religious martyrs, beatific and all-knowing. Ick!"

"Whew," Gus intervened, "that's tough. I've been the rejecter and the rejectee, and both situations suck."

"*You* mooning after someone like a puppy? " Marigold said. "Not *you*!"

"Yes me, and when I was your age, too, but tell me, you see kids 'in love' every day. From what you see in school, do you think romantic relating works better when both parties are besotted?"

"I don't know," Marigold replied. "A few seem to do okay as Romeo and Juliet, but soon, after a few weeks or maybe six months, somebody farts or gets mad and the spell is broken."

"Another human conundrum," Grace muttered, signaling her interest in changing the subject by narrowing her eyes and clearing her throat. "How's the human/canine communication coming, Gus?"

"Slowly. Yesterday I found Grizzie sitting on the computer keyboard, and Butterbean had her front paws on my chair, nosing Grizzie's tail. Her butt-hanging-out-of-a-litter-box-look flew across her face, and then she barked and leaped at Grizzie as if the cat should be in trouble. Naturally, they then dashed outdoors to safety. They're up to something, but nothing was disturbed."

"You might want to close the bedroom door, Gus," Marigold said. "I found Daphne with her nose on my keyboard one day. Saliva on the keys wasn't too bad, but she'd managed to change my language to Tagalog and lose most of my address book. She's smart enough to use the keyboard, but her nose is just too big!"

"Good idea. Anyway, I thought I'd make a dog-speak/English dictionary, describing canine behaviors and what they mean. For instance, one dog might scratch the door, another bark, another go in circles, but they all want out. Remembering and defining behaviors like that ought to give me focus and organization."

"Give me another example of dog-speak," Grace said. Hazel plopped next to her and Marigold settled on the tomb.

"I have a client with an old arthritic dog that also has thyroid issues. He was twelve when she inherited him, so his behavior patterns and attitudes were fixed, if not fossilized. This dog, Buster, loves the outdoors. He ignores heat and cold and comes in the house only for a drink or when it rains. She'll find him rolled up in the yard, shivering, and bring him in."

"So? He'll come in when he's cold enough, won't he?" Marigold asked.

"That's what she thought, and frankly, that's what I would think, too, but Buster doesn't operate that way. If she closes the doggie door, locking him inside, he gets nervous diarrhea. A doghouse is redundant. The answer turned out to be a sweater. Buster *loves* wearing it and she knows he's warm. Most humans can figure out things like this if they observe and *listen* to the dog. Is that different enough from the hundreds of books out there?"

"I don't know," Grace replied. "I think using your experience and human-on-human examples like the one about love messages is good. Or if you do James Herriot humorous tale-telling. You remember how his vet stories always contained valuable information or made an important point about the specific animal he was treating. If you use one, or all, of those methods, then it won't be the usual how-to training book."

"You could make your examples read like a play," Marigold added with enthusiasm. "It'd be fairly easy to write. Set the scene and the rest is dialogue or action between two or more characters. You could create the 'wrong' scene followed by the successful scene, very straightforward."

Hazel bounced with excitement, raising her hand. "Once you make your point, you could emphasize it with a one-liner or a limerick that would be memorable."

"Those are all good ideas. Could we write them down?" Gus grinned. "This is way harder than I thought." She looked at her watch. "Yikes! I need to get the vacuuming done today."

Grace looked at the sun. "What is it? Three-ish? I'm good until four. Oprah is having Ellen and Portia on, and I want to see that."

Marigold swiveled to look behind the bench at the dogs. "Maybe we'd better head out. Lady's asleep and Daphne's over there, but Art and Gwen are dashing about and I can't see Butterbean."

"Do you think I could write a book?" Butterbean asked shyly, addressing the canines assembled under an ancient willow oak, its branches tinseled with Spanish moss. While a warm breeze tickled the moss above, the restive canines had pawed the moss below until each one was properly situated in the damp earth for cooling and keeping watch.

"Write a book?" queried Queen Daphne, looking down her Roman nose as if she wore a monocle. "How, Butterbean, and what would you write? Our paws or noses aren't suited for keyboards, and we don't spell well."

"Speak for yourself, Queen Daphne." Butterbean stretched to her full height, nose-to-nose with the reclining Greyhound. "I can spell 'riboflavin,' 'catalyze,' and 'methyl-ethyl-amylase.' And I have plenty to say about freedom, murder, and inequity from a canine point of view."

"Well," Daphne conceded, "maybe you and Gus could collaborate. Tee Tucker the Corgi writes with her human, Rita Mae Brown." Daphne hesitated and then went on. "Unfortunately, the lead writer is Mrs. Murphy, a cat."

"Gak!" Butterbean rolled her tongue in and out a few times, as if she'd mistakenly chomped a rancid worm. "A cat as lead writer? Are you sure, Daphne?"

Gwen was sidling up to Butterbean when she heard this, and stopped mid-step. She startled her brother Art when she said, "Please don't write about boring things like canine nutrition, or care of hair, pads, nails, and eeewhew, anal glands. There's dozens of books about that, all so passé."

"No one writes about important things like registering Pit Bulls and chaining them from birth," Art said, moving to the other side of Butterbean, "or legislating against outdoor chemicals and carcinogenic carpet cleaners. I'm getting out my petitions, but if you'd put this in a book . . ."

"Art, how many Pit Bulls do you know?" Butterbean asked. "The two Pit Bulls in my Advanced Obedience class were sweeter than I am, but aggression *does* upset me, and I might say something about that, but right now, I'm in a quandary. In her book, Gus is saying she's the alpha leader and that it is a human's rightful position. What malarkey! *Everyone* knows canines are the leaders. How exactly do I refute my own human?"

"Oh poop, Butterbean, who cares what they think?" Gwen danced around Butterbean. "Forget all that serious stuff. Write about canine beauty, all the glorious, glamorous show dogs! By the way, there's some *eau de frogge morte* behind the next headstone. I rolled some on my shoulder. Isn't it lovely?"

"Thank you, Gwen," Butterbean replied, "but I prefer *cologne bouche de vache.*"

"Butterbean, dear heart," Queen Daphne broke in, "there are no farms here, thank heavens." She shifted position to drawl in Gwen's ear, "and Gwen darlin', *parfum septique* is what's worn this year. *Frogge morte* went out with tick dip."

Gwen jumped away, growling, to land on Art's back.

He responded with a snap, snatched his chewy, and marched behind the tree, griping so all could hear, "Fool females! Books, perfume, beauty! What about important things like my petitions? Maybe I *will* apply some *frogge morte.* I need to lift my spirits while I distribute my petitions against loose Pit Bulls."

Lady's gray muzzle and hind feet stopped twitching as she woke. She heaved upright and asked, "What have I missed?"

Butterbean replied, "Did you have a good nap? I asked for thoughts about my writing a book. What do you think?"

"Quite a concept," Lady said tactfully. "In all my years, I've not heard of a dog writing a book, but you could be the first. What would you write?"

Butterbean stretched and rolled onto her back for an upside down view of things. "I have yet to decide. So far, Marigold needs a functional relationship manual; Grace and Gus want a map of the Golden Years; Art would like a harangue against unchained Pit Bulls and chemicals; and Gwen favors a book about beautiful show dogs. Personally, I think canines need instructions for living with humans. In that vehicle, I could gently rebuke Gus with her alpha leader human nonsense, and also help those dogs who have intractable humans. If I followed a 'Training you to Train Your Human' format and combined everything we know, it would be quite a book, doncha think?" Butterbean flipped upright and shook.

"You might be right," Lady agreed, "though be careful what you say about human loneliness. From what I've seen, that's why they have us around. They don't need to know we know that."

"What do you mean?" Butterbean scratched her left ear.

"I mean, in spite of all the cooing about what a cute black bundle of fluff I was, I landed with Hazel because she couldn't stand being alone after she divorced her second husband. If humans found another solution for their loneliness, it'd be 'bye bye, doggies.'"

Daphne stood and stretched. "She's right, Butterbean. I got tangled up in the gate at the track and broke my hind leg. If Marigold hadn't been so lonely after Stuart left her, I'd be on the Rainbow Bridge with no one to wait for. Don't remind them about costs either. Getting my leg fixed was expensive, and so is our general upkeep."

"Ummmphf," Butterbean murmured, munching on an ant that mistook her foot for a mountain. "I see. My first humans couldn't care for all nine of us, but that doesn't explain Gus's motive in taking me, does it? Like the others, I think she needed company. What is it humans all say? 'I don't know what I'd do if I didn't have my baby, Fifi, Fido, whoever, to greet me!'"

"What about me and Art? What are we? Chopped liver?" Gwen squealed.

"Decorative," Butterbean answered, chasing another ant on her paw.

"Pooh!" Gwen snapped. "Bruce got us because we're cute. He wanted us. He didn't have to soothe some emotional deficiency!"

"Not!" Art snarled, returning from his petition distribution. "Bruce got us because Hazel had Lady. He was jealous and indecisive, so he took us both. How many humans have you seen lose one beloved canine only to come home weeks or months later with two? And don't forget the jerks who think we're animated furniture or status symbols. Their ways need to be exposed, so even inexperienced pups will know to stay away from them."

"Bruce sure didn't choose you for your optimism," Gwen needled, nipping at his cheek.

"Go away!" Art jumped on Gwen, biting the back of her neck. She twisted around, her pointy white teeth sawing on his right front leg. Amid shrieks and growls, they melted into a whirling caramel-colored mass.

"Stop it! Our humans will hear!" Butterbean barked.

Glaring and panting, Gwen and Art faced each other, speckled with saliva and flecks of blood.

"C'mon, guys, there won't be any treats if we get caught fighting. Worse, they'll get out the alcohol and peroxide, and turn us every which way to see if we're cut."

"Okay, Butterbean," Gwen gasped. "Let's get some *frogge morte.* That'll distract them."

"You go. I've got another ant to finish off," Butterbean said, licking furiously at her belly. "Your fight reminded me. Free-floating hostility represents the fraying of our canine cultural fabric. Life as we know it is being destroyed by negative forces, bad karma, and plain bad manners!" Butterbean stood, ears pricked, eyes alight, a picture of unleashed zeal.

Gwen and Art returned, their spirits much improved by the second application of *eau de frogge morte.*

Daphne noticed the humans and whined. The women had checked the canines twice in the last ten minutes, and now they were stretching and standing.

"I think they're ready to go," Gwen said, "and I want to say, Butterbean, I think you, or we, can write a book. A cat, with their flexible paws and claws, might be necessary for typing, but we can tell the story."

Butterbean trotted alone toward the car, intrigued with the cat-writer idea, but unconvinced about Gwen as coauthor. Queen Daphne slowed her regal pace to match Lady's arthritic gait, while the Poms raced ahead.

With luck, the humans wouldn't notice their dishevelment or the *frogge morte.*

9

A Fine Romance This Is

Marigold could cope with erratic, steamy, summer weather and afternoon thunderstorms, PMS, or full moons. But when, two days before the full moon *and* suffering from PMS, a loud thunderclap awakened her at one in the morning, Marigold disintegrated. She stormed and raged around her apartment, alternately cursing and begging for help from the gods for her situation in life: female, single, thirty-nine, and the corker, *alone!*

She wept in Queen Daphne's neck, made tea, read spiritually inspiring tales, even a few pages of *The Mabinogion*. Nonetheless, the moment Marigold put her head to pillow, her fears, doubts, and insecurities assailed her again. She tried computer solitaire, turned on Native American flute music, wrote in her journal. By four in the morning, Marigold fell into a fitful sleep, waking two hours later. In tears, she called Gus and made a date to talk over lunch.

Filtered through a stained-glass window at the Saints and Sinners Restaurant, the early afternoon sun framed Marigold's red hair with a rainbow. Gus was both enthralled and disturbed by the scene. Marigold seemed serene and content the past few weeks, but today she was an emotional mess, twirling her hair, examining the familiar menu as if it were written in Mandarin.

Lobster bisque and shrimp Caesar salad were still a $6.95 special, so Gus enjoyed the restaurant's ambience and awaited Marigold's epicurean choice. There were old tables and mismatched chairs painted bright red, blue, green, and yellow with a few pieces in fuchsia and chartreuse for visual hot sauce. Two plump sofas and a 1930s chair sat along the wall opposite a tiny sound stage. Near the dessert and deli case at the back were chrome and enamel kitchen tables with pull-out leaves and center utensil drawers, a wondrous collection in Gus's estimation.

"Where's our waiter?" Marigold asked, swiveling on her chair like a kid on a soda-fountain stool. She wanted his attention that instant.

Annoyance flicking at her mood, Gus reminded herself that Marigold was a child of flower children and could have had problems more serious than her sporadic lack of emotional discipline or her gypsy-like mode of dress with peasant blouses and dozens of silver bracelets. Watching her now, Gus realized anew how Marigold's feelings registered on her face, as if her mind were close-captioned.

"Gus?" Marigold asked, waving her hand across Gus's line of vision.

"Sorry, I was woolgathering. The waiter's behind you."

He took their orders and placed a basket of homemade breads between the women, closest to Marigold.

"I need to talk," Marigold said.

"I'm happy to listen," Gus replied, "but you might not like my response." She lined up her utensils like soldiers, their bottoms even on an imaginary line, wishing she could order her thoughts and words this easily.

"That's cool. Sometimes just talking de-clutters my thinking. I didn't sleep last night, and it's a bad time of the month for me, but the problem lurks even when things are perfect. Unlike you, I *loathe* being single and that loneliness hit me again last night." Her face puckered and her eyes glistened. A slight reddening of her skin blended her freckles into a solid coppery tan for a moment. "My best friend from high school just became a grandmother, and *I'm* not even dating! I can't forget the day we took Hazel to the deli, when you and Grace talked about aging. Do you realize, if I got pregnant this minute, the kid would finish its master's degree the same year I'd retire? That scares the crap out of me." Her voice veered into the whiny register. She dabbed her eyes.

Gus took a piece of banana bread and buttered it, thinking this conversation might require more than her normal quotient of tact, empathy, and wisdom.

Gus opened her mouth to say, "It's not you," just as Marigold leaned forward, shushed her, and said, "I *know* what you're going to say."

"What?" she asked.

"'Nothing's wrong with you,' is what you say. Others tell me, 'You're a late bloomer.' Or, 'Mr. Right hasn't materialized yet.' Those are true and awful answers."

Marigold clenched her jaw and leaned back in her chair, gesturing expansively. "Look around, Gus. There're some plain, ugly folks behind you, and we know couples who think intimacy is squabbling. Then there're cheaters, liars, and folks who turn a decent home into a trash heap, not to mention the felons." Marigold inhaled deeply, put her elbows on the table, and made a steeple over her nose with her hands.

"The other day," Marigold continued, "Oprah's theme was hoarding. A well-dressed, middle class woman had thirty-seven cats. Her fiancé and her daughter brought her on the show because, if the cats didn't go, they would. The point is this woman *had* a fiancé *and* a daughter. I've got a clean apartment, a degree, a job, an elegant Greyhound. I'm not Miss Universe, but I don't frighten small children, yet *I'm alone!*" Marigold rubbed her face, looking everywhere but at Gus.

"Here you are," the waiter said, plopping Gus's soup on the table, "lobster bisque." He positioned Marigold's salad with care, brushing her forearm. "Your entrées will be ready in a few minutes," he said, studying Marigold's face and hair as if there might be a pop quiz on eyewitness testimony.

Gus cut her eyes heavenward, wondering why Marigold didn't notice the waiter's interest. "Didn't you go to a workshop?" Gus asked, changing the subject. "What was it about?"

More composed, Marigold replied, "The focus was empowerment. Maybe it was good for others, but I could have *given* the workshop, it was so old hat!"

Marigold ate some salad and resumed, "I *am* empowered. Yes, I'm a space cadet at times, but I manage my life, and do it well, *I* think. I have friends and fun and I pay my bills. I like my work and I like the kids I teach. What's not to like about drama? Doing it all alone . . . day after bloody *day* is what makes me nuts! You have no idea how I want company, someone to hug me when I come home, to share in a decision."

Having no ready answer, Gus continued with her soup. Marigold, silent now, finished her salad.

"I'm hurt too," she added, wiping her mouth and pushing the salad plate aside. "In spite of my effort, Life with a capital 'L' keeps that door closed. It's unreasonable to think there're no good men left, so if *they* aren't jerks, the jerk must be me. If it *is* me, what's broken and how do I fix it?"

Gus sighed over Marigold's words and her empty cup. "Believe it or not, I said the same things at your age, younger, even. I can't vouch for 'Life' or 'The Universe,' but I came to terms with my singleness when I was moaning, 'Why me?' one day, and my therapist said, 'Why *not* you?' It felt like a pitchfork in my heart, but it rang true. In some way, being single seems to be my job in life. I have no idea why. Why am I a sober alcoholic? Why does Jane Doe have multiple sclerosis?"

Before Marigold could respond, the waiter delivered their entrées with great flourish, each order to the other person.

Looking as if Gus had described a bath in acid, Marigold exchanged their plates.

"It hurt a lot," Gus went on, "and the good news is that I survived. I got angry and decided if I was earmarked for living single, I'd make it a great life! Yes, ma'am, I wasn't gonna screw myself a second time by having a lousy attitude!" Gus felt a familiar energy surge and straightened her spine.

"Crap," Marigold said, picking at her entrée.

Gus attacked her salad with relish. "You remember that workshop you dragged me to last year, the one with the woman who had the open marriage?"

Marigold smiled wanly, "The woman who ate Prozac like candy and was bridge phobic? Sure. I also recall *your* antics too. You derailed a guided visualization for thirty minutes getting the leader to explain its purpose."

Gus laughed, "That's the one. The facilitator assured me I'd achieve nirvana if I attended other workshops and gave him my bank account and my body. Anyway, the Prozac woman was a reminder that most marriages aren't a Cinderella story. Couples don't seek help because they have too much harmony."

"You mean I might have a *lousy* marriage?" Marigold asked.

"Does a marriage license have a guarantee? What if you'd married Frank?" Gus asked. She finished her salad and all but two slices of bread while Marigold ate quietly. "I take it Fleming hasn't called yet," Gus asked, sorry she'd mentioned Frank. With luck, Fleming's name would dissolve thoughts of Frank.

"Nope, when I met him, ages ago it seems, he mentioned a long trip. I keep giving him time to get back, but it's been almost a month."

"That's a *really* long trip," Gus replied.

"I know all of you love me and want the best for me, but . . . " Marigold smiled at last, "sometimes your concern drives me *crazy*! Do you want dessert?"

"Thanks, I'll pass on dessert." Gus signaled the waiter, and Marigold asked for the check.

"I have a question for you. What's on your 'gonna do' list?" Gus asked, fishing for her wallet.

"Travel, but that's circumscribed by work." Marigold thought a moment. "I'd like to learn to play an instrument, and doing some acting instead of teaching would be fun too. Then there's the Outdoor Club. They hike, kayak, bicycle, and camp. I've done similar things in the past, but *with* someone. Alone, I don't finish the course or make the meetings. Then the guilt piles up. Now, I don't commit in the first place."

Marigold brightened as she pulled out a twenty and left a tip. "So, maybe Mr. Right is lurking in one of those places, waiting for me?"

"Maybe," Gus replied, thinking, *You aren't getting it, Mari. It's not about a guy. It's about you!* She snatched the check partly out of generosity, partly because she didn't want to hear another word.

Outside, Marigold said, "If I don't hear from Fleming in two days, I'll call the Outdoor Club and the Community College. Thanks for listening, Gus, I *do* feel better."

At home, Gus couldn't regain her emotional balance. Her usual pleasures seemed dull and insipid. When she thought of Marigold waiting for Fleming's call, her mind fixed on Frank, Marigold's last live-in, a menace in preppie clothing.

"No need to think about that," Gus said to Butterbean as she rummaged in the refrigerator. "Can I do anything for Mari now? No. I know how she feels, Beans, but I can't control her obsession with men!"

When the phone rang, Gus jumped three feet.

"Hello?" she answered, patting her heart.

"Gus, you'll never guess what," Marigold said. "I got home and there was a message from Fleming. We're going to dinner tonight! Wish me luck! Bye. Oh, and thanks again for lunch."

10

Grace Graceful

Because she had good genes, a lithe, wiry body, and a long career as a high school physical educator, Grace looked and behaved like a person twenty years her junior. She'd smoked a bit in the '50s and '60s when it was all but required, and the extra wrinkles and smile lines appeared on cue in her later years. While her marriage at forty was short, she had two daughters, one of whom lived in Snow Hill, the other in Minnesota. The Snow Hill daughter had two children, a girl in fifth grade and a boy who now drove and periodically visited Grace.

In early retirement, Grace's uncertainty about "finding herself" echoed the doubts of many of her high school students. How many times had she pointed out the freedoms, the choices, and the opportunities available to these young women if they made an effort? Even remembering that a decision wasn't written in stone didn't lift Grace's blanket of negativity about retirement. Instead of the glorious view of an open and free life Grace held for her students, she found for herself no purpose. Her best years were behind her, what more did she have to contribute anyway?

Then one day, she saw a demonstration of Tai Chi Chuan at the Woman's Club Park. Behind the spectators and beside a tree, Grace mimicked some of the slow, graceful movements. She knew she was awkward, but quickly realized this martial art required more than athletic prowess. She spoke with the instructor and began classes the next week. Soon she was singing in the shower on Thursday mornings.

Once she learned the first third of the Yang Long Form, Grace inveigled Gus into joining the class. She reminded Gus repeatedly that this form, while appearing like a dance, contained sequential blows and stances. Done correctly, these "soft hands" moves were as effective as the Tae Kwon Do actions Gus had practiced in her youth.

Together in Grace's poop-free backyard, they practiced. Gus caught on quickly, in spite of her knees and arthritis. In uniform, black mandarin-collared jackets and loose-fitting black pants with drawstrings at the ankles, they glided through the steps like one skinny and one well-fed stork.

Taking a moment to get centered in the T'an T'ien, a point two inches below the belly button, Grace and Gus stood with their feet shoulder-width apart, hands at their sides, and began measured breathing. Then breathing in, they slowly raised their hands, palms down with fingers relaxed like a drooping flower; breathing out, they lowered their hands to their sides; breathing in, they turned their left hands palm up at belly button level; breathing out, they turned their right hands palm down at breast level. As if cradling a beach ball, they shifted their weight from one foot to the other, leaning slightly from side to side as they did so, in tune with their breaths.

So simple, yet so difficult to execute properly, the Tai Chi moves impressed Grace, especially the more complex ones like "Needle at the Sea Bottom"—as the left knee bends and the right leg extends behind, the right hand makes a great swooping movement while the body leans toward the left foot and the fingers "pluck" a "needle" from the floor. Then the torso rises triumphant. Seducing her with that sequence, Tai Chi became Grace's lover.

The test on the final third of the Yang Long Form came the day after Gus's lunch with Marigold. Emotional wrecks, Grace and Gus parked in front of the dojo. Gus was typically a good test taker, and Grace expected her to be in a chipper mood, full of good-natured teasing. Instead, Gus was weighed down by her negative reaction to Marigold's dinner with Fleming yesterday.

Slamming the car door and leaning on the roof, she asked Grace, "Do you remember the order of that tricky part in the middle?"

Grace closed her door with a comforting thump. "Yep. First, Clouds, then Repulse the Monkey, Slant Flying, and Single Whip. After that, a couple of kicks to the south, a Snake Creeps Down, Shoot the Tiger, and voila, *finis!*" She looked at Gus across the car roof, "You okay?"

"I'm good. I need some advice about Mari, but first let's pass this test."

Lighter of heart with their certificates in hand, the women jogged to the coffee shop. The aroma of exotic coffees and baked goods, an olfactory siren song, slipped past the heavy glass door, snaring the women like a shepherd's crook. Gus snagged the last table and fussed with her chair whose rubber-tipped legs refused to slide. Grace got coffee and éclairs, remembering she had a question too, but it could wait.

"Thanks," Gus said, "I had lunch with Mari yesterday. We talked about . . ." Gus interrupted herself, ". . . Grace, it's probably me. She's been waiting forever for Fleming to call, and, as you know, she hates being alone. I suggested ways to enjoy her singleness and shared some of my experience, but, the net result of our conversation? Nada, zip, zero. Mari wants to meet someone, period, not to enjoy anything by herself. Then she called after I dropped her off, almost before I got in the door, to tell me that she had a message from Fleming, and boom, instant dinner date. I know I'm supposed to be delighted, but I'm sad and irritated. I feel as though I've wasted my time and words. Then I think, what if Fleming's like that Peterson jerk in the news who was very hard on his wives? He could be wonderful, but I don't get good vibes."

Grace exhaled for a long time. "You did all you could. You know we can't rearrange her mind like a pantry. She's got her lessons and her consequences. We get to stand by and support her or pick up the pieces."

Gus gave a weak smile. "I know, Grace. I do okay until Frank gets in my mind. Then I go berserk. Suppose I hadn't made the casserole? Suppose you weren't home? I know it worked out, but heaven forbid there's a next time. Some women don't survive, you know." Gus held her coffee mug, ruminating a minute. "I'll get more coffee," she said, rising.

Grace took a bite of éclair. Once Frank was out of Marigold's life, Grace hadn't given him another thought, so she was surprised by the sudden, intense memories that now shanghaied her peace of mind.

Movie star good looking, Frank was tall enough to embrace Marigold without looking like he was hugging a tree. To me, he appeared polite, educated, an excellent conversationalist. He even golfed with Bruce for a while. Turned out we were all snowed.

Over time, the three of us watched Marigold lose her joy, enthusiasm, and too much weight. She had an excuse for anything we thought amiss, insisting she was fine.

At the last gathering she attended with Frank, Marigold was quiet and had on too much make-up. Her every motion was fluttery and uncertain. In later conversations, we discovered each of us had noticed the looks Frank threw at Marigold, like she was trash.

The next day, Gus made her rare and famous macaroni casserole and decided to take some over to Frank and Marigold for dinner. When she walked up to the house, she saw Daphne tied to a tree. There was no water for the dog. Gus knew Marigold wouldn't do that, so she went around the corner and called me on her cell phone.

I arrived in an instant, screeched up to the curb and didn't even close the car door. Straight from gardening, I was a sight, hair every which way, sweaty face and dirty fingers, but I had Marigold's key. Gus untied Daphne and the three of us went in the front door without knocking.

Frank was about to open the hall closet door with a huge belt in his hand. He turned and saw us in the doorway.

"Get the fuck outta here, you meddling bitches."

Gus earned her black belt in Tae Kwon Do thirty years ago, but that day, that moment, those years vanished. She yelled, ran, and punched her casserole in Frank's face.

Beyond surprise at the attack, Frank fell backward into the wall, yelling, "What the fuck," as Gus snatched the belt from his fingers. The dish fell to the floor, its noise overpowered by Frank's bellowing and Gus snapping that belt. I picked up the dish and looked for an opening to clock him. Le Creuset Dutch oven became the modern iron frying pan.

Daphne scratched at the closet door and barked like a crazy dog. We assumed that was where Marigold was, but we had all we could handle battling Frank. Still leaning on the wall, Frank spit macaroni and blood. "You whore bitches!" he yelled.

How inventive, I thought, ready to strike. It is weird what runs through your head in a crisis. Frank clawed hot macaroni out of his eyes and gave a huge shake of his head. At that moment, Gus scooped a leg out from under him. He grabbed at her as he fell. She bit him and rolled away before he could latch on.

I saw my opening and seized it! I jumped him, banging the Dutch oven on his head. Suddenly, a brindle streak crashed into my chin. It was Daphne and she was going for Frank's throat. He threw his hands up in defense; she gnawed on his forearms.

He got wilder, yelling, "You fucking women's libber c---s!" Thrashing and bucking, he tried to choke a screeching, snarling Daphne, having dislodged me enough to half sit. Gus regrouped, grabbed the pan, and banged away at any part of him she could. I struggled to stay on top of Frank, and out of Gus and Daphne's way. He was rolling and yelling, "Get that mother-fucking dog off me!"

I considered poking at his eyes, but opted for a knee in his crotch instead. The pan came down one more time on Frank's head, breaking his nose and knocking him out. From behind us, I heard a croaky shout, "Hold it. Don't move, any of you."

Marigold had escaped the closet during the mayhem, somehow recalling what we had learned together in Citizens Police Academy Training. She stood there, shaking in ripped clothes, her hair chopped and her face bruised, but in perfect shooting stance. The .038 was leveled in our direction.

". . . expects way more of me than I have to give," Gus was saying, as she set steaming coffee on the table.

Grace snapped out of her thoughts, "Sorry, I didn't realize you were back. I got stuck in remembering the day we had Frank arrested."

"I was saying that I think Mari expects more of me than I've got to give."

Then, like a light turning on, Gus smiled and patted Grace's arm. "That was some day! I haven't felt that angry since I was a kid. I thought I'd kill him, or that you would, banging him on the head with that pot, and right then, I didn't care, though orange isn't my best color."

"I don't know what came over me," Grace said, "but if that pot had hit his nose the right way, he'd be dead. The cops had enough trouble with the macaroni, Daphne and us. A body would have been over the top."

"God yes," Gus chuckled, "once things settled down, I realized those cops could have been our grandchildren. It's a good thing you got rid of the gun." She reflected a moment. "It reminds me that Mari has an invisible tough streak—don't threaten her dog or her friends."

"Yeah, she got real feisty once Frank passed out, ordering us around, 'Gus, call 911,' 'Grace, hide this gun somewhere,' 'Daphne, bed, now,' until she glanced in the mirror over her hall table."

A moment passed, and the women's moods shifted. "I think this memory requires another éclair, what do you say?"

"Excellent," Gus replied, her face somber as she finished her coffee and Grace went for the éclairs.

"What *did* you do with that gun?" Gus asked before Grace could sit or put the éclairs down.

"I never told you?" she answered, surprise on her face.

"Nope, I didn't think of it all this time either. In truth, I don't think of that day at all. Done is done."

"I agree. I wanted to keep the gun secret, looks like I did," Grace smiled and went on. "The chambers were empty, but who knew? I dashed in the pantry looking for duct tape to secure Frank, and on the floor was an open fifty-pound bag of Daphne's dry food. It was almost full, so I shoved that gun down as far as I could and ran back with the tape. Mari must have found the gun, but she's never mentioned it, which is fine with me."

Grace passed an éclair. "After I called 911, I saw Mari sliding down the wall and stayed with her. As I recall, you began to tape Frank like a package, but he came to and was kicking macaroni everywhere."

"Yeah, he woke up as I finished his hands," Gus said, "and with his feet scissoring in that slippery mess, I couldn't do a thing! If the cops hadn't come right then, I was ready to clock him once more. Damn, I'm getting pissed off again."

"Me too. I can't believe it was, when, five years ago? Want more coffee?"

"Sure."

Grace set the coffee down and looked at the éclairs. "I have a question for you. Not related to Frank or Mari."

"Shoot," she said, all magnanimity.

Grace cleared her throat, "Would it be okay with you if my granddaughter wrote about our mission on the roof? 'The McClellan building: to demolish or not to demolish,' is the title of her fifth-grade essay competition. The children may take either side of the question. They'll be judged on cogency of argument, clarity, command of language, the usual English studies stuff." Inexplicably nervous, Grace patted back a strand of hair and fiddled with her coffee cup.

"Wow," Gus answered, scanning the idea for danger. "Who will read these essays? Will we be recognizable? Have you asked Hazel?"

"Whoa. It's a fifth-grade class in Snow Hill. The school paper would publish it *if* she won. Clarice is big-time excited about our 'operation.' In her ten-year-old mind, it's a sit-in similar to the sixties, and the fact that we're older women is 'way exciting,' she says." Grace split the last éclair in half.

"What did you tell her?"

"I thought about Hazel, and I thought about Clarice's enthusiasm," Grace said.

"Annnd?" Gus interjected, scooping the remaining piece of éclair.

"I told her she could write about me, but she'd need permission from you and Hazel. I figured it might not bother you, but we both know Hazel's sensitive. Besides, it's smart and polite to ask, and Clarice needs to learn that. If she becomes the journalist she thinks she'll be, she'll need tons of CYAs."

Looking quite serious, Gus replied, "Of course she can write about me, but . . ." her face then brightened, "I have to be twenty pounds lighter, blond, and able to sing."

"'The truth and nothing but' meets 'poetic license,' eh? She'll be thrilled she doesn't have to write the story as if I did it by myself." Grace scraped up a piece of éclair filling and a small dab of chocolate. "My plate could only be cleaner if I licked it."

"Want to get groceries?" Gus asked, her plate equally shiny.

Grace vetoed groceries in favor of a nap, leaving Gus with unwelcome free time.

"Crap!" Gus exclaimed, and Butterbean ran out the doggie door. Leaning on the counter in her kitchen, Gus looked out the window and continued the conversation as if the dog were still there.

"Like an irritating song, the Frank memory is playing in my mind, over and over," she said aloud. "Then I look at this place. "Gus turned to face the kitchen and the cluttered view through the dining and living rooms. "What a mess!"

Swearing by its restorative powers, one of Gus's friends cleans the grout in her tile shower with a toothbrush in times of stress. Scrubbing the kitchen floor seemed similar enough to Gus, so she bent down, reaching for the Simple Green under the sink.

When she opened the cabinet door, half the contents cascaded out, hiding her feet in a conglomerate of plastic take-out containers, scrub brushes, rubber gloves, wasp spray, and Clorox. No Simple Green in sight.

Gus used her favorite curse words and sank to her knees, holding the edge of the sink. She leaned in and pulled out the remaining junk, finding the Simple Green in the back, just out of reach. Mindful of the sink bottom and the pipes, she stretched until she could touch its cap. An extra lunge and determined finger wiggles brought the bottle into her grasp.

She hauled it out and sat down, tossing cleansers on the floor and shooting empty spray bottles, dead sponges, and other flotsam at the trash basket. Bending between her splayed legs, she arranged the keeper items, leaving empty spaces to facilitate visual inventory.

Finished and standing at last, Gus stretched and worked the kinks out of her back and filled a bucket in the sink. Butterbean stuck her head in the doggie door, sniffed the air, and scuttled to her water bowl.

When Gus put down the bucket of soapy water and began mopping, Butterbean stopped drinking and dashed back to the yard.

Scrubbing with a vengeance, Gus thought about her younger days, seeking a revelation that might catalyze Marigold's good sense. She found herself going over her mental Lovers Lost List.

Gus's search for the love of her life began in her college years. Fancying herself a writer and being enough of one to have a poem published, she needed no encouragement to embrace the writer image—clunky Royal typewriter, scotch, cigarettes, dismal and tortured insights, plenty of sex. It was the '60s. She recognized from her lofty view forty years later that she'd had great fun, but no substance in her relationships. Was it her, them, or both? Marigold's question exactly.

Sophomore and junior years brought Gus a fiancé who, soon after the engagement, chose a more conventional mate. Gus's bout with him was followed by one with a woman who, in a nanosecond, left Gus for another, wealthier, woman. Postgraduate, Gus engaged in a host of mismatched pairings in an alcoholic haze. Some were fun, some not: the racecar driver who couldn't get it up, the rich boy who couldn't get it down, and a few who tantalized but remained unrequited.

That frenzy ended in 1971, when Gus met George, a friendly and good man with a similar sense of humor and an ABD (all but the dissertation) PhD in Physics. Possibly trying on life on the wild side, George lived in a rooming house owned by a Lower East Side Jewish Psychodrama Guru with control issues and a Teflon zipper.

Gus got more soap and water, wondering as she did whenever she thought of George, why they had married. They could have been great friends. He was an unfocused city boy from Massachusetts. She was a country girl from south Jersey with tunnel vision, determined to have a farm. Delight in living in Philadelphia was their commonality.

Gus rinsed the floor, thinking, we nearly talked each other to death, each of us hearing what s/he wanted to, not what the other was saying, particularly about buying the farm. All too typical. Disappointed that she was making no profound discoveries for Marigold's enlightenment, Gus swiped a dry towel over the floor and dumped the dirty rinse water.

Butterbean poked her head in the doggie door, cocking her head as if to say, "You done yet? It's dinner time!"

Putting away the mop and bucket, Gus chuckled and said aloud, "Guess I'll practice making casseroles while Fleming develops."

11

Hello, I Love You, Won't You Tell Me Your Name?

As the sun transformed peachy dawn into blazing blue on a postcard perfect Thursday morning, Gus and Hazel resuscitated their war on fat.

"Good God, Hazel," Gus puffed, "this race walking is nuts! Look at us, arms flapping like wild turkeys, my knees shouting about the Geneva Convention."

"You're fine, Gus. We need to revitalize our routine. We haven't walked in weeks. By the way, how's Mari?" Hazel looked stunning in her stoplight red shorts with matching sneaks and chartreuse t-shirt.

Also well-attired, Gus wore denim shorts, a tee with painted sunflowers, and a flaming dragon sweatband. She wiggle-walked beside Hazel. "Grace and I talked about Mari after the test, which we both aced, in case she didn't tell you. I couldn't get past my exasperating lunch with Mari and, starting there, one thing led to another. We ended up talking about Frank's Final Episode. I hadn't thought about that in a long time, but now I can't let go of it. It haunts me." Breathless, Gus flapped on, watching the uneven pavement and noticing more trash at the curb than usual.

"Mari hasn't called since our gathering at the cemetery," Hazel said, the words carrying to Gus on the morning breeze. "Did you tell me she heard from Fleming?"

"I must have. I was pissed because he called her at last, while we were at lunch and left her a message. Here I am, talking about Life on Life's terms, with a capital 'L,' and how to live comfortably on those terms as a single person, and Mari just wants to land her prince. I was barely in my door after our lunch when she called to tell me they were going to dinner that night."

"You sure sound bummed," Hazel said, slowing down.

"I am. Oh, before I forget, did Grace ask you about Clarice writing the story of our 'operation'?" Gus stopped.

Hazel jogged back to her. "She did, and I said 'yes.' Don't look so surprised. Who in the state doesn't know by now?" Hazel started running in place.

Gus bent over, inhaled, and said, "Mari left a message yesterday. Would I keep Daphne this weekend while she and Fleming go to Asheville? I said 'sure' to her machine, if you call that a conversation. Fleming strikes me as a 'Man Who Came to Dinner,' and I bet we'll hear from Mari only when she needs us to take Daphne."

"Relax, Gus, it's just been a few days. Maybe a heavy dose of Fleming will be its own cure. 'Hello, I love you, won't you tell me your name' didn't work for us in college, and that approach doesn't improve over time. Let's finish this torture," Hazel said. "Fitness and immortality won't happen if we just stand here. We can yak at home where there's nourishment." She walked off, looking from behind like an emu on a mission.

The next three blocks were fraught with danger, uprooted pavement and plantings that reached out over the sidewalk to grab, smack, or slice the inattentive. Cans and bottles sprinkled the area, their escape from the recycle bins abetted by foraging humans and animals. They lay in wait for the unwary like lesser land mines. The trash cans treated the women to the smell of stale beer, cat litter, and diapers.

"Hold it!" Hazel ordered, grabbing Gus's arm, "I smell something."

"Me too," Gus replied, adjusting her shirt. "Bouquet of cat litter with an overlay of Budweiser. Let's go."

"Not that," Hazel said, standing on tiptoe, swiveling like a dish antenna.

"What then?" Gus, irked, wrung out her headband.

A breeze came up. "Ether," Hazel said. "They used ether when I had my tonsils out, and I threw up for a week. I'd know ether anywhere." She followed the odor across the street to a recycle bin in front of a classic brick Colonial.

"Ugh," Gus said. "When I began work as a vet tech, that's what we used to clean dogs' teeth. Tricky stuff, that ether." In the bin several cans of auto starter were visible.

Hazel picked up one of the cans triumphantly, "See? See, I told you I smelled ether! It's got . . ." she squinted to read the fine print, "it's got ether in it. Diethyl ether, to be exact!"

Gus pushed the can away. "Isn't it too warm to have car-starting problems? And who has carburetors these days? All the vehicles here are late nineties or newer."

"None of our business, I guess," Hazel said, tossing the can back into the bin. "I hear scones calling, and I smell coffee brewing."

"Not to mention the magnetic pull on your butt from your back porch rocker," Gus said, grinning. She dodged left away from Hazel's smack and took off for her house.

On Hazel's back porch, the breeze cooled the women's sweaty bodies, while the four canines lounged under the pecan tree a few yards away. Lady was asleep. Art, Gwen, and Butterbean shredded their rawhides, glancing slyly at one another in case someone's chewy went untended for a split second.

"What's your real issue with Mari?" Hazel asked as she sat, appreciating the comfort as well as the beauty of the new, hibiscus print cushions on her rocking chairs. She sipped her coffee and kept an eye on Gus whose body language was easy to read—tense as a stretched rope.

"I think she's a love junkie," Gus said, not wasting time on tact. "Her therapist pointed out that she's the common denominator in all her relationships. Mari said it herself, and I quote, 'I'll pick the only jerk in the room.' Not to mention, we all know she does the same thing over and over again anticipating different results."

"I see what you mean."

"The trouble with addicts is their personalities. The disease assures them that they are fine—the trouble is everyone else—insulating them from self-examination, personal accountability, and any sort of humility. To Mari's credit, she is beginning to think she might have some responsibility for the tenor of her life. But crap, Hazel, she's sitting on forty! Will it take another forty years for her to make changes?" Gus got up and began Picking Fruit, a Tai Chi exercise for stretching the arms and shoulders.

"Yoo hoo? Any one home? I know you're there, Gus. Your car's out front," Marigold yodeled.

"Back here," Gus yelled. Turning to Hazel, she said, "Now what?"

Marigold flew up the porch steps. "Am I interrupting? I'll only be a minute." She blew them each a kiss and twirled her long purple skirt, flaring and then wrapping it around her legs just below her knees. "Gus, can you take Daphne today . . . now? Fleming's free, so we thought we'd leave for the mountains a couple of days early. I know she'd love to be with Butterbean. We're boring her."

"Hi, Mari," Hazel chirped. "Would you like some coffee and a scone? I haven't seen you since the cemetery."

"Has it been that long? Wow!" Marigold's face flashed genuine surprise. "Sure, I'll take a scone, but Daphne and Fleming are in the car, so I've got to hurry."

"Get him to bring Daphne in," Gus offered.

Guessing what was coming, Hazel gave Gus "The Look."

Deftly ignoring Hazel, Gus patted the adjacent rocking chair, put a scone in a napkin, and said, "I'd like to meet him, you know, give him the third degree, in loco parentis, that sort of thing."

Marigold, her mouth full of scone, blanched.

"Is he single? What kind of work does he do? Does he exhibit at the Deco Gecko?" Gus continued.

"Enough, Gus," Hazel barked. "She'll answer another time. You heard her. They're in a hurry."

Marigold laughed and redid her ponytail. "I'll tell all after this trip. Oh," she said as an afterthought, "he *is* single." She turned to Gus, "I won't be thinking about living alone now. I think he's The One. Yikes, I better get going! I'll put Daphne's stuff in your car and drop her back here."

"You okay?" Butterbean asked after Gus left for work the next day. Yesterday, the dogs were occupied doing errands with Gus or lounging at Hazel's, but Butterbean, hyperaware of emotions, knew Daphne was off-kilter. She'd been eating and behaving normally, but it was the *way* she did those things. Butterbean could see Daphne was detached, withdrawn, and anything but regal.

"I feel dumped," Daphne blurted out without her customary élan.

Taken by surprise at Daphne's bluntness, Butterbean lost her tact as well, saying, "So, talk to me."

"This is confidential," Daphne said, circling the required three times in her bed in Gus's kitchen. "If you tell Gwen, she'll tell Art, and he gossips all over town, so please keep this between us." With majesty regained, she lay down.

"Of course, it's between us," Butterbean said, standing in front of Daphne. "Gossip is the exact and only reason I've decided Gwen can't coauthor my book. It'd be common knowledge before it's published." Butterbean stretched out on her belly in her bed, pushing her hind legs as far out as they'd go.

"It's my Mari that's upsetting me," Daphne replied. "I'm not here because she had a workshop or family emergency, you know."

"Let me guess," Butterbean got out of her bed and sat in front of Daphne again. "Fleming?"

"What else? A few days ago he finally called. They went to dinner that night, and they've been glued together since. He's never gone home and now they're having a fling in the mountains and here I am until Sunday night—no offense."

"None taken," Butterbean said, thoughtfully scratching her ear.

"You know people in general, and my Mari in particular, are so perplexing. Most people can't manage to have sex, enjoy it, and get on with their lives, and Mari . . ." Daphne flexed her neck and crossed her forepaws, searching for words. Cocking her head and facing her ears forward, Butterbean paid strict attention.

"My Mari thinks she would only have sex with a Prince. How could she allow such intimacy to happen with a lesser mortal? Ergo, the guy gets out of bed enjoying a terrific experience, and she gets up feeling a bottomless need to prove he's the kindest, gentlest Stud Muffin, damn any contrary facts."

Adjusting her hind legs, Daphne continued, "In my Mari's mind, they have to make a relationship, live together, and promise impossible things."

"I'm gathering that from listening to my Gus. She's disappointed after all the thought she put into their lunch. She thinks Fleming might be another Frank, and it makes her crazy. She really cares about your Mari, you know." Butterbean stretched out on the cool floor.

"I know. It's that damned Frank!" Daphne snapped. "If only your Gus had let me at his throat that day."

"Bite your tongue!" Butterbean shot back. "You'd both be dead, and he'd be stalking you at the Rainbow Bridge. I can see the headlines now, 'Killer Greyhound Attacks Abuser, Euthanasia Verdict.'"

"Oh, cat sausages, it would've been worth it."

"Wouldn't happen; none of the humans or we canines would let it. We'd dig tunnels connecting our houses, disguise you as a hairy mutt, and move you in with Irene. *Nobody* messes with Irene!"

"Oh please! Make me a Borzoi. At least they're elegant, if hairy. Back to topic: I think what's behind all this is Mari's need for children. What else could it be?" Daphne asked.

"Lots of things," Butterbean replied. "Maybe she honestly needs a fulfilling relationship. I know Gus does, though she wouldn't admit it if she were on short rations."

"Or maybe Mari truly can't handle living alone, period. She says it all the time, 'I am so over living alone.' You've heard her, Butterbean. She grew up in that commune with a gazillion people, so maybe solitude is too foreign for her."

Butterbean went back to her bed. Daphne kept on talking. "Because they don't have litters, or at least didn't until recently, people can use up seventy percent of their lives raising children. They have to be hard-wired to handle that. Why, we can comfortably have six to eight litters and spend only fifteen to twenty percent of our lives with puppies."

"No wonder humans need commitment," Butterbean said, perking up. "Once we got teeth, my Mom jumped out of our box and said goodbye. What's this Fleming like?"

"I'm not sure," Daphne replied. "My instincts are on alert, but I've got no hard facts. After dinner that first night, Mari fell into his arms like a sack of kibble, and they jumped in bed as if it were full of Greenies. From what I can tell, he gets high marks for mating performance, but so what? It's character, money, and dependability that matter."

"Hmmm, his lair and hunting abilities are also important," Butterbean murmured.

"There was just that one dinner out. Mari has cooked for him at our place since then. I don't mind. Due to their penchant for bedroom entertainment, I get plenty of leftovers. But does it mean he has no money or that he's stingy? Besides, I'll need more walks or more willpower if the leftovers don't stop." Daphne got up and began to pace.

"Oh pooh, you look your usual slim self except for perhaps a slight widening of your shoulders, which is quite becoming. The sturdy look is very in this year. But I digress. Mari has never been to Fleming's place?"

"Never," Queen Daphne rested her head on her forepaws, sighing. "Since they met, this is the first time I've seen you, and we haven't seen Grace or Hazel at all. I feel another mess brewing, a mini-Frank at best. Anyway, Fleming says he's a painter. I'd bet on house painter by his smell, but he has no fixed hours or paycheck. He says he goes to a studio while she's at work, but often he doesn't get past the VCR and Mari's movies. His kind of artist is spelled c-o-n, I bet. I know he's a parasite, but how to point it out? I thought having my portrait made might force his hand, but that's too complicated." Daphne rose and departed for the living room.

Butterbean bounced up and, racing between Daphne's legs, arrived first. Even with that momentum, she couldn't jump directly on the sofa without several false starts.

"May I?" Queen Daphne asked politely, putting one forepaw on the couch.

"Of course," Butterbean said. "You're family, you don't have to ask. I enjoy watching you merely step up here. You saw what I have to go through. It's exhausting, but if I don't wind up like that, I'll hit my chest on the edge, and fall back on my butt. That jars my back."

With admirable grace, Queen Daphne lifted each remaining paw onto the sofa, circled once, and lay down facing Butterbean, ready to listen and discuss.

"Maybe we can create a situation that would reveal Fleming's true colors," Butterbean suggested. "Does he drink? I hope he doesn't use drugs."

"He drinks some, but no drugs for sure. Our timing must be impeccable. If Mari thinks she's being herded, she gets angry and obstinate."

"Don't they all? You'll know when the time is right. Humans rarely admit we have faster and more accurate situational perception. Knowing we have better hearing and sense of smell damages their feeling of superiority as it is. We'll need time to perfect a plan. What if Fleming has an accident? Wouldn't his friends, boss, coworkers, someone, appear or call?" Butterbean swiveled her ears.

"You'd think. Remember those peculiar stairs leading into our apartment? Something serendipitous *could* happen." Daphne's eyes drooped and she sighed.

"Let's sleep on it. I get inspired after a good nap," Butterbean said, circling on her couch cushion and arranging the pillow just so for her jaw. "Please pardon me. I can only sleep back to the armrest, nose toward the front door."

"And I can only sleep rolled counterclockwise for some reason, so please excuse me also," Daphne replied as her footsteps bounced Butterbean's cushion fore and aft until Daphne was down and properly rolled up.

12

As Awful as It Gets

In a seeming instant, early summer arrived in Pine Crossing, slowing everyone's pace, encouraging a switch from hot tea to iced tea, providing a short but welcome time between heat and air conditioning bills.

This Saturday morning was one of the few cool and dry summer days in the Carolinas, and Hazel made the most of it. She returned from weeding and watering her garden in the dappled shade, envisioning each vegetable root gobbling a freshly fertilized meal. She peeled off her gloves and stashed them on the shelf near the dog port, at the same time slipping her wet shoes onto the boot mat below.

"Lady, Art, Gwen, breakfast!" she called, and was assaulted by two balls of caramel-colored fur. Lady Labrador hauled herself out of her bed with a twinkling eye and a wagging tail. Fifteen and arthritic, she still had the appetite of a two-year-old.

Bruce was visiting his son Greg in Virginia. Grace and Gus would be coming for brunch, maybe Mari too. Hazel had plenty of time to straighten the house, bake some scones, and relax in the tub, just as she wished. What a fine morning!

"Hi Hazel," Grace said, hugging her before closing the door and handing off a bag of coffee samples. Hazel gestured Grace toward the kitchen and pushed the door shut with her foot, hitting something that yelped.

"Oh, Butterbean, I'm sorry," Gus, in next, hugged Hazel. Behind her, Queen Daphne appeared, strolling up the porch steps, Marigold in tow.

"The gang's all here," Marigold chirped, unhooking Daphne's leash.

Inside, Hazel bustled about getting coffee and dispensing various bones and rawhide, the canine entertainment equivalent of Sesame Street.

"So Bruce is visiting Greg?" Marigold said, taking the Chai Lai. What prompted this trip?

"Aside from fishing and male bonding with Greg, he wanted to wrap up details about his will and give Greg the title to the cabin. Bruce is bypassing Greg's mother, who's still a problem twenty years after their divorce; can you imagine?" She got up to check the scones, "Almost ready!"

"I've been thinking," Gus said, stirring creamer into her coffee, "I'd like to play tourist in Seattle in the fall. Have any of you been there?"

"No," Grace said in concert with Marigold, who swiftly asked, "Would guys be invited?"

No one responded. Hazel concentrated on removing the scones from the tray, her fingers burning through the flimsy potholder. The doorbell buzzed and she jumped, the tray clanging on the floor.

Grace moved to answer the door, but Hazel, retrieving the cookie sheet, said, "I'll go, Grace. The yard's such a mess, I bet it's another landscaper after a job."

The buzzer went off again.

Hazel pushed aside a corner of the lace curtain on her front door. "Holy Mother of God," she whispered, "Sheriffs!" Her mind filled with images of her experiences at protest marches, uncalled-for traffic stops when she was full of youth and pheromones, and a nasty customs official. She straightened her back, inhaled, and stepped out, closing the door behind her, grateful she wasn't in her robe or spandex.

"Can I help you?" The Queen of England couldn't have been more regal.

"Is Bruce D. Winston here?" The baby-poop brown shirt and mahogany slacks accessorized with a belt of lethal weapons emphasized his rotund body and spindly legs. His badges and insignia weighed enough to make a gap between buttons two and three, revealing a net undershirt. His lankier sidekick deputy stood quietly behind him. A desire to be twenty, picketing something, and outrunning him fired in Hazel's mental synapses.

"No," she replied, moving forward under guise of adjusting her stance, reading his name badge.

"We have this as his residence, ma'am," Sheriff Alvin Outlaw said.

Hazel chuckled in her mind, wondering if it took stupidity or brass balls to be a sheriff with that name, while she stepped forward and stated, "This is *my* home. Who told you that?" More information was needed before she would hand out details of her life, or Bruce's.

"From the plaintiff, ma'am." As he moved forward into her space, Hazel did not move back. His belly was six inches from hers.

"Who is the plaintiff, and what is the complaint?" Hazel spoke without using contractions, clearly articulating her words. She pushed her chin forward, a model of deportment, politeness, and reserve that would have pleased Mother. Her stubbornness would not be approved of, however, for Mother always caved to authority, real or imagined.

"I can't tell you that, ma'am. Do you know where Mr. Winston is?"

"No."

"I must advise you, ma'am, if you are withholding any information, you may be subject to prosecution for obstruction of justice. I'll ask again, do you know where Bruce D. Winston might be?" In spite of his fuchsia face, his demeanor was also impeccable.

"I'm sorry, officer. I can tell you that Mr. Winston is in Virginia visiting family, but I don't know where. He is listed in the phone book, and I expect you could reach him there when he returns." Hazel, finished with this pissing contest, added, "I have company inside, and if there is nothing further, I am going." She reached for the doorknob behind her.

"In case you speak to him first, you need to know this matter, if not handled quickly, could have serious consequences. The boy over there," Officer Outlaw pointed toward the bright blue house next door, "the boy says Bruce has taken indecent liberties with him, molested him. The sooner we hear Mr. Winston's side of things, the better.

"You understand, since we have been apprised of the situation, we are legally bound to investigate and straighten it out." He handed Hazel his card.

"If you hear from him or recall anything, anything at all, you may reach me at this number." Officer Outlaw turned to go, and once his back was to Hazel, Mr. Skinny Deputy handed Hazel his card and winked. She reached behind her and turned the door knob, all the while staring at their backs moving down her walk to the cruiser.

The next thing Hazel knew, she was climbing out of a dark well similar to waking from a deep, deep sleep. "What's that God-awful ammonia smell?" she croaked, pushing away what seemed like hundreds of dog noses as she rolled off her back and sat up. She took a quick inventory. She was flat on her back inside her front door. Her three friends were yammering at once, as Hazel gagged and coughed, pushing Grace and her ammonia-soaked rag out of range.

Everyone else coughed, too. Gus pointed Grace and her rag to the kitchen.

"Are you okay?" Marigold knelt beside Hazel, putting an arm around her.

"What happened out there?" Gus asked, looking weird and sounding worse.

"What happened to you?" Hazel's eyes widened as she took in the bruises developing on Gus's cheek and her swollen nose.

"You fainted as you were opening the door to come back inside," Grace said. She planted a frozen bag of peas on Gus's face and continued, "Gus was watching through the curtain when you turned the knob and fainted. The door smacked her in the face as you fell. Luckily we all caught you."

"Silly me, I should have guessed," Hazel replied with sarcasm. "The sheriffs didn't see me faint, did they?" Energized at such a mortifying thought, Hazel scrambled up.

"No, they were gone," Marigold interjected as they grouped around Hazel, guiding her to the living room. "What did they say?"

Hazel sat on the sofa by the phone. Gus wandered to the mirror over the mantle, removed the peas, and put them back fast. Her nose was swollen, and purple bruises were everywhere. Grace sat in the wingback chair to Hazel's right.

"First of all, I knew better than to talk to them. At last, they told me what the trouble was." Hazel inhaled seemingly forever and took longer to exhale. Everyone, including the dogs, waited until Marigold said, "So?"

"It's Bruce they want. They said the kid next door, Mark, told them that Bruce molested him." Hazel watched her words change the women's expressions as a slap might. "Merciful heavens!" "Holy crap!" "Bloody idiots!" All of them spoke at once.

Taking a tissue, Hazel sniffed. "I told them I didn't know where Bruce was, which is true. Virginia's a big state."

"Breed," Gus butted in, stuffy like she had a cold. Her left nostril had swollen shut.

"I have to warn him," Hazel declared. "They can nab him anywhere if they run his license plate and put out an APB. He has to be prepared before talking to them. The word 'molest' is a death knell, way worse than our butts on TV. Your job, if you have one, disappears. So does your community involvement; no one wants to be connected with you in the tiniest way. It's like Amish shunning." Hazel, stunned by her own words, wailed into her tissue.

"Shhhh, it'll be okay, we'll work this out," Grace comforted and handed Hazel more tissues along with the phone. "Call him now."

"I dink you shud too," Gus said.

Next to Gus, Marigold turned and lifted the frozen pea packet. "Gus, this needs to be looked at. You might have a broken bone or two. What hurts?"

"Ebryting, d . . . doh ebrgency roob," Gus said, pulling away from Marigold.

"Okay, Gus, no emergency room, but we are going to Urgent Care." Marigold got up and searched for her keys.

Irritated because Bruce's cell phone was out of range, Hazel looked at Gus and so did Grace. Half her face was swollen and the color of a turnip.

"You need to go," Grace said in a no-wiggle-room tone. "You won't be able to breathe or sleep without medical attention."

Hazel nodded agreement as she thumbed through her phone book for

Greg's number. She'd let others think she was old-fashioned rather than admit she couldn't program numbers into her phone.

"You two go," Hazel ordered. "Grace and I will find Bruce."

Coffee in, coffee out, Bruce thought as he searched for his car, figuring he could get to his son Greg's house before "nature's call" became urgent. Fastidious to a fault, he hated public restrooms and always checked the silverware in even the finest restaurant. The mall he'd just exited wasn't the best, but it had a good jewelry store, a passable food court, and an excellent supermarket, all of which he'd found useful.

He'd gotten groceries for Greg and his family, a Starbucks primo-choc-latte with whipped cream and cinnamon as a personal treat, and a brash, colorful pair of earrings for Hazel. His car wasn't in sight. Then his phone rang.

"Hello, Bruce speaking."

"What's the matter with you? You sound winded." Hazel said, her tone oddly curt.

"I am sorta, Haze. I'm leaving the mall with groceries for Greg, and my car seems to have taken a trip without me. Oh! There it is! Row two after all. What's up, Love?"

"I can hardly hear you, Bruce. Are there mountains around?"

"Yeah, Sweetie, on three sides," Bruce yelled.

It came through to Hazel as, "Yeah . . . tie . . . eee . . . des."

"Call me from Greg's," Hazel yelled, not knowing what he could hear.

"Okay, from Greg's. Got that?"

"Yeah, from Greg's," Hazel shouted, adding, "It's urgent!" at the top of her lungs. She clicked off the handset in frustration.

Something's wrong, Bruce thought, unloading the cart into the back seat of his ice blue BMW convertible. Hazel never used the word "urgent" and she never hung up on him.

Bluetooth on, Bruce found good reception halfway up the last mountain toward Greg's house. He listened in disbelief while Hazel twice reiterated her encounter with Sheriff Outlaw and his Skinny Deputy. *Un-effing-believable!*

Though it repeated in his thoughts like a single loop tape, molesting a male minor wasn't computing in Bruce's brain, specifically not pimple-faced Mark, who was sloppy too. This has *got* to be a mistake. He'd call his attorney and friend, John Jackson, next.

"I've got a call in to John," Hazel was saying. "Sarah will get him off the golf course as soon as she can."

"Did you give her my cell number?"

"Of course, dear, please come right home. And don't tell anyone, not even Greg, until you and John get this cleared up. If anyone gets wind of this . . . Oh crap, the *media!* This *has* to be fixed right away!"

"It'll be okay, Hon," Bruce said. "I'll unload the car, grab my stuff and tell Greg something. As soon as that's done, I'll call you from the road. I'm sorry, I can't wrap my mind around this and I know you're upset. I'll call you and get there as fast as I can. I love you."

"I love you too, dear. Bye."

"What *will* I tell Greg," Bruce wondered aloud as he threw groceries in the refrigerator and left staples on the counter. *Do I write a note, call? This is FUBAR.*

He checked the guest room and bath three times for forgotten articles, tossed everything in his car, locked the house, ran back to use the bathroom, and at last, left for Hazel's. The BMW's performance lived up to the advertisements, winding around the mountain roads in safety, twenty miles above the speed limit as Bruce raced to the expressway and decent phone reception.

As he entered the expressway, Bruce took a second to note this splendid summer day, raced the Beamer through the gears, and settled in the outside lane. Then he got on the phone.

Hazel's line was busy. "Damn!" he said, the wind yanking the word out of his mouth. He didn't want to stop and put the top up. Maybe if he had to stop for something else, he would.

Next, Bruce called Greg at work and explained he had an urgent consult.

No lie there. He left John a message at his office, in case he went there after golfing. He tried Hazel again, still busy.

He called his two brothers, both football heroes grown into cops like their dad. He outlined his situation and paid attention to their advice. There was none of the customary teasing about Bruce's intellect or his resemblance to their nonathletic, paralegal mom.

Their advice ranged from SWAT team fantasies to hard facts about the court room game and its bias toward the prosecution, none of it encouraging. Bruce dialed Hazel again. Busy.

Okay, Bruce thought. *Pretend you're a client. What did you do to invite this? What might be a motive? Who would profit from my personal and professional disgrace? The McClellan building upset wouldn't produce this kind of venom, would it?*

Bruce tried Hazel again.

Still busy! With an equal lack of success, Bruce redialed John, then concentrated on speeding without being caught.

When John and Sarah returned her calls, Hazel had told them simply, "Sheriff Outlaw and his henchman came today looking for Bruce. Apparently Mark, the kid who lives next door, has accused Bruce of molestation." They assured her John would phone Bruce en route and they would be at Hazel's when Bruce arrived. Marigold had taken Gus home. Knowing the Johnsons would be there within the hour, Grace fixed Hazel a double Jim Beam on the rocks and warmed a scone, a desperate but effective combination.

Screeching into Hazel's driveway in record time for the trip, Bruce parked behind John and Sarah's Prius. Once inside, he greeted John and Sarah, ending with a bear hug for Hazel. Sarah had made several Black Russians.

"It's good to be home," Bruce exhaled like an untied balloon. "Everyone know what's going on?" Bruce picked up his drink, downing it in two gulps.

"Whoa, buddy," John said, taking the empty glass, "you need twice your faculties if half what Hazel said is true."

"Why don't you two talk in the dining room, while Sarah and I pull together something to eat? We'll all function better once we're fed," Hazel suggested. Making a meal comforted her in ways nothing else could. She pulled out a Dutch oven and colander, spaghetti on her mind.

Eye rolls came from the men.

"You can't wait a few minutes for personal dinner service?" Sarah inquired, smiling slyly. She winked at Hazel. "Okay then," John grinned, "we'll brainstorm in the dining room while you two make spaghetti and salad."

"Excellent idea," Hazel agreed, reaching behind her back to untie her apron.

Bruce and John hit the door to the dining room simultaneously, bumping their shoulders and losing balance, giving the women the last laugh of the evening.

Bruce's friend since law school, John Jackson still practiced criminal law, much of it pro bono. He was also Bruce's best golf buddy and a member of the Historical Preservation Society. He and Sarah were sailing the Caribbean during "Operation Wonder Woman" and Bruce's day in court. Had they been home, they would have been in the thick of things.

Sarah was one of Hazel's book club and Mahjong cohorts, and in the past, they had served at the local soup kitchen and on library committees. Usually when the two couples spent an evening together, except for the main event, they were as separate as Shakers at worship. Bruce and John liked to talk golf, law, or politics. Hazel and Sarah preferred discussing artistic endeavors, volunteer activities, and local events, liberally spiced with gossip. This night was different.

Once the dishes were cleared away by the women, coffee and its accoutrements appeared, compliments of the men. By then, disbelief in Mark's allegations had vanished and their talk turned to motive, focusing on background, neighborhood incidents, and community relations. John then asked routine questions, sounding like a TV detective.

"Have you ever had specific problems with them?" John inquired, yellow legal pad at hand. They had switched from booze to coffee, and were energized by the German double chocolate cake with chocolate frosting that Hazel had made while waiting for Bruce.

"Hazel sees more of them than I do," Bruce said, "but one time when I was here, Mark had their infernal floodlights on after midnight. He and his buddies were using the skateboard track in the side yard, which is okay, but one light shines right into our upstairs bedroom."

"I asked them a hundred times to point it anywhere but at the bedroom window, and they paid no attention. It's still in the same place," Hazel added.

"One night when we couldn't sleep," Bruce went on, "I yelled out the window to them. I'm sure I mentioned their education or IQ, but I also distinctly recall holding back other ten- and twelve-letter words about their parents or their behavior."

"You were charming, dear," Hazel said, putting her arm around his shoulder and smiling at his profile. She pushed a piece of his hair into place and turned back to the group.

"A few nights after that, Mark and his friends repeated the performance, again after midnight," Hazel said. "I was alone and I called the police. They came, and next thing, the lights were out and the kids were gone. That morning, I found a handful of dead firecrackers in my backyard. It wasn't a bright move, I guess, but I tossed them back over the fence. Since then I check the yard each morning, but I've not found anything else."

"You never told me that," Bruce said, his protective hackles rising.

"Wasn't your problem, dear," Hazel said, her tone scissoring that thread of conversation.

"You've lived here how long, Hazel?" John asked.

"She came about a year before we moved here," Sarah remarked, pouring him more coffee. "If it wasn't for Hazel, I'd still be floundering in this community."

"You're right, Sarah, but that's what, fourteen years, fifteen?"

"Sixteen for Hazel, fifteen for us," Sarah got up. "More cake anyone?"

Receiving three no-thank-yous, Sarah cut herself a sliver and put the cake away.

"I think I was here three or four years when the Lewis family moved next door," Hazel continued, "I griped a lot about the cars in their yard. I know you remember the community conflicts over the antics of the senior Lewis, Horace. He was a shade-tree mechanic until he was ordered to get rid of the junk cars. He'd stuffed seven in the backyard, had four or five along the drive, and two on the street, all unregistered. Then he applied for a bed and breakfast license and the Aldermen turned him down. Next came a dog-breeding business, Beagles, but the neighbors and the Humane Society went berserk. Without a kennel license, he was forced to cease and desist."

Sarah smiled at her memories of her early days in Pine Crossing. Bruce scowled at his recollection of all those cars. John shook his head in disbelief at the Lewis' combination of hubris and stupidity.

"Could he get a kennel license?" Hazel asked rhetorically. "Not in this part of town. Because I lived next door, I tried to stay neutral, but I signed a petition to remove the Beagles and found a home for one of them." Hazel grinned. "It's now the fattest Beagle in the county."

Hazel sipped some coffee. "At the end, Horace painted the house that pungent blue, thumbing his nose at all of us, I suppose. So far, things have been quiet, and I've been happy," she grimaced, "until now."

"Who else lives there? And what do you mean by 'quiet until now'?" John looked up from his writing.

Bruce answered, "There's Mark, who's almost eighteen; an older brother, who stays with his girlfriend, but shows up for a week or so whenever they break up. And the dad, Horace, is mostly drunk in the chair on his front porch. I never see the mother. Is there one?"

"I don't think so," Hazel responded. "I think she took off with another man a couple of years ago. 'Until now' means this ridiculous accusation," Hazel replied, keeping her anger in check.

"Does the dad work?" John asked, making a note.

"Odd jobs, demolition," Bruce answered.

"That's *it!*" Hazel screeched. "This jerk is the brother of the guy that owns the demolition company, the one from the McClellan to-do!"

"Damn, you're right, Haze," Bruce put his head in his hands. "I'd forgotten that."

"So?" John eyeballed Hazel.

"Normally, I'd think civil suit. The demolition company *could* sue the three of us and/or the Historical Society for whatever work they lost, although I gather it was only postponed. Am I right, Bruce?"

"Yeah," Bruce slumped over the table. "The Historical Preservation Society can't raise enough money to buy the McClellan. Probably the assorted Lewises realize none of us have that kind of money." Bruce turned to Hazel and patted her shoulder. "Demolition starts next week. Take lots of pictures, my dear, 'cause that's all we'll have."

"Still, if they sued us, for sure they wouldn't get millions, but they'd make us spend time and money, and cause us a heap of aggravation even if they lost," Hazel ran her hands through her hair.

"There's more," Bruce said, straightening. "Do any of you know who the third brother is? *Henry Lewis?*"

Everyone looked as blank as a ream of copy paper.

"He's married to my ex-wife's sister, Gloria, who likes me less than my ex because I didn't give her a tumble after my divorce from Sheila. I guess Sheila didn't let on that she got most of my money. Anyway, Henry's a brother of Herman, the Devoted Demolition Lewis, and next door's Horace Lewis. Horace, who wouldn't turn down a buck if it were covered in manure, is the sorriest of the lot. Who knows what Mark is being offered to make this statement?" Bruce looked at John, who scribbled like an EKG machine marking an auricular flutter. "Or is getting saved from," Bruce added as an afterthought.

"Let me get this straight," Hazel said, wondering in another part of her mind why she'd not realized this earlier, "Herman Lewis is Devoted Demolition, which we sorely aggravated over the McClellan building. His brother is Horace, who lives next door in détente mode, and his other brother is Henry, the guy who married your ex-wife's sister, Gloria, whom you dissed when she had the hots for you? These are all the same Lewis family?"

"Yeah baby," Bruce said, pulling her close. "Could there be more motives?"

John theorized Horace was behind Mark's allegations. Mark was seventeen going on eighteen and in the tenth grade. From Hazel's description of the activities next door over the years, the Lewis' only interest was in quick money. Horace's proximity to Bruce and Hazel afforded his more enterprising brothers excellent opportunities for revenge, Mark's allegations being just one choice.

"Chances are," Bruce suggested, "the lure of money is the bottom line." He paused a minute, "though ruining my reputation would appeal as well."

"I think they'd like to get rid of Hazel too," Sarah interjected. "Make life difficult for her in this town. Would any of them be able to buy this house?"

"Bite your tongue, girl," Hazel shot back. "I'd put flamethrowers on the roof before I'd sell it to a Lewis. Or an Outlaw! *Gott in Himmel!*"

Pouring more coffee, Hazel said slowly, thinking as she spoke, "Maybe it's political. Maybe one of the Lewises, or the Sheriff's office, or the District Attorney, maybe all of them, are hunting for the next rung on the ladder to success. And," she glanced at Bruce, fear, sadness, and anger flitting over her features, "maybe, dear, they think your ruin is that rung. Nothing changes lives like a male-on-male sex case."

Though they talked past midnight, the foursome produced no more worthwhile ideas concerning Mark's motives. All of Bruce and Hazel's "transgressions" added together didn't seem to warrant such a violent retaliation. John left word at the sheriff's office. He and Bruce would appear Monday morning at nine sharp to, as the sheriff had put it, "straighten this out."

13

Tropical Depression

Bruce and John appeared at the sheriff's office Monday morning before Officer Alvin Outlaw finished his first doughnut. To make the best impression, in spite of the summer heat, both men wore light sports jackets over their open-collared shirts. Their slacks were creased and belted.

Off balance because of the promptness and demeanor of his suspect, and because that suspect brought counsel, Officer Outlaw slipped into fundamentalist-cop mode. He had to make sure this case was airtight as a vacuum bottle. Wasting no time with niceties, the three men sat in the sheriff's inner office around a table with a voice recorder in the center.

Sheriff Outlaw turned on the recorder, stating the pertinent information: time, date, place, names of the participants, and allegations. "So, Mr. Winston," Officer Outlaw began, facing Bruce and ignoring the attorney, an attempt at intimidation. He had his questions all lined up in his mind. Getting a confession would be a feather in his cap.

"Hunnk-hmm," Officer Outlaw cleared his throat to begin again, "Mr. Winston, do you know what this is about?"

"Only what you just said into the recorder, sir." Bruce was sitting straight, doing his best to appear alert, but relaxed. John had an attaché case, legal pad, and pencil on the table in front of him.

"You have no idea what Mark Lewis is talking about?"

"No sir."

Silence dragged on. Officer Outlaw leaned back in his swivel chair, taken earlier from behind his desk. In the past, he would have lit a cigar, offered one, or a cigarette. He wanted to do that now, but thought better of it.

"Mark Lewis and his father, Horace Lewis, came to the office Friday afternoon, the tenth," he paused, swiveled around and picked up a sheaf of papers from his desk. Returning to scrutinize Bruce and John, he riffled the papers and said, "It says here that you used to spend afternoons with Mark after school watching movies. Is that true?"

"When?" John asked, and made a note.

"A couple of years ago, many afternoons over, oh, approximately a two-year period."

"Do you have dates there, Sheriff?" John was in shorthand mode.

"Yes, I do. Mark said it began in the fall, three years ago. The last encounter he mentioned was," Officer Outlaw flipped two pages, "last Halloween."

"What are the dates please?" John asked.

"Roughly, from September or October 2007 to Halloween 2009."

"You can't be more specific?" John inquired politely.

"Mark wasn't specific, sir. All this is general at this point. We'll get details after we deal with the substance of the matter," Officer Outlaw ruffled his papers again.

"We will, officer, for sure we *will* get specific," John said almost sweetly, cutting his eyes to Bruce as he continued, "Sergeant Outlaw, exactly what are the allegations?"

"I won't bore you with all the statute numbers," he replied officiously, "but I have a copy of them for you when we finish. The allegations range from fondling to oral and anal sex." The sergeant drew himself up to his full seated height and furrowed his brows. If his eyes were drills, Bruce would have been full of holes. "How do you answer to these?"

Bruce said nothing, thinking the room needed fumigation. He had a maddening desire to punch the sheriff. If it wasn't his life on the line, it would be a comedy worthy of Mel Brooks and Zero Mostel. He concentrated on his breathing.

"We're not in court, officer," John said, pulling his chair closer to the table and leaning toward Sheriff Outlaw. "Did Mark Lewis name any witnesses, anyone he might have told during these two years?"

"Not in this statement." The sheriff rose and went behind his desk, rummaging through more papers. He looked up and asked, "When was the last time you watched a movie with Mark, Mr. Winston?" John touched Bruce's arm, shaking his head, "no."

Bruce put his hand on John's shoulder, and quietly assured him, "Don't worry, John." He faced Sergeant Outlaw, "That's easy, never."

"You would swear to that?"

"Yes sir, I would," Bruce answered, realizing that truth *does* banish fear.

Returning to his seat, the sheriff asked, "What happened the night you met Mark Lewis at the playhouse downtown last August?"

Bruce gave John a quizzical look. John raised an eyebrow. The corner of his mouth moved a tad toward a smile.

"I was in the last group to leave the theater, and saw Mark standing by the ticket booth. It was raining. He was alone. He smoked a cigarette. I remember exactly what he said because I felt sorry for him. He said, looking everywhere but at me, 'Dad had to meet a buddy at the bar. I know he forgot me. Would you give me a ride home?' I did. I drove directly to his house, dropped him off, then turned into Hazel's driveway and had a night cap with her. End of story."

"He tells a very different story," Sheriff Outlaw replied.

"That's what we want to know, sir, Mark's story," John responded.

The rest of the baker's dozen of allegations were treated in similar fashion along with over twenty amorphous occasions that had no date or place connected to them. According to the sheriff's notes, Mark made those allegations with statements like, 'I remember it musta been lots of times that week,' or 'It seemed like we were together every day that month,' or 'If we were together, he was doin' somethin' to me.'"

At the end, John said, "This is no case. Mr. Winston was working, wasn't in town, or simply did a neighborly favor on these alleged occasions of molestation. That Mr. Winston invited Mark into his house in the middle of the night and committed anal sex on him? I won't even dignify that with a response."

John turned the page of his legal pad. "I want to be perfectly clear about this, sheriff. You have said that Mark has not seen a doctor?"

"No, not to my knowledge."

"And you have no forensic evidence to support his claims? No semen-drenched shorts, blood, hairs, nothing of that sort?" The sergeant looked through his papers once again. Both John and Bruce could see some of them were handwritten with many arrows and cross-outs.

"Mark claimed he threw the shorts out or they got washed. Even if we found Mark's hair in your car," Officer Outlaw looked directly at Bruce, "you said you gave him a ride. You'd claim that was how they got there, and as for anything else, well, you would certainly have cleaned *that* up by now. You wouldn't want your girlfriend finding stuff on your seats or ceiling," he finished with a sneer.

John smiled, "Since it didn't happen at all, you are more than welcome to examine Bruce's car. Just name the time and place. I have another question: Was anything ever done for Mark's welfare? Was he sent to a psychiatrist, given an AIDS test, or had any kind of treatment?"

"You'd have to take that up with Mark and his father. We just take the complaint."

"Well," John said, placing the pad in his briefcase, "anyone could concoct this pile of allegations against anyone. I wouldn't waste the taxpayer's money by carrying it one step further." He and Bruce stood.

"You're right about one thing, counselor," the sergeant said, standing also, "Anyone can say anything. However, we're duty-bound to see justice is carried out when a minor makes this kind of complaint." He shuffled his papers. "As I'm certain you're aware, counselor, once a charge is in the hands of the State through the district attorney's office, only the state can dispose of the charges. I appreciate what you've said, Mr. Winston, and you also, counselor, but this will now go before the grand jury. And I'll be over to collect the computer you have in your condo, Mr. Winston. Evidence, you know." Sheriff Outlaw shut off the recorder. No one shook hands.

The three men trooped downstairs to the magistrate's office, their footsteps and slamming doors the only sounds.

That Monday evening, a disconsolate Bruce decided to give Hazel the colorful, hand-carved earrings he'd picked up Saturday, seemingly centuries ago. He hoped it would lift both their spirits. After seeing the magistrate, Officer Outlaw had accompanied Bruce and John to Bruce's condo and taken his computer. Bruce began to understand how it felt to be robbed, raped, and violated. He still had his laptop at Hazel's, his main computer for several years. He couldn't quite fathom what they wanted with his desktop computer. *How odd*, he thought as he wrapped the small package in sparkly paper. *Only four days ago, the imminent demise of the McClellan building was my biggest woe.*

He came downstairs with the gift to find Hazel on the phone, cruising around the living room, dusting.

"Well, Gus," Hazel was saying into the portable handset, "I don't know what to make of it. Bruce's case will go to the grand jury next month. They decide in secret if it's fit to go to trial."

Bruce sat on the bottom step amid his buzzing Pomeranians, patting them and half-heartedly playing kissy-face with Gwen. *Gus must be speaking okay now,* he thought. Hazel caught his eye as she dusted her flapper floor lamp, the shade having six inch fringe, and signaled "just a minute" with her finger. Bruce could tell by the length of Hazel's silence that Gus was having a rant, so he got up. Maybe they had a movie in the den he'd like to see.

"I don't know, Gus. Our recent sentencing for the McClellan sit-in is my only experience with the justice system here, and that was a misdemeanor," Hazel said into the phone. "This crap is a felony charge. My experience was with the New York and New Jersey judicial apparatus, years ago. I'm sure it's different here, and there's at least thirty years of new laws everywhere.

"Bruce did divorce and family law, so while he knows more than I, criminal law's vague to him, too. Whatever, we'll be talking a lot with John." Hazel took a breath, waited a beat, and cut in, "Can we talk later, Gus? Bruce came downstairs a minute ago. I think he's got something on his mind. Would you call Grace and Marigold for me and tell them about Officer Outlaw and so on?" Hazel headed for the kitchen.

I'm sure we'll be up late. Bye, Gus. And thanks!" She put the phone in its cradle, got some wine, and met Bruce in the hallway. He fanned out three DVDs and she chose the middle one.

"I bought this for you . . . *before* the shit hit the fan," Bruce said, handing her the sparkly box. Hazel raised one eyebrow and he replied, "Yeah, Sweetie, I forgot about it until a few minutes ago, sorta anticlimactic." His face reddened.

Hazel opened the box, finding the earrings while Bruce fiddled with the DVD player. Each earring had a circle of gold, from which dangled eight hand-carved wooden fronds dyed a rainbow of bright colors.

"Darling, these are gorgeous," Hazel trilled, slipping out her pearl studs and putting in the new earrings. She tossed her head, making the fronds move, the sound reminding her of soft bamboo wind chimes.

"I got them just for fun, in case you felt like Carmen Miranda or . . ." Bruce's words and thoughts were cut off by Hazel's deep, delighted kiss.

"I'm leaving these on until this Nasty Business with Mark is over," Hazel said once they came up for air. "They'll remind me of ordinary days. Now," she added, pointing at the sofa, "let's watch *Mamma Mia*."

14

A Day at the Beach

The grand jury convened five weeks after Bruce's interview with Officer Outlaw. In that limbo, he was a free man, but warned not to leave the state. He became reacquainted with criminal law and updated his knowledge of similar cases and their outcomes.

Her speech recovered and face healed, Gus was out of hibernation and back to work. She wrote, wrote, and wrote, but even after hot baths and spiritual readings, her frustration with the contrast between Bruce's situation and her trusting belief in the American justice system undermined her concentration on "Dog-speak."

Immersed in running Such Happenis Adult Toys, Irene subverted Germy George's OTC ED salesmen, and launched into creating the world's best substitute penis.

Hazel left her earrings on, even when she slept, and everyone who knew Bruce well enough to be aware of the allegations against him, assured Bruce and themselves, that this was America, no one could get away with such wholesale fabrications and lies. Who would believe a marginally civilized teenager blaspheming an upstanding, seventy-something community icon? This was the United States. Not only would Bruce be exonerated, but Mark would get the help he obviously needed.

All the canines watched and waited, taking the temperature of every environment before seeking extra treats or attention.

Giving John only a few days notice, the grand jury deposed Mark and other family members under the auspices of Sheriff Outlaw and the district attorney. It elected to *indict* Bruce on a Friday afternoon. He was arraigned and released on his own recognizance with no bail requirement. The trial date would be set once the prosecution produced the Bill of Particulars, meaning the concrete, specific charges. Bruce and John were to check the court docket and appear whenever required, once each month usually, for a "setting," an unsubtle way of controlling the whereabouts of the accused.

Over time the initial shock their friends felt switched to creative resistance tinged with retaliation, focusing their diverse feelings into disillusion and outrage. Bruce's friends formed groups and committees to begin the lobbying, arm-twisting, and fundraising essential to any successful campaign.

The women, at the outset more naïve about legal matters, thought the grand jury would see Mark's constructs for the lies they were. Then they discovered the grand jury heard only the prosecution's side and had only one function: to determine if the *quantity* of evidence warranted a trial. Contrary to TV show stories, quality of evidence seemingly was not an issue. The women were mystified—how, with no tape, photo, witness, or expert evaluation, could the words of a seventeen-year-old in the tenth grade constitute a "quantity of evidence"?

The news of the indictment headlined the Saturday morning paper, and the women called Hazel to commiserate and lend support. Bruce had an early tee time with John and planned to spend the night at his condo reading cases. Marigold was with Fleming, so Grace, Gus, and Hazel decided to spend the day at the beach with the canines.

"Wonder who was on that grand jury?" Grace said from the back seat of Gus's Scion, the most dog-proof vehicle.

Gus drove, Hazel rode shotgun with the paper clutched in her hand, and Grace sat in the back with Butterbean, Art, and Gwen. Too arthritic for sand and sea, Lady stayed home in the air conditioning.

"Stupid people, whoever they were," Hazel spat out. "No wonder the grand jury needs more security than we give our nuclear weapons."

"No wonder no one wants to be on it either," Gus added, changing lanes.

Gus saw Butterbean in the rearview mirror lying on her side in Grace's lap, eyes glazed, tongue hanging halfway to the floor. The pair made a quick sketch of joy until Grace stopped scratching Butterbean's chest.

"These past weeks I've been as irritated as a cat in the shower." Hazel poked the headline. "Look at this, 'Attorney for Historical Preservation Society Indicted on Sex Charges'! Lying, incompetent bastards! I guess I'm glad Bruce and John are preparing for the worst. Maybe they'll find just the right cases to get this dismissed. Bruce is turning into Johnny Cochran before my eyes. He's all but moved into John's office, and he goes to the law library using John's card. When he's not doing that, he's riding his bike. He doesn't eat, and he's lost twenty pounds since this started. I'm surprised he chose golf today; he hasn't picked up a club since this began. It's always the bike, like he could pedal away from everything. When I tell him I'm concerned about his weight loss and his behavior, he tells me not to fuss."

Hazel turned sideways in her seat so she could see both Gus and Grace. "You know how it is when you know someone well? Sometimes you know they're in trouble before they do. Bruce is in trouble, and we've got to do something," Hazel wiped her eyes with the back of her hand, "and soon."

Hazel dropped the paper on the floor. "Mark or someone next door is up to no good in their basement. It's probably Mark because his dad's usually passed out in that disgusting chair on the front porch. They've been bringing in bags of fertilizer and lots of plastic plant pots, I think from neighborhood trash. I saw Mark with an armload of them one day when trash pick-up was late. The mulch man delivered a pile of topsoil and some compost and dumped it in their backyard last week. It smells like *eau de cow patty*."

"Maybe they're starting a garden," Grace offered, not believing it herself.

"I tried to think that until I noticed that their basement lights are on almost every night."

"Well, maybe growing pot will be added to their list of unfulfilled ambitions," Gus said, concentrating on the traffic ahead. An ambulance and a tow truck whizzed past earlier, and now the outside lane was at a standstill.

"Maybe," Hazel replied. "One thing's for sure, The Good Neighbor

Fence Company is giving me an estimate on an eight-foot-high privacy fence tomorrow. I'm getting it, cost be damned."

"Has Bruce discovered anything vital in his research?

"Not really, Grace," Hazel said, turning to face the back seat and scratch a frustrated Art. "It's all in the district attorney's hands. It's up to him, or his office, to hand over the Bill of Particulars to the defense. You can't mount a defense without specific charges, but there's no mandated time frame for the prosecution's delivery of the charges. So naturally, they drag it out to hinder the defense as much as possible. Next the machinery is set in motion for a trial date, supposedly agreeable to both sides. We'll see how that turns out. They do an awful lot of collaborating, the opposing lawyers. If John weren't a trusted friend, I'd be wicked skeptical."

"Of?" Gus asked. The traffic crept along now. She guessed there was an accident ahead.

"Who knows? Anything and everything, I guess. I watched a trial once, not a big one, and I didn't know any of the participants, but the most impressive thing was all the joking and laughing between the two attorneys, even at the sidebars with the judge."

"That is off-putting," Grace agreed.

"The only good news, if you can call it that," Hazel continued, "is the more time between indictment and trial date, the bigger the indication the case is flimsy, according to court scuttlebutt. A trial is still a trial in my book, and," Hazel retrieved the paper and smacked the front page, "with no evidence, no trial, no nothing yet, damage to Bruce has already been done by our glorious media. The Board of the Historical Preservation Society will let him go the end of his term next year or when the trial starts, whichever comes first. Big of them, eh? If it weren't for their eagerness to have that damn McClellan building, this wouldn't be happening in the first place!"

"It *is* piss-poor," Gus agreed, cutting sharply to the right and heading through a collection of connected parking lots. "I'm going to bypass whatever's up ahead."

"And this is a very unsympathetic time for sex offenders," Gus said, realizing as she spoke, how bizarre her words were. "Not that I'm in favor of sex offenders. This is *ridiculous*! None of us, Bruce included, is fond of sex offenders. How did reality suddenly get turned inside out?"

"Law enforcement making a reputation," Grace suggested.

"Yeah," Hazel choked on a mix of a giggle and tears. "And here *we* are, seemingly in favor of sexual predators because Bruce, who isn't one, is being charged as one. No wonder after all the sensationalism and lies, no one can get to the truth. Even Michael Jackson, resoundingly acquitted, is regarded with a jaundiced eye. When you look at the trial process up close, there's no way you can believe things aren't manipulated, even if you like the outcome."

"That's because no one sees the whole process. Much of it goes on behind closed doors with unidentified people who have who-knows-what axe to grind." Grace took a treat out of her pocket for each of the dogs. "Are we there yet?"

"Where are you going, Gus Roberts?" Hazel squeaked as they whooshed past the ordering line at McDonald's and cut across all lanes of traffic to stop, poised for a right turn back onto the main road.

"To the beach!"

Grace leaned forward, appreciating her backseat seatbelt. "I can see this whole sex offender frenzy leading to an even stranger situation. Suppose folks begin to use false accusations or threats of false accusations as a way to settle other disputes? Then the testimony of those who are truly innocent will not be given the weight, credit, or attention it deserves. What a boon for the real slime balls!"

"Ick," Hazel said, shredding the paper into long strips.

"Just one more thing," Gus said, "has Bruce heard *anything* about the exact charges?"

"Only that there were, Mark says," Hazel sneered, "fourteen occurrences of improper touching and one blow job. No times, dates, places even. He probably hasn't had enough time to make them up."

"Well then," Grace sighed as they pulled into the beach parking lot, "there's nothing to do about it today. Let's run with the dogs, catch a wave, and not talk about this until tomorrow."

"Scout's honor," Gus said, parking the car near the dunes. She held out her hand. Grace and Hazel piled their hands on top.

"Leashes!" Grace announced as each canine sat to be connected.

Water bottles went into back packs, hats appeared from behind the back seat along with towels, and nine pairs of feet made for the ocean.

Gus pulled into her driveway. An exhausted Butterbean waited to be lifted out of the car. The afternoon in the sand and water had been a rousing success, followed by a splendid seafood dinner. Gus had a short walk with Hazel while Grace let the dogs swim on their leashes. Not much was said, but intuition told Gus that Hazel thought more was going on in Mark's basement than pot production, something to do with chemicals. It was during the quiet of the ride home that Gus remembered the starter fluid cans and was struck with the two words, "meth lab." She decided to keep silent; no sense in alarming Hazel further.

In spite of being home while her face healed, Gus hadn't cleaned or straightened anything. When she walked in the door, she realized it would be impossible to tell if she were burgled. More likely an intruder would leave rather than paw through such a mess.

Her answering machine blinked as she passed it. There were two calls that could wait until tomorrow and five robo-messages which she sent to delete heaven. Butterbean ran in short bursts to the kitchen and back, nudging and drooling on Gus's foot, saying, "Dinner please," in Corgi language, whereupon she produced the proper amount of salmon, green beans, and kibble.

A glass of tea and a quick relax on the sofa appealed to Gus as a fitting end to a goofy day, but the phone rang.

"Hello?"

"That you, Doll?" It was her dad in Florida. The wobbly-old-man sound to his voice was new, or maybe she hadn't paid attention lately. Gus pulled out a kitchen chair and sat as if she'd been pushed. She had a hot flash and stomach twinges.

"Hi, Dad," Gus said, striving for a neutral tone. "How're you doing?" Something was wrong.

"I'm okay. It's your mom."

"What's up with Mom?" Gus started to pace. Dad worked up to things slowly.

"She's not feeling good."

"What part isn't feeling good? Has she seen the doctor?"

"She's got a urinary tract infection. We saw the doctor yesterday. He gave her antibiotics, which she can't take. Now she's really feeling punk."

"Rats. She didn't mention it when we talked two days ago."

"She thought it would go away, and she didn't want you to worry."

"I know, Dad, I know."

"She's got lots of blood in her urine, every time. She's weak, and she won't eat. Can you come down?"

He was wrecked, and Gus caught it quicker than a kid catches a cold in kindergarten.

"Sure, Dad, I'll come. Can I talk to Mom?"

"Okay, Honey, I'll take her the phone. She's in the guest room."

Audrey, Gus's mom, divulged one more fact. Her urine was bright red with clots. That meant she was losing fresh blood; something was leaking that shouldn't be, like a washer-less hose connection.

Audrey's tired voice and admission of illness made Gus promise she'd leave in the morning.

While Hazel, Grace, and Gus were at the beach, Irene coped with an aberrant boss. A smarmy salesman with what smelled like a pyramid scheme had popped in last week, convincing Germy George that his Miraq-L-Gro cream, liberally rubbed onto the penis, provided sexual salvation for middle-aged men. Irene had kicked the stuff under her desk, hoping her boss would forget about it.

The first task this morning when she arrived at Such Happenis Adult Toys was to check for the package under her desk. Sure enough, three packs of the cream were missing. The phone rang. The caller was Germy George, informing Irene that he was doing research and development on a new product, and he wouldn't be in until tomorrow. There was a to-do list on her desk, and he insisted she set up the display for Miraq-L-Gro, mangling his favorite French phrase as usual, "toot sweet."

Likely, today's research would be about massaging his penis between the legs of his mistress/masseuse, courtesy of Miraq-L-Gro, at the Bright Promise Motel.

Just after one o'clock, the dreaded smarmy salesman arrived, followed by a City of Pine Crossing natural gas man, who barged in yelling, "Ma'am, we've got a gas leak down the block. Y'all need to evacuate, now!"

Restless and anxious in her free afternoon, Irene channel-surfed, griped at the viewing fare, and shut off the TV.

Will I bake or fix my hair emergency?

An afternoon of baking cookies followed by a new hair color restored Irene's emotional balance. With a glass of merlot, she stretched out on her puffy sofa, her Golden Glow curls embracing her neck and covering her eyes.

Clunk! Slam! Woof! The sounds startled Irene awake at around nine thirty. She rolled off the couch to peer out the window at Gus's house. The floodlights were on. Gus was stuffing Butterbean's bed in the back seat, giving Irene a splendid view of her derriere. Irene saw a bag of kibble by the open hatch, and Butterbean raced between Gus's back door and the car, barking.

Wrapping her robe tight, Irene stepped out her back door. "What's up, Gus?"

"Eeeek!" Gus screeched, jumped a foot, and dropped several cans of salmon and green beans. "You scared the pants off me!"

Retrieving the cans, Gus stuffed everything in the hatch area, while Butterbean dogged her heels. "I'm taking Butterbean over to Grace's because Dad called and Mom's wicked sick. I don't know what's up exactly, but my inner voice says 'get going,' so I am."

"You gonna drive all night?"

"I don't know, Irene. I'll stop if I get sleepy, but I'm wide awake now. I'll feel better on the road than tossing and turning at home. It is a fourteen-hour drive."

"I guess you could stop whenever. I'll help you pack and batten down the house." Irene went back inside to dress and decided to make Gus a couple of sandwiches and some coffee for the road.

Gus knocked and pushed her way in, calling, "Irene, Ireeene?" She heard the toilet flush upstairs and waited.

"Coming," Irene yodeled, clomping down the stairs in clogs, her new L'Oreal Golden Glow piled high on the top of her head.

She handed Gus a bag of sandwiches, cookies, a coffee-filled thermos, an umbrella, and a dog-eared book of motels on route I-95.

Over at Gus's place, they checked the stove, raised the thermostat on the air conditioner, and put lights on timers. Gus changed her answering-machine message and gave Irene phone numbers of anyone she might need in case of hurricane, appliance malfunction, or Gus's early demise. Together, they cleaned out the refrigerator. Gus took what she could use, and Irene got the salad and veggies that wouldn't keep, not even in Gus's snappy new cooler.

Irene had no idea what Gus's mother's bleeding might mean, but she agreed it could be serious. Irene hugged Gus, who got in her packed car and then got out again for another hug.

As Gus drove away, "goodbye" and "drive safely" filled the air between them.

15

Mercury Retrograde

Faced with on-again-off-again sleep in a motel, Gus played and re-played the movie of her life in her mind: collages of her childhood, traveling with her parents, snapshots of them all over the world, especially of her mom on elephants, camels, hot-air balloons, and sky-sailing. Her dad did all that too, but he was the designated photographer, which he loved doing more. Her mom occasionally took photographs—the ones with people in the far corners or with their heads cut off. They just laughed and labeled those too.

Her parents, Audrey and Robert, were healthy, and the years had zipped by. Longevity was in their genes, so who was counting anyway? Though they looked and acted years younger, they were eighty-six and eighty-seven.

That her parents were eligible for a final illness hit Gus like a fist.

"I've never seen such a urine sample," the nurse said.

Neither have I, Gus thought. *It looks exactly like my miscarriage in '72.*

Audrey's face was white, not pink as usual, though she had on her regular makeup and her blonder-than-ever hair fluffed under an aqua-colored net scarf. *When had her hair turned white under the blonde? When had her red lipstick started looking like denial instead of normal?* Gus wondered, perturbed.

"It's a hemorrhagic urinary tract infection," the doctor said, talking to the middle drawer of his desk as he pawed its contents. "The nurse will give you an antibiotic shot. It should clear up in a couple of days." Audrey didn't answer.

Gus watched the doctor's attention ebb, and said, "Mom doesn't do well with antibiotics." She shifted in her turquoise, faux-leather chair. "The pills you gave her Friday made her feel worse. She isn't eating now." Gus gestured toward her mother, "You can see how pale she is."

"She looks fine to me. People are tougher than they appear. *This* shot will do the trick." Dr. Lee looked up from the drawer to the perpetual motion machine, the only thing on his desk besides the lamp and blotter.

"Not for my Mom," Gus said, struggling for civility. Audrey glanced toward the waiting room where Robert sat, and Gus noted her concern. "Dad's doing okay," Gus said, touching her mother's arm. Audrey treated her father's Alzheimer's like folks used to treat cancer. She wouldn't say the word and was upset by a forthright conversation, even with Gus. In spite of her mother's denial, Gus understood that her dad's situation was worse than the last time she saw him. *So far, Dad is okay in the waiting room. But if Mom doesn't take the shot, what do we do? Walk out? To where? How much fooling around can my folks handle?*

"Well," Audrey hesitated, returning to the matter at hand, possibly sharing her daughter's thoughts, "I'll do it this once."

The next morning, Audrey was worse, limp as a blanched pole bean. Gus propped her against the headboard, using every pillow in the house. Her mother ate one cracker and three sips of orange juice only to please Gus, who realized this was more serious than her mom's mononucleosis. *When was that? Twenty years ago?*

Gus called Dr. Lee, and his nurse said to bring Audrey in. Gus looked at her mom, who shook her head "no" and whispered, "I can't."

"No," Gus said, "my mother can't come in. She needs to go to the hospital." In short order, the conversation collapsed into an unresolved wrangle about admitting Audrey. Dr. Lee insisted on seeing her in the office first. Gus wasn't doing that, so she ended the call with a C-minus for cordiality.

Robert stood silently in the doorway, and Gus sat on the bed, massaging Audrey's feet. At last, Gus asked her mom, "Has your bleeding slowed any?"

"No," Audrey said quietly, "but maybe it will."

Robert took his wife's hand. "You'll be all right, honey. We'll get you fixed up, you'll see."

"You're right, Dad," Gus replied. "I'm calling an ambulance. That's the best solution right now."

Audrey raised her hand to protest, but dropped it. Robert looked first at her, then at Gus, who was dialing 911.

"I can't go looking like this," Audrey protested. She always rallied in favor of looking her best, like Butterbean always rallied for a treat. Gus smiled at the similarity, feeling deep love for both her mom and Butterbean, as she said, "Honey, if you look too good, they won't believe you're sick. We want them to take care of you!"

While giving the 911 operator information and directions, Gus realized a new person was speaking now. When she cradled the receiver, she had become her parents' parent.

After seven hours in the emergency room, Audrey was admitted to the hospital. Most of those hours were spent in the hallway, Audrey on a gurney with an IV pole in a row of similarly occupied gurneys. Gus and Robert perched on radiators or sank into folding wheelchairs. Once they traveled a labyrinth of halls to the x-ray room, but the main entertainment was watching others come and go. Robert dozed off at times. Gus, an inveterate people-watcher, passed the time creating stories for the folks in this peculiar wonderland. Nowhere did she see a Cheshire cat or a cookie marked "This Way Out."

Gus and Audrey made innumerable trips to the bathroom. Each trip, Gus helped her mom off the gurney into a wheelchair, and with an IV pole, traversed a hundred feet of hallway that included pushing through two sets of heavy swinging doors.

The lavatory threshold was designed for the public, not patients in wheelchairs, and initially, Gus and Audrey laughed at such engineering foolishness. On the last few trips, they were quiet, Gus intent on comfortable maneuvering, and Audrey bracing for the inevitable jostling. Gus willed her knees to hold out, and they both nurtured the futile hope that there would be less, or darker, blood in the bowl *this* time.

Between bathroom trips, the Queen of Hearts from billing pursued the family for information and a co-pay check, frightening and confusing Robert. Audrey needed more warm blankets and lots of water. Robert needed the men's room on occasion and couldn't go unescorted. During these hours, there was no sign of Dr. Lee or another physician.

Upstairs in a room and transfused at last, Audrey felt better. Audrey wanted her robe, makeup, and toiletries brought from home. Robert and Gus needed dinner, so he stayed in the hospital room with Audrey while Gus collected half her mom's bathroom and picked up two take-out dinners. By eight o'clock, exhausted, Gus and Robert kissed Audrey goodnight and went back to the mobile home, leaving their hearts in Room 105.

"Transitional cell kidney cancer," the surgeon said the next day, pointing to her mom's left kidney on the CT scan. Gus hadn't slept more than a couple of hours, but *a four-year-old could understand this CT scan*, Gus thought. Audrey's right kidney was a smooth oval while her left one looked like Pac-Man with a cavernous, black mouth. The cancer had eaten away a quarter of it, causing the bleeding. Too weary to concentrate on the surgeon's lugubrious description of the cancer's genesis, Gus brightened a bit when he said, "If it hasn't metastasized, removing the kidney will take care of the cancer. We'll know that when we operate."

"I understand if you don't operate, she'll eventually bleed to death, even with transfusions," Gus stated, just to be certain.

"That's right. This is Friday. I'll schedule her for first thing Monday morning. She'll be comfortable here until then."

Back in Audrey's room, after procuring another take-out dinner and more things from the mobile home, Gus crawled in bed behind her mom and rolled up her hair. Fingers shaking, all fluttery inside, Gus was honored to be doing something this personal for her mother, and terrified it would go wrong.

Later, on a trip to the cafeteria for dessert, Gus encountered the surgeon in the elevator. He said he had a surgical cancellation and would it be okay to operate on Audrey tomorrow? Could Gus be at the hospital in the morning by eight? Could birds fly?

The family waiting room was freezing. Robert and Gus had spent every pre-op minute with Audrey until she was wheeled away. Then they were ushered into a room lined with short-backed, wooden-armed, sparsely padded chairs. The ambient temperature seemed the same as a refrigerator. Tattered golf magazines interested Robert for a few minutes. After that, he and Gus had nothing to do but think, talk, or try to nap.

"Dad, I'm going to get some blankets," Gus said. "You wait right here, okay?"

"Okay, Darling, I'll be here. Where's your mother?"

"She's having her kidney out, and we have to stay here. I'll get us some blankets. I'll be right back."

"Okay, Doll." Gus closed the door and saw her dad looking at his watch for the gazillionth time.

Under two warm blankets, Robert finally drifted into a twitchy sleep.

Gus tried to nap, but her mind was over its occupancy limit. She reflected on their time in pre-op, making small talk, encouraging hope and good spirits, saying "I love you" to her mother in every possible way, dreadfully over-using those three words. Robert had held Audrey's hand and called her "sweetheart," "darling," "honey," thousands of times. They all knew this was tough, unwanted, and unavoidable. She and her dad each would have taken the illness. They were physically tougher, and besides, standing by and caregiving weren't their strong suits.

Another part of Gus's mind was behind the camera, capturing their powerlessness, feeling the fear and heartbreak that surpasses human expression. Weeping and wailing, all the ways a person could keen, faint, fall—none of it would be enough nor would be helpful. The only semiadequate expression Gus could conjure was a coyote's howl. Being an empathetic human was inadequate and thoroughly frustrating.

Four hours later, Gus and Robert, warm and relieved, were in the hospital room with Audrey. The cancerous kidney was gone. Having no idea how the next weeks would unfold, they reveled in their relief and delight. Audrey would be with them a while longer.

16

In the Meantime

High summer in Pine Crossing overwhelmed everyone. Outdoor enterprises, gardening, walking, house painting, were undertaken by most folks in the early morning or in the dusky evening. They saved mid-day for indoor chores or events. Movie matinees sold out. Torpor blanketed everyone, and "I'll think about it tomorrow" became the cliché du jour.

A quieter Pine Crossing meant quieter times for Hazel and Bruce. Marigold, in Chicago and accompanied by Fleming, conducted another drama workshop. Germy George, caught by his wife during a strenuous R&D session with his masseuse, made Irene a partner in the business so George could take his wife on a damage-control cruise around the world.

Since tempers flared in the heat, the police, and consequently the courts and attorneys, were on overload, pushing Bruce's case into the background. If the district attorney hadn't planned to retire soon, making a successful, high-profile case a tantalizing exit, or if Assistant District Attorney Kay Rapp hadn't been so ambitious, Mark's allegations against Bruce might have floated in legal backwaters and been forgotten.

John used every strategy to induce delivery of the Bill of Particulars, all to no avail. Bruce, frazzled by worry and research for similar case rulings, went to his office at the Historical Preservation Society each day, closed the door, and played four suit spider solitaire on his laptop or took a nap in the recliner. Fundraising, the one thing he could do, didn't appeal to him. He knew no matter what happened, he'd need more money than he had. His energy was sapped. He flirted with depression.

To break the ennui one evening, Hazel and Grace took the dogs down to a small park by the river that commemorated the heroism of a detective killed in the line of duty. A comfortable bench sat about three feet from the river's edge. The soft breeze and rhythmic lapping of water on the sand mesmerized the women.

The sun spread long fingers of red-gold light over the water, illuminating Grace and Hazel as they sat on the bench, their faces a photographer's dream of perfect planes and hues.

Absently Hazel patted Lady's head and asked, "Grace, have you heard from Gus?"

"Sorta," Grace answered, not wanting to break the mood. This was the first serenity she had experienced in weeks.

"There's no 'sorta,' Grace, you either talked to her or you didn't," Hazel snorted. "Don't be shielding me, good buddy."

"I had to worm it out of Gus. I didn't let her say hello to Butterbean until she told me."

Butterbean closed her eyes and growled at the memory.

"Audrey was operated on last Saturday," Grace continued. "She has transitional cell kidney cancer, whatever that is. I'll have to look it up. The real trouble is the surgeon found cancer in five other places, including her lungs and abdomen. Gus didn't have all the details because of those Hippo privacy laws."

"HIPAA," Hazel corrected.

"I know, I know. I think of them as hippos, growing ever more massive and unmanageable. Do you want me to finish?"

"Of course," Hazel said, digging a trough in the sand with her foot.

"Gus found out all she could by cornering the surgeon in the elevator. He didn't think much of the primary care physician, so he told her more than he might otherwise. The next shocker was Robert, her dad. He's more than 'slipping a little,' as her mom had told her. Gus told me a long time ago she finds Audrey's secretive ways frustrating. When confronted, Audrey claims she's simply being protective and private." Grace nudged Butterbean with her bare foot and looked around for the Poms who were deep in a bush, tails their only giveaway.

"How bad is he?"

"Well, his short-term memory stinks, but he's compliant, for Gus anyway, and he has some intestinal incontinence. When he has an 'accident,' as Audrey calls it, he goes into the men's room and washes out his jockey shorts. He wrings them out and puts them in his pocket or wraps them in a bunch of paper towels and . . ."

"Puts them in his pocket," Hazel finished for her, "bummer! Embarrassing too, I bet."

"Gus bought two six-packs of new jockeys, and she carries them in her bag like diapers. I don't know how she manages to keep up with the two of them in the hospital. Her plan is to set up 24/7 home health care for Audrey when they release her Friday, and then Gus will head home until they need her in Florida again." Butterbean pawed at Grace's foot.

"Is there a prognosis?" Hazel leaned back and Lady changed position, pushing sand in Hazel's shoe.

"I don't know. So far Audrey refuses cancer treatment, though she has an appointment with an oncologist on Monday. The home health care nurse will have to take her to that because Gus will be back here on Sunday.

While listening to the humans with one ear, Butterbean turned to Daphne. "Have you thought any more about what we can do with Fleming?"

"Not really, Butterbean," Daphne replied, crossing and uncrossing her forelegs. "For the moment, he seems to be treating Mari well. As long as he does that and Mari doesn't mind him mooching, who am I to judge?"

"Mmmm," Butterbean assented, her attention more on the humans. Her stomach growled.

"*However*," Daphne continued more stridently, "the first moment I hear any kind of verbal abuse or cheating, we'll make a plan and act immediately. How is your book coming? Is it easier with your Gus gone?"

"Actually, it is," Butterbean said after a minute of thought. "Initially I thought turning the computer on would be a problem, but Grizzie got the button pushed first try. Her little cat feet are amazingly dexterous. Grizzie didn't want to write without salmon, but a few hours of blocking the dog port took care of that. Unless Grace has me out or something is going on outdoors, I can get her to write whenever I wish. I've made quite a bit of progress. Are you interested?"

"Of course I am, but you'll need to turn the computer off before your Gus gets home, won't you?" Daphne rearranged her back feet.

"Gus will call Grace and I'll know at least a day ahead. Then I'll get Grizzie to shut it down." Butterbean looked at Grace, who was still talking. She sighed and lay down. "That cat, bless her heart, is very good at hitting the right letters when I stand over her and look at the monitor. If I tell her a word or two and don't look so I can correct her, it's often gibberish. When Gus returns, I have to share my salmon again."

"I won't be able to see your book until after my Mari gets back."

"That's okay, I have it memorized. I can tell it to you, and if I do that now, it'll take my mind off my stomach. Is that okay?"

Not wishing to be overheard, Butterbean moved away from the bench to the other side of Daphne and began. "The title is, *Four Things Every Human Must Know for Successful Living with Canines.* There will be four sections, the first explaining what the human must know; next, how the dog can teach humans without riling them; third, what can happen to the dog if humans are not properly taught; and last, common canine teaching mistakes and how to remedy them." Butterbean stretched and lay down.

"I like that, simple and straightforward." Daphne shifted her rump again. "Sorry I'm fidgety. My bad back leg gives me fits when the air is damp."

"I know. My hind legs get tingly sometimes, and I can't do a thing with them." Butterbean scraped at the grass with her front paws. "Somehow I need to include Rudimentary Human Language, Pack Leadership 101, and Advanced Alpha Techniques."

"How do you begin?" Daphne asked, swiveling her ears toward Butterbean.

"I think we canines have the most leverage in the first month with our new humans. If we get them when we're six to eight weeks old, we're cute and cuddly. The women's maternal instincts come to the fore, as do the men's protective urges, making that our optimal training period. They relate us to their babies, find our 'helplessness' irresistible, and think we won't comprehend much until we're about six months old. So I'll begin with day one in our new homes." Butterbean stretched, and Daphne flipped her ears backward.

Without warning, two Pomeranians circled the bench, leaped over Lady and Butterbean, and roared toward the honeysuckle bushes. Art had dug up a decomposing turkey leg bone, and Gwen believed in sharing. Her feet twitching in a chase dream, Lady slept through the commotion. Butterbean was irritated at the interruption, and not appreciative of their exuberance. So when the Poms began an encore, Butterbean, low and snake-like, shot herself right into their path.

Art, with the turkey bone, smacked into Butterbean's shoulder, tumbled twice over, and landed on his right ear, reflexively tossing the turkey bone high in the air. Gwen managed to leap over Butterbean, but with her eyes fastened on the sailing turkey bone, she crashed into Art. Gwen shook off the collision, but not her disbelief at the turkey bone's trajectory. In a beautiful arc, the bone landed in the center of a trash can. Lady woke up, looked everywhere and sniffed the air, wondering what she'd missed.

The women broke out in laughter while the three smaller dogs shook, grumbled, and behaved as if this was situation normal.

In the back of the car on the way home, Butterbean related Gus's experiences in Florida to Lady. Then she dramatized the Great Pom-Turkey Bone Race, especially its termination by a Super Corgi Body Block, which caused the turkey bone to fly into the trash can.

Understandably embarrassed, the Poms had matching pouts in the front seat with Hazel. Butterbean promised Daphne and Lady she would continue discussing her book at their next meeting.

When they arrived at Grace's, a puzzled Butterbean jumped out. During the drive home, she had quietly noticed a book tucked way under the passenger seat. Certain it wasn't beach reading, Butterbean spelled the title over several times so she wouldn't forget it: "A-d-v-a-n-c-e-d C-h-e-m-i-s-t-r-y."

Sunday arrived in a flash and thirty-seven minutes after Gus returned from Florida, a riptide of practical tasks threatened to drown her last reserve of energy. She had left Saturday at noon after introducing the home health care nurse and explaining her parents' needs and habits.

Spending the night in a noisy motel, Gus drove into Pine Crossing on Sunday just a few minutes past noontime. With Grizzie outdoors and the thermostat at eighty degrees, her house felt hollow and stifling. The telephone rang as she unloaded the car and Gus ignored its lengthy racket. Apparently, the answering machine was full. Inside, the house remained as she left it with bare cupboards, dirty sheets, clutter, and more clutter. It was both home and a foreign country after the intense two weeks with her folks. *Okay*, Gus thought, *I'll make a list.*

On her second day in Florida with her to-do tasks increasing exponentially and her stressed memory decreasing faster, Gus had purchased a fat purple notebook and an assortment of pens.

Skipping the first page, she had dated the next one, and began listing things her mother wanted brought to her in the hospital, questions for the doctor, groceries needed at the mobile home, and a list of folks to call in North Carolina.

For the next thirteen days, she had filled at least one page per day with similar notes and names, addresses, and phone numbers. Accomplishments were crossed out or boldly checked.

Today, on her third trip from the car to house, Gus found this blessed notebook and left it open on the dining room table, making notes as she passed by. The phone rang and stopped. Stifling the urge to rip it out of the wall, Gus emptied the car, turned the thermostat down to sixty-five, wrote down two pages of messages, changed the outgoing message, and turned the ringer off.

She had returned most of the calls and had written half her grocery list when the doorbell rang. Resigned to interruption, Gus sighed. The bell rang again. Gus yanked the door open to be greeted by Grace and a hyperextended Butterbean peeking in the screen, her butt about to wag off.

"Butterbeeaaannn!!" Gus squealed, getting down to Corgi height. "Thank heavens it's you and Grace," Gus exclaimed as Grace hopped around her and the wriggling, whimpering, wrong-side-up Corgi.

Butterbean flipped upright and dashed to check out the kitchen, while Grace put a pot of stew on the table and helped Gus stand. They hugged, Gus leaking tears and sniveling, and Grace trying to ignore it.

"Don't worry, Grace, this is my new normal. I weep for every reason and no reason, appropriate or not, so don't pay any attention." She lifted the lid and smelled the stew. Butterbean instantly materialized. "What's in this?"

"I ran into Irene at the grocery store, and she said she'd cleaned you out in the food department, so I got some beef cubes and threw in the contents of my vegetable bin. In other words, who knows?"

Gus replaced the lid as Grace continued, "What do you see in that now-blonde floozy anyway? Surely you're not seduced by the 'fallen woman with a heart of gold' stereotype?"

"Grace! Bite your tongue! She may manage Such Happenis Adult Toys, but she's no floozy and you know it. What's got into you? She *does* have a heart of gold. Who do you think fusses over me and tries to run my life like Portnoy's Mama?" Looking closer at Grace's expression, Gus got it. "Why, Miss Grace! Do I detect some jealousy?"

"One more word and that stew goes back home with me. You know I like her well enough. It's that damn hair. I never know who she's gonna be. She looked like Archie's Veronica for a long time, then came the Brenda Starr look, now she's Blondie."

"You're a control freak, Grace, and I love you," Gus said. They hugged and laughed, and Butterbean barked and nudged Gus's leg for inclusion. Gus bent to pat the Corgi, who turned upside down for another belly rub.

"I'm gonna go and let you finish here," Grace gestured to encompass the whole messy house, "but we all want to take you to dinner tonight and get the scoop."

"What a great idea. I need the scoop too. What's up with Bruce and Hazel? And Mari?"

"Not much has changed with the Nasty Business, as Hazel now calls it, and Mari still has Fleming camping out at her place. She said she invited him to move in. No matter, he went to Chicago with her, probably lounged around the motel room while she taught her drama workshop." Grace's face was a mask of disapproval. "Would six be a good time?"

"Super. I'll even have a moment for a nap! Can we do the Chinese buffet?" Gus asked.

"Sure," Grace said. "Oh! I brought Butterbean and her bed back two days after you left. She spent some daytime with me, so I kept some of her food, but she was here every night because Grizzie got lonesome and did some gross claw art on your wingback chair. I have plenty of dry food and green beans, but only two cans of salmon left."

Butterbean's ears flashed forward at "food," and they all trooped out to unload the car, many hands and paws making light work. Butterbean the Brinks Guard Corgi escorted the bag of kibble and cans of salmon once again to the safety of their kitchen cabinet.

No sooner had Gus gotten halfway seated in front of the stew when the phone rang again. Irked, she answered it to find Hazel repeating the dinner idea.

"Thanks, Hazel. I told Grace I'd like the Chinese buffet. Is that okay with you?"

"Sure, I want to hear everything." Hazel's cell phone crackled and spat, cutting them off and then back on. "I missed you and love you. See you tonight." Hazel was gone.

Gus looked at her phone as she hung it up. Hazel never said "I love you." *Maybe I'm not the only one with intimations of mortality,* Gus thought.

By five o'clock, Gus had run three loads of wash, straightened most of the house, made the bed, and had a short nap. She called Marigold at work to find Hazel had already told her about dinner. Marigold, too, was delighted Gus had returned.

Gus's list for tomorrow filled a page, making calls on her folks' behalf to various agencies, utilities, and banks. She also had a list of assisted-living places to call and visit in Pine Crossing. *For Dad, just in case,* she told herself, knowing better. The more she accomplished tomorrow, the less she'd have to do along with working on Wednesday. And she'd have a whole night's sleep, cool and uninterrupted by Dad. She danced a short jig.

Before dressing for dinner, Gus grabbed a glass of iced tea and dialed her parents' number. They should be home from the oncologist by now.

"Hi, Dad, how are you?"

"Okay, you home?"

"Yes, I got in a bit ago. How's Mom?"

"About the same. She's asleep now."

"Did she go to the doctor? Are the nurses there?"

"No, she didn't feel up to seeing the doctor. The nurses are here, but we really don't need them."

Gus closed her eyes and swore silently, "Sure you do. Mom won't be up and around for quite a while, and you can't do everything. She had a kidney out, remember? That's a big deal. She needs to heal, and you need to rest."

"Okay, honey. You want to talk to the nurse?"

"Sure, Dad, who is it?"

"I don't know. Here she is."

"Hi, this is Dahlia. Your Momma doin' okay. She sleepin' now. She dint go to the doctor. She say she not feeling good enough. I say to her, 'Miss Audrey, you have to go, keep your appointment.' She say, 'I don't have to do anything.' She comes out of her room and turns the a/c off, says she cold."

"Is she asleep, Dahlia?"

"Don' know, Gusta, I'll look. She not happy. She hurts, but wone use the commode or eat except soup. I'm goin' now."

The phone clunked on the counter, and the mobile home came to life before Gus's eyes. The guest room, with its white-paneled walls, green carpet and drapes, pink and green flowered comforter, and white Italianate furniture, used to be Gus's room when she visited. She knew it well enough to walk around in the dark. In a self-imposed exile, her mother now resided there.

The next vignette included Gus's greatest fear: Dad walking Mom down the long hall from the guest bedroom past "his" green bathroom to "her" pink bathroom at the end by the master bedroom. She'd seen this heart-stopping performance twice—the two of them unsteady on their feet, often lurching into the wall.

Gus had been their child long enough to understand this was how they would be. Her fears now mirrored her mother's fears for Gus as a child. She pictured her parents fallen and in a tangled heap in the hall with broken hips. Her words of caution would go unheeded. Mom wouldn't have the nurses walk her any more than she'd use the commode in her bedroom. Gus pushed back her exasperation.

"Gusta?" Dahlia returned and broke into Gus's thoughts. "It's Dahlia again. Miss Audrey awake and wants to talk to you."

"Hello?" Mom's voice was deep, tired. "Is this you?"

"Hi, Mom, it's me," Gus replied, trying for bright and cheery, but not brittle. "How are you feeling? Things any better?"

"Oh a little. Dahlia is very good, but the night nurse falls asleep and doesn't come. Dad hears and takes me to the bathroom. We aren't paying her to sleep. How was the drive home? You sound tired."

"The drive was great. I'm tired, but okay. I'll sleep well tonight. Are you using the bell? Surely she can hear that bell?" Gus asked.

"I try not to because sometimes it wakes Robert. She's being paid to be awake." The covers rustled; her mother sighed.

"You okay, Mom?"

"I'm fine. I can't stay in the same spot too long. When my mother was sick, she could stay in the hospital and had a private nurse who took care of her as well."

"I'm sorry, Mom, it's the twenty-first century. You have the best care we can get now. Dahlia is kind and smart. She's from St. Kitts, remember? She likes you and wants to help you. I'll have a baby monitor set up so the night nurse will hear you." Gus forged onward, not wanting to give her mother a chance to change the subject. She needed to hear it from the source. "Did you see the doctor today?"

"No, I didn't feel well enough to go. I don't want that stuff anyway. I want to live like I'm used to. I don't want to be here in bed feeling awful all the time."

"But Mom," Gus suppressed an adolescent whine, "a few weeks of feeling awful could buy years of feeling normal. The doctor planned to talk to you about odds and options. Then you'd make an informed choice. I thought we agreed, before I left, you'd get better information than you've gotten from Dr. Lee or your surgeon. Then you'd decide."

Clearly she hadn't conveyed the complexity of her feelings about Audrey's further treatment when she was there, so Gus didn't try it on the phone. In the end, what Audrey did was up to Audrey, but *damn*, Gus thought for the nth time, *at least try, Mom! Where're the guts and fire I've seen when you thought I was in trouble? Can't you do that for yourself?* Gus wished life had a computerized "restore" button.

"Well, Doll," Audrey said, "I can always make another appointment if I want to. Maybe that baby monitor will help if it gets here tomorrow. I'm getting tired, and they want me to eat something. Your dad is eating all right, but I can't stand their spices when the nurses cook. It smells funny in here for hours, and I know they are ruining my pots and putting the wrong things in the dishwasher."

"Mom, you can always buy new," Gus all but screamed, then softened. "After all this, who cares about dishes? *Your* getting well is the most important thing. If you and Dad get what you like to eat, what the nurses cook for themselves doesn't matter. If you don't get what you need, tell me and I'll take care of it, okay?"

"Okay. Dahlia is here with my soup. You take care of yourself. Don't get worn out worrying about us. We love you. Do you want to talk to your Dad? Here he is. Love you, Doll."

"I love you too, Mom . . . Hi, Dad." Gus started pacing. Goodbye was hard. No one wanted to say it.

"I'm worried about your mother, Doll. She seems a little better today, though."

"Yes, she should be getting a little better each day, I hope. Is your dinner ready?"

"Yes, Dahlia just put it on the table. Will you call us tomorrow?"

"You know I will. Is this a good time?" Gus started pacing faster.

"Call us tomorrow. About now, okay, Doll? We love you."

"I love you too, Dad. Bye for now." Gus hung up quickly. She needed to finish her stew. She wrote "baby monitor" on tomorrow's page, then put her head in her hands and sobbed. Butterbean sat on Gus's foot, offering love, hoping for stew.

17

Chinese Fire Drill

As Chinese dinner meant Gus would leave her alone again, Butterbean grabbed her purple fox squeaky toy and raced through the house, inviting Gus to a game of chase.

"I can't right now, Sweetie," Gus said, standing in the bedroom, one leg in her slacks and the other in midair. Butterbean, in an unusual fit of pique, snatched the dangling pant leg and pulled it with all her strength, making Gus hop until she regained her balance. Then Gus latched onto the loose pant leg, yanking it tug-o-war style, reeling it in closer with each pull.

Lost in her fury and the fun of irritating Gus, Butterbean didn't notice how close she'd gotten to Gus until it was too late. Gus was on her knees, one hand on Butterbean's collar, the other squeezing the hinge of her jaw. "Drop it," Gus ordered, the hem of her pant leg falling out of Butterbean's grasp in a punctured, sodden, wad.

Butterbean froze, ears back, flat on the floor, leaning as far away from Gus as she could get without strangling herself.

"What's gotten into you?" Gus asked, releasing the collar as she stood over the chastened Corgi. Gus imagined that Butterbean would place her paws over her ears and melt into the floor if it were possible. Gus relaxed and smiled, again getting on her knees and elbows to embrace Her Flatness. "I know you missed me. I missed you. I need to be with our friends tonight. You'll have me all day tomorrow, I promise."

Butterbean squirmed around and gave Gus's ear a huge slurp. When Gus moved back to her hands and knees, Butterbean pushed her body between Gus's arms, turned, and looked up at Gus's chin, tongue lolling, eyes glistening. Mission accomplished.

"Okay, girl," Gus said a few minutes later as she held onto the edge of the bed and levered up. "Heaven knows what I'll wear now."

Arriving a fashionable ten minutes late, Gus caught sight of Bruce's silver hair and Irene's L'Oreal Blonde Glitter. Grace wasn't visible, and Hazel might be "powdering her nose" because the chair next to Bruce was empty. He and Irene, who was on the other side of the empty chair, were deep in conversation and looked as if they were practicing semaphore signals. There was no sign of Marigold or Fleming, but the Jacksons were on the end of the next table closest to Bruce's seat.

Politely passing the line waiting to be seated, Gus pointed to the back tables. "I'm with them," she said, moving off before anyone interfered. Hazel, returning from the ladies room, saw Gus coming and grabbed a chair from a nearby table. She jammed the chair next to hers and waved at Gus.

John and Sarah Jackson, it turned out, were with Historical Preservation Society folks, celebrating that Lewis and Son Devoted Demolition dropped its civil suit against the society on Friday. Some members thought Herman Lewis dropped the lawsuit as a ploy, presenting Herman as a good guy, living up to the Christian aphorisms on his equipment. Logically then, there would be a bad guy, Bruce. Most members thought Herman had enough savvy to choose a contract in the hand, to demolish the McClellan, over the vagaries of a lawsuit. His choice more likely had to do with money, not Bruce.

Hurriedly taking in her surroundings, Gus fetched a wonton/egg drop soup combination and a plate of boiled shrimp from the buffet. She carefully carried these to her seat between Hazel and Irene.

"Gus, it's so good to see you," Hazel gushed, turning from her plate of broccoli and chicken. "I don't know where to begin, eating or talking."

"It's been crazy here," Irene chimed in. "We all missed you. Germy George got caught doing some R&D with his masseuse. His wife's got him corralled on a trans-Atlantic cruise and I've been made partner in the business!" She gave Gus a sitting hug.

"Wow, a lot can happen in two weeks, and it couldn't have happened to a nicer 'goil'! You can get at least half of the profit from your penis prop idea now." Gus peeled a shrimp.

At that moment Grace appeared, waved, and made her way to the only empty seat, the one next to Irene. Everyone within reach exchanged hand clasps and greetings before Grace went to the buffet.

"So how's the case coming?" Gus asked, directing her question to Hazel and Bruce on her right. "Have I missed anything?"

"Only the first setting," Bruce replied. "We wait, get called to the judge, and set a time to appear the following month. That arrangement keeps track of us 'offenders' with no effort for the state—a waste of time and money, sure, but who cares? The system can always squeeze more tax dollars from the serfs."

Hazel patted Bruce's arm. "Don't be bitter, dear. We promised not to let this get to us. The accusers want that. Living well is the best revenge."

He took her hand and squeezed it. "You're right, dear. One of these settings will produce a trial date. Shall we take bets on which one? Meanwhile, I'm going to get more food. The moo goo gai pan is terrific."

Hazel turned to Gus, "I went to this setting, and it's not as bad as Bruce makes out. There was someone who murdered a friend over a woman, and he got a trial date, but everyone else got another setting. It seemed old hat to them: sauntering, sighs, and then back to their business. The time we spent in court was only ninety minutes, but court starts at ten o'clock, so the morning is shot getting ready, and when you get out, it's time for lunch. If you happen to like naps," Hazel winked at Gus, "then the day isn't yours until after three in the afternoon."

"Well," Gus replied, "you remember our Citizen's Police Academy training years ago?"

"I do, Gus. We had a lot of fun. How come we didn't get more involved afterwards?" Hazel speared a broccoli.

"I think we were enamored with the soup kitchen then. Anyway, you remember the instructor said that most of the crime in this town is committed by the same 300 people? Bet they were your sauntering sigh-ers. Has John made any moves in terms of defense? Has the Bill of Particulars shown up?"

"No B-of-P, but John has been consulting with an attorney friend in Delaware who specializes, can you imagine, in sex crimes cases. He has a very high success rate, so John is interested in his MO and in creation of sympathetic approaches."

"That makes justice sound like a business: 'specializes,' 'high success rate'—same as medicine or insurance. Ick!" Gus said, peeling another shrimp. "Where is Bruce anyway? I thought he was coming back with more food."

Hazel glanced around the room, stretching her neck like a periscope. "There he is, next to John." She waited a minute. "I can tell by their facial expressions and gestures they're talking golf, probably discussing every stroke and nuance of their last game." Turning back to Gus, Hazel asked, "But how about you? How are your parents? Your mom's not having further cancer treatment? That doesn't sound like her."

"You just said it all. I'm surprised, too, that she doesn't want to fight. I can't wrap my mind around her acquiescence. I want to scream until I disappear, but it's not my choice to make. My job, if you want to call it that, is to make things as smooth for her as I can." Gus exhaled, popping a shrimp in her mouth.

Wanting to pat Gus somewhere, Hazel got up and touched her shoulder. "Can I get you something from the buffet? I'm looking for cheesecake and maybe another serving of fried rice."

"Thanks, how about some broccoli and chicken and a spoonful of Seafood Delight?" Gus looked at Grace returning with her appetizers and Irene finishing her second plate.

"I want to hear what's going on too," Irene said. "Let me get some cheesecake, and then you can tell us all at once."

"Good idea," Grace mumbled, slurping her beef lo mein like spaghetti.

Just as Hazel returned with her cheesecake and Gus's plate, Marigold and Fleming arrived. They forged through the filled tables, bending around protruding highchairs and outstretched baby fingers, speaking too loudly, "Hi, everybody. Are we too late?"

Bruce, who had returned from his conversation with John, rose in acknowledgment, he had to leave early to solicit monetary support from buddies at the Elks Club. He offered his seat to Marigold, who introduced Fleming. After the greetings were finished, Bruce said his goodbyes, gave Hazel a peck on the cheek, and said, "Don't wait up. We'll have a lazy day tomorrow, I promise."

"Yeah, yeah, yeah," Hazel smiled, returning the peck.

Bruce headed for the cashier, and Marigold and Fleming sat down. Hazel turned to them, "Hi, you two. You're just in time. Gus is about to tell us about her Florida trip, which was no vacation," she said for Fleming's benefit. "Her Mom had a kidney removed."

Gus, satiated, pushed back her chair. Everyone seemed settled, so she began. "Long and short is, it seems Mom has decided to die, and I don't think she has enough information to make that decision. I think she went off half-cocked, canceling her appointment with the oncologist. Anyway, I'll never get the full story. The surgeon told me she had five spots of cancer in her abdomen and lungs." Gus stopped for a drink of tea. "How big, what kind of cancer, how to treat, survival rate, only an oncologist could know or guess. Because the surgeon talked to Mom in private, I only know what she chooses to tell me, and she hasn't gone beyond what the surgeon already told me. Mom has never told the whole truth about her health. Why should she start now?

"I tried to present other options, posed the possibility that she'd buy good years with a few months of aggravation, talked philosophy, discussed euthanasia . . ." Gus ran out of words.

"Euthanasia?" Marigold interrupted. "She's not the family dog!"

"That's her *point*," Gus said, facing Marigold and speaking over Hazel. "Mom wants to be put to sleep like we did for Jamie, the family Cocker. I told her I loved her, but euthanasia is illegal. Then we went off on the philosophy of that illegality, ending with one point of agreement: We're kinder to our pets than to our old people."

"Your mom's right, Gus. I wasn't thinking," Marigold said. "I watched my grandmother die of lung cancer the summer before I started college, and I'll never forget what she went through. She had it beaten for a while, but then it reappeared in her lymph system and metastasized everywhere. The last two years of her life were round after round of chemo and radiation, sheer misery. She said many times, if she'd known how it would be, she'd have made a good morphine connection and lived her best until she died." Fleming sat next to Marigold, showing his discomfort by ignoring the conversation.

"Could this be psychological?" Grace asked. "I mean, what does your mom see as her future? You've said many times that she likes things the right way, which is her way, and maybe with your dad having memory problems and so on, maybe even a healthy future doesn't seem inviting to her."

"I imagine myself in her shoes," Gus said, tearing up, "and I know what *I'd* do. I'd look for the lesson in the disease, and then do all I could to work with it until I was sure dying was right. Then, I'd want euthanasia, too." She wiped her eyes and went on, "But I'm not Mom. I don't have her situation, her feelings, her experiences and ideas, or her possible future, should she live. She has a very different history, set of values, and goals. All I can do is help ease her journey. I strongly believe euthanasia should be available for people, but with stringent and long-term regulation. It shouldn't carry the negative emotional charge it does."

"I know this is tough for you," Marigold said. "Is there anything I can do? Will you be here awhile, or do you have to go back soon?" She put her arm around Fleming, who sat as if his chair seat gave intermittent electrical shocks.

The restaurant cleared, reducing the ambient noise a decibel or two.

Gus answered, seemed to shout, and lowered her voice, "I don't know, Marigold, what's coming next. My sense is that I'll be going to Florida often, but there are too many variables to know ahead of time. I may need a hand with keeping Butterbean if Grace goes away, but for now, I'm okay." Gus looked at Marigold and wondered what she was thinking. Her color wasn't good.

"We can't stay and eat, Gus, but I wanted to welcome you home," Marigold said, looking at Fleming. She patted his hand, reassuring him, "We can be a few minutes late. You know your friends won't be at the Deco Gecko until later." Fleming made a face and stood.

Marigold rose from her chair, and Fleming pulled it away from the table with an audible sigh of relief. Marigold embraced Gus, Grace, and Hazel. "I love you all. Please call me." Towing Fleming, she sliced through the tables like an Alaskan icebreaker.

Gus, Grace, and Hazel looked at one another.

"Was Mari annoyed with Fleming?" Grace asked.

Irene returned and settled in with a second piece of cheesecake, a questioning look on her face. "What just happened?"

Grace looked at the chairs deserted by Marigold and Fleming. They appeared quite ordinary, with no detectable defects.

"It was the euthanasia," Gus replied, returning to her seafood delight. "Mari isn't good with age or death, and from the looks of him, neither is Fleming."

"In that case, there'll be plenty of rockin' 'n' rollin' in the old bedroom tonight," Irene piped up.

"Oh yeah," Hazel affirmed. "Nothing perks up the old sex hormones like death. My second child was conceived the day of his granddaddy's funeral."

"Well," Grace said, retrieving her purse, "I remember a couple of hot times myself."

"You may have more coming," Irene added. "From what I understand there's a dapper, silver-haired gentleman interested in the house that's for sale next door to you, if they drop the price."

"Hmmpf," Grace snorted, unconvinced of the benefits of a new neighbor, no matter what his looks. "I've got to go. Can we get together in a few days when we're not so distracted?"

"Great idea," Hazel said, "I'm going too. I haven't fed the troops yet. Let's call each other and make a plan. I feel like I'm running out on you, Gus."

"Don't. I'll just be a minute longer."

After hugs all around, Grace and Hazel left, and Gus walked toward the buffet. Once they were out the door, she spun around, grabbed a cheesecake from the hands of a server and returned to her seat. Amid the debris of the others, she savored the taste and texture of both cheesecake and solitude.

"Kibbles and bits, I'm having fits," Butterbean mumbled and growled, pacing from living room to bedroom and back. "Humans can't find steak if it's in their food bowl, no wonder the world's screwed up. Gus needs rest, so she climbs on a social merry-go-round. Go figure. Hazel seems to be the only one paying attention, and that's 'iffy' today. Everyone knows she's going to the library in Centerville with Bruce, but not about her *Advanced Chemistry* book, and she's not talking." The slap of the doggie door interrupted Butterbean's rant, alerting her in time to deflect a full-steam Grizzie attack.

"Cut it out!" Butterbean ordered, baring her teeth. "I'm in no mood for cat crap! Can't you see I'm busy? No, you can't see. You're too self-centered to notice anyone else. You're a cat." She advanced on Grizzie, hackles up, her eyes narrow, shooting darts of disdain.

"Geez, don't be such an old fart, Corgi," Grizzie replied, sitting down. She raised a paw, ostensibly for cleaning, but kept it poised to strike in case she misjudged the dog. "You aren't the only one who's hip, you know. We cats have a grapevine too, and yes, Hazel's right. More than false allegations are happening at Mark's house."

Mollified in part, Butterbean sat down. Grizzie, taking that for peace, began bathing her paw in earnest.

"I'm sorry," Butterbean apologized, lying down. "Too much negativity makes me nuts. Gus is a nervous wreck in spite of her social smiles and laughter; Hazel and Bruce are strung out over court; and Marigold keeps Fleming hidden. Everyone ignores something dangerous next door to Hazel, and my Gus is as bad as the rest. Sure, she's been with her dying mom in Florida, but the telephone works, and I know she was with Hazel when she first saw the starter fluid on one of their morning runs."

"And this is your business, how?" Grizzie inquired with utmost seriousness.

"I'm a dog, my human *is* my business. Art, Gwen, Lady, and Daphne are my friends, so their humans are also my business—being too independent is clearly a feline shortcoming," Butterbean stated, her tone over-the-top condescending.

Grizzie stretched and flicked her tail, creating a snap at the end of each flick like the tip of a whip. "Nope, humans are humans' business. Cats are grounded in reality. For starters, humans don't use the brains Deity gave them, and they're unmanageable at best. We cats don't burden ourselves with emotional giving back. Our presence and our presents of hot lunches from outdoors are enough. Besides, purring gets them every time."

"So," Butterbean asked sincerely, "why do cats hang around? If it weren't for the emotional bond and my extreme loyalty, why, if I could feed myself, I'd be gone . . . some days, anyway." Surprised at her admission, Butterbean lay down.

"They're good providers," Grizzie answered. "Why would I want to eat sparrow every day and sleep in a pile of leaves under a porch when I can eat the same thing that fuss-budget Persian on TV eats and sleep on Gus's other pillow?" She arched her back and began a full-body, fore and aft stretch. "I may be young, but I'm no fool."

"No, you're no fool," Butterbean mumbled, her mind switching to writing issues.

"I guess I have to ask you for a favor."

Wary, Grizzie asked, "What about?"

"You writing with me."

"Not so fast, you conniving Corgi. I'm looking for parity here—you and me on equal footing. I know you'll never get enough salmon to pay me for typing it, especially not all the *rewrites*." Grizzie smirked. "I want a contract."

"Get real."

"Okey dokey then," Grizzie said over her shoulder, "I'm off to torment a lizard."

An hour later, a few feet from the doggie door, Butterbean was taking a snooze break when she was broadsided by a screeching cat with a lizard attached to her nose.

Butterbean snatched the lizard in its middle, giving it her best 'broken neck' shake.

"That's worth twenty pages."

"Ten," Grizzie sputtered, cleaning up her bloody nose.

"Okay. While you were getting in this mess, I was thinking." Butterbean hesitated. She needed just the right words. "You're right. We do need parity here. Give and take. One for all, and all for one."

"There's all that gush again. What's the trade-off?" Grizzie sat erect, a bubble of blood on the tip of her nose.

"Okay. I accept you as who you are, a mostly grown-up cat, a half-decent one at that, and in return, you write my first draft, salmon free, re-writes to be negotiated." Butterbean paused.

"Think again, poo-butt," Grizzie hissed, spraying blood on Butterbean's bright white toes.

Butterbean sighed and cleaned her feet at great length. She said, "You do the typing, you can be coauthor, and we'll split whatever salmon Gus hands out, fifty-fifty."

"We'll need some rules, though. I know about cat abuse from the newspaper, and there *are* strict labor laws," Grizzie purred.

"When do *you* read the paper? I know you sit on it so Gus can't read it. Do you absorb the news through your backside?" Butterbean stuck her nose in Grizzie's face, getting it rasped by cat tongue. "Phffft," Butterbean sneezed, "Don't *do* that!"

Ground rules established with minimum hisses and snarls, the coauthors next chose the subject of the book. Butterbean liked training humans as a topic, but realizing she only knew decent humans, she felt inadequate to discuss or train nasty humans.

Grizzie, being a cat, didn't give a rat's patootie about training humans, so they agreed on a book of opinions gleaned from practical experience, including insights into canine/feline/human relations and the occasional exposé. Grizzie would be more diligent about spelling and grammar, and Butterbean would take care of dictionary look-ups. They agreed to fight about the title later.

Walking side by side down the hall to Gus's bed/computer room, Grizzie laid her tail across Butterbean's back, their haunches swaggering in tandem.

18

Briefs: Legal, Lace, Cotton, Long, and Short

Dinner at the Chinese buffet, however fun and exciting, was not the place to exchange ideas or information. Two weeks passed before the women could spend a late Thursday afternoon together at Gus's house.

Settled in her backyard with plenty of drinks and Hazel's no-fat, sugarless carob cookies, the women conversed, while Gus relaxed on her glider and listened. The canines made the most of their outdoor playtime with treats and knucklebones.

"In brief," Hazel ranted in mock seriousness about the Chinese dinner, "it was too hectic to brief, debrief, or read a brief."

"I'm sorry I didn't stay," Marigold said, "Fleming's become a nuisance with his diet, changing what he eats every week. He was a vegan that night, so no Chinese. What did I miss?"

"Court is same old, same old. We've examined Bruce's every move from 2007 to 2009, hauled out every old record, bill receipt, and check stub to determine his whereabouts. We've devised rebuttals to every conceivable contingency and tried to second-guess what that twerp might concoct next. Our circuits are fried." Hazel took another cookie and went on, "John has filed every appropriate motion, and Bruce has prevailed upon his urologist to induce and certify certain measurable conditions, if needed."

"What do you mean 'induce and certify measurable conditions'?" Marigold asked. "I don't get it."

Grace patted Marigold's arm. "Think about it tonight, and call me in the morning."

"Oh my God!" Marigold sputtered, catching cookie dribble in her napkin. "You mean he had to get it up in front of the doctor?"

Hazel smiled ruefully, "You got it, girl. Pretty, huh?"

"Hey," Grace said, thinking aloud, "what if John had a penis line-up?"

"I hope you mean photos," Hazel bristled. Then she grinned in spite of herself.

Gus hooted at the image in her mind of men in suits with bags on their heads and exposed erections. *Now look carefully, Mark, and pick the one that molested you.* Gus shook the macabre thought from her head, "*I* hope this will get settled somehow out of court. Is that possible?"

"There could be a plea bargain, but I don't know what the 'Persecution' could offer that might satisfy Bruce. He's beyond reason about proving his innocence. He might accept a trespassing charge, maybe," Hazel said.

"How's Irene?" Grace asked. "Is she getting anywhere with her penis prop? She needs a simple and inexpensive gimmick, like the hula hoop."

"A sexual hula hoop," Gus demonstrated. "Great (pant, pant, howl) exercise (gasp) for penile (wheeze, gasp) blood flow."

Hazel whooped, then calmed down. "Since her boss made her partner, she picked up a line of realistic blowup men that come with three outfits: suits, sportswear, and work clothes. Older women driving alone, especially at night, are snapping them up. Not just single women, but married women whose husbands are away a lot."

"Not a bad idea," Grace responded. "Are they anatomically correct?"

Marigold, attempting dignity, turned purple.

Gus went off into another round of gasping laughter. "I so needed this belly laugh!" she choked out.

"Whatever," Hazel giggled, wiping her eyes, "I'm glad ol' Germy George got caught and had to make Irene a partner."

Lying beside Gus's new azaleas, the canines considered more serious matters.

Lady stretched out and dozed, flanked by Art and Gwen, who were engaged in earnest rawhide consumption. Daphne reclined near Gus's huge summer magnolia, enjoying the dappling of sun and shadow on her body. Butterbean rolled on her back, feet waving in the air as she worm-wiggled, scratching her back on the stiff grass. Then she relaxed, dropped her feet to her sides and let her flews hang open, exposing the inside of her cheeks and white teeth.

"Eek! *What* are you doing?" Gwen yelped, unused to seeing Butterbean's entire underside and dentition.

"Playing dead, humans' favorite doggy trick. I need to talk to all of you." Butterbean flipped right-side up. "Lady, you awake?"

"Enough," she murmured. "I'm listening."

Art stood up, chewy between his front legs. "Are you going to talk about what we've been seeing on our walks?"

"In a minute, but first I want to know about death. Gus's mom, Audrey, is dying. While my Gus puts on a good face, she's not at all herself. And it hasn't been that long since Sassy was almost killed." Butterbean shook out some grass scraps. "I know we won't see whoever's dead again, and that's the saddest thing, but what happens when you're the one who's dead? What's it like?"

"Don't be a dork! What's important is to enjoy every minute and make the world better, like with my petitions to chain Pit Bulls from birth," Art grumbled. He picked up his chewy and trotted nearer Daphne. "Think about it. Do we know anyone who's dead?" he said over his retreating shoulder.

"Whoopee dog biscuit, of course not," Gwen exclaimed. "Why would *anything* matter if death means disappearing?" She moved her rawhide closer to Butterbean.

Art sauntered back, chewy dangling like a cigarette, "Listen to our humans, laughing like hyenas over there. Let's talk about the trash."

"Okay," Butterbean said, rawhide firmly under a front paw. "What have you seen? What are you thinking?"

"Well," Gwen preened, "one day, empty Gro-lite packages filled the recycle bin next door, and you can see special soil stashed behind the house by the shed. At the house across the street where that geeky guy lives, we've seen bleach containers, lye bottles, brake and starter fluid cans, and strange literature. Hazel's noticed, too. She seems to think he's a chemist or salesman."

Gwen slipped beside Butterbean, tickling the Corgi's ear as she whispered. "Art doesn't know this. A catalogue came last week. It knocked me flat when it fell in the mail slot, and the flap closed so hard, it clanged like a cymbal right in my ear. I tried to drag the catalogue under the sofa, but Hazel heard the clang. All I saw before Hazel snatched it was the cover picture of black outfits, infrared heat detectors, and weapons." Butterbean shook her head ferociously. It felt like a beehive had moved into her ear.

Art looked up from his chewy. "I've got better news than that. My buddy, Butch Boxer, says there's good pot in town right now. His human, one of the assistant district attorneys, crows about arrests being up. Maybe some of the pot comes from next door."

"Very interesting," Butterbean said, the tingling out of her ears. She didn't mention the chemistry book in Hazel's car. She knew what chemistry was, but not how advanced "advanced" might be. She'd have to look in the book—fat chance of that with humans always hovering. "We'll have to keep our eyes and noses on the streets and the trash. My Trouble Meter is registering red."

"Mine too," Gwen said, lying down beside Butterbean. "Could we talk more about death? Since Sassy was attacked, I think about it all the time. Do you?"

Butterbean munched on her chewy. "I've heard there are no leashes, treats grow like grass, and there are personal petting machines. My cousin talked about being in a room full of Greenies when she had complications from back surgery and supposedly died for five minutes. We've all heard humans talk about seeing family and friends during similar experiences. Some humans theorize there are other lifetimes, both past and future. They use words like 'transition,' 'higher expression,' and 'eternal peace.' Damned if I know what that means. A few people say nothing happens, and they liken death to a good sleep. If humans haven't figured it out, how would we?"

"Is that why they whisper?" Gwen cocked her head. "Things like 'she died of cancer' or 'we had to put her to sleep' are always whispered. Maybe it *is* a long rest. That's not bad."

Butterbean sighed. "Maybe Lady or Daphne want to talk about it. I've got one unpredictable and very alive human on my paws. You have no idea how wild Gus is over Audrey choosing to die. First, she yells, and then she cries." Butterbean began vigorous groin washing.

Lady got up and limped over to lie down near Daphne in deeper shade. "I'll tell you one thing, my arthritis is so painful that sometimes, when I sleep well or have my favorite cat-chasing dream, well, if that's being dead, it's okay. Nothing hurts then, and I'm happy." She pulled herself up to scratch her ear, then slid back down. "Maybe Gus's mom feels like that, only worse. Maybe it isn't kind for us to will her to live when we don't know about her life."

Butterbean stopped lapping her foot. "Gus is letting Audrey do whatever she wants; it *is* Audrey's decision, but she's shattered by it. I can't go to Florida with her, or do much for her here either, and that makes me crazy. What *can* I do with myself?"

Lady made a sigh followed by a moan of pleasure at finding the right position. "How about writing your book?"

Butterbean didn't reply. She didn't know how to tell Gwen she'd been coopted as coauthor, and by a cat, too.

"Well, I hate to laugh and run," Grace said, "but I need to get home.

"Me too. Bruce promised he'd be home for dinner. Can I bum a ride with you, Grace?"

"Of course. The dogs will fit in the back."

"Well," Marigold said, fluffing her skirt and brushing off her bodice. "I suppose I should head out also. I've got class tomorrow.

Seeing movements of departure, the dogs meandered toward the back porch to sit near their respective humans.

Grace knew this laughter and riotous good humor, while refreshing, wasn't Hazel's original agenda for this gathering. Like a case built on circumstantial evidence, her suspicions about Hazel having another scheme had gelled, but she wanted to be certain so she dropped Marigold and Daphne first. Changing Hazel's mind was nigh impossible, but she would try. Besides, the air was sultry and smelled of honeysuckle, so Grace drove aimlessly in the twilight.

"Remember riding around when you were in high school?" Hazel asked.

"Sure do, though for most of us it was walking or biking. After dark, we searched out places to have a clandestine smoke, sometimes sneak a beer, too, where anyone who noticed wouldn't betray us. Wonder what kids do nowadays?"

"Keep their stash in their rooms and put all their information online," was Hazel's response. "Then they get trapped by *real* perverts." She turned in her seat to face Grace. "That's not why you're driving around. What's up?"

"It's a pretty night, and I know you've got something cooking," Grace replied, her attention on the road.

"You still have your night-vision goggles?"

"Yep," Grace drove 30 mph with the focus of an Indy racecar driver. The dogs enjoyed the smells coming in the back windows and ignored the tension up front.

"Well, I got an infrared detecting device from the same place, Law Enforcement Uniform and Supply. I still can't believe I don't have to identify myself as law enforcement. Remember the days when we'd have to use a guy's name for most everything?" Hazel said, hoping to find a less combustible topic.

"Sure do, Haze," Grace said, tight-lipped. "Our early programming is hard to overcome."

"Hmmm," Hazel agreed, watching the mansions slip by, realizing she had to take the risk. "That infrared heat detecting device is cool. I can tell something is going on in Mark's house, something that makes light and heat. It's probably Gro-lites and marijuana plants."

Grace sighed. "I've been watching too, Haze. You know the out-of-work-living-on-his-settlement chemist across from Mark's, the one who has no car and goes to the Christian Science church?"

"Yeah?" Hazel was curious now.

"Sometimes when I'm walking off my insomnia, I see him going into Mark's house. Keeping odd hours like mine. What would be the reason? Clandestine lovers? Chemistry lessons? Doubtful."

"That's interesting," Hazel shifted in her seat. "He has no car?"

"Nope," Grace muttered, turning toward the historic downtown area.

"I saw a bunch of used roadside flares in his trash one day," she looked at Grace and cut off her next question. "Yes, I wrote it in my diary. Do you remember the ether in the trash Gus and I found? That guy is a friend of Mark's dad."

"Very interesting," Grace admitted. "I've seen lots of empty Sudafed boxes in the chemist's trash too. Go figure."

"I figure meth lab. That stuff is volatile. You see those labs exploding all the time on TV. I can't be having that next door."

Grace slammed on the brakes and pulled into a parking space. "You're going in that basement, aren't you?" she shrieked. "How do you know all this meth lab stuff anyway?"

Hazel stiffened her back against the door. "How do *you* know about it?"

Relaxing somewhat, Grace replied, "Internet, though you can't believe half of it."

"Nan nah nan nah nah nah," Hazel chanted, "I get my info at the library while Bruce does his legal research, and you *can* believe that." Hazel smiled.

"Okay," Grace continued, "so we agree it's a meth lab. Even eight by ten glossy photos with circles and arrows and letters on the back would be excluded as evidence because we need a warrant. Our suspicions would be taken as retaliation, and we'd be laughed out of Sheriff Outlaw's office. Without a warrant, any photos would be evidence of *our* wrongdoing, breaking and entering. Not a good idea."

Not a word from a smiling Hazel.

"Look at me!" Grace commanded.

Hazel saw fire and ice, none of the camaraderie of the McClellan escapade, and shot back her own determination, The Look.

"You're going to do it anyway," Grace said, slumping in the driver's seat.

She gripped the steering wheel and stared straight ahead, fury muddling her aura and making her skin prickle.

Hazel answered the non-question gently and seriously. "Yes, Grace, I'm going to do it. Maybe the information I find will travel on Bruce's back channels, maybe not. I can't live with a bomb ready to go off next door. When I see what's there, I can decide what to do." She touched Grace's hand.

"You're a grown up, and you'll do as you please, I know, but you're talking felony and prison, not just a fifty-dollar fine and community service." Grace scowled and peeled away from the curb, realizing Hazel was in lioness mode, beyond seeing good sense if it was nestled in a bowl of chocolate covered truffles.

Hazel exhaled and silence reigned for the rest of the ride.

Later, Clarice told Grace she'd won the essay contest, and Grace called Hazel, who was happy for Clarice and wanted everyone at her house at noon sharp on Saturday. Then Grace called Marigold and left her a message about Clarice's win and Hazel's invitation. Last, Grace called Gus, whose voice was stress shrill. Robert and Audrey needed Gus in Florida, and she'd leave early in the morning. No more night driving, whether she slept or not. Grace told Gus about Clarice's essay and Hazel's gathering, and promised to care for Butterbean.

Late Saturday morning, Hazel ordered five large pizzas with a dazzling variety of toppings, and made sure she had ice cream and sodas on tap. She was sad but grateful Gus was back in Florida—one less person to ward off in this unpleasant think-tank business. She had her strategy mapped out, and she wanted hirelings to do her bidding, not colleagues with their own ideas. Even this early in the planning, Hazel could tell that Grace and Marigold were trying to usurp the operation. Marigold stuck to intellectual skirmishes, while Grace plunged into subterfuge and nefarious activities like a Navy Seal. Neither shared Hazel's interest in hard facts. Derailing her was their objective, and she knew it. She knew they knew she knew, and that foolishness had morphed into an elephant in the living room. Hazel wished she hadn't shared her plan.

Hazel wore black cargo pants with a black sleeveless shirt and enough gear in her pockets to sink her in a small swimming pool. She pursed her lips and surveyed her troops. The dining room table, littered with pizza boxes, cans, and paper cups, had returned to its pre-McClellan–mission ambience. Several open books and some notes rested amid the gastronomical gore. Exhausted and well-fed canines sprawled on the floor. Bruce had left long ago for golf with John, cautioning the women about legality. Hazel held small hope she'd have suitable "indians" to her "chief."

"Okay, back to the subject at hand," Grace said, waving some computer printouts. "We know Mark's growing pot upstairs, and it's a good guess there's a meth lab in the basement. But if he did online research, what I have in my hand is the type of garbage he'll find. In all of it, by the third step in meth production, you'll either get a useless result or get blown up."

"We also don't know how he's storing what he's got or what other flammables might be in that basement," Marigold added. "But from what I can tell here," she turned a page in the advanced chemistry book, "the correct procedure to make meth has to do with reductive reactions that require either nickel or lithium, neither of which is easy to get or manage in a non-lab setting. I doubt he's got those ingredients.

"It's been too long since I've studied chemistry to fully understand it, but for sure Mark won't be reading a book like this. What Grace is waving around from the Internet is more his level. Maybe not even, if he's only in the tenth grade." Marigold stretched, her feet deftly avoiding a sleeping Queen Daphne.

"For heaven's sake," Hazel spouted, walking to the refrigerator for another cola, "we've seen matchboxes, Vicks inhalers, and household cleaner jugs along with starter fluid cans and roadside flares. We don't know what Mark has stored in that basement. An explosion next door terrifies me, and that's what I want to short-circuit," Hazel skipped a beat. "If I know there's a meth lab in Mark's basement, for sure the cops will 'discover' it."

"I like Bruce's way best," Grace said. "Let's annoy them with unscheduled pizza deliveries, bogus calls in the middle of the night, and put our minds to disrupting their satellite TV, phones, etc., without being detected," Grace said. "Anything traceable to us could jeopardize Bruce's case, which is the last thing we want. Even hanging over your fence could cause trouble."

"I want to be perfectly clear here. I'm not into making trouble or blowing anything up. I want my house to be safe! Certainly charges against Horace might dampen Mark's ardor about prosecuting Bruce, but *the goal* for me is safety," Hazel said, then adding, "After that, I'll switch to nasty, underhanded, sneaky mode if I have to!"

Marigold and Grace exchanged eye rolls.

"I have a plan," Hazel went on, ignoring her friends. "I'll call and tell them they've won a rifle, a boat, a 52" plasma TV, something they couldn't refuse. They'd have to pick it up at a certain time out in the county. You know they'd go."

"Who'd make the call? They'd recognize any of us," Marigold said. "Maybe my neighbor Sam would do it. He's still got that crush on me even with Fleming around."

"That's okay," Hazel said. "I picked up one of those voice-altering gizmos."

"Not good," Marigold declared, fidgeting in her chair. "They're mechanical sounding and used for kidnappings. No one would offer a prize with a mechanical voice."

"The one I got," Hazel replied, "makes your voice either higher or deeper. With that and a wad of gum in my mouth, I'll be unrecognizable."

"Your phone won't be," Grace interjected.

"I've got a prepaid, throw-away cell phone."

"Oh great!" Grace covered her eyes and shook her head.

"Anyway," Hazel went on, "that would give us an hour minimum, and this nifty outfit is practically invisible. I've got latex gloves, night-vision goggles, plenty of tools. I'd do the search work and Grace would do the photography."

"I would *what?*" "Do you not hear me? NO! Not on your life, friend of mine. Sheriffs make me throw up, and I loathe jails. NO, Hazel, I am *not* your Kemo Sabe on this." Grace glowered at Hazel.

"Yikes!" Marigold said, looking at her watch. "It's late, and I have a dinner date with Fleming, his treat."

"Holy Toledo! What's he eating now?" Grace and Hazel said in unison.

"How did that happen?" Grace asked.

"What about his rent?" Hazel inquired.

"It's our three-month anniversary," Marigold said as she located her purse and Daphne's leash. "You can stop worrying about me. He's not fiscally savvy, but he's no Frank, and he's fun when he's not being artistic and finicky. Hazel, you look most impregnable in that outfit. Whatever you two do, I can only afford one bail at a time."

Marigold hugged both women and leashed Daphne, slipping down the hall and out the front door before Hazel or Grace said another word.

19

Summer Madness

Gus's life was not her own. July and August whirled by, consumed by tending to her parents, all action and no time to plan, reflect, or decide. When Gus arrived at their house on this July trip, it was evident that her mother wasn't treating her cancer. Moving her father to Pine Crossing now vied with preparing for her mother's death. *I'm a human doing instead of a human being,* was her frequent thought.

Knowing she'd be in Florida again when her mother died, Gus charted a double course. On the one hand, she managed all aspects of her parents' lives while she was there, and on the other, she established connections for her personal comfort and well-being. She moved to a motel with a Caribbean motif owned by a gay man named Ted and his two Labrador Retrievers. She found AA meetings she liked, met some of Ted's friends, and planned to refinish a small piece of her own furniture under Ted's tutelage.

During working hours, Gus captured officials—bankers, lawyers, home and auto insurance representatives, DMV workers—to wind up her mom and dad's affairs in Florida. She buttonholed her dad's doctors for last checkups or to get copies of his records. She learned the value of silence and spontaneous tears and developed an intuitive "officious bureaucrat" detector, doing what it took to avoid them.

At eight in the morning, she picked up banana boxes, which make the best packing cartons, from the supermarket and treated herself to the most caffeinated coffee available before she attacked a new day at nine. After offices closed at four thirty or five o'clock, she would hit the supermarket, a department store, or shoe repair.

Someone once said that Florida was God's waiting room, and Gus discovered the truth of that statement. She out-maneuvered fragile blue hairs piloting "driverless" cars, and the phalanxes of expertly coiffed, wheelchair- and walker-bound women as they fumbled with gnarled fingers in their purses and then counted out, sometimes in pennies, exact change. Beside those women often stood sad, old men competing with who they were thirty, forty, fifty years ago.

As a group, elders were irascible, forgetful, inconsiderate, and unmercifully slow. Individually, they were the bullies, princesses, rescuers, and wallflowers of second grade in cranky, frustrating bodies. Even though challenged by Alzheimer's, her dad was an anomaly. At eighty-seven, when he went with Gus for groceries, he called the slow drivers and change-fumblers "old geezers." The only change he counted was the change he received.

Driving in Fort Lauderdale was a hair-raising experience beginning with rotating traffic signals. Both directions on the same street didn't go through the light simultaneously; the lights were timed for one side and then the opposing one, and then the same for cross traffic, due to double or triple left turn lanes and right turn on red. Then, right lanes turned abruptly into shopping malls without warning or choice, and huge boulevards dissolved into one-way residential streets.

The location of drawbridges and mall entrances seemed inexplicable, and when her father was with her, he told Gus how the lights worked and what lanes to use. When alone, Gus sometimes ended up driving away from her destination. There was no recourse but to be funneled several blocks by grassy islands and erratic drivers before she could execute an electrifying cross-traffic U-turn.

The smaller, original downtown areas presented a lesser nightmare with their one-way streets in no order, but the ambience was more interesting. Here, a parking space was a fantasy.

Through all this, Gus roasted, the heat wrapping her like the tortilla wraps a burrito. She understood why in south Florida everyone, even those who looked better when dressed, wore so little. Though she hated her flapping arm wings, she bought and wore tank tops. Next, she purchased a cardboard sun-blocker—a bulldog face wearing sunglasses—for the windshield.

Gus learned she wasn't alone in this baffling world. In banks, she noticed other adult children toting large purses or briefcases stuffed with bank statements, certificates of deposits, and powers of attorney. Each person had the wild-eyed and dumbstruck look that comes from corralling social security checks in glove compartments, bank statements from piles of junk mail, and deciphering arcane scribbles on scraps of paper. Sometimes the financial situation resolved differently than expected.

Like Gus's parents, many of the elderly at an earlier point in life had suffered a monetary loss in the stock market or an investment not under the auspices of an FDIC-insured bank. This resulted in their emphasis on safety of capital over gain. They purchased certificates of deposit, especially in times of high interest rates, laddering their money among the bank specials, and getting the best rates for the shortest periods of time.

Over the years, banks escalated their competition; as a result, many retirees like her father had handfuls of CD books spread over six or seven banks. He tried keeping up with the quarterly changes, listing certificate numbers, bank, amount, and maturity date, but it proved too taxing. Dates passed, consequences occurred, frustration mounted.

Grateful to be sitting in the center of an air-conditioned bank instead of baking in the mobile home with her parents and their nurse Dahlia, Gus closed her eyes a moment and reflected on the day she met Dahlia.

The Saturday after her mother's surgery, Gus wanted to head home by noon to avoid driving in the dark. When the nurse who was scheduled to arrive at the mobile home at ten hadn't appeared by eleven, Gus called the agency. The nurse was "on her way," the agency told her. She called again at eleven-thirty. Again, the nurse was "on her way." After after a meltdown on the phone, Gus found out that no one had given explicit written directions to the incoming nurse, which accounted for her delay.

Gus marched outside to start her car and let it cool. She'd leave and pray the nurse would appear. She could do no more; she was worn to the bone. Just then, she saw an ancient Chevrolet turn the corner, all the windows open and the driver's arm out the window. *No air conditioner,* Gus thought, feeling sad for the driver. The woman in the car checked the house number, parked, and exploded from the car.

Mature and portly like Gus, she had cornrows, wore a flowered sundress, and was as black as Gus was white. Sweat and frustration stuck out all over her. Her cell phone needed charging, and this was her last try at navigating the maze of Arrowhead Gated Mobile Home Community.

Gus had on skimpy shorts and a tank top. She was so ready to go her feet were on fire, and her wet hair painted flat on her scalp. Sweat and frustration stuck out all over her too. They ran toward one another and embraced, delighted to find each other.

"I'm Dahlia," the nurse said.

"And I'm Gus. Welcome to the Roberts' house. My mom Audrey and my dad Robert are inside."

Smiling at the memory, Gus felt blessed to have Dahlia with her parents. They'd become closer over the phone, but especially on this visit. In the evening, with her mother fed and in bed, and her father watching TV, Gus and Dahlia washed the dishes and sang gospel. Dahlia with her splendid voice didn't flinch when Gus made it an off-key duet. Both women wrapped ice cubes in bandanas, tied them around their necks, rolled their eyes at the craziness of the world, and hugged a lot.

"Ms. Roberts?" Gus's reflections were shattered by a thin woman in a black suit approaching, ennui and resignation on her face.

"Yes," Gus replied, standing as she gathered up her tote bag and purse.

"Right this way." The woman turned sharply and headed toward the safe deposit boxes in the back of the bank.

Inside the vault, the woman opened box 94, pulled it out, and guided Gus into the "viewing room," where she placed the box on the table, and said, "When you're finished, just come to the door. I'll be outside." She left, closing the door with a sound much like a prison gate.

Gus opened the safe deposit box. Inside the long metal box lay a tri-folded document with a heavy, gray cover and a small, white box with "Denver Dry Goods" engraved on its top. Picking up the white box, Gus lifted its cover, realizing it had come from Denver to Buffalo with her mother when she had married her father, making it older than Gus. She smiled at that and at its contents, a dozen silver dollars.

When she looked at the document, Gus's smile turned to raucous, hysterical laughter. It was a power of attorney dated 1994—the very one she would have needed to access the safe deposit box had she not insisted her mother update everything last winter.

Back in Pine Crossing, Butterbean had her own issues.

With Grace's responsibilities, Butterbean was left "minding the house" with no pattern to which house it was—hers or Grace's. Her walks were out of order also. As Grace was an insomniac, walks happened anytime, even at two in the morning. Thanks to the doggie door, Butterbean's bathroom habits stayed regular, but her social life was a disaster, as was her writing.

"Phhhhffft," Butterbean sighed at Grace's feet one day when she realized her canine cronies were passing by. She scooted to the side of her chair and put a paw on Grace's calf. Cocking her head, Butterbean donned her most beseeching, brown-eyed pitiful look that cried, "Walkie?"

Finally Grace caught on. Butterbean was ecstatic as she pulled Grace down the block to meet her friends.

"Hi, guys," Butterbean said as she ran up to Gwen and Art, who were waving their matching ivory tails. "How are you? I've missed you."

Gwen turned briefly from her car-chasing stance to say, "Missed you, too. Where have you been?"

"Endless minding the house! It's great to be out. What have I missed?"

"What?" Gwen glanced at Butterbean and turned back to the street twice as fast. Art lifted his leg on each tree, a fence, the recycling bins, and on air.

"Pay attention, please," Butterbean snarled. "You can chase cars any day. Who knows when I'll see you again?" Butterbean sat at the curb, tongue hanging to her elbows.

Gwen pranced over and gave her jowls a few slurps. "I'm sorry. You know I have this car addiction. Pig ears are the only thing more important to me than cars."

"Fine, whatever," Butterbean murmured, ignoring the covert demand. She had no idea how or where she would get pig ears at Grace's.

They crossed the street a few feet ahead of Hazel and Grace, who were quiet today. Lady stayed at Hazel's side, Art at the end of his retractable leash.

"Now what's Hazel looking for in that recycle bin?" Butterbean asked. "She's trying to be nonchalant, but it's not working. Grace does that, too, when she can't sleep and we're prowling around in the middle of the night. Will things ever be normal?"

"Who knows," Gwen said, catching herself as a car passed. "Last week, Hazel collected the aluminum cans, got thirty-eight fifty for them too, but she's really searching for Sudafed boxes, starter fluid cans, and certain cleaning materials. When I put my front paws on the bin and look in with her, she pushes me down and says, 'No, Gwen, dirty, ick.' She doesn't understand I'm pointing out the stuff, not wanting it."

"What are these furtive conversations with your Hazel?" Butterbean complained. "One good thing is that Grace can't walk around with her phone and disappear in the bathroom like Gus does. She has a rotary phone on a gossip bench, though she does use her cell phone too."

The canines came to a corner and sat until it was time to cross. Butterbean didn't interrupt Gwen's concentration on passing cars.

Once across, Gwen resumed, "So with Grace hitched to her phone, what do you hear?"

"Mostly, Grace orders your Hazel to stop planning a raid on the Lewis's basement. If I've heard 'Hazel, you know that spells trouble' once, I've heard it more than I've heard 'too much noise, Beans.'"

"That's saying something," Gwen replied, stopping to sniff a gooey, dead frog. "No offense, but for a while I thought those were the only words Gus knew."

Gwen resisted as Hazel tugged at her leash, pulling her away from the carcass. "No dead frogs, Gwen!"

Butterbean sniffed the frog. "It's not ready anyway. If the sun stays out, it will be crunchy and quite tasty in another day or two. Humans don't appreciate gourmet road cuisine."

"For sure," Gwen answered, trotting ahead, "but I prefer to wear it. Even crunchy, frog upsets my tummy."

Gwen began eyeballing approaching cars, signaling the conversation was over. Art was almost out of petitions, and Lady whispered, "We're almost home. I hope Hazel gives me an aspirin for my arthritis after this walk."

"Only another block," Butterbean whispered to Lady. Then she retreated into thoughts about her book, but she couldn't do anything concrete until Gus returned. She couldn't write without Grizzie, the computer, and a room of her own.

20

Bruce, Fully Cocked, and Loaded with Barbeque

Always happy to be cooking barbecue, Bruce was ecstatic piloting a 17,000 BTU gas grill with side counters, gauges, and a full complement of long-handled utensils. He danced from cooler to grill to $7-per plates as the chicken halves flew into outstretched hands. Neither the heat wave—it was the week before Labor Day—the confusion, nor the occasional rude child dampened his high spirits. He was Chicken Chef at the Bruce Winston Legal Defense Fund Barbecue and Outing, a fundraising notion cooked up by Hazel and her book club friends.

Food and entertainment booths lined the end block of Glover Street by the river, including the Farmer's Market building. Some of the game booths were so hokey—that was their appeal. Hit the basket, a bushel basket placed ten feet from a taped line costing one dollar for two balls, put prizes in the hands of the smallest children, while older ones groaned good-naturedly at having to double the distance.

Hazel, Gus, and Marigold ran to the Dollar Store and the supermarket, keeping just ahead of the demand for prizes, chicken, and side dishes of potato and macaroni salad. Gus, back from her August Florida trip, forgot her stress and absorbed the pleasure of young people, laughter, and the fun carnival atmosphere. Irene made a sizeable anonymous contribution. Grace sold tickets for the children's carousel, and Fleming suffered in bed with a cold.

One of John Jackson's friends set up his food wagon, selling funnel cakes and drinks. Mere acquaintances had come as vendors, all of them donating their time and profits to Bruce's defense fund.

A Preservation Society member, part owner of the local gym, brought over the wall climber with lots of mats and scheduled each of his personal trainers for an hour of supervising. Eager citizens traded five dollars for a five-minute climbing experience. For most customers, five minutes was four minutes too long, but many youngsters went again and again, making an expensive afternoon for their parents and a windfall for Bruce. The personal trainers touted the advantages of hiring their expertise for sessions at the gym, winning a dinner for two when someone signed up for their services. One stunning trainer emerged from her hour of supervising and selling, hoarse, but certain of half a dozen free dinners.

Amused by the pretty trainer and fascinated by people wall-climbing, Bruce watched and shoveled more birds onto the plates of expectant diners.

After the food, the dunking cage was the most popular attraction. The Pine Crossing Police Department used this apparatus at festivals with great success. Cops would take turns sitting on a small platform that, if the contestant hit the target with a softball, would collapse and drop the cop into the tank of water. Rent for the unit was nominal as Captain Fox was an old high school buddy of Bruce's.

Bruce thought dunking volunteers might be few, but as the day went on, the heat worsened, and by one o'clock, dunking became a desirable experience. The high school principal, a pastor, and a tour buggy driver were among those who emerged considerably wetter and cooler. A few cops also volunteered to sit in the cage and cool off after their shifts.

Bruce had gathered some serenity in the past week, more or less accepting the limbo of no trial date. He didn't want to develop a false sense of security, but at the same time, an indefinite state of high alert was impossible. Besides, Hazel seemed preoccupied, flaky, and secretive since the grand jury indictment. Bruce suspected she needed some attention, though he hadn't a clue what kind.

Her travels to Centerville with him while he delved in the law library at the University seemed plausible for a while, but how much shopping, visiting, and club lunching could she do? Two days ago, he had run into one of her friends on campus, a woman Hazel had mentioned as a lunch partner last week, but the friend's questions and behavior told him she hadn't seen Hazel in months.

Bruce flipped some chicken halves. He had to face facts. Hazel never had enough bags for the amount of shopping she claimed, and he never saw their contents. As for her lunches, she had no doggie bags. To top it off, he recalled a whispered phone conversation where he'd heard the word "reconnaissance" or maybe it was "reconnoiter." Hazel was a schemer, he knew. Something was up.

Wondering how to broach this delicate subject, Bruce flipped half a chicken just as John arrived with a booming, "Hi, buddy." Startled, Bruce missed the airborne chicken, and both men, mesmerized, watched it plop on the concrete.

"Hi, yourself. Any news?" Grinning, he asked, "Want half a chicken?"

John pulled a face. "No news is still good news, and yes, but not that piece."

Bruce placed another half on a plate, raised one eyebrow, and gave it to John, who asked, "The secret's in the sauce?"

Bruce smiled, "Would that it were so, pal."

Near the end of the afternoon, Bruce turned grill duty over to John and strolled the two blocks to his favorite jeweler. The way to Hazel's heart was earrings, and he was sick of the ones he'd given her the day of the Nasty Business. They'd come close to ripping out of her ears in bed last night. And maybe, just maybe, with some fresh booty, he could seduce her into telling him what was up her sleeve.

Later, curled up with Hazel on the sofa after the successful day, Bruce shifted and pulled a velvet-covered box out of his pocket. He handed it to her near the end of *Cold Case*, when the commercials seemed endless. Inside the box lay an exquisite pair of teardrop, emerald earrings.

Hazel looked at the earrings, then at Bruce, then back at the earrings, making him nervous about her reaction.

"Had enough of the other ones, eh?" She said, fingering the emeralds.

"Unh-huh, Haze. They got in the way last night, don't you think?"

Hazel looked into his eyes and saw they were soft like Lady's when she wanted a pat. "These are beautiful, Bruce. You're right about last night, dear. I almost had a lobe-ectomy."

She took off the costume earrings and put on the emeralds. "These are real?"

"Yep, the fundraiser went so well, I thought you and I could celebrate." They both got up to admire the earrings in the mirror over the mantel.

"You're right," Hazel said, embracing Bruce, "we've been too serious too long. I never saw so many silly, wet people loaded up on chicken and carnival prizes. Did John say anything interesting?"

"Nope, just that no news is good news."

"These are beautiful beyond words. Thank you." She leaned over Bruce, gave him a kiss, and sat down. The two minutes of *Cold Case* had passed, and the commercials returned.

Hazel grabbed the remote, saying, "I was thinking today about digging into Mark's background. I know he was in trouble in school a few years ago, but I don't remember what it was, if I ever knew. He was a real juvenile then, so I guess the records are sealed. But someone must know something. How would I find out whom? I'd hire our local PI, but I think this is too deep for Billy Bob's Used Cars and Detective Agency. His forte is pictures of infidelity and injury fraud."

"Haze, darling, we're doing all we can do. John will find any background on Mark that's available, believe me."

"Maybe," Hazel replied, tossing her head. "What about current stuff?"

"What do you mean?"

"Whatever's going on in Mark's basement. Gus, Grace, and I have decided it could be dangerous, and we three are going to find out."

"Oh great," Bruce exclaimed in exasperation. "Just what this case needs—you, Grace, and Gus playing PI! You read too many detective stories and watch too much TV," he said as *Cold Case* resumed. "Case in point," Bruce added, pointing at the TV as he looked for the remote, finally realizing Hazel had it stashed in an intimate place.

"That's right, good buddy." Hazel wagged her finger and pushed it further between her legs. She caressed an earring and gave Bruce a sexy look.

21

Sudafed, Lye, and Vicks Nasal Inhalers

Summer didn't want to let go. Though darkness fell earlier now, October weather was hot and sultry. Inside Hazel's house, it was bright, noisy, and cooler.

For the past three years on the first of October, Bruce and Hazel held a BYOB potluck that verged on being an open house. Friends, neighbors, coworkers, and friends of friends were welcome. Because the barbecue fundraiser took place a few weeks ago, and because the allegations against Bruce polarized the citizenry of Pine Crossing, Bruce favored skipping the event.

Though understanding Bruce's point, Hazel felt strongly the event would, biblically speaking, "separate the wheat from the chaff," among their friends. A recent snub from two "blood brother" pals at the Historical Society changed Bruce's mind. He was innocent, so why should he behave differently than usual? The gathering was on.

The turnout both surprised and impressed Bruce. Fifteen or twenty people, a fifth of the total guests, were still present at ten o'clock, eating, drinking, and talking in small clusters.

Upstairs in a dark bedroom, two women changed clothes by feel—clothes versus bedspread, yours versus mine, front versus back.

"Damn!" exclaimed Grace, "I got this turtleneck on backwards even after all my practice." She squeezed and flapped, at last shoving her arms in the sleeves. "Are you sure these are my biking pants? They feel shrunken and short." Grace pulled the spandex in all directions away from her waist, crotch, and butt.

"Shhh, Grace, they'll hear us," Hazel cautioned. "I wish Gus were here too. I miss her good sense, and I have bad vibes about this trip she's making to Florida. It may be her last." The crotch in Hazel's pants only made it halfway up her thighs. She moaned, "I can't get these on. Are you sure you washed them in cold water? Why can't I wear my cargo pants? I'm gonna turn the light on."

Grace grabbed Hazel's arm, "No light," she hissed. "Put on your night-vision goggles." Grace grabbed the waistband of Hazel's tights and heaved upward. They stretched until Hazel was covered, though miserable.

"I can't walk like this," Hazel wailed. "My thighs rub and make noise. I could catch fire."

"Even you aren't that hot," Grace replied through clenched teeth. Her turtleneck didn't stay tucked into her tights. Every time she raised her arms, her white back and stomach flashed in the dark like Morse code. She needed a belt.

"Where are your belts?"

Hazel, slipping off her tights, answered, "In the closet behind you." While she snuck into her cargo pants, Hazel heard the swish of hangers and the plop of a suit landing on the closet floor. "On the left on the whirly rack, for heaven's sake. Where do *you* keep belts?"

Able to see the pastel belts, Grace chose one she couldn't see instead. If *she* couldn't see it, probably others wouldn't either. Cinching herself into a Scarlett O'Hara hourglass figure, Grace noticed the bedside clock. They had to hurry.

The women reconnoitered outside near Hazel's new privacy fence. Their plan was simple—go in the Lewis's basement with their flashlights and tiny camera, record what was there, and get out. Hazel had scouted out the bulkhead while checking her night-vision goggles. The hasp was broken and the hinges were rusty. She carried traveler-size WD-40 for the hinges, just in case.

"Do you have everything?" Grace asked.

Hazel felt around in her pockets, "Flashlight, check! WD-40, check!

Camera, bandana, latex gloves, pencil, teeny notebook, all check! You sure we don't need the walkie-talkie? And quit rattling that newspaper. We'll be heard downtown at this rate."

"And smelled down there, too, if we use the WD-40," Grace muttered. "Are the steps as ratty as the bulkhead doors?"

"Geez, Grace, I don't know. I've never been down there."

"Geez, Haze, you're crabby. You're the one who *has* to do this! I'll be right behind you, but you so owe me."

"Behind me?" Hazel squeaked. "You said you'd go first."

"In your dreams, girlfriend," Grace tugged at Hazel's back. "Pull down your goggles. They're no good on top of your head!" She gave Hazel a slight push saying, "Off you go then!"

Hazel opened the gate and reclosed it. "We didn't check your stuff. Do you have your camera and flashlight? What about wrenches, pliers, screwdrivers?"

"Got 'em all," Grace answered, placing Hazel's hand under her waist pack, hefting it up and down to illustrate. "But I won't be using them. This is a photo shoot, remember?"

"Okay, we look and shoot," Hazel agreed, her fingers crossed. She had a few thoughts about destroying the basement, accidentally, of course. Opening the gate, she whispered, "Come now, no lagging." She hugged the other side of the fence, made a sharp left and shot across open space to the topsoil pile where, balancing on one knee, she noted a distant rumble of thunder.

From behind Hazel, and referring to the bulkhead doors, Grace asked, "Right or left?" Hazel jumped, clocking Grace under the chin with her shoulder. "Ouch! Turkey!"

"I'm sorry," Hazel said. Her tone was contrite, her eyes excited. "This is scarier than I thought."

"Maybe we should quit now," Grace suggested.

"Oh pooh," Hazel said, fingers recrossed, "we're just looking."

Hazel dashed over to the bulkhead and raised the left door. It squeaked, and Grace promptly spritzed it with WD-40. First casualty of the evening, a dead squeak.

Then a few raindrops splattered quarter-sized spots on the closed door, and the women slipped stealthily down the steps.

No way could they have prepared for the mess. The mold and sludge coating the floor and partway up the walls was stupefying. There were workbenches the length of the basement along the moldy outer wall and shelves, stacks of boxes, cans, crates, and hooks with raingear and rags on the wall opposite. Everything mildewed to the perfection of Camembert. A narrow aisle went to the front wall where a sturdy built-in cabinet stretched floor to ceiling. It had a hasp but no padlock.

The cellar in the bilious green of the night-vision goggles stunned Hazel. Grace dismissed the mess to look to the right. Another set of steps led upstairs, and in the considerable space behind them was an old refrigerator, a water heater, and an ancient tank for kerosene or heating oil, sitting on short, rusty legs.

A web of phone, electrical, and unidentifiable wires traveled around these items and along the joists only six inches above their hair. Grace felt nostalgic about the round, button-like, white insulators with bare wires passing through them, same as in the attic of her childhood home. She hoped these here had fallen into disuse.

Grace turned to Hazel. "Who could make anything in this dump?"

"Men can," Hazel replied. "Listen a minute. Do you hear what I hear?"

In the quiet, they both heard hissing, dripping, and a louder, metronome-like ticking. Hazel probed the corners and joists, seeing only wires and cobwebs. For sure, no one tall came here. Grace examined the benches, covered with bottles, cans, pots, and a huge pan. To her left lay a Bunsen burner surrounded by flasks, decanters, titration pipettes, mason jars, funnels, sieves, and regular goggles and masks.

The containers on the floor and on the shelves emitted odors that could be ether, carbon tetrachloride, or burning clutch. Grace gagged. Hazel poked under some empty cans and came up with an old kitchen clock. The numerals were raised and the second hand stuck on them, thus the tick or tock every five seconds instead of the usual one. Hazel reached to fix it.

"No!" Grace yelled. "Don't touch *anything*!

"I've got my purple latex gloves on," Hazel said. "No one can tell the difference in this mess anyway. I can't stand that noise."

"They'll miss it!"

"I'll re-bend it."

"Okay, I'll take some pictures. You be stupid if you want." Grace snatched her camera out of her waist pack, dropping a wrench and screwdriver.

"Pick those up," Hazel ordered. "Bruce will notice if they're gone. She bent over to read the labels on some of the cans and bottles on the floor. "This *is* the stuff listed on the Internet for making methamphetamine. All that's missing is the antihistamine tablets."

Grace snapped pictures.

"Let me look through this cabinet." Hazel opened the huge cabinet at the front of the basement. "Eureka," she shrieked, standing back to reveal stacks of Sudafed, Equate generics, and Vicks nasal inhalers. She held up the newspaper and pointed her flashlight at each ingredient while Grace clicked away.

Back at Hazel's house, though the party was winding down, the living and dining rooms held two groups of friends engaged in well-lubricated end-of-the-evening conversation.

Lady got up from her spot by the hors d'oeuvre table and made her way through the assortment of legs to the kitchen. Her arthritis wasn't in the cranky range, and she had done well cadging morsels from the guests, but she was uneasy. The moon wasn't full, she noted, sticking her head out the doggie door; there was only the faintest sliver. On the porch, the Poms gnawed on pig ears in the dank air, nothing alarming there. She decided to get a drink and investigate the rest of the house.

Lady checked out the guests, the powder room, and the back stairs—nothing amiss so far. Then it hit her; she hadn't seen Hazel or Grace in a long time. *Where were they?*

Bruce was there. Marigold and Fleming had come and gone, but not a hint of Grace or Hazel. She sauntered to the front door and caught the barest whiff of Hazel going up the stairs. She didn't want to go up there with her arthritic legs, but *what if Hazel hadn't come down? What if she were sick up there?*

Lady sniffed the first two steps and checked the air. Hazel had gone up, not down, at least not this way.

"Oh, heartworm!" Lady cursed under her breath, putting her front feet on the first step and looking with trepidation at the rest of them. She hadn't been up there in months without help. Concern for Hazel overrode her fear, and she leaned forward to make the first leap up.

"Lady," Bruce called out. "Lady, wait! No one's up there." He came over and gently removed the elderly dog off the steps. "Maybe they went for a walk. You know they're not party people. Go lie down in the kitchen. They'll be back."

Finished photographing cans of brake and starter fluid, brick cleaner, boxes of roadside flares, lye, and the contents of the big cabinet, Hazel moved nearer Grace. With no one talking, Grace noticed the earlier hiss and dripping sounds had become louder hissing and a solid gurgle.

Hazel was about to ask "What's that?" when a sudden clap of thunder sent her midair. She grabbed Grace, and bit her tongue. Then came a sound like golf balls hitting the bulkhead door and bouncing down the steps,

"Look, Hazel," Grace pointed, "Hail!" Then she focused on the water heater. A small stream flowing from the rotted bottom made the gurgling sound. The women looked at their feet. They were standing in an inch of water.

"Crap," Grace said, snatching Hazel's arm, "we've got to get out of here before something shorts out in this water and electrocutes us. Let's go."

"Wait," Hazel resisted and pulled her arm away. "I don't want to get bonked with a hail stone. Besides, I need to see what's in the refrigerator first." Pushing past Grace, she wrestled the door open. No cold came out. She shined her dimming flashlight on the jugs of distilled water and spotted a carton of pistachio ice cream.

"That can't be ice cream," Grace sputtered over Hazel's shoulder. Hazel wheedled the carton past the jugs and opened it. It smelled like pistachio ice cream, but looked nothing like it. She laughed. "Grace, they made the wrong product! It's the other meth, meth-something-or another, I don't remember the name. Won't make you high, but still dangerous. Good for us!"

Resigned to Hazel's disinterest in *their* safety, Grace investigated one of the brown glass bottles while Hazel took shots of the pistachio-like faux meth. Unleashing the inimitable smell of toluene, Grace replaced a cap and headed toward Hazel, who closed the refrigerator door. That instant, the basement was illuminated as if by a thousand flashes, and simultaneously, there was a deafening, thunderous boom right there in the cellar.

The two women stared at the shattered water heater. Essentially it was no more. Sparks and bits of fire had flown in all directions, igniting some of the wood on the wall and a box of trash. Water gushed out of the pipe from the street, and the oil or kerosene tank was a whisper away from the burning wall.

Grace and Hazel leapt onto the bottom step, heading up and out. Step two broke under their combined weight with a terrifying noise, dropping them back in the now deep water.

"Crap!" Grace swore, removing the wood shards that poked her side. One big piece wedged itself between her belt and the bottom step, keeping her stuck until she undid the belt and wiggled back onto the bottom step.

"Help, Grace, help! I can't find my left foot. And we're on fire!" Hazel thrashed around, sending a shower over both women.

Grace wiped her eyes with her bandana, unable to see or to help Hazel. Then Hazel discovered her foot was in a sump hole.

The fire on the wall was on top of the old tank, and Grace thought of the toluene and other chemicals. Hazel was at a standstill, mesmerized by the fire and the missing step.

"Come on, Haze, go! Up and out," Grace ordered.

"I can't. There's golf ball hail out there, fire in here, and how will we explain our clothes? This was a stupid idea." She slumped on the step and began crying in earnest. Grace slapped her twice.

Shivering, frightened, banged, and bruised, a soggy Hazel and bedraggled Grace crept and crawled onto Hazel's back porch. Side by side on the porch floor, backs against the wall, the women panted from their exertion and patted Art and Gwen, who thought this was a nifty game. The dogs were uncertain about some of the chemical smells, but mulch, mold, mildew, and dirt were more delectable than ice cream.

"Now what?" Hazel moaned, looking at the smoke coming from the back of the house next door.

"What?" Grace replied, testily. "Haven't we done enough?"

"We did nothing," Hazel shot back. "The lightning did. What do we do about us?"

"We go upstairs the back way, dispose of these clothes, dress, and come down. If no one has discovered the fire and called 911 by then, *we* can notice it. We need to hurry. The rain won't be enough to stop the fire, and it could reach this house if the wind is right."

They stripped in the upstairs bathroom, passed themselves through the shower, and dressed in casual walking shirts and shorts, ignoring bruised ribs and wrenched knees.

Their story was this: they had been out for a walk, gotten caught in the storm and, not wanting to be seen disheveled, had gone up the back way and cleaned up. It would be "Yes, Bruce, it was awful out there," and "No, Sarah, we didn't catch our death of cold," and "By the way, did you see those golf-ball size hailstones? Come look, there may be some in the backyard . . . oops, oh my God! The house next door is on fire! Quick, dial 911!"

An excellent plan, the women thought as they descended the stairs, gaily greeting the crowd in their fresh clothes and damp hair. John and Sarah and a few of Bruce's golf buddies stood by the fireplace with drinks in hand and egos off leash.

Bruce returned from the kitchen with a beer and all the dogs in tow. Seeing Hazel, Lady stopped short and with a sigh of relief, enthusiastically nuzzled her left knee. Hazel lurched, reached for Bruce as she fell, causing him to lose his balance. He tossed the beer high and wide as he caught himself and slowed Hazel's fall.

Lowering to her side, Bruce whispered, "First you disappear, then you're just out of the shower, then you can't take a Labrador nuzzle. What's going on?"

Overhearing, Grace interrupted. "Let me get you another beer, Bruce. Then we'll clean this up. Hazel, what would you like?"

"Excellent idea," Hazel gushed, catching Grace's intention, "I'd like a cherry Dr. Pepper and some cookies. They're in the top right cupboard. Then we can tell everyone about our walk." Hazel gathered her legs under her. "Will you give me a hand, dear?"

Bruce gave her a curious look, but graciously helped her up.

The instant she was in the kitchen, Grace went over to the cabinet, peered out the window, and saw the fire. The Poms, already aware of the fire, danced around Grace's feet.

Gwen ran upstairs, nose to the ground seeking more lovely smells. Lady stood by Grace, her furrowed brow suggesting one more piece would solve her puzzle.

In the distance, Grace heard sirens.

Gwen rushed downstairs and dropped a pair of wet black tights in front of Lady, who sniffed them, and wagging her tail, looked at Grace with a most satisfied expression. Grace quickly folded the telltale tights, wrapped them around her waist under the elastic of her shorts, and stretched her navy shirt over everything. Then she yelled, "Fire! Fire! There's a fire next door!"

22

They're Only Human

They did *what?*" Queen Daphne barked, her left eyeball protruding through a knothole in Hazel's Good Neighbor fence. The Lewis house had imploded, spontaneously combusted, experienced a personal tornado, perhaps all three, in Daphne's estimation.

Reduced to charred timbers, the outer wall facing Hazel's house was but a frame for tortuously twisted wires and pipes. Unidentifiable flotsam floated in what used to be the basement. Each room could be seen, like a child's dollhouse, its proper furniture, appliances or bathroom fixtures in place, but painted with black plumes and psychotic splotches from smoke and water.

"Grace and Hazel couldn't have been in there and lived to tell about it. This is your worst joke yet." Daphne turned an imperial snarl on the group of canines hunkered on the back porch.

Lady, exhausted but curious, jerked her head up each time her lower jaw touched her forelegs, trying to keep awake. Though Butterbean had heard the whole story secondhand from Lady, she felt left out. She moped and put her head between her front paws.

The Poms yapped in unison, "Hazel and Grace were here patting us when the fire broke out, and then they went upstairs. We knew they were okay."

"I found Grace's tights," Gwen said, wriggling at the thought of their smelliness. "I brought them downstairs, but she took them away. I bet they're washed and ruined by now."

"*I* barked and ran in circles when I heard the sirens," Art added. "I heard them and saw fire before Grace came in the kitchen and yelled 'Fire' at full volume. That hurt my ears. So did the sirens when they got close, painful beyond howling, so I went under the bed." He sat down, perplexed by the distress on Daphne's long, aquiline face.

"Thank you, Art and Gwen," Daphne said. "I have one question that maybe *someone* who was here can answer. *What* were they doing over there in the first place? There was a luscious party going on here, *here* in Hazel's own house, a house filled with friends and hors d'oeuvres. What in Unholy Bathtime was the need to slog around in a slimy basement in the middle of the night in an electrical storm with golf-ball-size hailstones? Are they addled?" Daphne began to pace up and down by the fence, so upset she shed a clump of hair at the base of her tail.

Daphne's tirade abated, possibly finished. Butterbean looked at the others. *Hadn't they figured it out?*

"You haven't figured it out?" Butterbean asked, rising to her full height of twenty-two inches counting ears. She stretched first fore then aft, extending each hind leg as if she were at full gallop. She enjoyed creating suspense, making the others wait.

"What's to figure?" Gwen asked. "We know humans are undecipherable. They don't make sense and aren't likely to change."

Art and Daphne agreed with Gwen. Lady snored. At times, human behavior made a sensible dog itch worse than fleas.

Resisting an urge to pontificate, Butterbean said, "Think five-and-ten."

Gwen and Art looked blank, but Daphne answered in an instant. "They were on a mission, to prove what this time?"

"Remember the online chemistry, the book in the back of the car, the trash-picking?" Butterbean hinted.

"Holy Flea Treatment," Daphne exclaimed, "it *was* a meth lab!"

"Those tights smelled delicious," Gwen said sadly, "and now the source is gone for good."

"No, Gwen." Daphne stole the floor from Butterbean. "The source of those cool cellar smells is still there under the water."

"Lady told me they made the wrong thing," Butterbean said, regaining the spotlight, "but it didn't matter because the place was flammable in either case. That was the mission. If it *was* a meth lab, Hazel and Grace aimed to shut it down somehow, 'cause if it did blow up, it could hurt us or this house." Butterbean licked her chops. "You missed the best part this morning. Bruce was apoplectic. Then Hazel got angry."

"That's true," Art said. "I'd never heard such language. I had to go under the bed again."

"What a wuss," Gwen remarked, prancing up the steps to listen by the doggie door. "I think they're at it again."

Though Bruce and Hazel stopped yelling an hour ago, the air still crackled. Earlier, Marigold had dropped Daphne off for the afternoon and left, aghast at the disaster next door. Fortunately, she hadn't time to talk about it. Impatient Fleming wanted to check out rental storefronts. He wanted to open his own gallery.

Another half hour of arguing brought Bruce and Hazel no resolution. In the aftermath of the melee last night, Hazel had invited Grace to come over for lunch, and she now arrived with a loaf of fresh, homemade pumpernickel bread, a welcome diversion.

"Okay, Hazel," Bruce said, making a sandwich, "mustard or mayonnaise?"

"You *know* I like mustard with ham," Hazel snorted, her head in the refrigerator as she located the ham and iced tea.

"I apologize for our fracas earlier," Bruce said, slathering everyone's bread with mustard, "but I'm angry, still angry. Stop smiling, Hazel. I can't yell when you're smiling like a Cheshire cat!"

Hazel brought ham, tea, and pickles out of the refrigerator, looking at Grace and then at Bruce, smiling more. "We're sorry too. If we had any skill at this, you wouldn't have found out. The lightning would have set their house on fire, and we'd have been here, dressed and cheery, with you none the wiser."

Plunking the pickle jar on the table, Hazel quit smiling. In a much sterner vein, she continued, "I didn't know Mother Nature was going to throw a fit last night. I *did* know my home and hearth might be in danger and, if you haven't noticed, that includes you, buster. *And*," Hazel took off her apron, "the damn Lewis people ought to be grateful too. If they weren't out last night to pick up a free TV, as it said in the morning paper, the lightning would have struck and they'd be crispy instead of talking to their insurance adjuster right now."

"Is that who's over there?" Grace asked. "When I left last night, Horace and Mark were talking with the arson squad and the fire marshall. They were too involved to notice me. Did I miss anything?"

"This guy's an Allstate insurance adjuster," Bruce replied. "He's been taking photos, measuring, making entries in his laptop, and no, you didn't miss a thing, Grace. Naturally we didn't go over," he smirked and winced as he opened the pickle jar, "but we watched from the upstairs bedroom. Horace threw a few aggressive gestures toward our house, but the fire marshall's reply seemed to calm him down. That was well after midnight. Horace and Mark left a few minutes later, probably to stay with one of the brothers, who knows? Hazel and I were worn out, and once we were certain Horace and Mark had gone, we went to bed, letting the fire marshall and his colleagues poke around in the debris without our second-story supervision." Bruce swallowed a bite of his sandwich. "The *result* doesn't make me less angry with you two. It's the *danger* you were in." Bruce's eyes narrowed.

Before Hazel could comment, Grace intervened. "If the storm hadn't happened, Bruce, we'd right now be showing you photos of an operating meth lab. How *would* that be?"

Hazel looked up from her sandwich to see Bruce's jaw working, and asked, "Hmmm? Answer that, please. What *would* you do with that evidence?"

"Which I intend to download this afternoon," Grace chimed in.

Bruce considered the question while the women ate. What would he do if there were no fire, but plenty of meth lab photos? Charge next door with pistol or baseball bat? Any thought of an explosion in the middle of the night or when Hazel or the dogs were alone made him berserk, and he loved Hazel's house way more than his condo.

But the law's a ticklish matter, Bruce thought. The lab may be illegal, but so is trespassing, especially the kind of trespassing necessary to get the pictures. And of course, any macho move on his part would send *him* to the clink, not Horace or Mark. Worse, since the fire *did* happen, those photos suggested responsibility for the fire rested with the women, not the lightning. Not to mention the impact on his defense. Who wouldn't think this was revenge?

"Well?" Hazel said, breaking into Bruce's considering.

"Dammit!" he yelled, slamming his fist on the table, "I don't know!" The mugs and plates jumped, and the chips fell out of their dish.

Outside, Gwen jumped back from the doggie door, hitting Butterbean in the face, and Art ran under the porch. Daphne stepped back and shuddered. She didn't like loud noises or yelling. Lady woke up as if she heard a gunshot.

"I'm sorry," Bruce said sheepishly, rubbing his hand. "I was thinking about legalities. We'll be in serious trouble if your presence in that basement comes to light. Would people be satisfied the lightning caused the fire if they knew you two were in the basement? And what's to keep them from thinking I sent you to do it?"

"Whoa," Grace said, "are you suggesting we, in any way, had something to do with that fire?" Her anger, not yet noticeable, was rising too.

Two noses poked in the doggie door. Hazel took the empty plates to the sink. *Maybe we all need some schnapps,* she thought.

"Grace," Bruce said, "not for a second do I believe you two did any more than you told me. The fire marshall will corroborate the lightning strike on the water heater, and your photos will show what you found. *However*, the timing is tight, and if I were opposing counsel, I'd make a big deal out of the tools I found in a waist pack by the bed last night." The corners of his mouth crept upward, became a grin, and then a gulping belly laugh.

"Is he nuts?" Grace asked Hazel.

Sputtering, Bruce tried to explain. "I got an image of you two with pliers and a screwdriver bringing down an entire building," Bruce gasped, almost rolling out of his chair. Tears streamed down his cheeks, and he got redder and laughed louder.

"It's the stress," Hazel said, gathering up the mugs and utensils. "You know how it is, like a pressure cooker." Reliving some of the moments of last night, Hazel smiled, then grinned and laughed too.

Grace grasped Bruce's point of view: Mr. Machismo watching two middle-aged women make their way into a dark, dank cellar and demolish it with a nail file and a hairpin. Her anger dissipated, and she joined in the hysteria.

The doggie door flapped shut and five canines on the porch stared at one another, barkless. *Humans were hopeless, just listen to them.*

23

Will the Circle Be Unbroken?

The same Saturday morning that Hazel revealed her meth lab investigation, Gus's Florida trip took a negative turn in the first hour. She left as she planned on Saturday morning and would arrive around noon the next day. Practical matters were under control for the moment, so the intention of this trip was to "just be" with her parents, perhaps for the last time as a whole family.

In Pine Crossing, between the August trip and this one, Gus had reserved an efficiency apartment at The Homestead assisted living facility, making her father's arrival date flexible. While preparing to leave, for no particular reason, Gus packed these papers along with extra clothing and her CD player.

The evening before Gus's departure, her Mom, sounding like Tallulah Bankhead on the phone, assured Gus that she was okay, just tired, and the receiver was getting heavy. They ended their conversation as they did every day.

"I love you," one would say.

"I love you too," the other would reply.

At ten thirty-seven Saturday morning, Gus was chewing up the highway, way over the speed limit, when her cell phone rang. She knew who was calling, and she knew the message. She didn't want to hear it. If she didn't know, it couldn't have happened. She would stay in pause mode, suspended in the space before manifestation. Sounds like purgatory, Gus thought after a minute, and liking that less, she answered the phone.

"Gus? This is Virginia." *Yeah, the home health care owner,* Gus thought obtusely. *Damn! Damn!*

"Mom's dead, isn't she?" Gus said.

"Yes, Gus, I'm sorry. Are you driving? Pull over if you can."

"I am, and I can't," Gus replied, bursting into tears, "so just talk to me. When? What happened?"

"She died at ten twenty this morning. Your dad is upset but okay. When will you be here?"

That was seventeen minutes ago, Gus thought. *Where was I then, Swan Lake, Huntsville?* She said to Virginia, "Noon tomorrow at the latest. I'd drive through if Mom was alive, but if Dad's okay, there's no need now. Please ask Dahlia to come tomorrow."

"She'll be there Monday," Virginia reminded gently, "the weekend crew's on now."

"Shoot, that's right. Still, I'll need help with Dad and breaking up the house, however long that takes. If Dahlia would come days, I can handle Dad at night." Gus blew her nose, steering with her elbows. "I talked to Mom last evening. She knew I would be there around noon tomorrow, we had agreed. Maybe she didn't want me to see her sick, but I so wanted to see her." Gus saw a wide spot on the shoulder and pulled over. They discussed Dahlia, hospice, and her mother's body. Finished, Gus closed the phone and wept in earnest.

It was a one-car funeral procession. In the family Buick, Gus drove her father, Dahlia, and Virginia behind the lead car and the hearse. Humming "Will the Circle Be Unbroken," Gus listened to her father remark about the familiar streets while Dahlia and Virginia murmured in the back seat.

The instructions from Fletcher and Crisp Funeral Home were simple: Arrive at the funeral home on Tuesday morning by ten if you wanted a viewing, later if you didn't. The hearse would leave for the cemetery promptly at eleven, the burial would take place upon arrival, and then, well, then it was over. The bronze marker would be ready in several months. *How complicated could that be?*

Dahlia arrived Tuesday morning at her usual seven o'clock, served breakfast, and helped Gus deal with her father's one dress suit, now twenty years old. His blue plaid jacket fit well, but the gray trousers were too small and unsuitable for his pot belly. After thoroughly searching a house full of sixty-five years of married life, containing everything from an alabaster statue to a xylophone, Dahlia and Gus couldn't locate one safety pin.

Gus's outfit caused less trouble. Intuitively, she supposed, she had packed dress black slacks, but no decent shoes. Even Florida heat wouldn't excuse ratty sandals or flip-flops at a funeral.

Dahlia was resplendent in her beaded cornrows, royal blue dress, and black, strappy shoes.

They left early, purchasing dressy sandals for Gus and safety pins for Robert on the way to the funeral home. Exiting Eckerd's Drugstore with the safety pins, Gus found Dahlia and her father waiting by the car, watching the horrific traffic. Suddenly his trousers dropped—slapstick comedy on the busiest corner in Fort Lauderdale.

He grinned and chuckled. He bent to pull up his pants and butted heads with Dahlia, also grabbing for them. Gus struggled to pin the waistband comfortably, her father swaying as she tugged, and they laughed and cried at once.

Robert's trousers under control, and everyone now giggling, they climbed into the car. Virginia would meet them at the funeral parlor.

From the back of the viewing room, Gus saw her mother's open casket placed before an army of tan folding chairs, which made her wonder how many million tan folding chairs were in this world. Gus noted that the wallpaper, a comforting green, had the same swirling pattern as the upholstery in her favorite Chinese restaurant.

Looking closely at the casket, though unable to see her mother in it, Gus felt a deep gratitude to her Mom for preplanning her funeral. The casket was baby blue with silver handles, something Gus would have liked for herself, had she wanted a burial. But if she had tried to emulate her mother's taste instead of her own, Gus realized she would have chosen a pink casket with gold handles—clearly *not* what her mother wanted.

Picking the clothes Mom would wear for all eternity had been trying enough. A skirt for dignity, or slacks for comfort? Pink? Blue? Purple? Or

Green? Each had been a beloved of her mother's, and Gus had no idea which color garnered her most recent favor. She compromised by choosing a long-sleeved print blouse with all the colors and dressy white slacks. Her father picked out white strappy shoes, and Gus included her Mom's purse with all its important contents. Should she look in the casket now and make sure all was well? She didn't want to. No one Gus had ever seen in a casket had been improved by the embalmiing process, and she wanted to remember her mother out and about in the spring, before cancer.

Robert, holding the opposite view, insisted on seeing the love of his life for sixty-nine years, his wife for sixty-five of those years. Even in her casket, he wanted to see her. So he went into the room and stood by her, touching her hand. After watching him awhile, Gus couldn't stand the loneliness she felt for him, so singular in the empty room. She went where she didn't want to go and put her arm around him. He reciprocated, and they stood there, much as they had stood by Audrey on the gurney in the pre-op prior to her surgery. There in the hospital, they had chattered love and hope. Now quieter, they only could offer love and sorrow.

Her mother looked okay in the clothes Gus had chosen, but her hair wasn't right. At least her purse was there, Gus noted. Outside the house, her mother always carried a purse. Gus leaned in and kissed her Mom, leaving lipstick on her forehead as her mother had done to Gus for most of her childhood. She cried, hating every part of this situation, even the wallpaper.

Then it was time to go. Gus took her father's hand as they walked back to Virginia and Dahlia.

As Florida cemeteries go, this one was beautiful. Long-needled pines purred in the wind, and jacarandas provided color as did other flowering trees and bushes. Sounds and the smell of the sea, three blocks away, permeated the air, and the plot Gus's folks had chosen faced east under the largest pine. Here, they could greet the sunrise, and here the funeral procession stopped. Audrey in her casket was rolled to the open grave under a royal blue tent. Neither Audrey nor Robert wanted a service, so the funeral director, hearse driver, and the four mourners watched while the cemetery workers lowered the casket. Then the two drivers solemnly shook hands with the mourners and left.

Robert, Gus, Dahlia, and Virginia each threw in some dirt. When the grave was closed, Gus and Robert laid a bouquet of pink roses on the earth, and the four of them held hands. They stood by the grave and sang every hymn that came to their minds, "Amazing Grace" and "How Great Thou Art" among them.

At the last, Gus suggested "Just a Closer Walk with Thee." Everyone knew the first verse, but Virginia and Robert dropped out as the song went on, leaving Gus and Dahlia to their unique duet on the last verse: "When my feeble life is o'er, Time for me will be no more. Guide me safely, gently o'er, To Thy Kingdom's shore, to Thy Shore."

Back at the mobile home, dazed, sad, relieved, and wounded in their hearts, Gus and her father faced an enormous change in their daily lives. Paradoxically, their attempts to deal with Audrey's absence made her all the more present.

Gus's list mushroomed to two pages a day. She sent the deposit for her father's new place at The Homestead, "toot sweet" as Germy George would say. The only available space was large enough for two—if they liked each other, as there was no fightin' room—and priced accordingly. Gus took it. Robert could afford it and he wouldn't feel cramped.

Along with that, she collected his medical records from seven specialists, scheduled a last visit to his dentist, his hearing aid specialist, and to his primary care physician for a physical and the TB test required by The Homestead.

When she wasn't driving around with her father, Gus had plenty to do at the mobile home. She chose what furniture her father would need at The Homestead, what family things she wanted, and what things she knew friends needed. The rest she had to sell or give away, including the mobile home and the car. Paying lot rent on a vacant mobile home made her gag. Park management provided no service, made rules like rabbits reproduced, and raised the rent annually. Gus loathed Arrowhead's oligarchy.

Dahlia channeled most of the household items to needy communities through her neighbors and her church. Her church lady-friends took most of Audrey's dresses, blouses, and skirts. Audrey's purses, each with mirror, comb, and emery board, also had at least one pair of matching shoes. Gus adored the thought of many women wearing her mother's clothing in church together.

Neighbors in the mobile home park bought furniture and electronics, and Gus all but gave the car to the next door neighbor, who had been a good friend. One young immigrant couple, while taking apart a twin bed, discovered a wad of hundred dollar bills her father had stashed and forgotten there. Awash in embarrassment, Gus didn't know if it was appropriate to reward the couple, and if so, how much? When she decided to give them the bed, their faces lit up like kids having a birthday.

Friends came for square dance clothes and shared with Gus the fun of dance competitions they had with Robert and Audrey. Bowling balls, board games, and yard tools also triggered memories. Her mother had mentioned only a few of these friends, but Gus behaved as if she knew about all of them. She nodded so often, she imagined herself a bobblehead.

Amid this bustle, Gus reserved a U-Haul truck, deposited the family assets in her bank in Pine Crossing, and, with Dahlia's help, packed the household goods, labeling everything, "Gus," "Dad," or "Storage."

Audrey, ever vigilant against burglars, had continually warned Gus, "If anything happens to me, you go through everything, even soap-powder boxes before throwing them out. I've hidden cash and jewelry everywhere." In earlier years, that statement yielded giggles and jokes about the hiding places. When her mother said it the last time before her surgery, it was no joke—it was an order.

Gus followed that order to the letter. She found a false-bottomed tissue box holding a dozen silver dollars, rolls of bills inside toilet paper, jewelry in bras and empty shampoo bottles, hundred dollar bills under old cancelled checks. Her mother hadn't fibbed about soap-powder boxes either. Inside an Ivory flakes box rested a rolled up, rubber-banded plastic bag containing a pair of gold earrings that reminded Gus of Hazel.

The coup de grâce came when Gus cleaned out the walk-in closet in the guest room. Filled with luggage, winter clothes, extra blankets, fans, and heaters, that closet was the catch-all for seldom-used but necessary items. Gus had half-filled two suitcases on the bed with jackets and blankets, and cardboard boxes on the floor with small appliances, when she maneuvered the last two boxes from under the hanging clothes.

The first one, labeled "Cards," sagged in the middle as she brought it out. The next one, smaller but heavy, had a label, too. Raising it to the light, Gus read, "Orringer Crematorium, Edward L. Roberts cremated March 14, 1984." She shrieked and dropped it like the proverbial hot potato. Feeling foolish, she looked at it on the floor. If a box could be sad, this one was, stained from age and Florida damp. Probably her parents hadn't considered it since they put it there in1984.

Poor Uncle Ed, Gus thought. He was Dad's alcoholic brother and Audrey's perfect negative example of everything. She smiled and picked up the box of Ed, packing him with the cards, sweaters, belts, and miscellany to be sorted in Pine Crossing.

"You're out of the closet now, Uncle Edward," Gus said softly, laughing for the first time that day.

Irene called Gus the day after Uncle Edward's appearance. Her son was between jobs and visiting her for a month. They could drive down to help Gus move. Philip could load the U-Haul and drive it. Irene and Gus would drive the cars, and Robert could ride with whomever whenever. Gus wept tears of gratitude. She was over her last hurdle.

Twenty-three days, fourteen hours, and thirty-seven minutes after Gus last left Pine Crossing, she was back. First stop was Hazel's, where the hostess graciously supplied all hands with sandwiches. There were grinders for Gus and Grace (the New Englanders), hoagies for Hazel and Bruce (the New Jersey-ites), and submarines for Irene and Philip (native North Carolinians). Nobody remembered they were also called "torpedoes," and Robert only cared about eating at least two.

When the meal was finished, Bruce called two friends to meet everyone at The Homestead to unload Robert's furniture and boxes. Next stops were Gus's house and the storage unit.

By dinner time, Robert was safe in the hands of the certified nursing assistants at The Homestead, his bed, bureau, and clothes in place. The TV worked, and his recliner easily fit across from the bed. Gus made sure he would be taken to the dining room, kissed him goodbye, and promised to see him the next day. Now Gus understood how her mother felt the first day Gus went to kindergarten. In response, Gus focused on the tasks ahead and bolted to the car.

Soon Gus's living room held a stack of boxes, five feet high, ten feet long, and six feet wide in its center. Because the boxes labeled "storage" weighed little, she, Irene, and Marigold could unload them. Gus gave Bruce money for a couple of rounds and dinner platters for the guys, and watched as they stampeded to their vehicles in a race to catch the football game at the local pub. Their grins and waves were the thanks Gus needed.

The women unloaded the last boxes into the storage unit as dusk settled. Philip volunteered to drop off the truck and join the men at the pub, after first leaving the women at Gus's.

No sooner had the women seen Philip off and sat down to some tea, than Grace appeared with Butterbean and pizza. Hazel trailed behind with a huge salad and the rest of the dogs.

Everyone ate and talked, and Butterbean staked her claim to Gus by sitting on her left foot and snarl/smiling a warning at any intrusive canine. Shortly, Marigold left to meet Fleming at a gallery reception, and after much clucking and hugging, Grace and Hazel left, aware that Gus and Irene needed showers and an early bedtime. They made plans for a group walk tomorrow evening with the dogs.

Gus's covers were cool and exactly the right weight. The swish of the overhead fan and the Brahms Lullaby on the radio led Gus's thoughts, like the Pied Piper, through a watery past that transformed, as half-dreams do, into beguiling possibilities, clouds and wind and azure blue. She stretched and rearranged her body, her mind basking in a soothing place of gratitude and hope. Being in this place forever would be good, but Gus had moved too much—she woke Butterbean.

Butterbean heard the sheets rustle and woke with breakfast on her mind. She nudged the bed with her paws and nose, standing straight against Gus's extra-high bed.

She nuzzled Gus's hand as it reached out over the edge of the bed, heard Gus mumble something like: "Go back to sleep, Butterbean. Just a few more minutes."

Resigned, Butterbean dropped down to the floor, eye level with the plastic containers under the bed. There, she supposed, was every photograph taken by Gus or a family member since 1859. And every letter they had written too. In Butterbean's opinion, this was a terrible waste of a cool and spacious den.

Butterbean turned three times in her bed and finally dozed off again, but hunger overcame her fatigue. Apparently deciding those few minutes had passed, she took a more vigorous approach. She barked, waited, barked some more.

"Oh all *right!*" Gus grumbled. Her stomach and bladder now playing a cacophonous duet of hunger and urgency.

After tending to breakfast and bathroom needs, Gus gave Butterbean a medium-sized Greenie, guaranteed to satisfy the most discriminating Corgi, and went back to bed.

The last days Gus spent with her mother before her death replayed in her consciousness as she drifted in and out of sleep. A hectic and sad time, it created an intimacy that Gus and Audrey rarely expressed. In Florida and on the phone, Gus had left her mother on a loving note, but . . . what if she'd known it was the last time, would she have broiled in the mobile home another hour? Maybe she could have rubbed her mother's feet more often or been more cheerful, less exhausted, or more talkative. Dozing again, Gus realized she had done all she could. She hadn't withheld anything. She simply hadn't one more drop to give. *I can't even get out of bed*, Gus thought, *I'm beyond exhausted.*

In the afternoon, more rested but more negative, Gus surveyed the disaster she called home. She hadn't been able to reach her friends, so she took advantage of her irritated energy, and unpacked the boxes in the living room, moaning and complaining.

Butterbean disliked the tension she felt while Gus muttered and tossed newspapers and bubble wrap around, so she rousted Grizzie out of bed to write. Neither the cat nor the Corgi had thought of a catchy title, but they had created a premise. It was time for the introduction.

"Want to get on the computer?" Butterbean whined low so Gus couldn't hear.

"Sure, do you have the salmon?" Grizzie stretched one leg at a time, made a Halloween cat back, and began washing a front paw.

"I thought we'd share what Gus gave me," Butterbean replied. "That's what we agreed. You're coauthor, remember?"

"It's taken us a month to get the premise," Grizzie countered. "At that rate, we'll be dead before we get to chapter twenty. I understand the difficulties of writing, Butterbean, but being coauthor when I'm dead doesn't cut it for me. I want pay-as-you-go salmon. You can be sole author and take the dead glory. Salmon while I'm alive is what I want."

"Just like a cat," Butterbean growled in Grizzie's face, "indecisive, flaky, and demanding! I shoulda known. When you're in you want out, when you're out, you want in—a red flag the size of a matador's cape!"

"So?" Grizzie asked, raising her gaze from her front paw. "Salmon or not?"

Butterbean flopped on the floor, her back to the cat, grunted, flattened her ears, and closed her eyes. She did some math, figuring this might be an okay turn of events. Now she wouldn't have to tell Gwen that Grizzie was coauthor. *And* she could get back to her original idea about training humans.

"Okay," Butterbean sat up and turned to stare at Grizzie. "You can have the salmon from one of my dinners for every five pages you type. We'll mark the pages as paid the day you get the salmon."

"Every other page or type it yourself," Grizzie shot back, turning to wash between her hind toes.

"Go litter-box yourself," Butterbean exclaimed. "Five pages." Butterbean felt a snit coming on. "We've done so little. I've only got your word you can write. Maybe you can't spell and won't learn grammar, for all I know." She flopped on her bed. She'd find another way if Grizzie got puffy, Butterbean decided.

"Okay, *okay*," Grizzie spit, her toilette complete, "how about three pages?"

Butterbean turned her back, sulking. "Five."

"Four's an even number and typing is hard on my claws. What if they broke? I'd be defenseless, and you'd feel guilty."

"Ha! Not hardly!" Butterbean snapped.

Grizzie wiped her ear with her front paw. "Your meal of salmon every four pages is a fair exchange, I think."

"Okay, okay," Butterbean slid out of bed and fixed Grizzie with her stare, "four typed pages for one meal of salmon, final deal. Any changes and I type it myself."

Butterbean trotted over to the computer. "Let's go. I'd love to get Gus's rant on paper. Listen, she's still carrying on."

In the living room, Gus wielded the box cutter, fuming out loud about the current state of affairs, "And so far, no movement from the DA's office, Hazel said. How long can this go on? 'Speedy' trial, big laugh! In 1937 my great-granddaddy shot and killed a man, was tried and acquitted all in eight weeks. What's happened?"

Gus wound down enough to put a load of dirty clothes in the washing machine. Then she spied the box of Uncle Edward's ashes and carefully opened it. Inside was a brand new gallon paint container with a similar label, "Ashes of Edward L. Roberts, cremated 14 March 1984." Gus thought of getting a paint can opener to see if his ashes were placed in a plastic bag like dog ashes. In the middle of that consideration, she recalled the two letters she had received from Uncle Ed, written after her 1972 visit to him and her grandmother Roberts in Colorado.

"First," she interrupted herself out loud, "where did I put his Bible and wallet that I found in Dad's drawer?"

After locating Edward's effects, Gus entered the bedroom in search of the two old letters, surprising Butterbean by the computer and Grizzie on the keyboard. Grizzie strolled onto the chair as if being on the keyboard was totally appropriate, and Butterbean bounced over, barking and hoping she appeared to chastise the cat.

Were Gus more alert, she might have remembered a similar occurrence a few days after her trespassing conviction, or noticed the computer was turned on.

24

A Date! A Very Important Date!

"We've got a date!" Hazel shouted as the Poms and Lady dragged her down the sidewalk toward the café tables at Port City Java. Halloween decorations were up, and the humidity was down, at least today. Butterbean and Daphne, at a table with Gus, Grace, and Marigold, strained at their leashes, each one wrapped around her human's foot.

"What date?" Marigold asked, untangling Daphne's leash from Art's. Grace took Lady from Hazel and led her into the shade while Gus grappled with the macramé Butterbean and Gwen had made of their leads.

The canines settled, a moment passed, and Marigold answered her own question, "Oh, Hazel, *that* date! Yippee! When is it?"

"When Grace and Gus bring the coffee, I'll tell all. I never thought I'd be excited about a *court* date, at least I think I am. I'm scared too." Hazel sat down, Art and Gwen now at her feet.

"An end in sight is some relief, isn't it?" Marigold asked. "The damn trial is inevitable, so if John's ready, why wait? Your lives have been on hold for months now."

"That's for sure! We couldn't help Gus. We can't plan a vacation. Bruce is unemployable, even part-time at Lowe's, which was his intention after adjusting to retirement, and half of the Historical Society snubs him."

"Okay, gang, here's four super choc-lattes with whipped cream and cinnamon," Grace announced, placing the cardboard tray on the table.

"Followed by the last of the bagels and cream cheese," Gus said, setting out a plate of bagels, a pot of cream cheese, knives, and napkins.

"So tell them," Marigold said to Hazel as she spread a hint of cream cheese on a bagel half.

"We've got a trial date, the second Monday in December!" Hazel's eyes sparkled. "I don't know what I'm so damn happy about. No one controls a jury, and in this town, it could come out all wrong." Hazel's glee ebbed. "Besides, Greg's kids are being bullied—'Grandpa the Perv.' No matter how Greg explains Bruce's situation, the boys blame their predicament on Grandpa. For the moment, the boys are out of school, but now parents are getting in the act, and someone egged Greg's house."

In the thick silence of listening friends, Hazel wiped the perspiration from her forehead and neck, "It seems a classmate visited his aunt in Pine Crossing and saw the paper. Who'd think this would get all the way to Virginia?" She patted her eyes and stuck the soaked tissue in her pocket.

"How is Bruce handling the bullying?" Grace asked.

"Better than I thought. He's calling his brothers as we speak," Hazel slathered half a bagel with cream cheese.

"Don't even *think* a negative outcome," Gus commanded. "The trial will come out fine and the whole episode will be *over!*" She took a huge bite of her bagel, squishing a blob of cream cheese out the side. Grace swiped it with her napkin before it fell on Gus's knee, disappointing a hopeful Corgi.

Hazel sighed, some optimism returning, "We'll have almost six weeks to respond to the Bill of Particulars, which John has been assured will appear momentarily. Trials are formatted to take a week, and the court sticks to schedule pretty much. Of course, there's always the unexpected loss of a juror, violation of some rule, or death. These days, I suppose deranged shooters join the list of disruptions, in spite of the annoying security. Remind me not to take a purse. I don't want Officer Skinny looking in it."

Anybody experienced a trial?" Marigold asked.

"No, unless you count our misdemeanor appearance," Gus replied, "but that was just the judge. Wonder what a jury might have decided?"

"Objection! Irrelevant," Grace responded, grinning.

Ignoring Grace, Gus began, "If court's like it is on TV, well, I don't have to explain that, do I?"

"You mean opening arguments, witnesses, experts, cross-examinations, and a twist at the end with a surprise witness, new evidence, or a court-room confession?" Marigold's naiveté showed like a twentieth-century woman's slip might peek from under her dress.

"Yeah," Hazel said, swallowing a bit of bagel. "Except for the last-minute drama, Bruce says it's pretty much that way. Summations, or closing arguments, are given Friday morning, and the jury has Friday afternoon through the weekend for deliberation, if needed." Hazel ripped her bagel in quarters, cream cheese squirting everywhere. Gwen jumped up and down, almost in Hazel's lap in her effort to nab a glob of her favorite treat. Art gave a sharp bark, and Hazel came to her senses, feeding small bits of bagel and cream cheese to both Poms.

"The damned rules," Hazel continued, "like the 'objection' and 'overruled' business scares me. Half the time the 'overruled' question seems valid to me. Not to mention the sidebars and machinations in chambers. Sometimes the jury can't be told important stuff, and other times, if an attorney is clever, the jury hears things the judge then orders them to un-hear, as if that's possible!"

"Relax, Haze," Grace said, "we can't do anything today, so let's appreciate this." She waved her bagel to indicate the weather, the place, and the company. Gwen lucked out when part of Grace's bagel slipped to the ground.

"We'll be able to catch our breath between the trial and Christmas, too. It could be worse," Gus said, snatching the fallen bagel and passing pieces to Butterbean and Daphne.

Grace wiped her mouth and asked, "What's in the Bill of Particulars?"

Gus handed another napkin to Hazel, who wiped each of her fingers with great care as she answered, "Thirty-seven counts."

A beat passed. "Can you imagine?" Hazel whispered, her voice cracking. "They manufactured *thirty-seven counts!*" When a couple of tears escaped, she covered her face with a napkin.

Regaining her composure, Hazel went on, "Each supposed encounter, say, a reciprocal blow job, is two counts against Bruce, none against Mark. For three of those encounters, Mark made up dates and places. The rest are vague and should go away if John's motions are accepted. But those three are the kickers."

"What happened to 'innocent until proven guilty' or 'every citizen is entitled to a speedy trial'? Civics class was a waste apparently," Marigold fumed with palpable disillusionment. "This is wicked depressing!"

"How come everything is weighed so heavily in favor of the 'Persecution'?" Gus inquired, a wry smile denting her cheeks. "I think we're dinosaurs when it comes to our judicial system, or maybe just naïve.

"This mess isn't what we were taught, and not what we see on *Law and Order.* There, hordes of people work to prove the defendant's innocence." Hazel thought a minute. "Isn't trying to show you *didn't* do something proving a negative?"

"A logical impossibility!" Grace exclaimed and, suddenly aware of passing pedestrians, said no more. Subdued, she glanced at the others.

"What?" Hazel asked, looking around.

"Passersby," Gus explained in a low murmur. "We were getting some weird looks.

"I've gotta say just one more thing," Grace said gathering the debris the wind threatened to blow into the street. "First and foremost, cops and DAs have to appear tough on crime, and politicians need crowded jails to prove their commitment to public safety. There! End of soapbox!"

Hazel stood up. "And no one knows better than we three how the media keeps the whole pot boiling. Let's go back to my place. There's more privacy there."

"I can't" Marigold said, regret clouding her face. "I'm supposed to meet Fleming in forty-five minutes. Damn! I'm sorry, I've got to run!"

While the women were hugging and saying good-bye to Marigold, Butterbean stood by Daphne. "They still haven't told Gus or Mari about the lightning on the party night, have they?" Daphne asked.

"Nope," Butterbean replied, "maybe that's coming."

"Tell me if they say anything new."

"Okay. Daphne, how are things with Fleming? I'm guessing you haven't orchestrated your accident yet."

As she left, Daphne woofed. "Soon, Butterbean, soon."

On the way to Hazel's house, Gus screeched the car to a halt alongside the entrance to Cedar Grove cemetery. "Sorry, Haze, but I'm not comfy next door to Mark, and I don't want to be indoors on such a gorgeous day anyway. Let's find a place in here to finish talking."

The women and dogs tumbled out of the car, Grace taking the two frenetic Poms. A few yards down the path into the cemetery, she pointed to the left, saying, "There's a pleasant spot."

Releasing Art and Gwen, Grace strode off to where a raised, flat tombstone lay in state, surrounded by numerous phallic ones. Shade from live oaks garbed in faux Spanish moss dappled the area. Gus and Grace sat on the flat tomb and the dogs frolicked, keeping the women in sight.

Gus could wait no longer. "Whatever happened at the Lewis' house?

Hazel, seated on the grass, her back against the close marble phallus, readjusted her legs and said, "Well, they aren't staying there right now."

"I'd guessed that," Gus snapped. "The place is only fit for bugs and turtles."

"I'm sorry," Hazel replied. "We didn't tell you . . ."

"We didn't want to upset you," Grace interjected, touching Gus's arm. "You've had enough on your plate lately."

"And what I want to say about the trial is more important right now than the Lewis' stupid house," Hazel said, heading for a full pout.

"Geeze Louise, okay," Gus said in exasperation, "have it your way, but we *will* get back to this."

Thoughtfully, Hazel began. "It's the media, their adjectives, the way they say the word 'alleged' in a tone that suggests 'sure pal, alleged my ass, wink wink.' I'm so upset with all of them, radio, TV, newspapers, I could explode!"

Gus left the tombstone to stretch out on the ground and look up through the oak-leaf canopy. "I feel the same way, Haze, but I'm not sure if we can short-circuit them."

"Maybe we could get a reporter to address other issues like the right to a speedy trial and homophobia," Grace suggested. "Perhaps getting folks worked up about those things would be a divisive diversion. Like that alliteration?" She smiled.

"Perhaps," Hazel got up, inspired. "A countersuit!" she exclaimed. "Bruce *could* sue Mark and Horace for slander, libel, and false arrest."

"Right," Grace replied, unconvinced. She traced a few letters on the tombstone with her index finger.

"Maybe yes, maybe no to the countersuit, but Bruce could take the offensive," Gus said. Both women turned in her direction.

"I'm thinking this through as I speak." Gus leaned on an elbow. "Take the blow-job issue. If you were that up close and personal, you'd know what his penis was like, right? Size, shape, any moles or marks, hair amount and color, maybe even something about his testicles would be memorable." Gus sat up, a wicked glint in her eye. "*You'd* know, Haze, if Mark's description was correct."

Hazel made an unimpressive scowl. The corners of her mouth wouldn't stay down.

Gus continued, "Not joking—what about a penis lineup?"

"What an imagination," Grace said, grinning like a tooth-whitening advertisement. "Where would we get the extra penises?"

Caught by the idea, Hazel replied, "College students. They'll do anything for a buck. I like it, Gus, don't know what Bruce or John will make of it, but I *like* that idea."

"Anything else, Ms. Brilliant?" Grace asked.

Gus stood and stretched. "Not so fast, you two. No more subject changes, no leaving until you tell me about the Lewis house. What *did* you two do over there? It looks like Urban Renewal attacked the place."

"When did you see that? You came by and didn't stop?" Hazel asked, incredulous.

"More to the point, what makes you think we had anything to do with that mess?" Grace challenged. Her mouth was firm, but she had a twinkle in her eyes.

Gus leaned back against another stone phallus. "It may have been page eight, but it was in the paper and you two were in town. I'm no judge, but that's evidence enough for me." Gus smiled. "Tell me."

"Hazel hatched this crackpot idea, and I spent forever cajoling, coercing, and threatening her in hope that she'd get sensible and ditch the notion," Grace interjected, now tracing "Eldora Fitch" on the tombstone with her fingers.

"You were a pain in the ass," Hazel rebutted, "but I noticed you were there too."

"Gus, she made me do it. Somebody had to watch her. If I wasn't there, her body would've ended up in the rubble, too." Seeing Hazel about to object, Grace pointed and chuckled, "You *froze*, dingbat!"

Hazel made a shushing motion, "Jehoshaphat, Grace, leave it. This is one of those tail-eating arguments, like 'he-said, she-said.' Gus, here's the *real* scoop. Bruce and I decided to go ahead with our third annual party in spite of this Nasty Business. We were sick of analyzing our choices and strategies, of dealing with our doubts and anxieties. Everyone means well, but all the concern, the suggestions, and the soothing encouragement bored us out of our skulls. *You* know," Hazel gestured toward Gus, "the same as with your mom's death, everything is meant with good intentions, but so useless. You end up comforting those meant to comfort you! On top of that, we've gotten hate blasts from the most surprising people. So we thought we'd use the party to sort out our true friends and put the others on notice that we were living well and happily."

"*Annnndd* it was a conveniently moonless night, *annndd* Mark and Horace were conveniently out," Grace hooted. "The night-vision goggles, black cargo pants, and camera materialized by accident too, I suppose."

"Oh crap, Grace. Gus knows how you feel," Hazel said, then looked directly at Gus. "It was dark, and the party was going well. So *if* we were up to something, theoretically, here's how it might go. We would change upstairs, creep out the back way, go outside and down into their bulkhead, finding—GASP—a dreadful place full of mold, mildew, cobwebs. We would find and photograph the incriminating evidence," Hazel stood up and waved her arms across the sky, "but nature would intervene. We would then hear the hail going thunk on the bulkhead steps, maybe notice the water heater leaking. I might find faux meth in the refrigerator, but we would haul ass out of there way before the lightning strike. That's if we went there in the first place, which we didn't. Too bad no one noticed the fire before it got out of hand."

Gus broke into laughter. "Only my friends wouldn't do this," she gasped, holding her stomach. "I'm truly sorry I missed that."

"I'll show you the photos I didn't download to my computer," Grace giggled.

"We aren't being funny, Gus, we're being careful," Hazel admonished. "In the wrong hands, this information and those photos could send us way past trespassing and well into the land of felony. Bruce hopes he can use them, but so far, they'd cause more trouble and little gain. The good news is that the fire marshall officially proclaimed the lightning as the culprit. Horace's insurance should pay without hesitation, and there's no reason to look at us."

Having run until they could only pant and gasp, the canines lay in the shade of various headstones, keeping their humans within sight and earshot. Art ranted about the environment and Bruce's legal issues today, instead of his usual petitioning to chain up Pit Bulls from birth. Gwen rooted piglet-style after a smelly underground bug, and Lady dozed.

Watching the humans, Butterbean observed, "Looks like a big conversation. Lots of arm-waving and changing places. We'll be here a while, I bet."

Lady let out a big snore that flapped her jowls. Her feet twitched.

"She's chasing that cat again," Art said.

Butterbean shook. "Our humans are sitting on volcanic situations."

"Tell me more while I get this bug."

"There's the usual. Your folks have the trial and Gus lost Audrey.

Yesterday, Gus went on a goose chase after an imaginary cousin, I think, but," Butterbean lowered her voice to a soft growl, "there's more."

Bug legs in her chops, Gwen sat in front of Butterbean and blinked her eyes with pleasure. "What a tasty bug, never had that kind before. What's more?"

"Grizzie and I were seen on Gus's computer for the second time."

Gwen's ears pricked. "How'd that happen? Were you scared?"

Butterbean sat up. "It happened because that cat and I finally agreed on four pages per meal of salmon. So we got to work on the book, and Gus appeared like a genie. I wasn't scared, but we barely wrote down the title."

"Which is?" Gwen asked, tilting her head.

"*Human Management—Not for the Faint of Heart.* Jazzy, eh?"

"Totally cool," Gwen said, examining her dirty nails. "Are you going to reveal the truth about humans or stick to the usual concepts?"

"The truth and the whole truth," Butterbean answered. I have a secret and you can't tell Art. Swear!"

"On a bag of Greenies, I swear. I swear, I won't tell Art."

Butterbean whispered in Gwen's ear, "Fleming is about to have a serious accident."

25

The Assisted Living Motel

Painted yellow, Robert's new suite at The Homestead had double windows opposite the entrance, two mammoth closets, and a tiny kitchen area. Audrey would have loved the bathroom with walk-in shower, high-rise commode, and movie-star lighting.

Perhaps because he was well-traveled and perhaps because the heat/air conditioning unit in the wall below the windows resembled those found in motels, Robert decided he was just passing through. For the first four days, he packed after breakfast and waited amid a cluster of suitcases for Gus to pick him up. The staff unpacked his things each day before lunch, explaining this was now his home.

On the fifth day, Gus confiscated his luggage while he was at breakfast. She then remembered his love of solitaire. She set up his card table with a chair and half a dozen decks of cards. After that, her father settled in.

A few days before Halloween, Gus and Hazel went shopping. Gus bought a decorative welcome sign for her father's door, and wire and hooks for hanging his family photos on the blank wall opposite his bed. Gus called it his "Rogues Gallery."

Marigold met them in the parking lot, and the three trooped in with a pile of packages. Gus had Butterbean on her leash. In his room, Robert was watching golf on TV, so Hazel and Gus sorted the pictures, and Marigold commandeered the bathroom to change into a new dress she'd just bought.

Butterbean jumped in the chair, beside Robert. Unfazed or perhaps enjoying the bustle of activity, Robert watched the women and the golf, occasionally dozing like Lady in the afternoon sunshine.

"Dad," Gus asked, pointing at the row of photos she had just hung, "do you remember these?" She faced him so he could read her lips because, even with both hearing aids working, what he actually did hear was questionable.

Squinting, he answered, "Sure. That's my mother. From before I was born, I think."

Gus studied his expression. He seemed to be present to the moment, so Gus said, "Dad, did your brother Edward ever have any kids?"

His eyebrows moved closer to his nose, and his eyes almost disappeared as he thought. "Not that I know of, Doll," he replied, his face opening into a smile. "No, no kids."

"Did he ever marry?"

Again Robert's thinking face. "He had a couple of serious girlfriends. He was engaged once, oh, what *was* her name?" He scrubbed his face with his hands as if he could push the name into his mind. "Elaine. He was engaged to Elaine. Ed had a car, and your mother and I would double date with them when we could. It beat taking the streetcar."

That's what Mom wrote in her diary, Gus thought. Her mother also wrote that she and Robert had bought Ed and Elaine a small engagement gift in the early '40s. "They never married then?"

"Nah," Robert said without hesitation. "Ed drank too much. Couldn't keep a job and lost the car, too, I think. Once we moved east, we only saw or heard from him when he needed something."

"He visited you once in 1938," Gus ventured, "and didn't he come with your folks when I was about five?"

Quick-thinking face this time. "That's right. We were in Newark in '38. He came to look for work, had another car, but no gas money. We finally gave him enough money to get back to Colorado."

"Ta daaa!" Marigold trilled, entering the room in her new dress. As she twirled, the skirt flew out in a haze of mauve, chartreuse, teal, and royal purple. She then made a decent imitation of Marilyn Monroe on the air vent. When Robert's eyes lit up, Gus thought of all the times her mother similarly displayed her new clothes.

Everyone applauded. It was an exquisite dress, chosen for the annual college award dinner in two weeks. Marigold was neck-and-neck with the math instructor for "Teacher of the Year."

"You'll be the belle of the ball," Hazel said, hanging the last picture in the second row.

"For sure," Gus added. "Is Fleming going?"

"If I can make him," Marigold said. "He doesn't want to go anywhere. He found a gallery space he wanted me to rent for him. I said no, and he's been pouting since. I'm not sure I like him anymore, but I don't want to talk about that. What's all this about your uncle having a kid?"

Hazel sat on the bed with the same question in her eyes.

Gus pulled a chair closer to her father. "I thought I mentioned having Edward's ashes, but maybe I didn't."

"Nooo, do you really?" Marigold flinched. "How do you know they're his? What are they like?" She plopped beside Hazel on the bed and fluffed out her skirt.

"They're labeled, 'Edward Roberts cremated March 1984,' and they're in a gallon paint can in a box."

Marigold, disliking the conversation, went to change out of her dress.

Robert looked over, "What are you going to do with them, Honey?"

"That's why I'm looking for Ed's son, Dad. Do you remember I visited Edward and your mom in 1972? After that, I got a couple of letters from Ed, who insisted he had a son, Evan Roberts, an Elder in the Mormon Church on a mission in Finland at the time. His mother was named Carolyn. He sent me photos of the two of them with his car and a Chow dog. To answer your question, Hazel—if a son exists, he should have the ashes. If not, I'll think of something."

Marigold, now changed back to her comfort clothes, popped in the room. Hazel tore herself away from the TV golf tournament.

"You're the genealogist, Gus. Have you looked him up online?" Marigold queried.

"Yes, but nothing's turned up yet. I was hoping Dad could give me another clue."

"Well, let's hang the last of the pictures," Hazel suggested. Marigold backed up by the windows to survey the wall in its entirety.

"What's left?" Marigold asked.

"There's four of Robert and Audrey together. Looks like from the '30s to a couple of years ago," Hazel said, shuffling the pictures on the bed.

"And one more of me in my teens," Gus added. "We don't have to put that up."

"Sure you do. How about hanging you as an end-cap near the corner on the top, and then put your folks equidistant from each other for a third row. Your Dad can see all of them from his bed or his recliner, and it'll be chronological too." Marigold pushed over to hold a couple of the photos up for Gus to see.

"Good. Let's do it," Gus said. "I'm ready for lunch."

The women finished the project, gathered their things, and were deciding whether it was best to wake Robert or let him sleep.

He suddenly opened his eyes. "All done?" he asked, lurching up from his recliner. "That's real nice, Doll, thank you. Do you have to leave?" He put his arm around Gus, looked at his watch, and said, "Is it dinner time yet?"

"No, Dad, it's lunch time. We've got to go, but I'll walk you to the dining room." Gus embraced him and kissed his cheek. Hazel and Marigold were close to the door, checking out the kitchenette.

"Okay, Honey," Robert said, heading toward the door, "I'll walk you out. It was a good visit." Hazel and Marigold stepped back as Robert opened the door. "It was nice meeting you too." He smiled at Hazel and Marigold and walked them all down the hall to the main entrance. Butterbean went to the car with Hazel and Marigold while Gus took her dad to the dining room, kissing him goodbye once he was seated.

As she drove off, Gus's head spun with new ideas about finding Evan.

The doorbell rang. Gus left her computer to greet Marigold, Daphne, and her bed and food. Butterbean bowed, "I haven't the spirit for mannerly displays. Gus has been glued to the computer or the phone, and she just a minute ago spoke with her cousin Evan, who *does* exist. Need I say she's berserk? I hope your Mari isn't in a hurry. I don't think she can avoid hearing about this discovery."

"And then, on Family Search I found Edward had a living child . . ." Gus noticed Marigold looking at her watch. "Do you have a minute for some tea and the rest of the story?"

"I'm sorry, Gus, but Fleming's in a mood and I have to leave for my workshop in fifteen minutes. I'm surprised he's not honking the horn. Did you find Evan?"

"Yes! He lives in California and he might visit. We'll talk later, you go."

"Mayhem," Butterbean muttered to Daphne, "mayhem reigns."

"No decorum anywhere. This is not the world I was raised to live in," Daphne declared.

Butterbean curled up in her bed beside Daphne's, and they watched Gus flit past them, singing a very off-key "Oh Happy Day." Then she was on the phone again. The dogs huffed and closed their eyes.

Moments later, both pair of canine eyes flew open. It felt past dinner time.

"How likely are we to be fed tonight?" Daphne inquired.

"Chances are better today, I think. Yesterday I had been through 'cute,' begging, whining, dancing, circling, and was up to tripping her when my dinner popped in her mind. Was she lucky!"

"So, while we wait, tell me what happened today."

After describing the phone calls, Butterbean got a drink and said, "Now tell me about Fleming."

"In a minute," Daphne said, "I don't understand human preoccupation with paternity, bloodlines, and surnames. Unlike us, they're all mutts!"

"Who knows? I think the Daughters of the American Revolution and organizations like that are human versions of the AKC. To register there, just like us, they have to have pedigrees. How else does anyone claim royalty?" Butterbean wondered.

"Gwen mentioned the other day that you and Grizzie almost got caught on the computer. Is that so?" Before Butterbean could answer, Daphne shifted to her other side. "She also told me Fleming might have an accident. How did she get that information?" Her eyes were like darts headed right for Butterbean.

"I am so sorry," Butterbean apologized. "It slipped out in my excitement about my book. Please accept my apologies," Butterbean howled, imitating Brenda Lee's pleas in her fifties hit song, "I'm Sorry."

"It's okay," Daphne replied, "as long as the humans don't figure it out. So far this is my plan." Daphne settled deeper in her bed and Butterbean stretched partway out of hers for better hearing.

"Mari's at a workshop this weekend and Fleming didn't want me underfoot. When she gets home, they will reconnect, which involves wine and sex, in that order these days. Fleming tends toward insomnia, or he thinks his creative juices flow best in the middle of the night, so he roams around sketching and mumbling and having more wine."

"Interesting," Butterbean snorted.

"To continue," Daphne said, arching her neck to look down at Butterbean, "whenever he seems the most addled, I plan to leap up and bark as if there's a burglar. When I'm really upset, I can slip and slide on the hardwood floors, and I can 'accidentally' knock him over the coffee table. Better, he might open the door to look for the intruder, and in the excitement I can see to it that he tumbles down the stairs."

"Hmm," Butterbean, murmured, "your stairs have a landing and turn right after the first five steps."

"There's no guarantee he'll have enough momentum to make that turn, but he could go fast enough to knock himself out if he banged into the wall." Daphne stretched fore and then aft, and stood up. "What do you think?"

"I like the idea," Butterbean replied. "Can you be sure you won't be hurt too? Wouldn't he grab you or fall on you as easily as anywhere else?"

"It's a small risk, but well worth it if it gets rid of him. I know Mari doesn't tell the other women, but he isn't working at anything. Beyond his sketches, there's no paintings, sculptures, or whatever happening. And no junk job to help with the food and utilities, never mind the rent."

Daphne whined a little and paced, "He has a small trust fund, but the income isn't enough to keep me in dog food. He uses that money to buy her trinkets and Starbucks lattes, and she thinks that makes her a princess. It is way too disturbing to watch her money go for that slug. And he controls her every way she'll let him, which is plenty. That new dress she bought for the award dinner? He made her take it back. Too revealing, he said. All the signs are there, a mini-Frank blossoming!"

"Okay," Butterbean said, slipping out of her bed. "Let's practice your plan on Gus. My stomach says she's forgotten our dinner. I'll herd, you block, lean, and push until we get her in the kitchen. Then we can bat our dishes around and scratch at the food cabinet. That always works. She thinks scratching ruins cabinets."

26

Humpty Dumpty Had a Great Fall

The Sunday before Halloween Marigold returned home from the workshop "Family of Origin Dynamics in Present Day Intimate Relationships." With the clearest view of herself since prepuberty, Marigold barreled into her apartment to greet Daphne, whom Gus had dropped off, per Marigold's request. Once she and Daphne bounced and danced their hellos, Marigold felt Fleming's absence.

"Where is he, girl?" Marigold asked Daphne as she opened the Greenie jar. "Where is he?"

Daphne whined, possibly implying Fleming should be seeing a proctologist to find his head.

Marigold took it for a genuine answer, and replied, "Getting some wine, is he? You know everything, don't you, your Royal Highness?"

"Helllloooo?" Fleming yelled up the stairs. Marigold ran to the open door, saw him with two boxes of wine and flew to the landing where she took one box and gave him a wet, sloppy kiss. Daphne shuddered and retreated as they came up the last five steps.

True to Daphne's prediction, Marigold and Fleming began the evening with wine and sex. There was no food for anyone, not even Daphne, who, in a pique, rolled up on the sofa while the humans rolled in the bedroom.

In an hour, they were watching a docudrama on personality disorders, addiction, and divorce in America. Once the humans emptied the second box of wine the Greyhound's illusions of dinner vanished completely.

Under the influence of the wine and TV, Marigold mentioned Fleming's financial irresponsibility. He retaliated, presenting his passivity, languor, and detachment as healthy self-care, making it clear that other women found his innate, laid-back attitude adorable. Obviously, Marigold caused their problems by being a controlling, castrating female. The rest of the argument fell in the gutter, drowning in wine and acrimonious repetition.

Marigold locked herself in the bedroom, weeping, cursing, and shredding Fleming's clothes. Unaware of impending wardrobe disaster, Fleming sprawled on the sofa in his jockeys and socks with a Margarita. He flipped on the football channel.

Daphne twitched, sighed, and shifted in her queen-sized bed with memory foam under a sheepskin cover. She flinched with each reflection on the scene tonight, and with every flinch, her resolve strengthened. Tonight was the night.

By two in the morning, Fleming had been up, and then back on the couch, for the third time. Snoring from the bedroom told Daphne that Marigold was asleep. She jumped out of her bed, nails clacking on the floor, and barked at the front door, accidently bumping the umbrella stand. It thumped against the wall.

"Whazzzat? Whoooossse there?" Fleming groaned from the couch.

Daphne hit the umbrella stand again. Thump. Fleming, on his feet, but off balance, reached for the lamp, and instead of turning it on, knocked it to the floor where it smashed. He flailed and righted himself. "Daphne, where are you?" he bellowed. "Who's there?"

Flustered, he grabbed the Buddha from the coffee table and crept toward the front door. Daphne hit the umbrella stand twice, barked, and dashed at Fleming as he opened the door. He lurched forward as she blocked, and he stepped hard on her front paw. She screamed, snarled, and pulled back instinctively, leaving Fleming only air for support.

In slow motion he fell, head first, and rolled down the five steps to the landing, legs jammed against the wall, his head and arms dangling over the remaining stairs. It was time for serious canine alarm.

Not realizing the extent of her own injury, Daphne bounced on her left front paw with her first bark. She slipped and tumbled end over end, clawing air, to land upside down on top of Fleming.

Marigold heard the whole ruckus through the closed bedroom door and the fog in her head. Certain the Huns were invading, she found her phone and punched 9-1-1, all the while yelling, "Daphne! Daphne!"

She opened the bedroom door, half in her robe, and ran through the broken lamp shards in her bare feet, stopping at the open front door. Queen Daphne had extricated herself, but not before Marigold saw the indignity of Her Royal Highness upside down on top of Fleming.

The paramedics said Fleming had a sprained wrist, bruised ribs, and a leg broken in three places. The leg breaks were likely from the impact of an airborne Greyhound. For sure, his leg required surgery. One EMT looked at Fleming's eyes and tsked, "Some way to avoid a hangover."

Marigold let the cutest paramedic bandage her bleeding foot, but wouldn't go in the ambulance. Daphne needed to go to the Animal Emergency Clinic first. Then, Marigold promised, she would appear at the emergency room for stitches. She smiled and touched the EMT's hand, assuring him she knew how important stitches were in the first hours and the dangers of leaving wounds like hers untreated.

"Will you be there?" she asked, but he didn't hear her.

Marigold dressed and loaded Daphne in the car in time to see the EMTs leave with Fleming in the ambulance.

As she drove, Marigold gave thanks for automatic transmissions, and thought whoever was in the ER, vampire or yahoo, if he could sew flesh and dispense pain meds, he would be knight enough. Her left foot throbbed, and she saw blood on the bandage. In the back seat, Daphne moaned, closed her eyes, and wondered if the Emergency Animal Clinic could restore dignity.

As all doctors do, the vet and techs on duty asked how Daphne got her injuries. When Marigold related the tale, the tech asked to be excused, and Dr. Truman, hunky-looking even in his white coat, turned an interesting puce, failing to hold back his laughter. Soon Marigold laughed too and Daphne, flat on the examining table in pain and suffering from damaged pride, began wagging her tail as she remembered Fleming flying through the air. If you didn't have the broken tail and the sprained paw, it was funny.

Soon, full of canine valium, Daphne lay across the back seat, with a splint on her tail and a metal support cast on her front leg that looked like an aluminum snowshoe. She thought she had heard "bacon, egg, and cheese biscuit" while the doctors set her tail. And instantly she and Marigold were at Bojangles eating just that. Lost dignity had its compensations.

"You were lucky, young lady," Dr. Laughinghouse said. "A millimeter more and you'd have cut a tendon." He wrapped and wrapped gauze around her foot, taped it, and tightly velcroed a walking cast. He cleaned the small cuts on her right foot and bandaged them with ordinary band-aids, covering that with a surgical sock. "This should heal well enough for regular activities in two weeks, unless you dance or skydive."

"I love dancing," Marigold replied. "Do you?"

"I do, but no dancing for you for at least a month." He looked at Marigold's devilish expression and added, "Or mountain climbing, strenuous gym workouts, nothing that involves feet. If you have a question about an activity, don't do it, especially no swimming or water sports. For this week, keep that foot elevated every possible moment, the higher the better."

"Oh, doctor," Marigold said, flirting now, "I bet you say that to all your patients."

Her gaze slipped to his hands as he wrote her a prescription for antibiotics and a pain-killer. He was a southpaw with a wedding band.

27

Reprise at Shear Charisma

A few hours before Daphne's next appointment with Dr. Truman, Dr. Laughinghouse pronounced Marigold able to proceed in her normal life without bandages on her foot. Still no skydiving, he admonished. Thrilled, she skipped and tapped up the walk to the vet's office, her footwork punctuated by the clank of Daphne's cast.

Impressed by Marigold's skill at caring for Daphne and deafened by Daphne's impatient stomping, Dr. Truman hustled to remove the offending metal. Grateful for the silence, he made an appointment for Daphne the following week. If things progressed as expected, she too would enjoy regular life, minus stair-diving of course.

Eager to show off their good health and not be late for afternoon tea and scones, Marigold and Daphne rushed over to Gus's where, after some showing off, Marigold joined Gus, Grace, and Hazel. Daphne trotted into the yard to visit with Butterbean, Lady, and the Poms.

The approaching holidays and the impending trial required extreme organization, so the women sat on Gus's front porch, submerged in tea, scones, calendars, and appointment books. Under the azaleas Bruce planted, the canines lounged with pig ears and rawhide chewies.

"That cast was more important than I thought," Daphne, tired from showing off, whined as she lay down using one front paw. "Ouch!" She flopped on her elbow in a most undignified manner.

"You'll get used to it," Butterbean encouraged, though a tad gleeful about seeing an un-royal Daphne.

"Stiff upper, old chap, what?" Daphne mocked, hoping to retrieve a wisp of grace.

"Cut it out," Lady ordered, flat on her side in the shade. "You wanted to dispose of Fleming and you did. A stellar job too, I say."

"True, true," Daphne preened a bit. "I haven't seen any more of those cheap wine boxes around either, the ones with the scenes of smiling people toasting each other. Maybe, just maybe, Mari sees through that advertising."

"Amen," Butterbean grumbled. "Those oughta be scenes of people fighting, falling down, or throwing up, things that *really* happen after a box or two of that rotgut. Why, I saw a spoof on the Marlboro Man once, a cowboy and his oxygen tank . . ."

"Whoa, gang. No time for tirades," Gwen interrupted. "Our women are planning the next few weeks and we should too. There's a lot coming up."

"Good idea," Butterbean replied, "but first I have a question for Daphne, two to be exact. What happened to Fleming, and do I sense something going on with Mari and Dr. Truman?"

Resting her aching paw on the other one, Daphne said, "From what I overhear when Mari's on the phone or I happen to see her Facebook page, she and Dr. Truman are simpatico, but busy and gun-shy about relationships. I think they're too put off the dating scene to do anything."

"Over here," Art yapped at full volume, startling the others. "Our humans are saying important stuff, the trial!" He whirled and darted back.

"Sam told Mari that Fleming's out of the hospital and staying with the fat floozy owner of Deco Gecko. No surprise." Daphne snorted, hoisting herself to a sitting position. "Butterbean, don't gobble that pig ear. The slower you eat, the easier it is to keep slim."

"So you think I'm fat!" Butterbean challenged. She grabbed her pig ear and trotted after Art.

"You're the one complaining about your tuck-up," Daphne growled, her pig ear dangling from her jaws as she limped after Butterbean.

"Hurry up," Gwen shouted, circling Daphne. "I heard the words 'grooming' and 'tomorrow.'"

"Hi, Ruthie," Gwen squealed with joy, "It's been forever! How are you?" Gwen dragged Barbara, the groomer, to the last drying cage on the bottom row where Ruth, the black Pomeranian whose human was a court reporter, yelped "Hello" to a soaked Gwen.

"You like each other?" Barbara asked. "I'll put you next to her, Gwen." After setting a medium dryer on Gwen, Barbara scooped Butterbean out of a midlevel kennel and told Art, caged beside her, "You're next, buddy."

Lady lay in a large crate, and Daphne, now grateful to be without her cast, stood in the crate next to Lady. The air was filled with undercoat from the Husky on the other side of Lady. Art's Boxer friend, Butch, soon arrived and settled in on Daphne's right. Because his human was one of the assistant district attorneys, he was popular and highly sought after. For a minute, the four big dogs discussed the weather and panned the most recent dog food commercial on TV. Then they settled into the routine.

Art asked about the upcoming Aldermen's vote on canine matters. He'd heard there were ordinances pending about poop-scooping, leashes, and a proposed dog park. Most of the canines had definite opinions on the issues and took bets on how the humans would vote. Two to one the humans would vote in favor of leashes and poop-scooping, but a dog park? They could go either way on that one.

Bruce's predicament was *the* hot topic. Having listened to contradictory conversations in their homes, on TV, and on the street, the confused canines wanted facts from the horse's mouth, so to speak. There were no better "horses" than Lady, Art, and Gwen, along with their friends Butterbean and Daphne.

When Lady woke to change position, Henrietta asked the opening question, "How is Bruce doing? My human knows him from the Historical Society, and she can't believe what she hears. She's rabid that the media takes such a negative stance, all but pronouncing him guilty before the trial. So am I. Is there anything I can do?"

Lady lumbered up and shook herself. "Thanks, Henri. First and most important, Bruce did none of the things Mark alleges. Mark's story is true like the times our humans say, 'Let's go for a ride and get a treat,' and next thing, there you are at the vet's office getting shots."

Henrietta switched shoulders in front of her dryer and barked, "Amen. Go on."

Lady did. "One of Mark's uncles is the owner of the demolition company that wrecked the McClellan Building, and that brother didn't appreciate our humans' sit-in. Then the sister of Bruce's ex-wife, who's married to the third brother, hates Bruce because he didn't fall in love with her after divorcing her sister. Makes me grateful canines don't have these family issues."

"I remember hearing about the sit-in on the roof," the Husky said. "My family thought your women were dynamite."

"The demolition guy didn't apparently," Lady replied, "and Mark's dad has hated the neighborhood and the town since he moved here. He wanted to live in an historical area and have a junk yard, own a bed-and-breakfast without red tape and taxes, and breed Beagles without a kennel license. If he can get money or help his brothers with revenge, he'd be pleased. It seems that hurting Bruce and Hazel is fun for that bunch."

"Thank heavens Hazel stopped the Beagle business," the Husky intervened. "The Beagle she rescued is my neighbor, and she's a special pal."

"Cool," Lady replied. Lying down, she continued, "We can't understand what Mark was offered or saved from that could motivate his garbage accusations."

"What personal reason could Mark have to persecute, I mean prosecute, Bruce?" Daphne broke in. "Bruce, a seventy-something poop-scooping, heterosexual attorney with a smart and sexy significant other, a kind neighbor to a pimply faced, overweight sixteen-year-old! I understand the three brothers' interests, but *how* could they motivate Mark?"

"Maybe Herman promised Mark a place in his company or a car," Henrietta guessed.

"Or promised him he could quit school and have a sex slave," the Husky interjected.

"Herman could afford to give Mark a stipend for life," Art chortled, "though if Mark grows good pot, he won't need it."

"With a pot operation, he'd either be rich or in jail," Gwen added. Then, with a flirty wiggle, she said, sotto voce, "Butch, you didn't hear that from us."

"No problem, Gwen. The cops and my human know all about the pot," Butch Boxer answered. "Oddly, they appear to be ignoring it. I know the district attorney has ambitions, and ADA Rapp wants to bust chops, but in my estimation, the prosecution and the grand jury have overstepped this time. I don't think my human is, or wants to be, involved, but I'm watching him carefully. Bruce's case may be a career-maker, but it's also a conscience-breaker."

"What breaks *my* heart," Lady said, "is how the media smeared Bruce's reputation. His career here is over and maybe his life too, no matter if he's acquitted five times or if folks shout 'innocent' from the roof tops. It shouldn't be, but it is—the words 'molest' or 'homosexual,' stain worse than blood, ink, or berries."

"Too true," Daisy, a Terrier mix added. "My human's church voted to launch an anti-homosexual campaign. They say such things are 'an abomination in the eyes of God,' whatever that means. I love my human, and I don't think she truly believes this; she can't because her nephew is gay, and she's very kind to him. But she loves her church, so where they lead, she follows. Mom has no idea why I try to bite the minister."

Henrietta spoke again, "As far as my mom can tell, the Historical Society is split fifty-fifty about keeping Bruce. Even if he's found innocent, half of the members don't want to be 'tarred with the same brush.' At times, I don't understand the best of humans."

Spun dry at last, Art shook, and jumped into the conversation. "We need to both support Bruce and protest the grand jury finding. If a majority of the dogs in Pine Crossing went berserk every time the trial is mentioned by humans, in the paper, or on the news, maybe *Homo idiotus* will get a message."

Butterbean adopted her best big-dog stance, adding, "That's a good idea.

Specifically, we could chew up the particular articles in the paper or turn off the TV by biting the remote. But it has to be done the instant words about Bruce or the trial are spoken. We all know how dense humans are. If we wait even a minute, they won't get the connection. Anybody have more thoughts?"

"One," the Husky said. "I don't know how to research this, but where I live, out in the county, some families have feuds that last for generations, like the old Hatfield and McCoy story. Is Bruce's family from here? Could there be an old resentment from his father's or grandfather's time, some ancient dealings with the Lewis family or the Outlaws?"

"An excellent thought to investigate," Butterbean said. Lady agreed, though neither had a clue how to check out Bruce's family history without Gus's help.

Daphne lay down only to jump up again. A kennel girl dragged Kurt, the Jack Russell Terror, into the room for his pedicure, put him on the counter and muzzled him. Gwen stuck her nose through the cage wire, showing every one of her sharp, white teeth. Art called him names the others had only heard once or twice.

Unused to Kurt's ways, the kennel girl released his muzzle before setting him down. He lunged at Art's cage. Mid-fall, the girl caught him, and he turned and bit her for her efforts. The clamor in the drying room reached full volume as Kurt lifted his leg on the door jamb and snarled to Art, "Bruce's face looks just like Hazel's butt."

28

It Comes This Time Every Year

Thanksgiving approached at warp speed. A late friend of Grace's often said, "Of course it's Thanksgiving! It comes the same time every year. It's not a surprise, you know!"

This year, with Bruce's trial scheduled for the second Monday in December, the women moved their annual Christmas Wrap to the second Saturday in November instead of after Thanksgiving. Having the most spacious living room of the three women, Grace hosted the event. Card tables served as stations for paper, ribbon, and tags. Bows, ribbon, and paper garlanded the room. In the front entry, each woman stashed her bags of unwrapped gifts, which after passing through the appropriate stations were finally placed in a pile on the kitchen table.

Gus had a dozen small things for her cousin's grandkids, and a cherry red velour shirt for her dad. Hazel wrapped few gifts besides those for Bruce and for her two children's families. Cards stuffed with generous checks suited everyone, so Hazel created masterpieces each year. While the cuts on her foot healed, Marigold had made an afghan for her mother and a vest for her dad, and both needed wrapping. Grace was in a funk.

"C'mon, Grace," Gus wheedled, "what's bugging you? And please put your finger on this ribbon so I can tie it."

Grace plunked her finger on the indicated spot and grimaced as Gus tied the knot.

Grace sighed. "It's my niece, Belinda. She's pregnant in jail!"

"She got pregnant in jail?" Hazel asked, her voice rising in disbelief.

"No, turkey, she got pregnant before jail," Grace said, her tone coated with sarcasm.

"Excuuuse me!" Hazel shot back, slamming another card on the table.

"Sorry, Haze. I'm upset. According to Belinda, it'll be nip and tuck whether the baby comes before she's out of jail. In any event, her current boyfriend is the baby's daddy." Grace wandered among the tables. "I can't get into the spirit of this. I keep thinking that I should have taken things in hand earlier, that I could have done *something* to prevent this!"

Gus stopped wrapping, went over to Grace, and put an arm around her. "Stop beating yourself up, Grace. What do you tell me all the time?"

"I know, Gus. I always say, 'all you can do is watch and be ready to pick up the pieces,' but I'm finding out how hard that is to do."

"You can lead a horse to water . . ." Hazel said from her seat at the tag table as she drew, pasted, and stickered her cards and wrote the checks. "What does your sister intend to do about this incipient grandchild?"

"Yeah," Marigold wondered aloud, wrapping her afghan, "Is Belinda using now? What if the baby's born addicted? Where will Belinda and the baby live?"

"Don't forget the baby daddy," Gus interjected. "He'll get out of jail sometime, too, and he'll be involved for better or worse."

"You can say that again," Hazel added. "Nothing marries you like a baby."

"I raised all those questions to my nutty sister," Grace said, pacing around, "and she blew me off. Made me feel cut out of their lives, and I want to be included, though why eludes me. My sister and Belinda spread heartache and disillusionment with the speed and élan of kudzu strangling a forest. I think I'll cancel Christmas this year."

"Did your sister win the lottery? Does she have a clue what all this will cost?" Marigold taped a big bow on the wrapped vest and headed for the kitchen table where she plopped it on top of the wrapped afghan. Without the secret Santa gag gift she needed for work, Marigold was done for today. She went into the kitchen.

"What about your Minnesota daughter, doesn't she deserve a gift?" Gus asked, finishing the seventh of her twelve presents.

"We give each other magazine subscriptions, so all I have to get is whatever I'm going to get for you guys."

"Oh no! Not this year! We promised!" Gus stomped her foot on the floor.

"Graaace!" Marigold yelled from the back door in the kitchen. "There's a cute kitty out here, a teeny, tiny kitty." She cooed, picked it up, and kissed its little head.

"Put it down, Mari. I don't need a cat."

Marigold turned so Grace could see the kitten in her arms. "He's Siamese, I think." The kitten yowled and tried to escape from being held. "Yep, that's a Siamese yowl."

Grace strode over to collect the cat and put him out. "He showed up yesterday. He's in good shape and might go home if I ignore him," Grace said.

The kitten saw Grace extend her arms, and as Marigold turned toward the outdoors, the kitten launched himself over her shoulder to land on Grace and dig in.

"Yeoowtch!" Grace scruffed the little guy, detached him from her chest, and put him down on the back steps. "I don't need a cat!"

"Maybe your new neighbors will. Look." Marigold pointed at the woman taking up the For Sale sign from the front lawn next door.

"Great. I guess my peace and privacy had to end," Grace complained as she turned to go inside. Seeing the door still open, she looked under the nearby bushes and across the lawn. "Where's that cat? I hope he didn't go in! Siamese cats are worse than monkeys. They're on everything like a tent."

Shaking her head in wry bewilderment, Marigold followed Grace inside, bagged her wrapped gifts, and prepared to go.

Marigold leashed Daphne and waved to the women in the living room. "Talk to you tomorrow, bye," she shouted.

"Bye Mari. Bye love. Cheerio," echoed behind her as she closed Grace's back door.

Grace stalked around, poking and peering under furniture. "Did a cat come in here? A Siamese kitten? A *male* Siamese kitten?"

"No," Gus and Hazel echoed each other.

"Why?" Hazel hazarded as she put her finger on Gus's last package.

"I'm sorry," Grace said, "this day is going from bad to worse. First my lulu sister and niece, then this kitten shows up—again." She flopped in her recliner. "I think he lives nearby and took a fancy to my porch. Marigold saw him right before she left, picked him up, and insisted I should keep him. While that was going on, we spied a woman removing the For Sale sign next door. Goodbye peace and privacy. Then I noticed the door was open and I didn't see the cat outside. Daphne didn't go into her 'cat fit' on the way to the car, so I'm pretty sure the little bugger is holed up somewhere in here."

"He'll come out when he's ready. Like mice, they can hide anywhere. You'll wear yourself out looking." Gus stacked her last package and moved to the tag table. Hazel had finished her cards.

Grace ran her hands through her hair. "Want a quick tea?" She thought a second. "Or something stronger? I've got some of your favorite Bloody Mary mix, Gus."

Hazel stretched and Gus signed her last tag. "Great idea, what's stronger?" Hazel inquired.

"Beer, bourbon, a nice merlot."

"Merlot is good. I'll straighten this up after."

"Let's do it now," Gus suggested. "I'm not worth much now, but later I'll be worth less." She grabbed the wastebasket and began tossing in ribbon snippets, teeny hunks of paper, and a pile of cellophane.

"Okay, slave-driver," Hazel rolled up the paper and replaced the bows, ribbons, and tags in their proper containers.

Grace took the tape, scissors, and pens to her desk as she headed for the kitchen where she bagged Hazel's gifts and cleared the table before she got out the merlot, Bloody Mary mix, and a beer for herself. She put out a plate of cheese and crackers as well.

As the women sat down, Gus took a gulp of her Virgin Mary and exhaled with pleasure, Grace doing likewise with her beer.

Hazel leaned into the center of the table as if someone might overhear, "What's a good way to dispose of a cell phone?"

Gus and Grace's expressions were blank. Gus glanced at Grace and made a stirring motion near her ear, intimating Hazel had gone cuckoo. Then enlightenment struck.

"*That's* how Horace and Mark were conveniently absent!" Gus exclaimed.

"I *knew* it!" Grace burst out, "In spite of your denials, I *knew* you called them."

"BFD!" Hazel rejoined. "That call kept them alive as it turned out."

Gus gulped another draught of her Virgin Mary. "If I'd come home to find you two dead, I'd really be pissed, cheated out of killing you myself for such a stupid move."

"Let's not go over old stuff," Hazel sputtered. "I need to figure out how to get rid of it, and Grace, you need to clear your computer. We can't have anything surfacing like it does on *Law and Order*."

Seeing empty glasses, Grace tossed her empty beer bottle and brought over the bottles of merlot and Bloody Mary mixer and the five-pack of beer, putting it all on the table. "This is all there is, gang, so pace yourselves," she announced, sitting again.

"How about if we hammer the phone to pieces, have takeout fast food at different places, throw a few bits in each bag with the wrappings, and put it in several different dumpsters?" Gus offered, shaking her head.

Taking a slug of wine, Hazel replied, "Not bad, Gus. Any better ideas, Grace? I thought about taking it deep-sea fishing, but it's too cold now."

Smashing might do it," Grace responded. "I changed my hard drive after making one disc with the basement photos on it. I don't know how it works, but I've been told that just deleting something doesn't really do it."

"It doesn't?" Hazel said, her voice rising in incredulity. "Where does it go, then?"

"Don't know, but I think we can't be too cautious. Where's your phone, Hazel? I've got a splendid four-pound sledge hammer!" Grace grinned. "And I'll get my old hard drive."

"I'll go get it. Let's finish this off now," Hazel said.

"Whoa," Gus interjected, "Grace, why do you have a disc of those photos? You don't think you can hide that from a subpoena do you? You want your house torn apart by sheriffs or some kind of SBI or CSI officers?"

"All I'll say is, we don't yet know if those photos will be useful and the disc is not in the house," Grace replied, distributing the last of the drinks. "Get that phone," Grace ordered, hauling out her wallet, "and pick up some more refreshments. Gus and I will make sandwiches—and find that cat."

In spite of full pantries and cleared schedules, the weekend before Bruce's trial fell far short of its intended use as time for preparation, centering, and focus. Bruce reviewed his testimony with John, examined every imaginable prosecutorial question, outlined John's motions to the court, and concocted strategies for either the court's acceptance or denial of those motions. Bruce's suits, altered because of his weight loss, hung in his closet, cleaned and pressed. Still wired on Sunday afternoon, Bruce rode his bicycle into the next county and back.

Hazel prepared and froze ten days worth of meals, baked several cheesecakes, six dozen chocolate chip cookies, and two pound cakes. At a second's notice, she could produce a batch of scones. Fence or no fence, she was leaving the dogs at Gus's for the duration of the trial, and she had their food packaged and labeled. She selected five stunning outfits with matching shoes, bags, and necklaces that would go with her emerald earrings.

While Bruce was riding his bike, Hazel talked with everyone she knew, collected a wicked headache, and retreated with the dogs to a silent, darkened, bedroom.

Grace, her wardrobe as ready as it ever would be, also froze quick meals and spent most of the weekend in her garden, partly because she wouldn't get to it during the trial, and partly to work out her anxiety and anger. The Siamese kitten hadn't turned up since Marigold tried to bring it indoors, and the new neighbors turned out to be one neighbor, a man about her age, she guessed. He seemed quite pleasant, yet Grace foresaw helpful friends fixing them up, which set her teeth on edge.

Exhausted from gardening and thinking, Grace went indoors for a beer and a nap. On the second swallow, she heard a yowl in her dining room and rushed to investigate. She scanned the sideboard, the sheer-curtained windows, and the table. Seeing nothing, she turned to her right and looked at her china cabinet filled with glass figurines hand-blown by her late brother. On the top shelf, almost invisible behind the larger figurines, crouched the Siamese kitten. Grace's mind seized—how to remove the cat and save the figurines?

Gus, too, dealt with clothes and food, being extra choosy about her attire in case she had to testify about Pomeranian behavior in terms of their watchdog skills. In no way did she want her disrespect for the court to show. She did what she could to calm Hazel, walked a couple of miles with Butterbean, and cleaned her house to white-glove standards.

Irene, piqued that she wouldn't be able to attend the trial all day every day, completed every aspect of her work except, of course, incoming orders and shipping. She put Germy George on notice that she'd do what she could, but as full partner now, she was leaving at two each afternoon "toot sweet." Tasks that couldn't wait until the next morning, he could do.

Irene's church, The Right Hand of God, supported Bruce in the same offhanded way it didn't judge her job. "God bless everyone, no exceptions" could be their mission statement. They planned to demonstrate in front of the courthouse each day, carrying signs on neon paper with large print in contrasting colors. The signs' content focused on wasted taxpayer money, the absence of hard evidence, the presence of homophobia, sprinkled with comments about abdication of Christian principles by other churches. That Sunday evening, she made a margarita and relaxed on the couch, watching the news.

Saturday afternoon Marigold had returned from her workshop, picked up Daphne, and worked on her class plans for the next week. She felt better being alone than she had in years. She also had a call from Dr. Truman, Daphne's vet. Maybe they'd have dinner one night soon.

During Bruce's trial, Marigold planned on eating her lunch out. She'd repurchased the dress Fleming had made her return and planned to wear it all week. Twenty of her friends and colleagues were slated to attend the trial, and Marigold and the more adventuresome teachers planned to join Irene's picketing group when they could.

Itchy, anxious, and emotionally untethered Sunday evening, Marigold took Daphne for a long walk and phoned Gus, Grace, Hazel, and Irene. Then she vacuumed, dusted, cleaned her bathroom, and sat down to surf the web.

In contrast to their humans, the canines were delighted. They had overheard that they'd spend each day together at Gus's, feasting on Greenies, rawhide, and pig ears. Food and safety was a good thing. So was freedom from distraught humans.

29

The Rain, It Raineth More Upon the Just

"Oyez, Oyez. All rise," the bailiff intoned. Judge Bendix entered the courtroom.

All rose, coughing and rustling. Then silence. The bailiff announced the rules of the court, emphasizing the consequences of any violation.

The pew-style seating, the floor, and the walls up to the chair rails were made of golden oak, circa 1800, as were the railings around the judicial area, and the tables and chairs allotted to the plaintiffs and the defendants. An oak forest gave its life for this room.

The walls above the chair rail were ivory, showing off ponderous, gold filigree framed portraits of dour judges, whose wigs and scowls lent an air, likely intended, of solemnity and disdain. Gus remembered ministers of her childhood looking that way when she asked how "God the Father of All Creation" could banish thousands of the folks He had made to everlasting damnation just because He made them in a time before Jesus, or in a place where Jesus was unknown. She hadn't received a satisfactory answer then, or since, and she didn't suppose these painted characters would have had satisfactory answers to Bruce's situation. Not every judge was King Solomon.

The observers were on the bride's side (the left), of the courtroom and the prospective jurors on the groom's side (the right). Once the jury was selected, people supporting the plaintiff would move to the groom's side, with the defense supporters remaining bride's side. Just below and facing the judge's bench on the left, Bruce and John sat at the defense table, and on the right, Sheriff Outlaw and Assistant District Attorney Kay Rapp sat at the prosecution table.

Seated in the front row behind the defense table, like the monkeys of hear-see-speak-no-evil, sat the tightly wound trio. Gus had the aisle seat, with Hazel to her left, then Grace. John's wife Sara, Bruce's brothers, and his son Greg filled in the rest of the row. Behind them sat Bruce's golf buddies, members of the Historical Society, Hazel's Mah Jong group, and the usual court habitués. In the last row was Mark, his father, and both uncles. Mark's mother was conspicuous by her absence, as was Bruce's ex-wife Sheila, but her disgruntled sister Gloria was there, showing cleavage a notch short of a dress code violation. The air curdled from her perfume.

The assistant district attorney was up first for jury selection. An otherwise unremarkable woman, Kay Rapp had a nasal twang and wore a urine-colored suit. Her hair, a red-auburn shade meriting Irene's clucking disapproval, lay on her shoulders in varying lengths. She questioned prospective juror number one about her job, life, and beliefs on many issues, especially homosexuality. Then John asked his questions.

Bruce and John conferred about each juror's responses, as did ADA Rapp and Sergeant Outlaw. When twelve jurors and an alternate were deemed satisfactory by both the prosecution and the defense, the others were dismissed, and Mark's family moved to the right side of the courtroom, still in the back row.

The one juror Gus knew, she disliked. Still, she had confidence in John's knowledge and skill. Her horror at the counts listed—twelve counts of sexual offense, thirteen counts of indecent liberties with a minor, and thirteen counts of committing a crime against nature—she kept to herself, though she saw her feelings mirrored in the faces of the others as she glanced down her row of seats. *Were her feelings that transparent also?* she wondered.

The judge instructed the jurors, "While you sit as a juror in this case, you are not to form an opinion about the guilt or innocence of the defendant, nor are you to express to anyone any opinions about the case until I tell you to begin deliberations. You must not talk or communicate in any way with any of the parties, any of the lawyers, or any of the witnesses in this case. This applies both inside and outside the courtroom.

"Communication with anyone in the courtroom except the bailiff by the jurors is forbidden, even to ask about the restroom," Judge Bendix went on, next explaining the consequences. His required investigation of the matter would appreciably extend court proceedings, even if the communication was innocent. If the communication pertained in any way to the trial, the trial could be derailed, and the offender would face appropriate charges.

"Media coverage of this trial, either by newspaper, or television, or radio—you are not to look at it, read it, or watch it," the judge continued. "Your verdict must be based exclusively on what is brought out in this courtroom. You may not do any independent inquiry or investigation about this matter, nor are you to visit the scene or places which are the subject matter of this trial, or will be brought out during the course of this trial. With that, I'm going to excuse you."

"Whew," Hazel whispered to Grace, "some jury. Best of the bunch, though, from what I can tell."

The attorneys approached the bench to discuss legal and procedural details with the judge, their words inaudible even to the women in the first row. Finished, the judge addressed the courtroom, "Those people who are here, who are interested in the outcome of this trial, again, I am going to give you the same instructions I gave the jurors." He reiterated the consequences of talking with any juror for any reason, reminding all that he would have to stop the proceedings to ascertain the conversational content. Courtroom observers, too, would be charged if they were found to be out of order. Gus rolled her eyes, supposing, despite the extensive admonitions, someone wouldn't get it and gum up the trial.

Hazel looked at her watch—almost one o'clock. The background noise level had risen. People were hungry and fidgety.

A few more comments passed between the ADA and Judge Bendix, and then, at sweet last, court recessed until the next morning. The TV crew deconstructed to film outside the court for the five o'clock news, and the local newspaper reporter disappeared.

After an animated lunch at Applebee's, Bruce and John departed for John's office to prepare for the next day. Greg and his uncles decided to play tourist at the behest of Sarah Jackson, while Gus, Grace, and Hazel went home, stopping at Grace's first.

"Can you come in a minute?" Grace asked as she got out of the car. "I want to show you something."

"Can it wait? I'm whipped," Gus said.

"Me too," Hazel echoed.

"No, it can't," Grace retorted. Dispensing deep sighs and protracted eye rolls, Gus and Hazel shadowed Grace into her dining room. There, in a round bed on the sideboard by the window, slept a tan ball with chocolate feet. When Grace went toward it, the ball unrolled, stretched, and yowled. Grace picked him up and put him on her shoulder. Gus and Hazel grinned like the kitten's Cheshire cousin.

On Tuesday, court opened promptly at nine thirty. The attorneys wrangled for an hour before the bench about discovery and the prosecution's late disclosures to the defense. Mark had made a change in his statement about the occasions of certain acts, and that change, coming late as it did, became more part of pretrial preparations in the estimation of the ADA, than part of the Bill of Particulars. Disclosing that to the defense, Rapp argued, would then make it possible for her to be called as a witness, an untenable position for the prosecutor.

"So Mark changed one set of lies for another," Hazel whispered first to Gus and then to Grace. "What difference does it make *when* he said *which* lies? Why did John let them take so long to deliver the Bill of Particulars?"

"He couldn't stop them," Gus whispered. "Sure their procrastination stonewalled the defense, but what could John do? Go over and wring it out of them? ADA Rapp just said about interviewing Mark, 'I mean, I never got into specifics until I was getting ready for trial . . .'"

Hazel whispered back, "So what was she doing for six months?"

"Shush, just listen," Gus hissed. "I can't pay attention and talk at the same time."

The judge said, "The defense's motion to dismiss on grounds that they were denied proper discovery is denied at this point in time."

Hazel's eyes shot poison at the bench.

John's next motion was to dismiss as evidence certain male-on-male pornography on Bruce's computer, citing several recent cases where this type of evidence was ruled inadmissible because it lacked connection to the accusations and because of its inflammatory nature. Mark had not mentioned pornography, the computer, or Bruce's condo in connection with his allegations.

John explained the reasoning behind the decisions of inadmissibility in each of the cited cases. In addition, there was no way to prove Bruce had personally viewed the pornography sites on the computer or that the presence of said porn wasn't accidental. That computer had been in Bruce's office before it was retired to his condo, and in both places, many people had access to it.

Rapp replied, "Judge, I have two hurdles here. I have to prove first of all that he likes males, and I have to prove that these crimes occurred. And I understand that normally the courts would keep this out. After all, just because you look at pornography doesn't mean you therefore molest kids."

She mentioned the pornographic website, and then explained, "So we would introduce it, not to show that because he likes porn, he molests kids, but to show that because he likes specific types of pornography, he has a proclivity for young boys."

"So these websites are gender-specific?" the judge asked.

"Yes, Your Honor. And they include young boys. I've got it down to, like, 101 pictures of naked men and women. I have narrowed down the pornography of interest to those including just young boys. It corroborates what the victim has said about their sexual relationship."

The judge then asked, "Is there any evidence or testimony that you are going to offer which shows that they, the accuser and the defendant, talked about these websites or that the victim viewed these websites with the defendant?"

"No, Your Honor," was the ADA's reply.

Hazel turned purple. "Judge *Bendix* is even using the word 'victim' after he said not to! Mark's *not* a victim! Bruce is innocent," she whisper-screeched in Gus's ear. "So much for being innocent until proven guilty," Hazel wiped flecks of spittle from her lips.

"John just said there were no allegations that Bruce watched porn with Mark; Kay Rapp just said she had no evidence that mentions such mutual viewing of these porn websites. And, Rapp said there were women in the various porn shots, but that she narrowed down her 101 images of these men and women to include just young boys!" Gus adjusted her skirt, crossed her legs, and re-crossed them, fidgeting in frustration. "Judge Bendix must be deaf!"

More vehemently, John again reminded the court that this pornography had not been used in any way around Mark. Bruce had not invited him to view it, mentioned it, nor did Bruce, with Mark, have any other imaginable connection with it.

"I agree the judge is deaf," Grace hissed. "Rapp herself clearly explained why the porn shouldn't be allowed. We've got Dumb and Dumber running this show." Hazel ripped up a tissue.

John continued, "The cases that I cite and have copied for the court to support my motions also recognize that the closer the case, really the more careful the court has to be in weighing the prejudicial effect of this evidence in determining the—"

"What do you mean by 'the closer the case'?" the judge interrupted.

"Well," John replied, "I really mean the less evidence the state has." Letting those words have their effect, John gestured toward the bench and the papers he'd just given the judge. "In one of those cases, the court said, and I quote, 'We find that this is essentially a case of who and what to believe.'" John paused, looking at the prosecution and then back to Judge Bendix. "To paraphrase the rest, the court further explained that because the state presented no medical or other physical evidence, and no eyewitnesses of the alleged events, the outcome depended solely on the jury's perception of the truthfulness of each witness. Therefore, the court ruled that inflammatory evidence such as pornography, which could cause a verdict to be entered on an emotional rather than factual basis, would be prejudicial and *not allowed.* We have that exact situation here, Your Honor."

Rapp countered by saying the cases John cited *did not* count because they weren't about same-sex relationships.

For another quarter of an hour, the prosecution and defense argued before the judge, who then weighed the various issues. Would a heterosexual lifestyle override homosexual issues or bisexuality? Did the court need to sequester witnesses? Could both the prosecution and the defense continue without a ruling on the pornography? In the end, the court denied John's motion to sequester witnesses and his motion for the inadmissibility of the pornography.

Hazel left for the ladies room in the basement, and Gus followed her.

The jury was empanelled and given copious instructions regarding their comfort, conduct, and court proceedings. Gus and Hazel missed that absurd instruction, always given on TV: "If The Court grants a motion to strike all or part of the answer of a witness, you must disregard and not consider that response which has been ordered stricken."

In the restroom, Hazel wouldn't come out of the stall, so Gus stood on the toilet in the adjoining one and peered over. Hazel still had her pants on. She sat with her head in her hands, elbows on her knees. Her shoulders were shaking. "Haze," Gus called softly, "what's the matter?"

Startled, Hazel looked up. "Go away. I'll come upstairs when I'm ready."

"Unh-uh, Hazel, first you tell me what's wrong."

Gus waited, hanging over the top of the stall, the toilet seat slipping under her feet. "C'mon, Haze, I know this is rough." She watched Hazel stand and blow her nose.

"Get down now, Gus," Hazel ordered. "I'm going to use the toilet."

At the sink, washing her hands, Hazel groaned. "I'd forgotten all about it. I can't believe she did it."

"Who? Did what?" Gus asked.

Facing Gus as she wiped a paper towel over her hands, Hazel all but spit. "Damn that Sheila! I know where the idea for this whole trial came from. Double damn that Sheila!"

"What?" Gus fumed.

Hazel sighed from her toes. "This is so old, I'd forgotten about it. Bruce had an affair with a guy in college. Typical story, Bruce cast aside, heartbroken when another man, prettier, richer, better connected came along. Bruce loved the man, not the lifestyle. He told Sheila about it in the first flush of their relationship."

Gus slapped her forehead, "Oy vey, I get it! A midnight, just-screwed, be-close-and-share-confession! Do *they* ever bite later! This is one big alligator in the swamp!"

"A long time ago, Bruce told me he told her. Who'd think it would get used this way? We were all children of the sixties; sex stuff was no biggie." Hazel checked her hair, her eyes narrowed in the mirror. "Crap! I can see them all plotting this, snorting and hee-hawing about Mark being a minor, how this would bring Bruce down."

"And we'll let them?" Gus squared her shoulders, reclaimed her lost half inch of height, and said, "Back we go in full regalia. Head up, girl!" She linked arms with Hazel and smiled at her. "My friend Hazel says that living well is the best revenge." Gus let the restroom door slam behind them.

When they reached the courtroom, the judge was announcing ". . . so instead of breaking up the witness's testimony, I thought it best we take our lunch recess now."

30

Because the Unjust Hath the Just's Umbrella

A deluge of Mark's testimony opened the afternoon session—what was done to whom and with which body part on three particular occasions. To show fabrication, John attacked the discrepancies between Mark's first alleged chain of events and his later depiction of them, forcing Mark to admit his initial statement to the sheriff was incorrect. John examined Sheriff Outlaw's handwritten notes versus his later typewritten ones, finding them conflicting and confusing. What did Mark *actually* say? Was the initial version the truth? The second? Or none?

Condensed, Mark's testimony amounted to three specific sexual encounters with Bruce. The first alleged occasion of molestation took place one night when Bruce, leaving the local theater, found Mark standing in the rain, looking for a ride home because his father was drunk at a nearby bar. According to Mark, instead of driving home, Bruce parked at a secluded boat landing, and there they performed reciprocal oral sex. After that, Bruce dropped Mark at his residence and went into Hazel's house. The descriptive adjectives Mark used came straight from popular porn literature.

Hazel whispered, "Now we know what he reads!" Sarcasm dripped from her words like blood from a knife. "That covers a dozen or more counts," she added.

The second encounter happened during Mark's community service for a high school drug bust. Part of that service included setting up and breaking down the tables and chairs in the library auditorium whenever there was a speaker. One night, Bruce lectured about preserving historic sites. When the Q and A session ended, Bruce and another man, who had a fatal heart attack two weeks later, were the last to leave. According to Mark, Bruce stayed behind, and they racked up a few more counts in the storeroom with the chairs.

Irene and her church group entered along with Marigold and her colleagues in time to hear about the third occasion. They squeezed into the remaining seats on Bruce's side of the courtroom.

Seeing this influx of people, especially those from the church, and catching the eye of two members of her Mahjong group, Hazel's ability to smile in greeting faltered. Torn with feelings of gratitude for the support and mortification about the testimony, she turned eyes front.

Gus tapped her on the arm, "Don't look," she said, "our local newspaper reporter is sitting to my right, next to Channel 20's reporter with a video camera. I'd hoped their absence meant they couldn't tape inside, but it looks like they're rolling."

"Crap," Hazel exclaimed. "At least you're in their sights this time."

"Pay attention!" Gus pinched Hazel and impaled Mark with her gaze. His eyes, a startling cold blue, magnified by his glasses, appeared uncomprehending. His expression seemed disconnected from the words oozing between his narrow, worm-like lips. Properly dressed for the courtroom in a white, long-sleeved shirt and dark slacks, he fidgeted on the stand, uncomfortable as if he wore a toga or dashiki; yet, overall he delivered his lines well. Gus remembered Mark had sometimes acted in the local theater youth group.

The third incident, Mark testified, happened on a night the previous spring—after midnight when Hazel was sleeping in the upstairs bedroom. Bruce sat on her front porch because of insomnia. Mark had been beaten by his father and tossed out of the house in his pajamas. Upon seeing this, Bruce called him over. After they talked a while, Bruce invited him in. They sat on the couch in the dark, not wanting to wake Hazel or the dogs. After a while, Bruce reached over and unbuttoned Mark's skivvies.

ADA Rapp then asked, "What do you mean by 'skivvies'?"

Mark: Sleep pants.

Rapp: Do you remember what kind of sleep pants?

Mark: They were red with grey stripes. I pulled them down.

Rapp: How were you positioned?

Mark: Lying half sitting, half on my side.

Rapp: Then what?

Mark: He kind of turned me, and I assumed he wanted anal sex. He removed his shorts and stroked his penis a few times, and then he performed anal sex on me.

Rapp: How long did that last?

Mark: A few minutes, not long at all.

Rapp: Was any type of lubrication used?

Mark: I don't think so.

Rapp: Why do you not think so?

Mark: It was very, very painful, and I didn't feel any.

Rapp: Do you know if the defendant ejaculated?

Mark: I believe he did.

Rapp: And why do you believe that?

Mark: Because pretty soon my sleep pants got wet near my anus.

"What a crock," Hazel announced outside. "He must have gotten that from a book. You can't get in our living room without Art and Gwen going off. He had unlubricated anal sex there? I don't think so!"

"Anus?" Grace added. "He wouldn't say 'anus.' I bet they coached him big time."

Worn out from listening so intently to the proceedings, Gus, Grace, and Hazel stood in a circle of friends and latecomers on the steps of the courthouse. Gus put away her notepad; she'd need a new one for tomorrow. "What's with *this?* Mark undoes his pants, says nothing, and assumes sex is on the menu? Does he approach every unrelated male that way?" Gus said. It was rhetorical and no one responded.

"I'm concerned about all the questions that *aren't* getting asked," Grace fumed. "It's one thing to point out, which John did very nicely, the discrepancies in Mark's various statements, but can't John get to the real thing, that *none* of this is true? Everyone, even us, gets balled up in refuting instances rather than the whole thing. Yes, unlubricated anal sex is painful. No, actual sex doesn't last a few minutes, maybe three minutes on a good night. Who cares what pants Mark did or didn't have on? None of it *happened!*" Grace's face reddened dangerously.

"I don't understand why a plaintiff doesn't need some qualifications," Marigold said, flanked by her teaching assistant and a math teacher. "Mark's been to a psychiatrist. He's had drug run-ins at school, and in the sixth grade, he declared to all and sundry that he was gay. Doesn't a person have to exhibit *some* stability and sound reasoning to accuse others? Is every ordinary citizen subject to anyone else's whims, resentments, and lies via the justice system? And, to be fair, why isn't someone helping Mark? He's got to be hurting to do all this, coerced into it, or not."

"Good questions," Grace said, her visage regaining its normal color.

A wedge of demonstrators led by Irene and the minister of her church came around the corner. Their signs declared, "God loves gays too," "God blesses everyone, no exceptions," "Liars come in all sizes," "Free Bruce," and "Hatred is a Christian value?" Circling in front of the courthouse, they shouted, "Oyez, Oyez, A-D-A, Go Away!" and sang peace and love songs.

The Channel 20 videographer twirled like a pinwheel in a typhoon. After following Bruce and John, who gave them the slip as they left the courtroom, he dashed out to film people exiting the courthouse. Next he ran down the block to capture The Right Hand of God demonstrators.

"All we need is the high school band and a dirigible," Gus muttered as they bounded to their cars.

The last three days of the trial were a Machiavellian endurance test. John repudiated Mark's sex story with simple questions about sequence and his skivvies. He highlighted the lies in Mark's conflicting statements to Officer Outlaw and ADA Rapp.

Under oath, Gus testified that the Pomeranians bark and scratch at the closed bedroom window every time she and Butterbean pass on the street. She could not comprehend how they would have been silent if Mark and Bruce had entered Hazel's living room and had sex. "The sex never happened anywhere," she managed to insert.

Hazel testified to Bruce's actual whereabouts and behavior that evening. When Bruce was sitting on the porch and saw Mark tossed out of the house next door by his father, Bruce went upstairs, told Hazel what happened, got his keys, and drove Mark to his brother's crash pad a few miles across town. Bruce's absence from her home that evening lasted fifteen minutes, start to finish.

Grateful she had no reason to be in the witness box, Grace turned to her kitten during these disheartening days. She'd named him Tonto, and in the evenings, she fell asleep to his purr.

On Wednesday morning Judge Bendix stunned the defense, denying John's several motions against showing the eight pornographic photos on Bruce's computer to the jury. The court threw him a bone, however. He would be allowed to dissect the prosecution's methods of retrieving these files.

Hazel, Gus, and Grace listened closely to the explanation set out by the State Bureau of Investigation computer expert. After fifteen minutes of technical discussion about cookies, pathways, and free space, it came clear that SBI Agent Arthur had used another program, accessible on the web, called www.waybackmachine.org. He viewed, from its archives, the particular pornographic website that contained the eight images accessed by Bruce's computer.

Questioning the agent further, the defense revealed there was no reliable way to ascertain the exact makeup of that web page on the particular day Bruce allegedly looked at it. No sooner did Judge Bendix, at last, grant a motion in John Jackson's favor, than ADA Rapp called FBI Special Agent Epistle, a cyber crime investigator.

"Holy crap!," Hazel exclaimed, quickly covering her mouth, "the *FBI* got into this!"

"It's okay," Gus whispered, patting Hazel's hand. "Listen. He just said he didn't get the computer until October. Who had it all that time?"

"Stop it, you two," Grace hissed. "Epistle just said the sheriff had it until then, and they hauled those images out of free space. Listen, don't talk."

The agent set up a projector and screen only the jurors could see, but there was an audible gasp in the courtroom as the spectators saw the expressions on the jurors' faces. Lunch break followed immediately.

On Wednesday afternoon, more supporting witnesses, a social worker, a therapist, a urologist, Bruce's colleagues, and other character and alibi witnesses appeared for the defense. The prosecution paraded a bevy of teachers, relatives, and students along with Mark's therapist. All were examined, crossed, and redirected when necessary.

Thursday morning, Bruce testified. John Jackson asked questions pertinent to Bruce's current life situation, his relationship to the plaintiff, and segued into the present circumstances concerning Mark's allegations, starting with the night at the theater.

John: Were you at the theater on the night in question?

Bruce: I was.

John: What time did the play end?

Bruce: Between 10:30 and 11:00. It was a long play.

John: Was anyone else with you?

Bruce: Yes, I left with James. We were the last two out of the theater.

John: Was Mark present that evening?

Bruce: Outside the theater. When James and I came out, he was standing beside the ticket booth.

John: Did you speak to him?

Bruce: I nodded at him. James's wife had pulled up, and I was saying goodbye to them. It was raining and raw, and I was wishing I'd brought my umbrella.

John: Then what happened?

Bruce: James got in the car and left. Mark came up to me and asked if he could have a ride home.

John: Then what?

Bruce: Mark looked embarrassed and said, 'I'm sorry to bother you, but my Dad's in the bar down there and won't leave. I need to go home.' Mark pointed toward the end of the block. As he and his dad lived next door to Hazel, and I knew drink was a problem, I said, 'Sure, let's go,' and dashed for my car. Mark followed, got in the passenger side, and I headed toward home.

John: How long a drive is that?

Bruce: Five minutes unless there's a train. Then, who knows?

John: But there was no train that night?

Bruce: No, no train that night. They usually pass during the day or wee hours of the morning.

John: You got to Hazel's and then what?

Bruce: I pulled past her house to the next one, Mark's house, and he got out. I think he said 'thanks,' but I'm not sure. Then I backed up, pulled into Hazel's driveway, parked, and went in.

John: And what time was that?

Bruce: 11:15

John: How do you know that?

Bruce: Hazel's mantel clock was chiming as I came in and I looked at it. It said 11:15.

John: Did you stop anywhere along the way?

Bruce: I did not.

John: Did you in any way touch Mark or make any kind of comment that could be construed as sexual in nature?

Bruce: I don't recall touching Mark at all. I said I liked the play and he said he wished he could have seen it. I made a comment about the weather and the local high school basketball scores. I'm not sure Mark replied.

John: Thank you, Mr. Winston, your witness.

Rapp: You've been in this courtroom all week, haven't you?

Bruce: Yes.

Rapp: And you acknowledge Mark's testimony about the night at the theater differs from what you just said? You are under oath, you know.

John: Objection!

Judge Bendix: Overruled.

Rapp: Mark testified that instead of going directly to his house next door, you took a side trip to a construction site, a deserted site, and there participated in mutual oral sex. Did you or did you not go to this place and commit these acts?

Bruce: I did not go anywhere but to Mark's house and I did not, then or ever, commit any acts of a sexual nature with Mark.

Rapp: Didn't you testify that you left the theater between ten thirty and eleven, and that you entered Hazel's house at eleven fifteen?

Bruce: I did.

Rapp: And didn't you say it was a five-minute drive from the theater to Hazel's house? If you left at ten thirty, that gives you more than thirty minutes unaccounted for. How do you explain that?

Bruce: I believe I said *the play ended* at ten thirty or eleven. Won't the record show that?

Rapp to the court: Can I have the beginning of the defendant's testimony read back, regarding his leaving the theater?

Judge Bendix: "Yes." He nodded to the court reporter.

Court reporter: The defendant said, "Between ten thirty and eleven. It was a long play,' in answer to the question, 'What time did the play end?"

Rapp: There's still a lot of time there, Mr. Winston. How do you explain it?

Bruce: The theatre was packed. James and I sat in seats G5 and 6 as I recall. We hadn't seen each other in a while, so we were in no hurry to push and shove our way out. We'd easily spent fifteen minutes exiting the theatre. Then, as I said before, a few minutes passed before James's wife arrived, then Mark asked me for a ride, and so on.

Rapp: So you refute Mark's testimony about that night's events? You say that nothing more than a ride transpired between the theatre and Mark's house?

Bruce: That is correct. I did nothing more than give Mark a ride.

ADA Rapp continued her cross-examination in the same vein regarding the other alleged incidents. She also delved into the nature of Bruce's relationship with Hazel, presenting it in such a way that Bruce seemed an unsavory character because he and Hazel weren't married, that he was an avid porn fanatic, and that refuting Mark's testimony showed Bruce to be a slick and clever liar.

John shot holes in Mark's other occasions of molestation, but all his objections to the ADA's tactics were overruled. The defense began to wonder if there was more than met the eye in Judge Bendix's handling of the trial, but couldn't fathom his motivation.

Keeping count of the overruled and sustained objections, Gus, too, noted something awry. Rapp had thirteen sustained objections and nine overruled, a total of twenty-two. John had twenty-seven sustained objections and forty-two overruled, a total of sixty-nine. Grace, Gus, and Hazel were exhausted. Bruce and John appeared numb and haggard.

In spite of her irregular attendance, Irene agreed something was fishy in this trial. She also found it interesting that several jurors were regular customers of Such Happenis Adult Toys. Outside the courthouse on Thursday afternoon, without uttering a word, she took a swing at a woman juror who was saying to another exiting juror, "I know he made that poor child gay."

When Gus watched the TV coverage that night, the story seemed to be about a different trial, but there she was, in her green dress with toucans and birds of paradise. Wednesday's biased report in the local paper had made her nauseous and she discarded it halfway through the article. Until now a great supporter of free press, Gus found the media to be presumptive fear-mongers at best, puppets or fools at worst.

Friday morning, the attorneys delivered their closing arguments. ADA Rapp, back in her urine-colored suit, played the same old one note—Bruce was at least bisexual, did terrible things to Mark, and needed to be in the clink forever. The porn proved it all.

John's closing argument, clear, concise, pointing out the impossibility of Mark's allegations, exhorted the jurors to use logic and common sense. The State's evidence was as substantial as the Emperor's New Clothes.

Judge Bendix admonished the jury yet again about their communications and conduct, then sent them to their chambers to deliberate. They'd be served lunch shortly. The rest of the courtroom was excused, too, but could return at will until the verdict was delivered.

The media, initially distracted by the church demonstrators and a few radical gay protestors, got back on point, polling the citizens' opinions and reiterating the counts, which during the trial were reduced to seventeen. The TV and newspaper reporters subtly projected a guilty verdict by using every inflammatory adjective available to Anglophones.

Bruce and John ate in a private room behind the courtroom. The women, after a quick lunch at Port City, returned to the courtroom to wait.

Exhaustion and stress clouded everyone's thoughts. After deliberating until six o'clock, Judge Bendix sent the jurors home for the weekend. Court would resume Monday morning at nine o'clock and they would continue their deliberations at that time. Until then, no communications with anyone about the trial, blah, blah, blah, allowed.

At Hazel's kitchen table, Bruce laid his head on his arms as kids do in second-grade timeouts. Hazel massaged his neck and shoulders. Grace and Gus picked at the vegetables and dip. Irene cleaned up the used napkins and empty plastic cups. The dinner table overflowed with plates, empty pizza boxes, and the bagged remainders of pretzels, chips, and cheese puffs. Family and friends had joined them earlier, eating buffet-style. Opinions dropped like bird poop, but no one had the energy to refute them.

The dogs, overfed by well-meaning guests, lounged quietly under the table or by the air conditioning vents.

"Bruce, you were brilliant on the stand," Grace offered, taking over the neck massage from Hazel. "You and John couldn't have done one more thing with that mess."

Gus looked at Bruce's cheerless face, adding, "It'll be okay, Hon. There might be a couple of stupid jurors, but not all twelve. Reasonable doubt is all we need."

Wearing bracelets that out-jangled Marigold's, Irene drew Gus aside. "I wish I felt that confident. I know three of those turkeys, numbers two, five, and eight. They're consummate liars. Number two was the class tattletale and teacher's pet in first grade with me. Number five picketed Such Happenis with that fundamentalist church a few years ago, and all three of them buy sex toys not for their wives. They'll condemn Bruce with smug virtue." She struck a pose. "Unless he's fully acquitted, they're no longer my clients."

"Too much information, Irene. I know one of them, number nine, who is the most arrogant fundamentalist you'll find. Still, that's only four jurors." Gus mentally thumbed through her estimations of the jurors, and said, "It'll be okay. Six of them, minimum, appear to have good sense."

"I hope so, Gus. How about we get everyone together Sunday afternoon?" Irene suggested. "I don't think it's good for Bruce and Hazel to be alone all weekend."

Gus poured a Pepsi, and Marigold touched her shoulder. "You okay?" Marigold asked.

"I'm tired," Gus confessed, taking a slug of soda. "By the way, what kind of workshop are you attending next weekend?"

Surprised because she didn't recall telling Gus, Marigold answered, "It's about living alone, given by a woman for women only. I'm skeptical, but serious. I've heard from Dr. Truman only once. He's cute and a wonderful vet, but he's always busy. If I want to see him, I need a sick dog." Marigold pondered a minute. Gus waited to see where this was going.

"I suppose I could join or start a canine rescue group," Marigold mused. "Anyway, you want to go next weekend?"

"Go?" Gus snapped, blindsided by her hurt feelings over Marigold's past rejection of her wisdom. "I should be giving it," Gus said. *Damn, I'm testy,* she thought.

"I'm sorry," Marigold stammered with obvious contrition and red cheeks. "I should have consulted you as we'd planned back in the spring instead of chasing Fleming. I am truly sorry."

"That's okay," Gus replied, hugging her. "I'll keep Daphne if you want. Butterbean would enjoy it. We'll all be in better humor after Monday."

Marigold stifled the "or not" that zoomed into her mind.

At that moment, the canines, sprinkled about the room, perked up. Something in the ambience had changed.

Gwen lay down nose-to-nose with Butterbean, and Daphne bent closer as Gwen revealed, "Art heard from Butch Boxer, who said Ruthie, the court reporter's dog, said, 'Beware the pornography.' What could that mean?"

Butterbean snorted. "More chicanery and muddled thinking, like asking jurors to disregard what they hear. People go berserk over pornography, becoming mean and fearful like we see on TV. The 'Persecution,' which is how I think of them, took advantage of that fear superbly, and the judge let them."

"There's no proof of Mark's allegations. No witnesses, no medical, technological, or psychological corroboration of alleged events. No forensic tests like on *CSI* or even *Hill Street Blues*." Butterbean explained, losing patience. "So, in lieu of facts, the Persecution brought in porn—fear and disgust convicts as well as facts in certain cases."

Daphne interjected, "The FBI computer expert had to use a special program on Bruce's computer to locate the porn in free space."

"What does that mean?" Gwen tilted her blond head.

"It means that the porn on Bruce's computer was inaccessible by normal use. He couldn't look at it like a magazine, if he ever looked at it," Daphne replied. "Who knows what folks did in his condo when they were renting there? He hardly knew half of them."

"But didn't ADA Rapp admit there was no connection between the porn and Mark's accusations? I thought I heard my Gus and Hazel yelling about that." Kinking her neck to look up at Daphne, Butterbean cocked her head.

"Yeah," Art interrupted, belligerently standing over his rawhide. "She did say that. John and Bruce said it too. Even the FBI computer expert said no one could access the porn without his program."

"Why couldn't the FBI or someone plant something there?" Gwen chirped. "They had the computer for months. Who goes in and out of their offices, ADA Rapp, Sheriff Outlaw? I may be pretty, but I can think too."

Rising to her elbows, Daphne replied, "Obviously someone wanted a case badly enough to manufacture one. The question is, who and why?"

Butterbean stood and shook, her hind legs going in all directions on the hardwood floor. "All I know is my salmon doesn't sit well, and I'm sleep deprived. I understand PTSD now because I'm disordered, disorderly, out of order, and surly, too." She plunked down again and squeezed her eyes shut.

Gwen looked defeated and sad as she turned to Butterbean to Daphne and back again. All the canine cuteness, or brains either, couldn't return their world to the old normal of treats, walks, and cheery humans, Gwen curled up beside Butterbean and remained immobile for the rest of the evening.

31

"Lawsuit, noun: a machine which you go into as a pig and come out a sausage."

— Ambrose Bierce

Humidity was high and nerves humming Monday morning in the courtroom. The jurors had filed in, close to the wall, along the far edge of the courtroom and into their chambers just before nine o'clock. No one had reported the juror who flagrantly read the paper on the courthouse steps.

The rest of the courtroom occupants rose when Judge Bendix entered and sat when he sat. The instructions were simple: Maintain decorum in the courtroom and the bailiff would notify the judge when the jury reached a verdict.

Gus read a book, Hazel knitted a scarf she'd neglected since the last century, and Grace practiced meditation. They rotated trips to the bathroom, fretted over Bruce and John, only a few feet away but in a separate world at the defense table, and shared meaningful glances. They'd used up all their words over the weekend.

The prosecution table chatted and passed papers back and forth, obviously chipper. Working on their next victim, the women surmised, returning to their respective endeavors.

Gus heard a knock minutes before eleven o'clock, but since no one responded, she passed it off. It came again, louder, and the bailiff went to the door of the jury room and returned the knock. It opened and the bailiff conferred with the foreman.

Like a flurry of autumn leaves in a strong wind, people rushed about. The bailiff went to get the judge. Conversational knots untied, and people raced out of the courtroom to locate others in the restrooms or drinking soda in the hall. More than one person was outdoors smoking.

"All rise! Court is in session." Judge Bendix sat and ordered the prosecution and the defense be seated also. The jury exited their chamber and settled in their respective places. Silence prevailed while the foreman of the jury handed a piece of paper to the bailiff who carried it in front of the witness stand to the judge.

Hazel's eyes popped. Grace twiddled her thumbs like they were pushing a ship upriver, squeezing her eyes shut. Gus held her breath, and John and Bruce imitated statues.

"Will the defendant please rise?" Judge Bendix intoned. In seeming slow motion, Bruce and John complied.

"Have you reached a verdict?" Judge Bendix inquired, exactly as judges do on TV.

"We cannot, your Honor," the foreman replied, not what foremen say on TV.

The three women turned into bobbleheads, looking at the judge, Bruce, the jurors. What was going on? They plucked each other's sleeves, patted hands, fluttering like small birds. The courtroom had never been so quiet.

Judge Bendix motioned to the bailiff, who approached. They conferred. The bailiff went over to the foreman of the jury. They conferred. The bailiff returned to the judge, who asked the two attorneys to approach the bench for more conferring.

Hazel wilted, her skin glazed with sweat. Gus forced a breath. Grace's mind churned, projecting. Looking at her friends, Gus realized she'd never seen Hazel look so ill or Grace so gaunt. They exchanged glances and held hands, trying not to be alarmed.

"Ladies and gentlemen in the courtroom," Judge Bendix said, "it appears the jury is as deadlocked this morning as they were on Friday. I am going to poll the jurors and see if there is any chance of change."

The judge turned to his left, toward the jurors. "Juror number one, do you think that having more time to consider the evidence brought out during this trial would in any way change your mind?"

"No, Your Honor, it wouldn't."

Judge Bendix asked the same question eleven more times and received the same answer eleven times. Bruce and John could have been Buckingham Palace Guards.

"Then," the Judge said, "you heard the responses of the jurors, and therefore, I will not require further deliberations on their part. I declare this trial has resulted in a hung jury. The attorneys may approach the bench. As for the rest of you in the courtroom, I thank you for your patience and decorum. You may leave at will."

Stupefied, Bruce left the defense table and joined the women while John spoke with Judge Bendix and the ADA. Sheriff Outlaw and Mark and family vanished as did most of the spectators. Hazel embraced Bruce, the women embraced them, and Bruce's family encircled the five people, making a three-layered hug.

The newspaper reporter scribbled a few notes and turned off her recorder. The TV camera rolled on.

"How could the jury be hung?" Gus roared that evening, pacing in Hazel's dining room. The animals fled through the doggie door while the humans sat tacked to their seats around the table.

Gus was purple, spitting her words. "How could anyone, with five minutes life experience, believe Mark? What made that judge admit the porn pictures? Who has unlubricated anal sex without shrieking? It's the goddamned gay thing. Show someone homosexual sex, and they think they've seen the devil incarnate."

"Amen!" Irene said. "I should've decked that juror when I overheard her saying, 'I know he made that boy gay!' Did you see her, number ten? She needs a midnight visit."

Grace sighed. "The media had a dreadful impact, emphasizing the porn over and over. They need *shooting*. Whatever happened to the truth?"

"I couldn't get past Judge Bendix," Marigold added. "Whenever I was in the courtroom, he overruled all John's objections, but only one or two of ADA Rapp's." She turned to Bruce, "I know about everybody's motives, your ex-wife's sister and all those brothers, but still, Bruce, do they have enough clout to rig the trial? This is way too off. Someone's finger's in the pie!"

Grace's face was puce, and Hazel was making noises like both a gulp and a belch. She'd cried most of the afternoon. Bruce put his arm around her and repositioned himself in his chair. Everything about him had become more deliberate in the last half day. "Let's all calm down. John thinks they'll retry the case and take their own good time about getting to it. My gut instinct agrees."

"The first morning," Gus said "Rapp's answer to Judge Bendix's *direct* question, 'Is there any evidence or testimony that you are going to offer that tends to show they, Mark and Bruce, talked about these websites or that the they viewed it together?' was, and I have it right here in my notes, 'No, none at all.' Yet in comes the porn!"

"That's what sticks in my craw the most too," Bruce replied. "Neither John nor I understand why the Judge did that. It wasn't done to create grounds for an appeal. The proceedings had enough irregularities for that. Unless there's a conspiracy against Yankee preservationists with a past and of a liberal persuasion," Bruce held up his hand. "And don't dismiss that notion, but more likely I'm caught in someone else's drama. Not to mention the religious and political climate."

"Enough! Shall we sit on the porch?" Hazel asked. "You can see the trellis we put up Saturday. I'll plant morning glories on this side, and soon not an inch of next door will be visible. I can pretend no one's over there." Hazel sat in the padded double swing, her back to the trellis. Bruce joined her.

"And," Hazel's face brightened, "I might not have to pretend much longer."

"How so?" Grace asked.

"We talked about what to do in case I wasn't acquitted," Bruce answered, pushing the swing, "It's going to take deep pockets to get out of this fix, so Hazel and I will move in together sooner than we planned, and to smaller quarters. I won't be able to get a job, even at the grocery store, until this is over, and probably the Historical Society won't keep me even as a volunteer, but I can start an Internet business and consult. We're going to beat this thing." Bruce looked at Hazel, who reached over and took his hand.

"You're right about that," Gus said, relaxing a little. "Let me tell you a quick story, and then I'm off. A long ago friend of mine, a diesel mechanic, was asked by an acquaintance to work on a boat engine in the marina. The acquaintance wouldn't be there, but he gave the mechanic the key, the slip number, and the name of the boat. The mechanic went, got into the engine room, and noticed a few bales of MJ. He did his work anyway, locked up, and left."

"Wait, wait, what's MJ?" Hazel asked.

"Oh, you know," Grace cut in glibly, "grass, boo, pot, that stuff. MJ stands for Mary Jane, which was a huge code name in the forties. Mary Juana, I guess, is how it started."

"Anyway," Gus continued, "A few days went by—"

"Holy Toledo!" Marigold choked, "I'm sorry, Gus, but I just got it about my name! My folks smoked a lot of dope before I was born and the best was called 'Gold' then. Mari-Gold. My oh my! Sorry, this is too much."

Gus giggled as she tried again. "A few days passed and the mechanic was arrested as an accessory to the crime of possession with intent to deal that marijuana. Why? Because he didn't rat out the boat owner, and someone told the cops he'd worked on the engine. Can you imagine? This mechanic spent the next three years of his life, a hundred twenty-five *thousand* dollars, and two trials to be declared not guilty. It sounds depressing, but I take it as a sign of hope."

"You would, Gus," Marigold said, still chuckling.

32

Chinese Christmas

Emotionally numbed and physically exhausted from the months of stress, Bruce and Hazel rested and treated themselves well, but found no peace. "Hung" jury was an apt description Hazel thought, adding "twisting in the wind" whenever she thought of Bruce's status.

Gratitude for Bruce's freedom vied with a maelstrom of anger, self-pity, and second-guessing because he wasn't acquitted either. Never far from their thoughts was the nightmare of a future trial. The fact that their friends were swinging on the same emotional pendulum was cold comfort.

On a dull Christmas morning, Hazel called Gus and Grace for dinner ideas. They decided to meet at the Chinese restaurant at three o'clock and to invite all and sundry, hoping some welcome camaraderie could overcome post-trial ennui.

Crammed into Bruce's condo for the weekend, Greg and his family accepted the dinner invitation gladly, thinking Chinese on Christmas was so weird, it was cool. Gus, Grace, Marigold, and Irene would be there too.

This past month, Greg's sons put their martial arts skills to good use against their schoolyard tormentors. The boys wouldn't tell who had taught them a few "super secret" fighting moves, but "persons of interest" were Bruce's cop brothers.

The week after the trial, Grace visited Belinda, finding her quite pregnant and subdued in her behavior. Wanting to be near the baby's daddy when he was released from prison, Belinda elected to stay with her dysfunctional mother after serving her sentence. If she behaved, she'd begin the New Year with her freedom and a new baby. Disappointment with Belinda's decision to stay with her mother didn't dampen Grace's delight in finding her thirty days clean and sober, going to AA meetings in prison, and studying for her GED.

Dropping one drama class, Marigold increased her volunteer efforts at the local animal shelter, donating three afternoons a week and all day Saturday. She worked with Dr. Truman who provided shots and spay/neuters at cost when the dogs and cats were adopted. Marigold tended the animals and investigated the prospective adopters. Barbara, the head groomer at Shear Charisma, showed Marigold how to properly bathe the animals and to handle rudimentary "all-off" clips on the matted dogs.

Gus holed up with her writing between the trial and Christmas, except for the one day on her way for groceries when she scooped a six-week kitten off the freezing street. A trip to Dr. Truman's office trumped grocery shopping, and to her surprise, Marigold opened the door. The kitten, a champagne color that shone pink in the afternoon light, won Marigold's heart that instant.

Marigold named him Fred, and Dr. Truman gave him the necessary shots and worm medicine. Arms loaded with litter box, cat food, and Fred in a carrier, Marigold trudged up her steps that evening. When she set everything down to greet Daphne, Daphne smelled Fred in the carrier, said a gross canine word, and lodged herself in Marigold's closet.

Irene, thrilled with the success of her blow-up male dolls, kept one in the passenger seat of her car at all times, slipping him into the office when no one was looking and squashing him under the dashboard at night when the car was in her driveway. He appeared so real, she couldn't risk blowing his cover by leaving him unattended in a parked car. Questions about her new boyfriend raised her spirits and added bounce to her curls.

Hazel, feeling hurt and rejected by all of Pine Crossing because Bruce hadn't been exonerated, resorted to rage, frenetic activity, and food. In the mornings she wanted nothing more than to start at one end of the bakery and devour her way to the other end.

Though quite generous with Bruce about his billable hours, John had to consider his partners. Bruce's legal expenses required decimating his retirement funds or selling his condo.

Much to Bruce and Hazel's chagrin, the Lewises chose to rebuild. Contractors poured a new basement the day after the trial, and now carpenters hammered day and night. Staying in Hazel's house bordered on stupidity according to Bruce and invited bad karma in Hazel's opinion.

Hazel insisted they'd make do in his condo, but Bruce thought the dogs and he would be uncomfortable and cramped. At last he decided he'd buy the biggest, best, downtown condo he could afford and both names would go on the deed.

When Bruce proposed this idea, much to his surprise and delight, Hazel agreed, but only if she contributed equally, saying she could stand being that much married. They would move her family antiques and favorite furniture to the new place, and Bruce could bring or buy the rest, his choice.

On Christmas day, after she'd organized Chinese dinner, Hazel experienced a surge of energy, put the dogs in the yard, and attacked the kitchen with rags, mop, and bucket.

"Bruce!" Hazel ordered, barging into the den, gnashing her teeth. She had cleaned every other room to her mother's white-glove standards and wondered if Bruce was still alive. He didn't look up from his laptop, just waved a finger in the air, "In a minute, Haze, just a minute."

"A minute, my eye," she exclaimed, promptly closing the laptop on his knuckles. "You're over it as of now! It's Christmas Day! Your sulk is officially finished! Maybe life sucks and then you die, but you *could* be in prison right now, eating rubber turkey and worrying about a shiv in your back. We're going to the Chinese buffet in two hours, and whatever it takes, I want my regular Bruce back."

Bruce looked at her as if he were emerging from a well, a dark, black, deep place, and shook his head. "You're right, dear. I got sucked into a bog of remorse and resentment. I can't get all the way back in two hours, but I'll work on it." He stood up and she embraced him, tears sliding down her cheeks.

She held his elbows at arm's length. "A shower and a shave will fix the outside. Let's be with our friends this afternoon and talk tonight. My emotions are a mess too, but decisions don't wait. We need to muddle through."

Hazel wiped her cheeks, and Bruce gathered her close. "You're right, dear. I haven't been totally absent. I have some ideas." He let her go, saying, "Shower and shave it is, Admiral!" He saluted smartly and left the room. Hazel smiled, wiped her eyes, and unplugged the laptop, putting it in the closet.

The Chinese buffet was as crowded as the night Gus returned from her first Florida trip. A huge, decorated Christmas tree adorned the far end of the restaurant. Red and green fortune cookies dotted the tables, and jolly Christmas music skipped through the air, all to please the American clientele. The women's extended family absorbed the cheer like sponges and ate as if they were dieting tomorrow.

Stuffed full of food and conviviality, Gus, Grace, and Hazel dropped Bruce and Irene at their respective abodes, and picked up the canines for a bracing walk around the park. Investigation of the downtown condos beckoned. Gus and Grace always steadied Hazel in her decision-making, and now she needed to be fearless leader in choosing their new home.

A speedy walk four times around the park seemed a superb idea to the women, but Art, Gwen, and Butterbean sat down after the first loop, preferring to be on "stay" under their favorite tree. Gwen and Butterbean hunkered down between two large roots, shielded from the bluster that turned the seagulls' feathers backward and askew. Art's personal version of "stay" included two benches and the children's swings.

In a snit over Gus monopolizing the computer, Butterbean complained about everything, her food, the weather, Grizzie, and writer's block.

"What do you mean, 'writer's block'?" asked Gwen, cocking her head. "I thought you had to write something first."

"I *did* write something," Butterbean snapped, "before the trial. Now Grizzie's on a salmon strike. Busy with her own book, Gus has forgotten to get salmon, not that it matters. With Gus on the computer all day, a *frigate* of salmon wouldn't help!"

"Maybe you can offer Grizzie something else," Gwen suggested. "She can't *give* you help, though she likes you. She *is* a cat, you know."

Butterbean winced. "I know, dammit, I know! Cats are unmanageable and not companionable. That Fred kitten is making Daphne's tail hurt."

"So tell me about the writing," Gwen said, steering away from the subject of cats."

Butterbean looked at the women taking their third turn on the road. "I suppose you're right, Gwen. Griz does want to help, but we're *still* working on her alphabet. We sing the alphabet song each morning while we wait for breakfast. She thinks 'u' and 'v' are the same, confuses 'z' and 'x' and can't manage 'm' and 'w' at all. "Maybe she's dyslexic and has faulty short-term memory circuits. What was Gus thinking when she brought her home last year?"

"Okay, so needing a good 'cat writer' is a logistical problem, not a 'block.' I don't get it. Do you enjoy being morose?" Art sailed around the tree, bumped into Gwen, and knocked both Poms flat and breathless.

"Sorry, sorry, Brutus the Pit Bull is right behind me," Art puffed. "He doesn't like my petitions about chaining up Pit Bulls from birth."

"Maybe because he *is* one," Gwen wheezed, as Art dashed behind the tree. Gwen caught her breath in time to be pummeled again, this time by Brutus, a maelstrom of energy. Gwen rolled over and over while Butterbean hunkered down into her famous Corgi Rock Block. Tripping over Butterbean, Brutus's front feet flew from under him, to leave him lying at the feet of a furious Corgi and a baffled Gwen.

"What the hell?" The Pit Bull gingerly sat up, shook, and flinched as the motion hit his right shoulder. He shook again, not believing he had fallen over two small dogs, females too, if he guessed right.

"What the hell what?" Butterbean challenged, standing to her full twenty-two-inch height including ears, hackles up, every hair puffed straight out. "You don't look when you run around a tree? Are you some kind of special?"

"Yeah," Gwen yapped from behind Butterbean. "Are you a playground bully or something?" She thought Brutus would be cute if he were three feet shorter and had manners.

"I got nothing against you two. It's that twerp Pomeranian who has been distributing petitions about chaining up Pit Bulls from birth. Like I couldn't break any chain made. Where is he anyway? He's gonna answer to *me!*" Brutus struggled with his anger.

"Shut up, Gwen," Butterbean snapped and Gwen did.

"Your size and threats are scary," Butterbean said to Brutus.

"You act first and think later, like now. Would it have been so hard to ask us politely where Art was?"

"Yeah," Gwen said, peering around Butterbean's flank. "You could have killed me rolling me over like that, twice! What if I had a bad neck or arthritis or PTSD from a puppy mill? What if me and Butterbean were psychotic? We'd have bitten you up one side and down the other by now. Still could too." Gwen barked with the bravado of second in line.

Butterbean snarled in her best don't-push-me voice, "Gwen, *will* you shut *up?* Brutus, I think your rollover has affected her. She's usually mannerly and gracious."

Brutus looked at Gwen's defiant shoe-button eyes staring around Butterbean. His heart felt funny, and he relaxed. He had no words for it, but he bet this was love. *Such fire she has, so brave for so small,* he thought. *Of course, she's behind the Corgi.*

"Okay, I am truly sorry. I'm not going to hurt you ladies and not even your buddy Art with his berserk petitions. Please, let's start over." Brutus lay down to be on nose level.

"I'm Gwen," she smiled and shimmied. *His eyes are wooonderful,* she thought. *And he is handsome in a hairless sort of way.*

"I'm Butterbean," the Corgi said, blocking Gwen and her feminine wiles. "I am a Corgi, Pembroke Welsh, to be exact. I write, herd, and guard. I'm pleased to make your acquaintance. Perhaps we'll meet again, but we'll be going soon. Those are our humans over there." Butterbean gestured with her head toward the women seated at the picnic table. "Does your human bring you here often?" she asked less stridently. Gwen stood beside her, wagging her ivory plume and winking.

"No," Brutus admitted as he stared at Gwen, "I come here alone when I escape from my kennel. It's an okay kennel, just not very interesting. The only thing worse would be a chain. Oops. There I go again. Every time I hear or think the word 'chain' I get mad all over again. Maybe I shouldn't meet Art today. I want to shake him like a rat." Brutus glanced at Butterbean. "Did you say you were a writer? Maybe you could give Art a note for me."

"What would you say?" Butterbean inquired, feeling safe enough to sit. "Nothing lengthy, I hope."

Gwen stepped forward. "She won't help you, Brutus. She has 'writer's block' and can't write a thing. She says it's because her cat writer isn't working correctly, but it's more than that. Probably she can't write at all." Gwen smirked at Butterbean and stood by Brutus's front leg, peering up, way up, at his face.

"But if you tell me, I can tell Art and then tell you his response. Art's my brother, so sometimes he listens to me, especially when I threaten to tell our human, Hazel, what he does when she isn't watching."

Puffing, but invigorated by four swift turns about the park, Gus, Grace, and Hazel sat at a picnic table near the dogs, alternately checking on them and watching the gulls ride waves and fly up an instant before they broke over the fishing docks.

"I think moving in together is a terrific idea," Gus chuckled. "When was the last time Bruce stayed in his condo?"

"Last year when we had a spat over handling our income taxes, seems so silly now," Hazel replied, rewrapping her scarf. "None of these downtown condos are for sale yet, but Bruce heard a friend-of-a-friend rumor that one will come on the market next month. Waiting until January is somehow to the owner's advantage tax-wise." Hazel smiled. "What a difference a year makes."

Grace turned back from watching the dogs, "I like the idea too, Haze.

Living next to Mark and Horace would be the Inmost Circle of Hell in my estimation. Here you'll have a whole new set of neighbors and be by the water, this park, and lots of shops."

"No excuse to not meet me at Saints and Sinners Restaurant either," Gus grinned.

"Except my flab," Hazel remarked. "You *know* I can't have just one bowl of their lobster bisque!"

"How is Bruce holding up? He seems withdrawn and somber lately," Gus glanced at the waves.

"He's been in 'The Slough of Despond,' and I had enough of it this morning. I slammed his laptop shut on his fingers and told him his wallow in self-pity was over. He agreed. We'll see. Did he seem better to you today?"

"Pretty much," Gus said and Grace agreed. "I can't imagine what he must feel after the trial, the hung jury," Gus continued. "Does he know living well is the best revenge?"

"He will after we talk tonight," Hazel replied. "Ye gods! There's a Pit Bull with Butterbean and Gwen, and I don't see Art." Hazel launched herself from the table, flanked by Grace and Gus.

At the same moment, a stout man with a tam askew on his head, frost from his breath in his black mustache, and flapping coat and scarf, lumbered toward the dogs from the opposite direction. "Brutus," he gasped. "Brutus, come!"

As Brutus was being leashed, the women came close enough to holler greetings. "Merry Christmas," Hazel shouted and waved. "Beautiful dog," Gus added, followed by Grace's, "Lovely day for the park."

Gwen wouldn't leave Brutus, and Butterbean wouldn't leave Gwen, so Gus, Grace, and Brutus's charming human exchanged Christmas greetings while Hazel chased Art around the tree.

33

Auld Lang Syne and Senior Sex Olympics

January and February passed, carrying the usual baggage of tax preparation, insurance bills, last minute pruning, snow shoveling, Valentine's Day, and multitudes of charity solicitations and seed catalogs.

Marigold and Dr. Truman began to date discreetly. Marigold had her history, and Dr. Truman had two divorces under his belt.

Impressed with Belinda's progress in prison, Grace nearly burst with surprise and happiness when Belinda named her baby girl "Grace." Now living with her mother, Belinda stayed clean and sober, and Grace visited whenever her dysfunctional sister wasn't home. The baby's daddy would be out of prison next month and that would be the real test of Belinda's resolve.

Germy George, in spite of, or perhaps because of, taking his wife on an around the world cruise, couldn't stave off a divorce. He sold the rest of Such Happenis to Irene and moved, leaving no forwarding address.

Hazel and Bruce meticulously revitalized their respective abodes and signed a purchase agreement for a three/two end unit condo by the river downtown, contingent on the sale of one of their homes.

Gus hibernated and wrote, and the canines and cats waited or slept.

The early days of spring knocked everyone's blinders off, the humid warmth tasting to their souls like the succulent first fruits that refreshed their bodies. It was the Ides of March, and the cosmos was in motion.

A persistent buyer insisted Hazel's house was the only one for her family, making an offer Hazel couldn't refuse. She and Bruce weren't quite ready to move, but so what? Who knew what might happen after a second trial? Bruce and Hazel no longer believed in a secure future.

The condo had two stories—kitchen and great room downstairs, half bath tucked under the stairs, and three bedrooms and a bath upstairs. The whole upstairs had wall-to-wall carpeting, the down sported refinished hardwood floors. Hazel bought an Oriental rug for the great room, perfectly matching the color of the sofa that had been her mother's. Presently, the great room was strewn with boxes, full ones in the dining area, empties blocking the front door.

Sitting or lying wherever there was comfort, the women munched on treats from the bake shop and drank coffee so old and strong it tasted like stale espresso.

Fortified by chocolate, too much coffee, and a lot of frustration, Marigold brought up a touchy subject. "I didn't tell you about my last workshop, did I?"

"Nooo," Gus responded. She'd wondered why Marigold hadn't given her a blow-by-blow description, but chose not to mention it.

"Nope," Hazel replied, wiping her mouth. "With all this," she waved her arm around the room, "I forgot, but that doesn't mean I'm not interested."

"Well, it was a good one; the same stuff you guys keep telling me, but I heard it differently this time, and a lot of it I'd never heard before. I'm finding I like being single except for one thing, and you can tell me to mind my own business, but how do you manage with no sex?"

"Count me out," Hazel pulled herself up on some nearby boxes and strolled off to rinse her hands and face. "I don't know about 'no sex.'"

Marigold's eyes narrowed as she looked at Grace and Gus. Gus grinned, "Who says we do without sex?" Marigold's jaw dropped.

Grace made a face and joined Hazel.

"Think a minute. There's obvious ways to handle that part of being single." Gus got up, gathered some trash, and said, "Be right back."

Grace returned and sat next to Marigold whose face mimicked the color of a stop sign. "You know about vibrators, the 'M' word? That's sex too."

"I mean real sex," Marigold blurted out. She clapped her hand over her mouth.

Grace ignored her and shouted over the boxes. "Y'all recall that gentleman who moved next door to me? I have a tale to tell," Grace intoned in her best southern drawl.

"Wait for me," Hazel yodeled back. "I've got refreshments."

"How do we single folks deal with no sex?" Grace asked rhetorically. "I don't think you mean the mechanics of it," Grace gazed at Marigold. "I'm guessing you mean the emotional, intimate part that requires another human being. Am I right, Mari?"

Gus suspected this was a boomerang question.

Marigold glanced quizzically at Grace, then Gus. Hazel came in with some iced tea and a carefully preserved plate of scones, saying, "Sex isn't just all that heavy 'luuvv' stuff. Its fun, it's soothing, it's serious, and sometimes it's all laughter and foolishness like being a kid again." She sat in a chair across from the three on the sofa.

"What about sad sex or procreative sex, the kind with thermometers and calendars?" Gus added. "Or what I call 'wartime' sex amid catastrophe, intense and desperate, calling forth goodness and life to counteract calamity."

"My favorite was our childhood explorations," Hazel ventured. "Young bodies going through all those wild puberty changes fascinated me. We would look at each other in wonder over breasts and hair and penises. And the roller-coaster kind of scariness of first kisses and touching over clothing—before judgment set in about how far to go or what was the right kind of sex," she added.

Gus rebutted, "How about elder sex? I can see how I've relaxed over the years. Physical details don't matter, and performance carries very little weight; it's the emotional connection that counts for me."

Bracelets jingling as she motioned for silence, Marigold said, "That's all fine, but how are you managing *now*? What can I do *now*?" She studied Grace and the answer came. "You *are* having sex!"

The women watched Marigold's expression brighten as she said, "It's Daniel, your new neighbor!"

"You said it, Mari," Grace responded, admitting nothing. "Daniel. He's dapper and a sharp dresser, has a cool mustache and a devilish beard. He comes equipped with a snazzy cane, fiberoptic hearing aids, and gets bonus points for a handicapped sticker and easy-in, easy-out van."

"Yep. We thought that too," Marigold interjected, marveling at the idea of Grace and Daniel naked.

"Can't beat that easy parking," Hazel added. "He's financially well off too, judging from his antiques and the stock tips he passes out. I heard he paid cash for his house."

"Okay," Grace said. She stared into the distance, gathering her thoughts. "Certainly those things are inviting, even to me." She got off the couch and leaned against the sideboard in the middle of the room, its contents in the boxes piled on top of it. "Let me tell you a story."

Grace closed her eyes and began. "Let's say we've been on a hot date, Daniel and I. Date number seven. Dinner was excellent, preceded by exactly one drink, timed after Daniel took his heart medication, but early enough for him to drive home from the restaurant.

"To counteract the sauces and spices in a restaurant meal, I ate a pre-date bowl of oatmeal and stashed antacids in my purse. And in case of post-date exercise, I took a dose of Extra Strength Tylenol for arthritis. After dinner, we had a short stroll around the park, enjoying the evening air.

"Reaching home with no traffic tickets, no turned ankles, coronaries, or bathroom incidents, I asked him in for a nightcap. He declined alcohol due to his sensitive stomach, but said he'd like warm milk and perhaps an antacid. I mentioned scones and he scampered, euphemistically of course, up the steps.

"One thing led to another as it does," Grace went on, "and after careful ascent, and awe on his part that I put up with a two story house, we arrive in my bedroom. His face is puce and I can't tell if it's desire or the stairs. I elect desire.

"Several ardent kisses later, he sits on the side of my bed, takes my hands in his, and whispers, 'Darling, will you please untie my shoes?'

"I bend down, but only manage to unlace one shoe before I must straighten up. He pushes the shoe off with his other foot, and I plunge down again, removing the other shoe. He hangs his cane over the bedpost.

"I sit next to him, about to nibble his ear, but his hearing aid is in, and I fear electrocution. Maybe the other ear later, I think. He turns to help me with my blouse, and I begin to unbutton his shirt. We kiss, and it leaves us breathless. He begins to cough and spits in his hanky.

"He stands, removing his undershirt, and I work on his belt, my fingers not so nimble at such tasks. He embraces me and reaches to undo my bra, but the number of hooks is way more than I had in high school, and I come to the rescue. I don't want him to know I hook them up in the front and then turn the bra around, so I hurt my right shoulder reaching the top three hooks.

"We're half naked, kissing, panting, but where's his penis? I can't feel it against me. Simultaneously, I realize that bra-less, my breasts, firm and voluptuous in my mind, now imitate twin window shades fully extended. I want the light off before he notices the same thing, but he undoes the bottom three hooks and my bra falls away.

"His nipples are small, and his chest has three hairs below his throat. As we hug and rub together, my nipples fall in and out of his belly button. He's puffing now, and thinking as Victorian as I feel, I reach for his 'manhood.'

"I can't find it! In a panic I look down at his South Park boxer shorts, seeing also his spindly legs, knobby knees, and ungainly toes. I really, really want the lights out!

"I march over to the light switch. While my eyes are adjusting to the dark, I hear rustling and realize he's in the bed, on my side!

"He pats the bed beside him. 'Come on, sweetie, hop in!'

"Sure, I'll leap, gazelle-like, across the room and land beside him, size two and perky. What if I land on his bad leg or hit my shoulder or knee?

"I walk, with declining ardor, around the bed, and climb in on the wrong side. We kiss and rekindle. I feel wet and desirable. He caresses my shoulders, slides his hands down, down, my 'mound of Venus' being just a hand span away from my nipples. I like attention to my nipples and one advantage to 'not perky' is you can play with both of them at once. But he doesn't spend time there, despite my body language and verbal encouragement.

"Then I yell, 'Yeouch!' He's got no manicure? I bring his hands up to the splash of streetlight crossing the bed. Square nails. 'Sorry, Honey, let's do something else," I murmur.

"I locate his penis and he gasps. I try to catalyze and focus his sensation onto that area, hoping that 'erection' is still in its vocabulary. He moans and sighs and heaves and holds the base tight. I slide in and out of desire until I yearn to brush my teeth and get into my pajamas.

"He senses this and sits up. He caresses my hair. I look at his face, the snazzy mustache, devilish beard, and a bald pate. 'Bald?' I shriek to myself. Stymied, I cast about. My eyes note a furry mass on the night stand. A toupee!

"He holds me and I want to relax, but this is a bad position for my back. I suggest the good old missionary position. Maybe I can get some friction without nails.

"After fussing with the covers and arranging good legs and bad legs, we take off. Up and down, up and down. It feels really good in a squishy way, and with the right fantasy, I might come. The clamor of pain in my right hip begins to overcome the pleasure between my legs. Meanwhile, Daniel's foot cramps. He rolls off me, yowling and grabbing his leg.

"'Stand on it!' I command brusquely. I clutch the covers to my chest while he hops about, holding onto the mattress. His cramp recedes, taking with it my ardor. My bladder is full. We look at each other and shake our heads. How did it get to this?

"'I need to pee,' I say and get up with the spread covering my body. When I have my robe on, I toss the spread back to Daniel on the bed . . . bewildered, baffled, who knows?"

Grace exhaled, sat, and sipped her tea, her expression neutral.

"*Then* what?" Marigold bounced on the couch.

"So I went to the bathroom," Grace said, deciding how to continue.

"Then what?" Hazel asked, agog with wonderful possibilities. "Get to it. Did he sleep over? Will you try again?" Suddenly, less positive endings occurred to her and her face darkened, "Are you two still speaking?"

Gus, her imagination focused on a cartoon image of Daniel in Grace's Den, looked like she was pretending she wasn't ticklish. "Did it end okay?" she sputtered. "He *is* your neighbor. Ungainly nights can be tricky in daylight."

Marigold had a mental meltdown. What she just heard so contradicted her ideas of love and romance and "happily ever after." She felt as if she had been told, "Sit still, dear. We're going to shave your head. It'll be fun."

Observing Marigold and listening to Hazel, Grace asked, her voice full of dramatic tension, "How *did* we pull ourselves out of this bedroom mess? What *really* happened after we went to the movies?"

Grace's face lit up and she explained, "Over tea and brownies in my kitchen, Daniel and I and toted up our foibles and infirmities, slipping into how they'd fit in a bedroom scene. It was such fun, we embellished until no truth remained. We both hurt from laughter. Would we produce it in reality? When pigs fly!"

34

Will I Still Love Me When I'm Sixty-Four?

"Dork!" Hazel said to Marigold, laughing as she read Marigold's computer greeting card for Gus's sixtieth birthday. "It's 'milestone,' not 'millstone.' I see Gus standing on the roadside with a sixty-mile marker around her neck like the Mariner's albatross." Hazel giggled and handed the card back to Marigold, thinking Marigold would see the humor.

"So?" Marigold looked up from the box-cake directions she was reading. "I think the sixty-year milestone *is* a millstone. There aren't any milestones after sixty except one." Marigold's tone of voice made it clear she didn't appreciate humor about aging. "Unless, I suppose, you repeat yourself."

Hazel sat at in the kitchen table. "Aging is weird for us too, you know. Being older is not an elective. We never thought we'd live so long, or that it'd be so short. Any age past thirty was ancient, and part of me still feels that way. Also, many of us had lifestyles that precluded old age. Drugs and AIDS stopped lots of my generation in their tracks. I prefer thinking of myself as forty with twenty-nine years experience."

"That does sound better, Hazel. Gus's birthday is when, Monday?"

"Yes, the party's on Sunday so everyone can attend, and Gus won't expect it the day before."

Hazel and Bruce's new condo, spacious as it was, couldn't accommodate a party this size, so they decided Marigold would hire a caterer and Hazel would get permission to use the gazebo at the town park. The day before, Grace suggested her grandson's local garage band might play sixties music, what he called "old fogey songs," and she'd make sure he showed up on time.

Marigold finished reading the cake directions. "Do you think one cake will be enough? I could make a couple if it's as easy as this says. I didn't mean to be grouchy earlier, but have you noticed how quickly we seem to go off the rails these days?"

"For sure," Hazel agreed, sitting on one end of the sofa with her tea. "I'll clear the table in a minute."

Marigold sat at the other end of the kitchen table, slouching as her students often did. "I don't miss Fleming a whit, but I'm edgy and off balance. I love the pet rescue work I'm doing, and Daphne lets me take in a small dog for a short while. She's even accepted Fred, the kitten. Dr. Truman's fun to work and go out with, but I'm not into dating like I used to be. I feel like a stranger lives in my body. Of course, I *am* looking at forty this year."

"I notice you don't wear bracelets now and I rarely see you in a skirt either. Is that a good thing?" Hazel asked.

"Yes. The bracelets are too noisy for frightened animals, and skirts get in the way. I don't care if an animal pees or poops on old slacks or sweats, but most of my skirts need dry cleaning."

"I like your hair short too," Hazel added, taking a swallow of tea. "What do you think of my new do?"

"I like it a lot. Dare I say the blonde streaks take ten years off your experience?" Marigold smiled. "I got cured about having long hair when a kitten climbed my braid and sat on my head. I hope I don't bore you talking about my feelings. Sometimes I feel like a child and other times . . ." Marigold trailed off.

"I like to hear about your feelings, Marigold. Every age is the first time for everybody, and it's new and scary. Gus and I talk about this a lot. By the time we learn how to do a decade, it's over, and the rules have changed. It's the little surprises that throw us, I think, like one day you can't pick up the fifty-pound bag of dog food. Or you get a bag of loam loaded at the store, but you have to slit the bag and empty half of it into a bucket to unload it at home. My least favorite change so far was the day I discovered, no matter what, garlic and I were no longer friendly."

"Well, this *is* a banner year for decade changes. I'll be forty, you seventy, Gus sixty. What about Grace?"

"If not this year, she'll be eighty next year. I'll have to look in my birthday book."

"I'm getting a few unwelcome changes already," Marigold went on. "I pee more. I need more workout time to stay the same weight, yet I don't eat one more calorie than I did last year." Marigold pulled up from her slouch. "This position isn't as comfortable as it used to be either." She grunted. "By the way, have you seen Gus this week? She seems so, so *somber* lately."

Hazel sighed. "She isn't herself. Maybe its Audrey's death, maybe it's tending to her dad, though she seems to enjoy that. Maybe it's the upcoming six-oh. Some decade markers are harder than others."

"It *has* been a wicked year," Marigold agreed. "She got way into Bruce's trial, and I know she's still furious he wasn't acquitted. Listen! It's the Beatles on the radio, isn't it? Can I turn it up?" Marigold leaped up.

"Sure, I didn't know you liked the Beatles."

"With my hippie parents, surely you jest. They love sixties music and *still* play nothing else. They swear it keeps them young." Marigold sat again and tapped her foot to the music.

"Will you still need me, will you still feed me, when I'm sixty-four?" they sang.

Hazel got up and danced, inviting Marigold to join her. When the song ended, Hazel said, "Let's call Gus."

"Good idea. Before she gets here, I'll make a bake shop run. We've eaten all your good stuff."

While Marigold was out, and before Hazel could call Gus, Grace popped over with Tonto.

"Are the dogs out?" Grace asked when Hazel opened the door. Tonto perched on Grace's shoulder and yowled. Decked out in a royal purple harness, the kind that tightened if the cat tried to back out, and a purple leash with rhinestones part-way up from the clasp, he looked like a pet monkey.

"Yes," Hazel replied, chuckling at the sight. "Does he actually walk on that leash/harness contraption?"

Grace entered and put Tonto down. "Sort of, we're practicing."

The canines, having gobbled their rawhide strips, scanned Hazel and Bruce's new yard. Daphne appreciated cultural conversations with downtown dogs as they passed the fifty feet of Filbert Street fence.

In deference to Brutus, Gwen openly threatened the remainder of Art's genitals if he posted one more petition to chain Pit Bulls from birth. Not nearly as upset as he let Gwen think he was, Art decorated the length of their fence with legal questions, receiving interesting replies.

Lady did her usual amount of sleeping, but from her nose to her toenails, she enjoyed smelling the river in the early mornings.

Swiveling her ears as she sniffed the air, Daphne said, "I smell Tonto. Grace must be here. The world is being overrun by felines! I never thought Mari would subject me to a *cat!* Now I understand Butterbean's issues." Daphne snorted in disgust and marched toward the doggie port. It was closed.

"Your Fred will grow up at least," Gwen offered, her eyes unfocused, her mind clearly elsewhere. "That Tonto is hopeless with his Siamese yowling and arrogance. I like this yard." Gwen continued dreamily, "I see Brutus every day when he and his human walk by here."

"Cut the crap, Gwen. You're not Juliet," Art growled. "There's way more important things happening in this neighborhood than Brutus, you love-struck ninny."

"Art!" Daphne chided from the back deck.

"It's true," Art snapped. "Maybe you all don't want to hear what Butch boxer said this morning?"

Gwen pounced on Lady, "Wake up, wake up! Art has news!"

"He hasn't announced it yet, but the district attorney is retiring very soon," Art pontificated. "ADA Rapp, wanting to become DA, had to distinguish herself from the other assistant district attorneys. What better way than to take on a slam-dunk, high-profile salacious case? Enter Mark and his gift of allegations about Bruce. But the jury fooled her, and she wants to retry the case. Butch's human and two other ADAs know it's a phony case and want to scrap it, so the office is deadlocked in a political and ethical uproar." Art panted, pleased with his insider information.

"We'll have to find a way to tell Bruce and Hazel," Lady said.

"Want some tea, Grace? Mari's getting more baked goodies. I'm about to call Gus, but if she comes over, remember, no party talk." Hazel's eyes sparkled, and she felt better than she had all morning. The sight of that foolish cat; *tsk, tsk, this is what aging comes to,* she thought, grinning.

"Sure, Haze, I'll have some tea. I'll stay as long as Tonto remembers his manners. Then we'll have to go."

Grace sat in the wingback chair and let Tonto walk around dragging his leash. She could see his nose flaring as he took in all the canine scents. He would look up now and then as if to ask, "Where are they?"

Lulled by Tonto's docility, Grace and Hazel went over the guest list for the birthday party. It was hard to believe Sunday was just three days away.

"What's Mari doing here?" Grace asked, "Isn't this Thursday?"

"Some kind of optional day, she said. I've noticed she takes more time for herself now. We talked about her other changes too, short hair, no bracelets. What do you think?"

"I love it," Grace said. "She seems more substantial and competent, not flighty like she can be."

"I like it too," Hazel agreed. "She says she's not comfortable with her new self yet, but she's going with it. I remember changes taking me a while too."

"Some of them years," Grace said. "Call Gus, would you?"

There was no answer. Hazel left a message, imitating Hyacinth Bucket, "Sweet Tooth Satisfaction at Chez Hazel served with feline entertainment, attendance required at once."

Marigold appeared with two boxes of decadent sweets, and Tonto, left alone for a minute while the women examined the booty, undertook vertical exploration. He pounced to the china cabinet and the world was his from there. In the kitchen, the women heard a crash and elbowed each other into the living room.

Two of Hazel's drapes and rod lay on the floor with no cat in sight. Then Grace spied an inch of purple leash peeking from under the couch.

Thirty minutes and good giggles later, they synchronized watches. While Grace took Tonto home, Marigold and Hazel would stuff the canines in one car, and *all* of the baked goods in the other. They would meet at Gus's and see why she wasn't answering her phone.

"Golden days, full of sunshine and full of youth," Gus bellowed as she soaked in the tub, phone ringer turned off, Grizzie and Butterbean tubside for company. Her mother sang that song while dusting the apartment during Gus's early childhood.

At age twenty, Gus held interesting notions about the future—she was going to be at least ninety-six, but no below-the-knee floral polyester dresses and "old lady" shoes with clunky heels. Grey hair and blue veins would be okay, but declining bodily functions or depleted energy never crossed her mind. She would be twenty-something for seventy years.

Today Gus admitted the impossible had come true. In four days, she would be sixty. Because she kept diaries as her mother had, she could thumb through the pages and see she had participated in each day, all eighteen thousand six hundred of them, more or less. Folded into books, though, the impressiveness of that number dwindled, and six decades seemed but a fleeting few months.

She'd done her best for her mom and dad, helped Bruce and Hazel through their twist of judicial fate, moved stuff and moved more stuff, but she had accomplished precious little on her book, hadn't done much genealogy, hadn't finished reading her mother's diaries, or crossed everything off her annual to-do list. Worst of all, her body, without her permission, had painted itself with an inch-thick layer of fat everywhere.

"What a crashing bore!" she exclaimed to Butterbean and Grizzella, both of whom stared wide-eyed as if wondering why anyone—even a human—would *willingly* submerge in a tub of water.

Curious, Grizzella hopped on the edge of the tub, entranced by the bubbles. Suddenly, she leapt high in the air, intent on grabbing those fluffy bubbles with all four paws. Gus caught on and drew legs into her body.

Grizzie landed, *splat!*, in a foot of bubbly water. She flew straight up, turned in midair and vanished. She roared past Butterbean, past her toys, past her food, out the dog port, and up a tree.

Gus dried and dressed, remembering as she looked in the mirror that she needed to change her driver's license: "brown" and "brown" were now "grey" and "hazel." She enjoyed not needing to pluck her eyebrows any more or shave under her arms, but the slight droop to her jowl line and a mini-wattle made her think again, *too bad you can't iron a wrinkled birthday suit.*

In fact, she thought, looking more closely, *I'm a walking genealogy chart.* She had her mother's profile, her uncle's lower teeth, her other uncle's incisors, Great Aunt Helen's hairline, Grandma Maude's cheekbones, and, oh yes, Grand Mary's knees.

"Well," Gus said later to the wondering animals, "since only four days of my fifties remains, I need some spiritual nourishment. It's time I digested this year and made peace with it. Perhaps it will make a decent story."

Butterbean glanced at Grizzie, ears forward. Grizzie looked blank and meowed, "What does that mean?"

"It's the human equivalent of hairball remover," Butterbean replied, thinking she'd never get this cat properly raised. "Gus goes over the past, throws it up by writing it on paper then, like we do after a good vomit, she feels better."

Pleased with her analogy, Butterbean swaggered down the hall, following Gus into the computer/office/guest room, Grizzie beside her, tail over the Corgi's back. "I think the surprise party will help too, as long as it stays a surprise. She gets funny at every birthday, but this year's been such a doozy, I don't know what to expect."

Butterbean and Grizzella sat in the doorway, both alert, resembling decorative porcelain figurines.

"I hope she doesn't steal from our book on the computer." Butterbean whispered, "You did save it under 'chores,' didn't you?"

Grizzie thought a minute about their last session. "It seems like I did," she replied, carefully washing her left front paw, "but you were so critical of my spelling, and I was so flustered, well," she switched paws, "honestly, I could have saved it anywhere."

Having opened the Word file and the "book" folder, Gus was flummoxed by the last entry. "Whatever was I doing that day?" she muttered. "Why, how, how could I have written 's hpyjov mpbr;'?' and '"yesd s fstl smg dypt,u mohjy . . . ?' Am I catching up with Dad?"

Butterbean pounced on Grizzella, barking right in her face, "You saved it under 'book,' not 'chores,' imbecile!

Slipping out of her grasp, Grizzie batted Butterbean on the head, one, two, three! She hissed and screeched about cat abuse and dashed down the hall, Butterbean snapping at her tail.

Gus deleted the whole mess and charged after the maniacal animals, not trusting them to settle their affairs in safety. Then the doorbell rang.

35

What a Difference a Year Makes

Grace invited Gus to lunch at the Saints and Sinners restaurant, hoping to get her to the park attired in something other than sweats. She also wanted to talk about Belinda and baby Grace and Gus never vetoed a chance to eat lobster bisque.

Marigold sang and danced around her apartment as she baked. The cakes were splendid: one Dutch chocolate with cream cheese frosting and the other a swirl cake with dark chocolate frosting. She wrote "Happy Birthday Gus" in rainbow colors and split sixty relighting candles between them.

The caterers brought fruit, salad, lasagna, chicken, three vegetables, and three kinds of ice cream. Bruce and John provided tea, coffee, soft drinks, and all the necessary paper goods.

Tweaking, prodding, and being a cheerful general nuisance, Hazel orchestrated the event. And exactly as she had requested, the day began with a warm breeze and sunny skies.

Grace picked up an excited Gus and a quizzical Butterbean at eleven-ten. Grace stopped at a convenience store to get Tonto's Fancy Feast. Gus plopped the cat food in the back and suggested that Butterbean might enjoy a short walk before guarding the car during lunch. Grace zipped to the park right on time.

"Holy cow!" Gus exclaimed as they reached the entrance. "Look at the gazebo! It's full of balloons and streamers. Someone's having a real bash!"

"Let's go see," Grace replied, struggling to keep a neutral expression. Butterbean hung her head out a back window. How could she be scenting Daphne, Lady, Art, and Gwen? Why would they be here?

Hazel, at the gazebo, watched Gus and Grace appear in the distance. All the partygoers sat or stood with their backs to the park entrance. Hazel hunkered down behind the wall of the handicapped ramp, peeking, as Grace and Gus crawled along at five mph. The dogs were leashed out of sight on the river side of the gazebo, as excited as the humans.

Grace pulled over so Gus could take a gander at the gazebo and, unable to control herself, Butterbean leaned too far and tumbled out the window, doing a perfect belly flop. She caught her breath and shot across the road, following her nose. Barking and jumping at the limits of their leashes, but still hidden from Gus's view. The ecstatic canines became a messy pile, tangled like a handful of worms.

"What is wrong with you, Butterbean," Gus shouted as she ran after the dog. The sound of barking, like would be heard in a kennel at feeding time, penetrated Gus's concentration and stumbling, she looked up from her focus on Butterbean's butt to see her friends as they leaned over the gazebo railing shouting "Surpriiiise!" She burst into tears.

Pleased with the surprise and no longer famished, the guests lounged around tables in the gazebo or strolled in groups near the river. Various grandchildren played with the dogs, and Grace paced up and down the path by the river, calling her grandson for the thirty-seventh time. His voicemail box, full, accepted no messages.

"It's okay, Grace," Hazel said, walking up to and putting a hand on her shoulder. Startled, Grace jumped, her cell phone fell. Though both women dove for it, the phone bounced on the pavement, under the railing, and into the river.

"You scared the crap outta me, coming up behind me like that! Dammit! First my moronic grandson, 'Oh yeah, Gram, you can count on me,' with his full voicemail box and next my phone's in the river." All Grace could see were huge chunks of marl, concrete, and discarded building materials in the coffee-colored water. No chance of finding her phone.

"I'm sorry, Grace. I'll replace it. Who do I call?"

Out of the corner of her eye and over Hazel's shoulder, Grace saw

Marigold approaching with Sam at her side, each carrying a cake. Grace spun Hazel around, pointing.

"Oh, thank heavens," Hazel murmured. "I'd begun to think the cakes weren't coming either. I'm so sorry, Grace."

On a seat by the railing above the dogs, Gus regained her composure after weeping and hugging each guest. Good food and a giggly conversation with Irene helped, but she still quivered on the inside. A surprise party—what an awesome, heart-stopping, fun, generous, tsunami of a gift! So far, there were no presents, cake is enough. Presents and blowing out candles were fun for the onlookers, but for Gus being the center of attention that way was crazy-making. Content where she was, Gus observed others, like John and Bruce, who were having a lengthy conversation. John's wife, always the social butterfly, cheerfully worked the crowd for her pet projects: the soup kitchen, the library, and the Historical Society.

Gus looked down at the dogs. She'd untangled and rearranged them twice. Now, neither Daphne nor Lady, were visible. She got up to investigate.

Marigold and Sam each carried a cake across the grass to the gazebo.

Here's cake! Two cakes! Gus skipped down the gazebo steps to greet and assist Marigold and Sam in time to see a rabbit whizz by. Frightened witless when Daphne broke through the gazebo lattice work into its hiding place, the rabbit zigged and zagged around guests' legs, barely ten feet ahead of a Greyhound zeroed in on bunny tail. Gus lunged for Daphne as she passed, missed, and watched an episode of *America's Funniest Home Videos* unfold, hoping someone had a camcorder running.

The rabbit sprinted between Marigold's legs. Seeing Daphne heading straight in her direction, Marigold sidestepped to the right, trapping the rabbit between her ankles. She lunged sidewise a few steps, lost her balance, and belly-flopped in the grass, cake still intact on its tray.

Emulating the rabbit's turn, Daphne hit Sam's knee with her rump, and stopped short of trampling Marigold. Sam buckled on the spot, sending his cake up and over, in a bell curve, to land squarely on Daphne's shoulders. The rabbit escaped under the gazebo, and Gus wet her pants laughing.

Hazel and Grace caught the scene from their spot by the river and joined

Irene, who had rescued the one intact cake. The others helped Marigold onto her feet and to peel the second cake and frosting off a bewildered Daphne.

Irene lit the candles on the remaining cake and led a raucous rendition of "Happy Birthday." Startled by a booming thunderclap, the group fled to the gazebo seconds before celestial housekeepers dumped buckets of water on eastern North Carolina.

36

Breath Deeply, Relax Each Muscle, Empty Your Mind

April in Pine Crossing brought forth an overpowering floral abundance. Blossoms forced trees to stoop under their weight, yellow jasmine on the sidewalk snaked around the feet of joggers, and the potpourri of pollen bedeviled allergy sufferers.

Hummingbirds arrived and hormonal squirrels ran amok.

Grace, Gus, and Hazel felt their limbs loosen and their minds, unbidden, entertain ideas and plans outrageous even to teenagers.

Was it only a year ago that 'Operation Wonder Woman' went into effect? Everyone survived the dubious results, everyone except Bruce. The entanglements of selling two homes and buying the downtown condo on the river had provided panacea over the winter. Then he realized the trial left him with no business and very little credibility. People were polite on the street, and his circle of true friends were as tight as ever, but other attorneys were chosen for divorces and the Preservation Society forgot his name once the McClellan Building became rubble.

The month of March found Bruce riding fifty mile trips on his bike and playing Four Suit Solitaire into early morning hours. Day by day, Hazel despaired of enticing him away from his fears of a re-trial. Due to conflicts within the DA's office and an embezzlement scheme allegedly carried out by several town government officials, no information existed about Bruce's status. Attorney John Jackson's contacts were willing to share information, but there was none to share.

The deck at Hazel and Bruce's new condo had a southwesterly exposure that made it cool and refreshing on summer mornings, especially when the wind blew in from the river. Hazel added white rattan furniture and contrasting cushions printed with Elephant Ear leaves and Bird of Paradise flowers provided eye candy. The cushions turned out to be so comfortable it took the strength of Hercules to leave their embrace. Hanging plants and citronella torches completed a scene reminiscent of a tropical camp in the "Survivor" TV series.

After the women voiced their opinions of current events and lamented or rejoiced in their physical status, only the sound of soft munching of scones and slurping of hot coffee prevailed.

Gus broke the spell. "So, what's up with Bruce? And are you okay? Haze, you look tired."

"I am. Tired and frustrated. Bruce isn't busy enough now that we are settled. All he does is ride his bike and fret. It isn't because something is up and he can't find out, it's because nothing is up. I remind him that the longer his case isn't on anyone's docket, the more likely it is to vanish. He sees it as the Sword of Damocles, hovering over his head, able to drop at any moment. He's both anxious and paralyzed, if you can imagine it."

Grace pulled Tonto's leash, saving Hazel's Ficus tree from his claw sharpening. With a Siamese yowl of disapproval, he leaped on Grace's lap and surveyed the items on the table. "For sure no one knows anything?"

"So Attorney John says. A couple of judges have retired and not been replaced, so the Court calendar is jammed and the ADA's are in fierce competition to be elected DA, Rapp being the most vicious at the moment. Bruce trusts John, so that's a non-issue."

"Does he have other interests besides the Preservation Society? Legal Aid? Mentoring? Some kind of athletic competition?" Grace patted Tonto and came up with a handful of cream-colored hair.

"I dunno, Haze," Gus mumbled, struggling to finish her scone and hang onto her thoughts. "I know Bruce is a man, but, has he considered therapy? Not Freudian stuff. There's a bunch of useful stuff out there now that deals with current events, feelings and reactions."

Hazel tried to respond, but Gus was on a roll.

"Cognitive Behavioral is a case in point. You are taught how to identify and then change your thoughts and behaviors. Or there's EMDR. I forget how that works, but Marigold tried it once and she felt it helped. Not sure why, but yoga, tai chi, or any of the 'hard' martial arts come to mind. He's not going to influence whatever trajectory 'the System' is on, but he can improve his ability to live with the unknown. Even reading Krishna Murti and other philosophy books, Victor Frankl, for one…"

Hazel set her mug down with a thud. "I know, Gus. I know. But he doesn't get it and I'm not able to reach him." Tears leaked down her cheeks and she fumbled for her napkin. "Let's all think on it a while. Meantime," Hazel sniffed and blew her nose. "We've got a bunch of big birthdays coming up. Yours was such a success, Gus, I thought we could each celebrate." She brightened and slipped her napkin into her pocket. "Marigold will be forty, that's a biggie, and she needs a good surprise. You, Grace, eighty is a fine accomplishment and a good excuse for lots of cake!"

"I think surprising Marigold is a super idea. Let's work on that," Gus exclaimed, feeling a bit chastened. "We've only got a few weeks and she made the best cake for my party. How do we get her to do that again and keep the recipient secret?"

"I can think of a couple of ways," Grace said, "but no party for me. Too stressful and a fire hazard…."

In the yard below the women on the deck, the canines enjoyed the scents on the spring breeze. Marigold and Dr. Truman had taken their relationship to the next level and were camping on Oak Island, so Daphne was spending the week with Butterbean and Gus. Lady Labrador relaxed her arthritic hips under her favorite tree while Art and Gwen had a Pomeranian sibling spat; all sound, no fury. Butterbean, lying near the regally recumbent Greyhound, watched the Poms with equally royal disdain.

"Uh-oh," Gwen stopped her argument with Art. "They are talking about birthday parties. Listen up." She sat with her head cocked, ears at full upright.

"Oh boy, more parties! Hope they have it at the Gazebo again. Daphne, you were the hit of the day! I never saw a more glamorous serving table!" Butterbean stretched and grinned at the memory of Daphne covered shoulder to tail in fallen birthday cake, thirty candles turning her into a porcupine.

"Zip it, Butterbean," Daphne snorted, now staring down at the Corgi from a perfectly arched neck. "You knew better than to listen to me when I asked you to chew my leash so I could chase that rabbit. You're an enabler, big time. You need Al-A-Pet."

Butterbean settled back under the hydrangea and changed the subject. "Wasn't it a day like this last April that our women sat on the McClellan building?

"So?" Art grumbled, now scratching in a pile of leaves. "Another year gone and humans still use carcinogenic chemicals. Besides, that building rubble got used to cover the landfill. What's so special about that?"

"We had more exciting days last year than ever before, brother of mine. Chewies every day the week of the trial, walks and walks looking for chemicals in the trash, those wonderful smelly tights I found the night of Lewis's fire, a new house…"

"I didn't like Gus being gone that month after her Mother died," Butterbean whuffled, "I know Grace can't help being an insomniac, but my schedule stayed messed up for weeks after."

"Enough recapitulations," Daphne ordered, recalling her injuries from creating Flemming's 'accident' on the stairs. "Let's be grateful for some peace and quiet. Look at this great place. Trees, bushes, scents on river breezes, and new downtown friends. We're moving on up, friends, upscale now, we are."

"Right, Daphne, Brutus for one, is a new friend." Gwen looked dreamily through the fence. "I hope he'll come by this morning."

"Excitement isn't over yet," Butterbean prophesied. "Gus is not at an Agility Trial in Asheville and Marigold isn't leaving with Dr. Truman until tomorrow. As we speak, they are installing an unauthorized stop sign at the corner of Jefferson and Grover. It *is* a dangerous intersection, but where did the sign come from? Did they steal it? It reeks of 'Operation Wonder Woman.'"

"Shh," Gwen panted. "I hear something."

Art stopped chewing his found rawhide.

"Here," came a low bark outside the fence.

Stiff-legged, hackles up, the dogs trotted to the shadowy end of the fence. Jasmine covered the chain-link and mixed with Wisteria on that corner. Brutus could, and did, stop there unseen, but this morning it was Ruthie, the black Pomeranian with the Court Reporter human.

"Hi Ruthie," they chorused softly, observing the no-bark laws in this neighborhood.

"I've got big news." She pranced and addressed Art with a flirtatious grin, "Is that a rawhide you have there?"

"Yeah." Art clamped his teeth around its middle, creating the semblance of a handle-bar mustache.

Butterbean, Daphne, and Gwen shifted from paw to paw. Lady woke up. "What news?"

"I see sharing the rawhide isn't an option." Ruthie turned to the rest of the canines. "We had a special session yesterday after regular court. The DA, ADA Rapp, and Judge Bendix asked Mom to stay extra and record it. I was hungry and needed to go out, but never mind, I know where my kibble comes from."

Butterbean nosed Ruthie. "So? Get on with it. What did they say?"

"Here's the damned rawhide," Art grumbled, pushing it through the chain link. "Now tell us!"

Ruthie grabbed the rawhide and exploded with delight. "Rapp offered 'misdemeanor contributing to the delinquency of a minor, no fine, no court costs, three years unsupervised probation."

"Okay, that's settled. Since Marigold's birthday falls on a Monday, we'll plan the party she knows about for the following weekend. The Sunday before her birthday, I'll say it's Belinda's birthday, could she come and, oh, by the way, bake one of her splendid cakes? She shouldn't expect a celebration the day before her birthday." Grace half rose, then sank back into her chair. "I have got to go, gang. Tonto probably needs his litter box, and I've got enough to do for three people." She extracted herself fully from the chair. "If I don't get in before Daniel gets back from his volunteer work, he'll be over and I'll not have a moment's peace."

Hazel and Gus murmured similar statements and were clearing the table when Bruce and John Jackson burst through the sliding screen and clacking vertical blinds onto the deck.

Bruce grabbed Hazel and spun her around, knocking the Ficus tree over the railing into the yard. Alarmed, a phalanx of canines caromed up the steps. Everyone shrieked or sputtered except John Jackson who said, "We were offered a plea.."

"Misdemeanor contributing to the delinquency of a minor, no fine, no court costs, three years unsupervised probation," the canines woofed in unison.

"Shush!" Bruce said to the dogs. "And I took it!"

About the Author

A graduate of Rutgers with a degree in English, Sharon devoted her first career to canine coiffure in the clients' home, observing canines and humans in their "natural habitat," in New Hampshire and North Carolina.

After her parents' passing, she retired, built a small home in the woods of Alstead, New Hampshire, and resides quietly with her Corgi and cat, enjoying writing, genealogy, and photography.